CINDERELLA IS FAKING IT

DILAN DYER

Copyright © 2023 by Dilan Dyer

All rights reserved.

No part of this book may be reproduced in any form or by any electronic or mechanical means, including information storage and retrieval systems, without written permission from the author, except for the use of brief quotations in a book review.

This is a work of fiction. Names, characters, places and incidents either are products of the author's imagination or are used fictitiously. Any resemblance to actual events or locales or persons, living or dead, is entirely coincidental.

Cover design by @andersartig_designs

First Edition: 2023

Prince Charming is overrated!

Cinderella
IS FAKING IT

PRINCESS CROSSOVER SERIES

BOOK ONE

DILAN DYER

CONTENT WARNINGS

Heavy

Mental Illness (Anxiety, Panic Attacks) • Injury • Physical Violence • Sexually Explicit Content

Moderate

Abuse through Parent • Drug Use (unknowingly ingested, no negative consequences) • Gun Violence • Harassment • Hospitalisation • Self- Harm (skin pinching)

Minor

Financial Abuse • Mentions of Death of Parent • Mentions of Terminal Illness • Mentions of Attempted Assault

For a full list of themes, tropes and kinks explored in this novel, please visit **WWW.DILANDYER.COM**

Dicktionary

These chapters get spicy.
Read at your own comfort level:

Chapter Fifteen
Chapter Nineteen (solo)
Chapter Twenty-Two
Chapter Twenty-Seven
Chapter Twenty-Eight
Chapter Thirty-One
Chapter Thirty-Six
Chapter Thirty-Nine
Chapter Forty
Chapter Forty-Seven
Chapter Fifty
Chapter Fifty-Four
Chapter Fifty-Five

PLAYLIST

INSPIRATION

- **Cruel Summer** • Taylor Swift
- **Free** • Florence + The Machine
- **Gorgeous** • Taylor Swift
- **Untouched** • The Veronicas
- **Think Twice** • Eve 6
- **She Looks So Perfect** • 5SoS
- **Late Night Talking** • Harry Styles
- **Touching Yourself** • Japanese House
- **Starving - Acoustic** • Hailee Steinfeld
- **Stripper** • Sohodolls
- **Bad for Business** • Sabrina Carpenter
- **Are We a Thing** • Leidi
- **Pillowtalk** • ZAYN
- **Mr. Blue Sky** • Electric Light Orchestra
- **Watermelon Sugar** • Harry Styles
- **Call Me** • Shinedown
- **Wicked Game** • Gemma Hayes
- **Baby One More Time** • Britney Spears
- **The Right Kind of Wrong** • LeAnn Rimes
- **Francesca** • Hozier
- Hey There Delilah • Plain White T's

*For all my neurodivergent girlies
who just want to get railed.*

ONE

Delilah

MY EYES WERE TRAINED ON THE CLOCK WHILE PARKER CAUGHT his breath, face pressed against my neck. Every hot gasp fanned out moist against my skin, but I couldn't push him off just yet, so instead I ran my fingernails over his back in circles, up and down, which had him humming in delight. I'd worked out early on that he needed exactly three minutes to cool down after climaxing and he liked my nails on his skin as long as I didn't scratch him.

Two minutes down.

I watched the seconds *tick tick tick* past, ignoring the ache in my hips from his cold weight pressing down on me. Usually, I wasn't that jumpy. Sometimes the cuddling afterwards was the best part. But I had places to be and people to convince that I was employable. 2-minutes-52. 2:53. 2:54.

"Thank you," I whispered and kissed the top of his floppy brown curls, "that really calmed me down." Not really, but I wasn't going to tell him that while he was fumbling my breasts, I'd been going through potential interview questions in my head.

What kind of culture was I looking for? Well-structured with a team that works together to make the students' well-being and academic development a top priority.

Why did I apply specifically at Truman Academy? Because it had a great extracurricular program focused on culture and arts, and as an avid reader, I would like to work for a school that values and fosters a love for literature.

Why did I leave my old school in the middle of the year? - Why did I leave my old school- Why did I- yeah, at that point I'd faked my orgasm, so I could get ready.

"See? I told you I could take your mind off the interview for a bit." Parker stole a quick kiss from my lips and smiled down at me, his brown eyes all golden honey in the late afternoon light.

Okay, maybe one more minute. "Thank you." I drew him back to me for a longer kiss, sighing as he finally pulled out of me and lifted his weight off my aching hips.

"You're going to ace the interview, babe."

"I'll do my best." The problem was rarely the interview itself. I was great at those because I could talk about English lit for hours. He just didn't know that, because I usually didn't even get this far, and I hadn't told Parker why I'd been fired from my last job. That had happened like two weeks before meeting him and it had been too early for that kind of conversation. I seriously hadn't expected to get an interview at Truman Academy - which was one of the most prestigious private schools in the country - but I'd been desperately applying to every single job opening, and they'd replied.

Parker disappeared into the bathroom to take care of the condom and I swung my legs out of the bed, jumping back when Fitzwilliam tried to hook his claws into my calves. "Goddammit," I mumbled. He hissed at me, then scurried back into the shadows under my bed. That cat was a demon sent from hell, but he had been returned to the shelter so often that this was his last shot. And no matter how many times he'd bite me, I was not letting them harm a hair on his huge, gray body. Once I had a steady income again, I might have to invest in a cat whisperer though. My ankles could only take so much.

"You look great," Parker slung his arms around my waist from behind as I studied my very safe black jeans and white blouse combo. I'd add the blue blazer later, but I'd sweat through it on the overcrowded subway if I put it on now. Everyone would be coming back from work, sweaty and exhausted, and I had to look presentable like the day had just started. No pressure. I hadn't done anything with my hair, just letting the blonde bob frame my face. The whole look screamed I*'m a safe choice. I won't cause trouble.* Maybe the red lipstick was a bit much, but it was my lucky shade. You could claw Ruby Woo from my cold, dead hands.

"Thanks," I sighed and shot another look at the clock. I had to go in less than ten minutes. My stomach dropped as the anxiety clawed up my neck. I shouldn't even bother going. It was going to be yet another bust.

"How about I stay, and we grab pizza when you get back tonight? On me. It'll either be celebratory or commiseration pizza." He pressed a kiss to the back of my head.

Commiseration pizza. Great. Amazing. Loved the idea. "Okay," I said, voice wavering, and turned out of his hug to grab my bag and double-check its contents. I was a big believer in bags-within-bags. So, I had a blue pouch for pens, a pink pouch for emergency meds and band-aids, an orange polka dot pouch for cereal bars and chewing gum… I slid my notebook in between, alongside the folder that contained copies of my resume and references.

"I'M SURPRISED YOU DIDN'T APPLY SOONER. WHY MAKE THE switch from public to private school now?" Principal Baker was a large man with a soft face and a big smile that put me at ease within two minutes of walking into his old-school office. The office itself helped too, with an oak desk and dark wood bookshelves behind him, aesthetically ticking all my boxes. This was, however, the first time he even remotely asked about my employment history instead of my teaching style, and my heart was ready to leap out of my chest. It hammered painfully against my ribs.

"I love the energy teachers bring to public schools," I replied, hoping my smile didn't tremble too much. The interview had gone amazing up until now. Baker and I agreed on so many things, and it was refreshing to talk to someone in school admin, who actually valued cultural subjects, not just STEM and sports. Teaching here, I could actually show students how much of a difference the written word made on a personal and cultural level, instead of dragging through the curriculum to make sure everyone somehow got passing grades. "I went to public schools myself and I'm beyond grateful for my teachers' commitment over the years. Sometimes, however, as a teacher, it feels like that energy isn't reciprocated. In private schools, there's a sense of community and shared identity that goes beyond school sports."

"I agree," he nodded, "at Truman, we want everyone to feel like they are part of something bigger. Many of our alumni stay in touch with each other and with the school because of that." His eyes flicked to the clock on the wall. "I would usually ask you if you have any questions for me, but I'm afraid we've already been talking longer than anticipated. I'm attending an event tonight, actually hosted by one of our alumni."

"Of course, thank you for taking the time to meet me," I replied, getting to my feet when Principal Baker stood.

"I must thank you, especially for coming in during your summer break." He'd mentioned how the position had already been filled, but then the other person had to drop out due to health concerns. "If you have any further questions, please don't hesitate to email me." He motioned me towards his office door.

"Thank you," I replied and shook his hand goodbye, making sure to add just enough squeeze to convey that I may be short, but I was not too weak to take on a bunch of high schoolers.

"We have yet to hear back from all your references, but once we do, I will be back in touch with further steps."

Smile. Smile. Smile, Delilah, goddammit. "Great," I breathed. I nodded. I smiled. I turned and waited for the door to his office to shut between us, before I bolted down the hallway. I shouldered past some guy in a suit and into the girls' bathroom. I barely made it into the stall before my lunch wrap came out the same way it had gone down.

Of course, I'd never stood a chance.

Of course, they hadn't heard back from my references yet, because it was the middle of summer.

Of course, I had to go through the best interview of my life just to be shot down with one sentence.

When the sour retching stopped, another sound broke through my thoughts. Sobbing. And not mine for a change. I straightened, knees wobbling, wiping my mouth with soft, multi-layered toilet paper that I didn't even splurge on myself, before flushing down my misery and stepping out of the stall.

The uncontrollable sobs belonged to the most beautiful woman I'd ever seen, gracefully tall, blonde hair swept into an intricate updo, body clad in a dark blue gown that cascaded down her body in layers of tulle and beads. Her skin was covered in red splotches though, and her breathing hiccupped through the sobs.

"Hi," I whispered as I stepped up to the sink next to her, "do you need help?"

"No. I just- I can't. I can't." A bitter laugh broke through her crying, and she pulled a handful of paper towels from the dispenser. A whole pile of them already lay crumpled in the sink before her. She blew her nose while I rinsed my mouth out, my own panic fading in the face of someone else in distress. "Do you? Need help?" Her voice was so hoarse, I hardly understood her.

"Not unless you know someone hiring an English teacher," I replied, trying to sound more light-hearted than I felt.

Her pale blue eyes, rimmed in red, raked over me, then dropped to her own getup. We were so not dressed for the same occasion. "Did you just get fired?"

"I actually just interviewed here, but I won't get the job," I replied, watching her breathing slow as her attention shifted to our conversation. I knew that feeling so well. When your heart raced, and your lungs ached, and your brain was caught in its own spiral - and it was so hard to snap out of it if nobody was there to help you. I could distract her a little. "I was fired a few months ago, so this sucks. Hence, the throwing up."

"Hence," she mumbled, gasping another laugh, "you really are an English teacher."

"Well, not right now." I shrugged and pulled out the polka dot pouch from my bag. "Gum?"

"Yes, please. Have you ever had an anxiety attack? Because I feel like I can taste it."

"Yeah, I know the feeling." I dropped an Orbit into her open palm and watched as she started chewing and leaned back against the wall, eyes closed. Her mascara had run down her cheeks and her glowing foundation had gotten wiped off the tip of her reddened nose, but she was still gorgeous in the way that only rich people could afford. Not due to surgery. Just... enough sleep, expensive skin care, someone to pluck your brows into a shape that matched your face. (Hers were high arches.) We shared similar enough features, blonde hair, blue eyes, round face, but if she was Barbie, I was Polly Pocket. "Anything I can do to help?"

"Not unless you can get me out of here." She didn't open her eyes. "Unseen."

"The hallway looked pretty empty. I think there was just one guy. Do you want me to go check?"

"No, it's fine." Her head snapped back up and she wiped the tears from her lashes with another paper towel. "There's photographers outside, and I was able to avoid them on the way in, but now the event planners are swarming around like bees, and they want you to get photographed."

I hadn't seen signs of either just an hour ago, but that probably didn't mean anything. Principal Baker had mentioned an event. I just hadn't thought twice about it being held on school grounds. It made sense in relation to my last answer though. Allowing alumni to make use of Truman's gorgeous gothic buildings during summer break? The courtyard alone would make a beautiful backdrop for wedding pictures. "You sure that you don't want to go to the event? Because you look amazing. It would be a waste of a beautiful dress if you went home now."

"I can't. I just can't. There's too many people. It's too much. I don't- I just-" Her voice hitched as another bout of panic hit her.

"It's okay. You don't have to," I shot out quickly. God, I had not seen myself talking a random stranger through a panic attack when I'd gotten out of bed this morning. "We can just hang out here until the event is over. I have snacks and I have Netflix on my phone."

She picked at her skirt and sniffled. "Cordelia Montgomery," she said after a moment and stretched her hand out for me.

"Delilah Edwards," I replied and shook it, a little less energetic than with the principal. Cordelia seemed like she needed a bit of a soft touch.

"Delilah, do you want this dress?"

"I'm sorry?"

"It's an Elie Saab dress, costs around fifteen grand," Cordelia said as if that made more sense than her question. She shook her head at my quizzical stare and inhaled deeply. "Would you please switch clothes with me? I can probably get out of here if I look like a teacher."

Before I could fully compute her outlandish request, my brain latched onto the logistics of it. "You're way taller than me. I don't think that would work."

"Can we try? If it works, you can keep the dress."

Now the $15,000 detail clicked. This woman was ready to part with fifteen grand worth of designer tulle just to get out of this event. She either had the worst case of social anxiety I'd ever seen, or she was rich enough for that to be pennies. Possibly both. "Wouldn't you prefer to just wait it out? You can wear the dress some other time."

"Please. I just want to go home."

I recognized that tilt in her words. The one that begged people to understand that even though it seemed irrational, your brain wasn't able to handle a situation. I hadn't seen myself ending the day in a designer dress either, but considering how most social situations threw me for a loop, I couldn't deny Cordelia's request. "Okay, we can give it a shot."

Ten minutes later, Cordelia's ankles poked out from the bottom of my jeans, and the buttons of my blouse strained against her chest, while she stood behind me, lacing me tighter into her dress. It was the heaviest thing I'd ever worn, and it swished over the bathroom tiles, but even just seeing my upper half in the bathroom mirror took my breath away. I'd never regretted wearing a plain dress to prom until this moment. The way the dress curved around my body hid my usual box shape. It hugged the dip of my waist and flowed over my hips in a stunning blue wave.

"Done." Cordelia clapped her hands. The second she'd been able to button my jeans, her shoulders had relaxed and a bright smile had unfolded on her lips. "You look amazing."

"Thank you, I feel…" I let out a long breath.

"I know. I love the dress. If I could, I would wear it at home, on my sofa, watching TV. Actually, I did that yesterday." She grinned at my reflection over my shoulder. "Do you want to know the best part?"

Her hands snaked around my hips, and I tensed, but then they disappeared into the folds of the skirt. "No way! It has pockets!" I pushed my hands into them the second Cordelia's were gone. Best. Dress. Ever.

"Here, you should take this, too. It's not worth much, but I bought it specifically to match the dress." She took off her necklace and dropped it into my hand. It was gold with a single blue pearl pendant that had rested in the dip of her collar bone.

"Thank you," I replied, mentally weighing the cost of a cab home because I was not taking the subway in a ball gown. The necklace alone would probably pay for that because it sure didn't feel like costume jewelry when I fastened it.

"Can you give me a two-minute head-start?" Cordelia smiled and backed towards the door. She'd washed off her ruined makeup, and looked younger now, just around my age.

"Of course," I nodded, "I'll just keep looking at myself in the mirror for a bit."

"Hey, Delilah?" I winced. The words too close to that goddamn song. Cordelia continued, unfazed: "Thank you so much. I hope you get that job."

My insides tightened again. I'd just forgotten about that whole thing. "Thank you. Get home safe."

Cordelia disappeared from the bathroom, and I sighed and took my phone out, just to see that I'd missed two calls and three texts from Parker, asking how it had gone and what kind of pizza I wanted. I texted him back to apologize and told him that I'd be running late, and that I wanted Hawaiian pizza - as if I'd ever ordered any other kind. Just because he didn't like pineapple, didn't mean I'd change my mind anytime soon.

I took around 60 pictures of myself in that dress before leaving the bathroom and angling for the exit. A tall redhead with a headset stood in the middle of the hallway, clipboard hugged tightly to her chest. That would likely be one of the event planners Cordelia had mentioned.

"Okay Joey, if she's a no-show, that's everyone," she barked into her headset before her attention landed on me, "halt, I got eyes on her."

Eyes on me?

"Ms. Montgomery."

Oh no. Right dress, wrong person. "No, no, I was just leaving."

TWO

Delilah

"THIS WAY PLEASE. THE FIRST COURSE WILL BE SERVED IN LESS than two minutes." The woman pressed a hand into the back of my waist and pushed me forward. "I got her, Joey," she hissed into her headset with all the bravado of someone who had found a wanted war criminal.

"Sorry, I think there's been a mistake. I'm not supposed to be-"

"Nonsense Ms. Montgomery, you'll have a great time. Let me put this in coat check, room 105." My bag was taken from me and I was pushed through a side entrance into the school's dining hall and lost my train of thought. I'd googled the hell out of Truman, of course, but that didn't compare to walking under the centuries-old, vaulted ceilings, painted in pale shades of blue with clouds streaking the space. The splendor didn't end there. Two dozen round tables with decadent floral pieces, cream tablecloths and golden chairs dotted the room and its center had been cleared as a dance floor.

The place was decked out like an expensive wedding, except every woman wore a gown prettier than the next one.

"Here, sit." The event planner shuffled me into a seat between an older lady with a sharp chin-length red bob and some guy in a suit, whose toned back was turned to me, so all I could see was his neatly coiffed thick black hair. I stood out like a sore thumb simply based on the fact that my last haircut had been two months ago, and my hair was in two perpetual waves from being pushed behind my ears. I'd had it to a bob similar to the lady next to me, but it had since grown to skim my shoulders.

"As I live and breathe," the woman exclaimed as I sat down. She ran a hand over her very chunky diamond necklace, but my attention wandered past her to where the event planner was positioning herself in front of the door like a security guard. "Cordelia Montgomery."

The other six people swiveled in their chairs to stare at me. Oh god, oh god, oh no. This was bad. Alright, Delilah, be polite and get out. "Good evening, everyone. Unfortunately, I think there's been a mix-up."

"I believe that's my fault." The low, rumbling voice dripped a honey shiver down my spine.

I turned to the man sitting on my other side and forgot to breathe for a moment. Some people were just pretty on another level. Pretty sprang to mind because of his long lashes and the high cheekbones. But then his nose was just a little crooked… coupled with his tan skin and a dark, trimmed stubble, maybe *pretty* wasn't the right word. He looked like he belonged in a perfume commercial. "…so I messed with the seating arrangements."

Ohmygod. I had totally missed the start of that sentence. Before I could reply, servers flurried around us and placed bowls of soup in front of everyone. I took the chance to scan the room. There was another door at the back of the room, the main door, but my eyes caught on the person sitting at the table right in front of it. The principal. Who had just seen me in a blouse and jeans. Shit. I quickly whipped back around, hoping he wouldn't recognize me by the back of my head.

"I must recommend you finish your soup, Cordelia - can I call you Cordelia? - because they never prepare the meat right at these small dinners. You'd think the smaller the crowd, the less overwhelmed the cook, right?" The lady next to me tattled on and my eyes dropped to her place card. Rachel Sallow. Considering the event, likely tied to the Sallow Sweets company. My father had spent 20 years in their packaging department. Probably no point in telling her that he perfected the crinkle of their chocolate wrappers.

"Thank you. That's good advice," I said, trying to sound somewhat like a polite socialite who belonged at this kind of event. I had no experience with these sorts of people outside the pages of my books.

The man to my left chuckled but didn't meet my eyes when I looked over. Ass. What did he think was so amusing? He was in his mid-thirties and dressed like a penguin for the benefit of… of… I glanced around, trying to pinpoint who exactly benefitted from this benefit dinner. Orphans? Endangered animals?

"Not a fan of soup either?" he asked.

"Hmm." I had other things to worry about than my soup getting cold. It wasn't even *my* soup. Oh god, someone here had to know the real Cordelia. I'd get kicked out as an impostor and the principal would see and then I could kiss even my last chance at a job here goodbye. My heart was fluttering fast enough to be painful. I pinched the back of my right hand in my lap, trying to snap myself out of my own thoughts, but it didn't work. Of course, my good deed didn't go unpunished. Of course, I had to end up at the most ridiculously lavish dinner under all the wrong circumstances. Could I end up in jail if I ate soup that I didn't pay for? No, wait, you didn't pay for the food at these events. You paid by seat. Did that mean I could land in jail just for sitting here? My spine straightened, detaching itself from the chair.

I jumped when a hand folded over mine. I looked down. Between all the fabric of my skirt and the thick tablecloth, the man next to me had slipped his hand over my fingers, stopping me from pinching any harder.

"You'll hurt yourself," he whispered just loud enough for me to hear, eyes on the blonde woman across the table who seemed deep into a story about her cats? Her kids?

"I'm fine," I breathed and pulled my hands out from under his. A deep, red groove bloomed where I had pinched the skin with my thumbnail.

Not fine, but not for him to judge. Instead of removing his hand from my personal space, he lifted it slightly. "I'm Beck."

Well... I glanced at Cordelia's name card. At least my introduction wouldn't be a lie. "You can call me Del." I slid my hand into his and flinched when his thumb traced over the sore spot on my skin.

"We should take you to the school nurse." His dark charcoal eyes pierced me in place, while one corner of his mouth twitched up. Was he... flirting? Nope. Surely not. This was a very proper dinner among proper people. Right?

"I'll be fine, thank you." My voice came out surprisingly breathy and I pulled my hand back. *Goddammit Delilah. Don't let some handsome, rich, older guy throw off your focus with a smile.* I had to get out of here. Parker was probably wondering where the hell I was. Unless he was sleeping already since he had the early bird shift all week. That usually meant he was in bed by eight.

"It's just food," Beck said, still speaking low.

"It's dinner."

"Dinner is food."

"Dinner is food plus people plus conversation plus expectations plus…" I cut myself off before I could spiral down a similar road to the one Cordelia had taken earlier. No wonder she had locked herself in the bathroom. I would have liked to study a 50-page manual for handling a dinner like this before even thinking about attending.

The servers were back to take away our dishes. My eyes followed his bowl as it was lifted away from him, still untouched as well. Not a fan of soup.

I could not take my chances on a second course. Sooner or later, someone would track that I didn't even know which one of the three forks in front of me I should use. Maybe I could walk sideways past the principal. "Excuse me," I said and scooted my chair back.

"Thank you all for coming!" A voice boomed over the sound system. On the dance floor, a man with thinning white hair had taken the mic, and all heads turned.

"Seriously?" I hissed under my breath, drawing another chuckle from Beck. I squinted at him, but he was looking at the speaker like everyone else.

The man waffled on and on - only to get to the point that this was about historical building conservation. I couldn't even get myself into trouble for a really noble cause. Just crumbling facades upheld in the name of luxury condos.

He had just finished speaking when the next course landed in front of me. My insides twinged at the sight of cheese-stuffed mushrooms. I had perfectly good pizza at home but how could anyone resist hot, melted cheese? I almost picked up the fork, but Rachel Sallow of Sallow Sweets was digging into her mushrooms, and a mixture of ham and nuts and some other meat spilled out from under the cheese. That was a 'no' from me.

I blinked at the ceiling and squeezed my hands together until my knuckles ached. My eyes were beginning to burn dangerously.

"Eating the food is also an integral part of dinner, you know?"

"Can you please just- I don't mean to be rude, but I'll just sit here until this thing is over."

"You're just going to sit there and stare at the ceiling for four hours? That's one hell of a neck workout."

"Four hours?" I gasped and snapped my head back down. "But we're already on the second of four courses."

"There's breaks for dancing, there's speeches, inevitably something goes wrong, and we'll be forced to sit through a 65-year-old man's temper tantrum," he said with disinterest, picking up the bottle of wine from the center of the table. He leaned in to pour, but my hand shot out to cover my glass just in time.

"Thank you. I don't drink."

"Pregnant?" he asked with all the empathy of stone, pouring his own wine instead.

"No." Anxiety. And it was bad enough tonight without any help. I didn't need to add a panic attack to tomorrow's agenda. "You don't sound like you particularly enjoy these types of events."

"These are networking events. I'm not here to enjoy myself. However, Del, sometimes I'm lucky enough to be seated next to the most beautiful woman in the room."

If he hadn't delivered the line in all seriousness, I would have laughed. If he hadn't been looking at me with those dark eyes that hardly let you gauge where iris ended and pupil began, holding my gaze steadily, I might have even called him out on the line. Instead, it sent a ripple of heat down my spine that pooled in my lower back. "You weren't lucky though," I said, recalling his earlier words, "you messed with the seating chart."

"True." He cracked a wide smile that softened his sharp features, and my heart skipped a full beat. It was unfair for a single human to be this beautiful. My body was reacting in ways I would have preferred to stifle. I had a perfectly good Parker at home. "Every once in a while, you have to make your own luck."

"I let you have the first one, but that one was too cheesy."

He took a sip from his wine, and it really shouldn't have worked, but something about the way he held that wine glass oozed the confidence to talk about *light bodied notes of cherries mixed with earthy texture* or something without sounding like a total douche. "At least we agree that you're the most beautiful woman in the room. I like a woman who knows her own worth."

That one was so thick; I gasped a little laugh. "Alright, Casanova, cool it."

"Cordelia, have you tried the stuffed mushrooms at Chez? They are divine." Mrs. Sallow leaned over smiling conspiratorially. "I'm sure they would be able to deliver to your house, considering you prefer to stay there…"

Alright so Cordelia's social anxiety was clearly not a secret. These seemed like the type of people to gossip hard about each other and to make a big deal about every shrivel of new information. When you had no problems, you had to create them yourself, right? I couldn't give her too much of an answer or I'd be throwing Cordelia to the wolves.

"Unfortunately, I haven't had the pleasure yet." Nailed it. I had to tell Tabitha that reading Jane Austen was *not* useless. Then again, my best friend never would have gotten herself into this kind of situation.

"Oh, and you have to try their truffle ice cream. Although I suppose getting ice cream delivered all the way across town might be a little more difficult." Oh, she was rubbing it in now. What a snake. I pasted on my most polite smile and waited for the waiters to clear off the dishes - this time mine being the only one untouched.

"I could never indulge in ice cream," I said. "The combination of sugar and dairy has such devastating effects on one's hair density. I applaud anyone who's able to enjoy such a treat, but I'm too vain about my hair. I know, I know. Vanity is a horrible vice." I let my eyes click up to her hairline for just a split-second, let my smile waver, then pasted on the same polite expression as before.

Rachel Sallow of Sallow Sweets, whose entire fortune was built on sugar and dairy, touched her perfectly styled bob, with a silent 'oh' on her lips. "Well," she huffed, "yes, it is."

Oh god, I had just burned a bridge, hadn't I? The second I realized what I'd said, the heat shot to my cheeks. I had to apologize. I had to say something. I had to-

"Come on, Blondie, let's dance." Before I even had time to react, Beck's hand curled around mine again and he pulled me to my feet. His skin shouldn't have burned on mine as much as it did, just from holding my hand as he led me onto the dance floor.

Between a lush display of flowers, a string quartet had set up and played covers of pop songs, Bridgerton-style.

"Wait, did you just call me Blondie?" My thoughts finally caught up with me and I pulled my hand out of his.

"I thought you'd like the name since you're so vain about your hair." Beck turned and stepped in front of me, and my breath stuttered once again. Seriously. Handsome and rich *and tall*? How was that fair? It wasn't hard to be taller than me, but with my 5'1" I came face to face with his chest. He had to have more than a foot on me.

"I actually love ice cream," I said, standing awkwardly still as he directed my left hand onto his shoulder and placed his own on my bare back, "but truffle ice cream? Come on. Caramel fudge is where it's at."

He grazed his fingertips across the palm of my right hand to open it enough to slip his own into it, and my stomach twisted. No. Nope. Being attracted to someone was one thing, going through a whole spiel of touches with that person- He tugged me closer against his chest and started moving us. *I* was very much not dancing. My feet just sort of skimmed the floor as he danced and took me with him.

Not how I'd imagined my first proper dance in a proper ball gown to go, but I let myself be swept into the music and into the swirl of luxurious dresses and dapper suits. This close, the fresh scent of Beck's aftershave filled my senses, mild citrus mixed with something a little darker, more masculine, adding to the lush elegance of the moment. "I personally prefer good, old vanilla," he said once my stiff shoulders somewhat relaxed into the movements.

"Really?" I scrunched my nose at him. "I would have pegged you for a rocky road kind of guy."

"How so?" The corners of his eyes crinkled in amusement.

"Dark, rich, with a bit of a soft spot, and potentially a little nuts." A grin stole its way onto my lips. Oh no, wait, was this flirting? Was I teasing him? Retreat. Retreat! "Anyway, I shouldn't have said those things to her." I shook my head and closed my eyes for a moment, strangely confident that he wouldn't drop me.

"I disagree." His fingertips traced the vertebrae between my shoulders, sending a shiver down my spine. "You're a wild card on the social playing field. She tested your boundaries and you put her in her place."

Except I wasn't *me* and I had no idea what the fallout would be. Should I even be dancing with the man I was sitting next to? I tried to get a glimpse at the other dancing couples but spotted the principal's face near the edge of the dance floor instead. Shit. I lowered my eyes and shook the hair free from behind my ears, letting it fall around my face like a curtain. But if the principal was *there* that meant the door was unwatched.

"Thank you, but I'm all danced out." I tapped his shoulder. "I'm going to go find a bathroom."

"Have dinner with me on Sunday." He maneuvered us around

the other dancers to the far end of the dance floor and stopped there, but didn't loosen his position, his warmth lingering.

"We're having dinner today." I slipped my hand from his.

"I have a feeling I won't see you for the main course," Beck said, his touch moving up my vertebrae again until his index finger bumped against the clasp of my necklace. It wasn't even a touch. It was barely more than a brush over my back. And yet goosebumps raced up my arms. Traitorous stupid skin.

"Thank you for the dance." I sighed and turned out of his embrace. "Enjoy the rest of your night."

I grabbed the weight of my skirt with both fists and booked it out of there.

THREE

BECK

"The girl showed up just long enough to get her picture with you taken on the dance floor and then left?" Julian rubbed his temples and closed his eyes. I'd told him a hundred times that he'd be less prone to migraines if he didn't insist on the corner office with all the light streaming in, but God forbid he didn't have the largest office on the floor. "What kind of move is that? Did she even talk to Doyle?"

"No," I replied. "For what it's worth, I don't think it was a move. I think she just panicked."

"She should have panicked after getting the zoning rights for the M Elements."

Considering how jittery Blondie had been just after telling Sallow to shove her ice cream opinions up her ass, I doubted she'd have made it through a discussion about why the plans for the Montgomery's budget hotel had yet to be approved. That conversation with William Doyle merely wandered onto my to do list for after the merger. "Not my priority right now."

"I haven't heard of any more public appearances so far. You might just have to send her roses. That girl from the Roxy was obsessed with these roses in a bucket. Apparently, that's a thing now."

I chuckled at my brother's attempt to come up with a romantic solution. I hadn't seen Julian in a single romantic relationship since his wife died. But that had been fifteen years ago, and he had gone from grieving widower to someone who didn't even bother learning the names of the arm candy that never lasted more than a month.

"Don't worry," I said, even though I wasn't much more of a romantic, "I made sure to have an opening just in case she'd go back into hiding."

"Good. I'm not letting this slip through our fingers, Beck. Fuck Gregory fucking Montgomery."

"Hmm, I'd rather not." Cordelia's father had tied up his company in so many legal documents, all to ensure it would sink or swim with the Montgomery family long after his death. The egocentric bastard would rather throw billions of dollars out the window than have anyone outside his family take over his company. "Del on the other hand…" Those full, pomegranate red lips had me imagining a whole variety of ways one could fuck with the Montgomery legacy.

I got out of the armchair in front of Julian's desk and wandered over to the window. You could see the roof of the first ever Montgomery hotel from here, but despite the Montgomery family - now reduced to Cordelia - living here, their main business was handled in New York nowadays. The Axent Group HQ, however, had been in Boston since my grandfather had started this company.

Their name had all the grandeur of old money attached to it, including Cordelia's great-great-grandmother, some British duchess, having survived the Titanic. Axent had grown fast over 70 years because we expanded way beyond luxury hotels, but even a 5-star Axent Grand didn't hold the same prestige as an old Montgomery. Merging the companies would combine classic and modern luxuries on a global scale. Everyone involved would benefit.

"I've been meaning to ask whether you want mother's ring," Julian said.

"Jesus fuck, no." I laughed. "Unless you want the merger to fail. That thing is cursed." Getting a ring wandered on my mental to do list though. Might as well get that out of the way.

Just because the old man had made sure nobody could take the hotels off Cordelia's hands, didn't mean nobody could take Cordelia's hand. Once I was part of the Montgomery family, I'd be part of the business. It'd be smooth sailing from there. I'd just have to get her to the altar before she fucked up the whole company.

After catching Julian up on last night's progress, the rest of my day was a blur of meetings and negotiations. Summer was usually quiet since the tourism season was well underway and any further strategies would be discussed in September, once the numbers were in. On the day to day, that just meant I got out of the office around seven instead of nine.

I'd bought the gym across the street a few years ago. For convenience mostly. I'd not even considered keeping it open to the public, but then I was never one to leave well enough alone. Vortex had turned into a solid side project. Even now, it was filled with the sounds of leather smacking into skin, gloves slapping into punching bags.

"Oh, bugger off," Isaac groaned and pushed himself into a sitting position. He rubbed a glove over his chest where my foot had landed after he screwed up his defense.

"You're not giving up, are you?" I asked when he didn't get back up.

"Unlike some other jobs, my work requires movement beyond typing out a few emails. So, I'd like to keep my ribs intact, thank you very much." He let me pull him to his feet despite glaring at me. "That was brutal. Who spat in your beer?"

Swear to God, the more punches I landed, the stronger his Scottish accent broke through. Like I was knocking almost 20 years of living stateside right out of his system. "Didn't get as far with the Montgomery girl as I'd hoped." Not that I'd admit as much to Julian, or he'd take it upon himself to help.

"Poor little Beck. Did you meet a girl that didn't drop her pants the second she lay eyes on you? Do you actually have to put in some effort?" He chuckled and pulled his gloves off. Apparently, that was our workout for the day. We'd only been going for 30 minutes. Isaac usually lasted at least 45, even though we always scheduled an hour. "Welcome to the realm of mortals."

"Hilarious." I rolled my eyes at him. He was one to talk when he'd had his dick in just about every nurse at his hospital. Somehow that accent had them all swooning for him.

"Oh, hello, darling. Do you need help with that?" For fuck's sake. He'd stopped in his tracks to help some redhead in pink yoga gear with her pink boxing gloves. So much for the realm of mortals.

I left him there and hit the showers. Kicking the shit out of Isaac had eased my frustrations a little. I hadn't expected a famously reclusive woman to drop her pants - as Isaac had put it - the first night I met her. Considering that she left her house so rarely, however, every minute of quality time lost put a dent in my plan to put a ring on her finger by Thanksgiving. I'd given myself four months to charm her pants off. Her inheritance would likely be out of probate by then, but even as her fiancée, I could probably keep the company from sinking without proper leadership.

CINDERELLA IS FAKING IT

Once dressed, I waited for Isaac at reception, pulling my phone out to do something that would actually help with my mood: Fix this.

"Hello," a clear, female voice picked up when I'd fully expected this to go to voice mail.

"This is August Beckett for Cordelia Montgomery." I still had her father's number on file, and had figured they'd either transfer it to her, as the new owner, or would let it go to reception.

"Oh. Mr. Beckett." The woman paused, the line going silent long enough for me to check my screen, making sure she hadn't hung up. "She's not available at the moment, can I take a message?"

"She dropped her necklace last night. I'd love the chance to return it in person."

The woman sighed. "I'm afraid Miss Montgomery is opposed to taking personal meetings. I'm happy to arrange for a messenger to pick it up whenever convenient for you."

"I'm sorry, I didn't get your name."

"Uh, I didn't... I'm..." Another pause. That woman needed a lot of time to process her thoughts. "I'm Page, Miss Montgomery's assistant."

"Hi Page," I said, putting on my most charming smile, hoping she could feel it ooze through the speaker, "I'm not sure whether you believe in fate, but I think it's fate that Cordelia's necklace came loose, and I happened to pick it up. I would love the chance to talk to her again. Could you *please* put in a good word for me?"

Page gasped a little giggle. At least my charm was working on some silly assistant even if Del didn't want anything to do with me. Yet. "I'll see what I can do."

"That's all I ask for."

"I'll get back to you with her reply as soon as possible."

"Thank you, Page. I appreciate it."

"Goodbye, Mr. Beckett."

I hung up to see Isaac's shit-eating grin, arms crossed in front of his chest. "Really? Fate?"

"Oh, hello darling, do you need some jolly help with that?" I mocked him with my best English accent. "Maybe later you can let me be your tampon."

"Wrong country." He tsk-ed and pushed out the door. "I just realized something. You're basically a prostitute."

"If that's the case, you should pay for my company *and* my drinks tonight." He'd pay for the drinks anyway. He'd tapped out before our 60 minutes were up. If he'd made it, I would have paid. It had started as a challenge of who tapped out first, but the fact that Vortex was two minutes from my office, but 45 minutes from Boston Memorial, and his job required more triple shifts, meant that I outlasted Isaac every single time. I'd stopped giving him shit for it though because he once collapsed 20 minutes in. Only to find out he'd spent almost 72 hours without sleep. He'd seemed fine one moment and then his lights went out. He was a pediatrician, so his game face was unmatched. If he tapped out after 30 minutes, he tapped out. No questions asked as long as he paid the bar tab.

"You're shackling yourself to a woman, not knowing whether you'll ever get laid again. Your cock might be worth 20 billion dollars, but it does have a price." The old lady walking past glared at us, but Isaac shot her a big grin, a wink and a 'hello darling' and I fucking swear, her wrinkled cheeks blushed.

"If the sex sucks, I can always come over and introduce myself to your nurses." Besides, people had gotten hitched for much more frivolous reasons than a business worth 20 billion.

"They wouldn't touch you with a ten-foot pole. You're not nice enough." He laughed. "Then again, you do believe in fate now."

"Shut up before I drag you back and wipe the ring with your ass."

FOUR

Delilah

"It's gorgeous," Defne swooned.

"It looks heavy." Tabitha tilted her head of short brown curls sideways.

"I wish I had another occasion to wear it," I said, running a hand down the ball gown hanging on my closet door. In daylight, it was even more stunning than it had been at dinner last night, the waves of blue fabric shimmering in all shades from aquamarine to dark violet.

Thankfully, Parker had been asleep by the time I'd made it home, and back at work by the time I woke up. Thank God retirement homes served breakfast at like 7am or I would have had to explain last night to him - and I wasn't sure I even had a good explanation. This way, I could just hide the dress in the closet.

My two best friends, however, had come over first thing to marvel at the gown that cost more than both their cars combined.

Granted, they had crappy cars, but still… They were perched on my bed between all my throw pillows, staring at the masterpiece of sequins and pearls. I'd lost the necklace somewhere in my sheets last night, but I hadn't found it and hadn't gotten the chance to check under the bed yet, for fear of getting my arms sliced off by Fitzwilliam.

Defne clapped her hands together. "Oh, Del, it could be your old, borrowed and blue for your wedding." Both Tabitha and I turned to look at her with incredulous expressions. I had started seeing Parker all of three months ago and I hadn't even used the L-word yet. (Parker had once - on our second date.) Tabitha, on the other hand, generally thought weddings and marriage were bullcrap. "I'm just saying." Defne shrugged.

"Google says you can get ten grand for it." Tabitha tapped away on her phone, then snapped a picture of the dress.

"Hey, am I in that?"

She waved me off. "I'll edit you out. There. Posted on stories. Maybe someone will bite right away." She tossed her phone behind herself on the mattress. Despite treating that thing like an old toy, it was also part of her job. She had somehow made a living out of being the gruffest yoga teacher online. No crystals or meditation music, no pastel yoga shorts, just one woman yelling profanities at her camera while doing the downward dog.

"I think you should keep it. The blue must look lovely on you." Defne blinked her long lashes at me. If Tabitha threw rocks to make a point, Defne smothered you in cotton balls. She was 24, three years younger than me, still in grad school, and posted daily puppy videos on the GC.

"It makes no sense for me to keep it." I dropped onto the mattress between them.

Defne patted my shoulders. "But it's pretty."

"No job, no money," Tab pointed out. "Designer dress, lots of money. It can tide you over in case Childs keeps-"

"No!" I yelled at her loud enough for Fitzwilliam to poke his head out of the cat tree. I was not going to think about *that*. My stomach churned at the mere mention of his name, and I pushed down the memories threatening to resurface. I was done with that version of myself.

Defne pouted at the dress. "If you're strapped for cash, I can send you that site where you can sell your worn socks."

"You would rather keep selling your worn socks to men that jerk off in them than sell a designer dress?" Tabitha had her phone back in her hands but blinked at Defne.

"Of course," Defne scoffed, "I don't care what they do with my socks. I wear socks anyway and don't think twice about it. This? I would never stop thinking about this dress if I gave it away."

"I'm sorry did you guys come here for a debate?" They were acting like the angel and devil on my shoulders.

Neither of them had the chance to reply before my phone started blaring an old Jonas Brothers song and I scrambled to my feet to grab it from my bag. Boston area code. Could be Truman Academy. This fast? That was *not* good news. "Hello."

"Hi, I'm calling for Delilah Edwards." The chipper female voice on the other end didn't belong to the Truman principal.

"This is her," I replied, feeling two sets of eyes burrow into the back of my head.

"Oh, perfect, hello, this is Cordelia. We swapped clothes last night." No, no, no, no, no. Oh god. What had I done? I twisted around and furiously pointed between the dress and my phone to get Tab and Defne to understand what was happening.

"Uh-huh." My voice screeched up my throat. "Hi."

I had googled Cordelia after coming home last night when Parker had already been asleep. Cordelia Montgomery was the sole heir to the Montgomery hotel chain fortune, and since her father's death a few months ago, one of the richest people in the

US. Unlike most heiresses who seemed to flaunt their wealth in Ibiza and date F1 racers, Cordelia was apparently famous for being a recluse. Her mother had been fatally shot in a mugging when Cordelia had been 13 years old, and she disappeared from the public eye after that. Nobody had seen her in years. There weren't even any socials. Which explained Rachel Sallow's jabs last night. And the fact that nobody had ID'd me as an imposter.

"Could you come to my place? I want to talk to you about last night."

Shit shit shitty shittest shit. I may not have been caught last night - but word clearly got through to Cordelia. "Of course," I breathed, "my schedule is wide open."

"Amazing! My driver will pick you up in thirty."

"How did you-" The phone beeped at me. Hung up. "How did she get my number?" I stared at the phone in my hands.

"Who?" Defne asked.

I threw my hand towards the dress as if I hadn't been gesticulating the crap out of myself here. "Cordelia freaking Montgomery. The woman I was mistaken for."

"She's rich." Tabitha shrugged as if that was the obvious answer. "Enough money can buy you any information. Oh, stop looking at me like this. Have none of you watched any true crime ever?"

Thirty minutes later, Tabitha shoved me into a town car even after I protested because the driver was as beefy as a young Arnold Schwarzenegger, in a fitted suit, and tattooed from neck to knuckle. Plus, I had definitely never given Cordelia my address. Creep factor: through the roof. It didn't help that the guy didn't speak a word beside the short "Miss Edwards" greeting.

"Any idea what your boss wants from me?" I asked, trying to catch his eye in the rearview mirror but he kept 120% of his attention on the road.

We stopped in front of a gorgeous white, Victorian town house on Beacon Street. Nestled between red brick buildings, it practically glowed with decadence. The driver got out first and had my door open before I was even unbuckled, motioning me towards the building. While he unlocked the door, I dropped my location in the group chat. Better safe than sorry.

Inside, the house was very… pink. Not popping bright in a Barbie way. More in a strawberry macarons and porcelain vases, Marie Antoinette sorta way. I personally would have added a few more pastel colors, but if I ever had the kind of money for an interior designer, I'd have to ask for Cordelia's.

My eyes were still caught on the sparkling, pink glass chandelier, when the driver opened the first door on the left and nodded his brown buzz cut for me to get in. Right. Business. I was either going to die from shame or be killed for my sins. Had to get it over with. Heart thrumming, I stepped into an equally pink home office. Cordelia sat behind a huge glass desk that was covered in piles upon piles of papers and folders and smoothie bottles. My eyebrows twitched at the mess. Cordelia herself was perfectly put together, with glossy pink lips, bangs that sharply contoured her brows, and a puff-sleeved polka dot summer dress.

"Delilah, come in, come in." She shuffled papers aside and grabbed a stack of them before beckoning me over into the seating area by the window, which resembled a gold and pink explosion of fluffy throw cushions and velvet armchairs. "Coffee? Tea?"

"I'm good, thank you," I replied, taking my seat across from her. I'd rather get my impending death over with.

"Are you sure? Victor makes amazing tea." She pointed at the stoic man by the doorway, who had the kind of bulky arms that suggested any teacup would crack at the touch of his pinky. And those eyes were such a venomous shade of green, I wasn't keen on the idea of consuming anything he prepared.

"Thank you, I'm fine."

"Actually, now I'm craving tea. Would you be so kind?" She smiled at Victor and pulled her shoulders up.

He nodded, not breaking his blank expression. "Of course, Miss Montgomery."

I couldn't help myself. Once he was out of the room, I had to ask: "Personal security, driver or butler?"

"A little bit of everything, depending on what's happening." She shrugged. "Not a great chess player though. He cheats. A lot."

The snort broke through before I had a chance to suppress it. Okay, I wasn't here for chit chat. Time to get this over with. "I need to apologize. When I came out of the bathroom in your dress, someone whisked me into the dining hall. There was food and there was a speech, so I couldn't just leave. Also, the school principal was right by the exit, and he's the one who interviewed me, so I couldn't just walk past him. And then this guy asked me to dance. It kind of spiraled. I'm sorry."

Cordelia pursed her lips. "You made the news."

"Oh no." My heart sank. Imposter caught at high society event. Anna Delvey 2.0. There went my job chances. Again. "I'm so sorry."

"No, no, no, sorry, in a good way. Here." She pulled the first page from her stack of paper and handed me the printout of an online article. It detailed the event and included a picture of me and that Beck guy dancing. He was photogenic but the picture didn't hold a candle to the real version. The way I smiled up at him. Ugh. Like I was 16 all over again, meeting Harry Styles at a fan event, eyes bugging out of my head. Some people's superior genetics really turned your brain to goo. I read the caption out loud: "Power couples for a powerful cause: Cordelia Montgomery and August Beckett sweep the dance floor."

"We can debate whether or not conserving old buildings really is a *powerful* cause, but this is good press for me."

Really? "You're welcome?"

"You don't go to these events to help any cause. If you want to help a cause, you donate to a charity directly instead of attending a $10,000 dinner. These events are about being seen." She tapped the picture. "You got me seen and I didn't even have to be there."

Right. Networking not food. Beck had said as much. I blinked. "Those three stuffed mushrooms per person were not worth ten grand."

Victor came back and put a dainty floral teacup down on the side table next to Cordelia. She offered him a smile and a quick 'thank you' before turning back to me. "I want to hire you."

"What do you need an English teacher for?"

"No, silly. I want to hire you as a double. A stand-in for public appearances."

I wasn't sure what to reply to that kind of offer, so I said the first thing on my mind: "You're way taller than me." Granted we shared some of the same features, but not in a double-take kind of way.

"Nobody knows what I look like. There have been no public pictures of me in over 15 years. And the ones from back then… blonde hair, blue eyes, stubby nose. Close enough."

That seemed… what in the… "I can't. I'm a teacher."

"You're not. You're looking for a job."

"A teaching job."

"I can get you the job at Truman."

"No."

"What do you mean, 'no'?"

"I mean, no, you can't get me the job. And no, I'm not going to be your stand-in. People at the school would recognize me. I mean, you. Me as you." The idea alone had me pinching the back of my hand because of all the things that could go wrong.

"Oh please, the princess of Spain could walk through any American school and not a single person would know who she was. I don't want you to become a socialite or fashion-icon. It's a handful of events this summer. That's all. Look." She shoved the rest of her papers under my nose.

"No," I said again, not even looking down. What could it be? More articles about me? Her plan for me to get a boob job, so I could fit into all her designer dresses?

"Oh." She pulled the papers back, her shoulders sagging as she smoothed a hand over them.

Goddammit. My curiosity won out when I caught a glimpse of a pie chart. "What is it?"

"I made a PowerPoint presentation."

The only thing better than a PowerPoint presentation was a color-coded excel table. If there was one thing I couldn't resist, it was good organization and planning. "Can I see?"

Cordelia's chest swelled and she jutted the stack of paper back at me. "Why don't you look through it on your own time. You don't have to decide right now. Are three days enough? If so, we can reconvene here in three days."

"Sure," I sighed. Considering the Elie Saab dress hanging in my closet and the fact that she wasn't downright suing me for identity fraud, I could come back and say 'no' again in three days. Besides, maybe Truman would have called up my references by then, rejected my application, and I'd be in desperate need for *any* income. And I'd rather pretend to be Cordelia than sell my socks like Defne did.

FIVE

Delilah

Nothing had changed in three days. Parker stayed at his own place. I still hadn't heard from Truman. I kept sending my CV to schools that never replied. But at least one of Tabitha's followers had deep enough pockets to buy the Elie Saab dress, so I would be able to pay my rent this summer.

That also meant I could confidently reject Cordelia's job offer even though her PowerPoint presentation had been very compelling. It was an intricate outline, detailing eight weeks of social events. It basically came down to her father's estates still being in probate. A multi-billion-dollar company, set to be inherited by Cordelia alone, currently completely up in the air. Tied up in the legal proceedings of processing an inheritance that huge. Stakeholders were beginning to get cold feet because they didn't trust some young woman they had never seen, and the second the company was out of probate, its value could plummet unless

Cordelia showed everyone by then that she was totally capable of rubbing shoulders with all the right people. From there on out, she had a whole business model that I'd only skimmed because I wasn't cut out for corporate jargon.

I expected to find Cordelia in her office again that afternoon, but Victor wordlessly led me to a conservatory at the back of the house. It was filled with large, exotic plants that covered all the side windows, and a small fountain gurgled in the corner, but sun still flooded the room through the glass roof. Cordelia wore a fitted pink summer dress and sat in a wrought iron chair with her little, floral porcelain teacup. I'd always wanted one of those, not just the chunky mugs I'd accumulated over many birthdays and Christmases.

A second cup was set out for me on the other side of the table. Along with a folded piece of paper.

"What's this?" I sat down and unfolded the paper, finding a name inside. *Roger Childs.* My fingers jerked on reflex. I swallowed the sour taste welling up my throat and forced myself to draw my brows deep into my face. "Is this name supposed to mean anything to me?"

"Delilah, you don't have to play coy with me."

"I'm not." Tabitha's words echoed in my ears. Rich people could find out just about anything.

"He'll be gone by the end of the week."

I froze, unable to breathe. If she could really make that happen... "Why?"

"Because I owe you."

"You don't owe me anything."

"Beckett is a very powerful man. A picture of *me* dancing with him? Being called a couple? Let's just say other powerful men trust me more now that I have the Beckett seal of approval. At least for the moment. I'm not saying it's right, but that's how the game is played."

I had googled August Beckett since my last visit here. He was the CEO of the Axent group. Whereas Montgomery was all hotels, Axent was luxury hotels, luxury clubs, luxury restaurants. Basically, anywhere you'd spot a mega celebrity hanging out. However, after reading all that, I spent a lot more time on the google images tab… I couldn't help it. He was so damn pretty.

"As soon as Mr. Childs is out of the way, I will write you a personal letter of recommendation. My name still holds some weight."

"Cordelia-"

She didn't let me speak. "You were right when you said that I can't get you the job at Truman Academy. I can't guarantee you the job, but I can do this much for you. You deserve a chance to prove your worth without your past hanging over you."

"One event," I said, surprising myself. I was too soft. But Cordelia deserved a chance to prove herself, too. "I'll go to one event for you."

"Really? Delilah, thank you so much!"

"Del," I sighed, "you can call me Del."

"Do you know your measurements?" She pulled her phone out and tapped her fingers against it faster than should be humanly possible. Not even Tabitha typed that fast.

"I don't. Why do you need to know my measurements?"

"So I can get a dress for you, obviously." She blinked, stopped typing, and grimaced. "Sorry. I do that sometimes. I need to get better at explaining my thought process. I'm still working on that."

"That's okay." I felt that in my bones. Even slowed down, sometimes my thought process still didn't make sense to neurotypicals. But Cordelia had my neurodivergent radar flashing. "I'm a size four, and five-one, so I usually have to buy in the petite range." I finally worked up the nerve to pick up the dainty teacup, even though it looked too expensive to be handled. After one sip, I put it back down. Whatever tea Victor was brewing in that kitchen had to contain the bitter caffeine of ten espresso shots.

"Thank you. I can work with that."

An hour later, Cordelia had coordinated five dress choices to be delivered to her doorstep, along with matching shoes and accessories. I'd gaped at the prices, but when I'd suggested I could just wear my own sandals, Cordelia scrunched her nose at my feet.

All that was left for me to do was to cancel my Friday date night with Parker and show up here an hour before the event to get ready. I'd shake some hands, smile for the pictures and I didn't even have to stay more than 45 minutes. No biggie. No problem. I could do that. I was going to be a *great* version of Cordelia Montgomery.

I just kind of, sort of felt like throwing up. A little bit.

It was going. To. Be. Fine.

"I MADE RESERVATIONS AND EVERYTHING. I FEEL LIKE I DESERVE an explanation, Del." Parker crossed his arms in front of his chest, glaring at me across my studio. He was leaning against the kitchen counter but shrank aside when Fitzwilliam launched his huge body to the countertop. As if this weird cat wasn't weird enough, he only drank from the sink - which made doing the dishes a life-or-death experience in case he got thirsty. Parker had only ever gotten scratched once, but he kept two feet between himself and my cat at all times now.

"Is this about the cancellation fee?" I asked because Parker got upset over wasted money quickly. I'd gotten very good at never throwing out leftovers over the last three months. "I can pay the cancellation fee."

"Oh, you will, but what on earth could you have coming up on a Friday night?"

Okay, that stung a little. He wasn't wrong, of course. "I met this really rich lady at the Academy after my interview last week," I said, trying to steer clear of details, since spilling the whole truth now felt like admitting to lying. I hadn't lied. I just hadn't shared. "We talked and she's offering to write me a letter of recommendation since she has some pull with the school administration. That's why I'm meeting her again on Friday." Technically, none of that was a lie.

"Right, she's just writing you a recommendation letter out of the blue?" He laughed. "Please be serious."

Again. That stung even though he wasn't wrong. It was illogical for a random rich lady to write me a letter of recommendation. But the way he said those words. "I am serious. I helped her through a panic attack if you must know. She's grateful."

He threw his arms out and jerked them back when Fitzwilliam meowed because his hand had come too close to the sink. "Why didn't you just say that?"

"Because her mental health is none of your business, and I really shouldn't be sharing it."

He furrowed his brows and shook his head. "It's for work. I always tell you about the stuff I'm dealing with at work."

"Well, maybe you should keep some of the residents' medical issues to yourself. Maybe Mr. Peters wouldn't be too happy knowing that you talk to me about his epileptic seizures."

"Really? Now I'm not supposed to talk about work?"

"That's not what I said," I moaned and dropped onto the sofa because I was tired of this conversation. Was it so hard to go '*It sucks that we have to cancel our dinner but thanks for the three alternative date nights you suggested for next week*' or was I being overly sensitive? Did I owe him some huge explanation? Keeping Cordelia's secret was already messing with my head.

"I'm sorry, babe." Parker walked the five steps over to the sofa and knelt before me. "I shouldn't have yelled."

He hadn't. He'd barely raised his voice. Instead of pointing that out, I cupped his beautiful, soft sunshine face in my hands and offered him a conciliatory smile. "I'm sorry that I have to cancel last minute." Although three days in advance wasn't really that short notice if you thought about it.

"I'm glad that you're getting the recommendation. I want this job for you, baby." He kissed my bare knee, looking up at me through those pretty dark brown lashes, and my stomach fluttered. He was so pretty.

"Thank you," I breathed and leaned forward. "Kiss and makeup?"

He tilted his head to put a quick peck on the tip of my nose. Not the kiss I'd envisioned. "I think we should celebrate your recommendation, actually." His next kiss landed on the inside of my thigh, and he hooked his hands around the back of my knees.

"Uh, Parker…" Oh for goodness' sake. I'd told him I only ever wanted *that* for celebrations, important occasions, and the like. To keep it special or whatever. "You don't have to do that."

"I want to." He pulled my legs apart, which made my skirt ride up my thighs like a traitor. His mouth wandered up my leg and I tried to ignore the fact that he was trailing spit over my skin. Moist spots of saliva clinging to my leg. "Enjoy your victory, Del. Getting a personalized recommendation like that is a big deal."

"We can celebrate together." I smoothed his curls back from his face, trying to get his attention without outright yelling at him to stop raking his tongue all over me. It wasn't his fault that I was messed up about this, but he sure would take it personal. They all did.

"Don't worry." He smiled up at me, his face so goddamn close to my panties. "That comes later."

Oh. Great. I got to fake two orgasms tonight.

His head dropped between my legs, and I stared at the ceiling. Oral was the actual worst. Hence, the special occasion lie. At least sex felt good, and I got to hold him and kiss him. Oral was all fluids and weird sounds and not knowing how long I had to sigh and moan before I squeezed all the muscles between my legs and shouted 'oh god yes' a couple of times.

At least I'd mentally compiled my weekly shopping list by the time it was over, so I considered that a win for productive multi-tasking.

SIX

BECK

A FEW DAYS AFTER OUR PHONE CALL, CORDELIA'S ASSISTANT forwarded me an internal Montgomery memo. Note to self: Fire Page once the Montgomery-Axent merger was through. Not very trustworthy. For now, however, she was very useful.

The memo was three paragraphs of empty phrases, before it got to the point: Cordelia would attend the grand reopening of the Montgomery Hotel in Boston, which had undergone major renovations over the last 9 months. It had closed when the old man was still in charge, and her cutting that big red bow would be the perfect photo op to symbolize the torch being passed on.

Del's outfit that night was a whole business lesson in and of itself. She was clad in a sleeveless, fitted black jumpsuit. It had a high neckline and cinched around her waist. Despite her red lipstick and red pumps, she would have no trouble being taken seriously by any business partners in attendance tonight. But when she turned, the same jumpsuit allowed a look at the entire slope of her back, fastened around her neck and middle with thin straps, but baring every inch from her shoulders to her tailbone. The message was clear: it was a new, young era for the Montgomery - and she had it handled.

The message wasn't quite as clear to my dick, because Del had those two little Venus dimples on her lower back, and my mind conjured up images of wrapping my hands around her hips from behind and running my thumbs into those grooves.

The entire second floor of the hotel was event spaces, from the ballroom with a view of the Public Garden, to smaller rooms that had been decked out as bars, photo op rooms, and whatnot. If I hadn't been on a mission, I might have spent more time taking note of the event and the hundreds of attendees. But I wasn't letting Blondie slip out of my grasp again.

When I found Del, she was chatting to a young server, pointing back and forth between her champagne flute filled with orange juice and another full one on the man's tray that had her red lipstick marks on it. Micro-managing the wait staff? She spotted my approach when I was a few feet away and her shoulders straightened. "Thank you." She dismissed the server with a touch to his arm.

"I believe this is yours," I said by way of greeting, pulling her necklace from my pocket. The golden chain dangled from my finger, blue pearl swinging back and forth.

"Where did you find that? Never mind. Just: Thank you." She sighed and gave me a small smile. "Hi. Familiar Face."

"Hi Blondie." I opened the clasp of the necklace. "May I?"

"You don't have to."

"But may I?"

She blinked up at me as if I had requested something utterly outlandish before she turned. Oh fuck. I'd forgotten the back of her jumpsuit when I pulled the necklace move. All that smooth, milky skin. Which also meant she wasn't wearing a damn bra. Then she lifted the hair from the nape of her neck and her scent unfolded in the narrow space between us. Whether it was her shampoo or her perfume, the mixture of jasmine and amber shouldn't have worked - sweet floral and bitter earth - but it did. I allowed my fingertips to linger on the soft skin of her neck just a moment longer than it took to fasten the necklace.

I was fucked.

In the whole seduce-the-meek-little-heiress plan, I hadn't considered that the woman I'd be pursuing might look and smell this tempting, making it almost impossible to keep a straight thought.

"Thank you," she said and turned around again. I had to get an award for not looking at her tits after putting together that they were bouncing freely. That would really fuck up the plan.

Like Isaac had said. I had to play nice. "I'm not a fan of chitchat, so I'll come out and say it: I think you're beautiful and I would like to take you to dinner." There. That sounded nicer than 'let's get a room so I can bend you over, slot my thumbs into your Venus dimples, and make you scream'. Actually, a room wouldn't cut it. I'd have to get her into the stairwell and put her two steps above me, because even with heels she was so much shorter than me, her hips and mine were not aligned.

"Uh…" Del laughed and shook her head, wiping away my insanity. Fucking Venus dimples clouding my brain. "I'm flattered but I don't go out with men who want to spend time with me based on how attractive they find me."

"What kind of rule is that?" I asked, unable to reign in the gruffness in my voice.

"The one that got me a boyfriend who values me for more than my pretty face."

"Is he blind?" Wow, my niceness had lasted all of five minutes, but the way she'd said that sounded too sincere to be a lie. That meant she had a boyfriend I knew nothing about. And that was a problem.

"No. A little nearsighted, but he's not blind." She furrowed her brows at me.

"Did he see your face in any capacity when you first met?"

"Yes, but-"

"That means he thought you were cute before he realized you were smart."

"You don't know that." She crossed her arms in front of her chest, pushing her tits up under that flimsy fabric. I really shouldn't have looked. Fuck.

"Of course, I do. I'm a man. I'm assuming he's a man. I promise you, he was looking at your face or your body before he was thinking about what a great conversationalist you are."

She narrowed her eyes at me, fingers stiffening around her glass. "He read my profile and liked the quote I used, so he messaged me about that."

"Was the quote the first text right beneath your picture?" She sucked her cheeks in, pursing her lips. "I'll take that as a yes. He didn't read your profile, Blondie. He thought you were cute and knew that a 'hey, what's up' wouldn't get him anywhere with a woman as beautiful as you."

"Thank you for returning my necklace, Mr. Beckett," she huffed and threw back her glass of juice as if it was a stiff drink before placing it on a circulating server's tray. "If you'll excuse me. I have hands to shake." She brushed past me, shouldering my arm out of her way with all the force of a baby tornado.

Shit.

I royally screwed that one up.

Between her lower back triggering an apparently very specific fantasy, and the surprising boyfriend reveal, Del had thrown me for a loop. Maybe I should have taken improv classes before agreeing to court Cordelia Montgomery.

I got myself a drink at the bar, shook a few hands myself before deciding ten minutes was more than enough time for her to cool off - but not enough time to make her run.

Turned out, finding a Smurf of a girl dressed in black, at an event filled with men in black suits? My new personal hell. Thirty minutes of circling rooms and promising people whose names I didn't even know that I'd talk to them later, I was almost ready to give up for the night. I'd just call Page again. She seemed eager to help. But then I spotted her. Away from the crowds. Not shaking hands or mingling, pressed into the alcove by the fire exit. I almost would have missed her if her platinum hair hadn't caught a light from outside.

Her eyes were squeezed tight, and she was pinching the back of her hand. She'd done the same thing at the charity dinner and her skin was already an angry shade of red. Jesus. That girl was not cut out for stakeholder meet and greets like this.

I wrapped my hand around hers and her big ocean eyes flew open, a little too glassy. "How about this?" I asked, voice lowered. "I'm willing to negotiate the terms of our dinner."

"Negotiate?" She pulled her hand from mine and examined the angry swollen skin. "How about you take no for an answer?" Despite her words, her voice wavered.

"Instead of going out in public, I will cook for you myself." I dropped back, leaning against the other side of the alcove.

Del slipped her irritated hand behind her back and shook her head. That seemed to clear her thoughts a little, because her eyes had found their focus again when she narrowed them at me. "That's even more of a *date*-date than going to a restaurant. If you wanted to negotiate, you would have to meet me halfway."

"See? You have so much to teach me." I grinned. "We definitely should spend more time together. What's your counteroffer?"

"If I say breakfast, will you leave me alone?"

"Breakfast usually comes after dinner."

"Watch your tongue. God." She reached up to push her hair behind her ear, but it was sleeked back and clipped into place.

"Counteroffer: Drinks." I lightly knocked the tip of my leather shoe against her stiletto.

"I told you that I don't drink."

"Why?"

"Messes with my head. I had one accidental sip tonight and that will be all for me for the rest of the year." That explained her earlier conversation with the server. That boy was lucky to still have a job. How stupid did you have to be to mix up the alcoholic and non-alcoholic drinks? Not only that, but to serve the owner of the whole hotel the wrong drink? I wouldn't have let that kid get away with a pat on the arm and a 'thank you'. Del sighed. "Fine. I'll play." She clicked her shoe against mine. "Counteroffer: Brunch. You can have a mimosa if you want drinks."

"I accept your offer. Brunch it is."

"Wait, what?" Her mouth fell open.

"You're a great negotiator. I'm taking you out to Brunch tomorrow. Where should I pick you up?"

Her mouth formed silent words, before she caught a train of thought to verbalize. "You're not picking me up because it's not a date. If anything, we'll meet at the restaurant."

"Fine by me. I'll see you at eleven at Bumble by the Sea." I pushed myself off the wall and leaned down to kiss her cheek, a startled gasp escaping her throat. That sound sent a bolt of lightning straight down my middle and made me wonder what other sounds I could pull from her if this was how she reacted to a chaste peck on the cheek. "Try to enjoy your night, Blondie."

I left her there before she could come up with any excuses for not meeting me. I could only hope that she wouldn't totally wreck her hand over the next couple of hours, or I'd have to spoon-feed her on our first date.

SEVEN

Delilah

Cordelia's smile, when I FaceTimed her from the bathroom and told her about the impromptu brunch plan, was wide enough to rival the Cheshire Cat. She told me to have fun, make a good impression, and wear the red dress, then hung up.

Victor picked me up half an hour later, trunk of the car filled with all the stupid-expensive clothes I hadn't worn tonight, including a red skater dress Cordelia had deemed too casual and too short for the party. Victor also waited outside my door at 10.40 the next morning to take me to Bumble by the Sea, a small but popular Harbourside restaurant renowned for its waffles and smoothies. (Thanks Google.) Except when I got to the door, a sign announced the place was closed for a private event. Amazing. And I'd skipped breakfast for the blueberry pancakes that had looked mouthwateringly delicious on the website.

I was fumbling my phone from the tiny, beaded bag that

matched the dress, when the door swung open from inside. "Miss Montgomery, please come in."

I blinked at the white-bearded man who could have passed for Santa Clause if Santa wore jeans and henley shirts. Oh. Right. *I* was Miss Montgomery. "Thanks." I slipped past him into the restaurant. It looked exactly like it had online, except all the wooden tables had been cleared off, safe for one by the windows, which was still decorated with wildflowers and set with mismatched vintage tableware. The brunch buffet was fully stocked, and Beck was filling his plate with an assortment of mini muffins. He was in a suit again, just like the last two times I'd met him, but this one was light grey and fell a lot more casually around his wide frame.

"Do you already know what you want to drink, or would you like a look at the menu?" The bearded man asked with a bright smile.

"I'm just…" I blinked back and forth between him and the empty restaurant. "Apple juice please."

"Of course. Coming right up." He disappeared through a side door, leaving me with a preoccupied Beck. He only looked up from his pastry choices when I stepped up next to him.

"I was going to open the door for you like a gentleman, but I didn't want you to think this was a date." The corner of his mouth turned up, mischief glinting in those gray eyes of his.

"Good morning." I picked up one of the bowls from the end of the buffet. "Care to tell me why this place is empty?"

"I didn't want anything ruining our non-date." He shrugged and popped a mini donut in his mouth, with no reason to look as good doing that.

"Did you just call up a random restaurant and book the whole place with less than 24 hours' notice?" I filled my bowl with fresh fruit: strawberries, grapes, melon cubes, the whole shebang. "How much did you pay for that?"

"Actually, I bought the place this morning," he said, and I dropped a kiwi slice into the breadbasket. His eyes followed the splash of green between perfectly toasted golden brown. "People don't like doing things they perceive as an inconvenience, like clearing out a restaurant for a day on short notice, even if they get paid for it. People *do* like making a huge amount of money in a snap without having to ask for it, if all they have to do is one little task, like clearing out a restaurant on short notice."

"You bought this whole restaurant because you didn't want any inconveniences?" I asked, still dumbfounded.

Beck properly turned to me for the first time that day. I almost shrank back under the intensity of his slate eyes as he stepped in front of me. His long fingers wrapped around my right wrist, and he pulled my hand up, running a warm thumb over the back of it. "Seems to be doing its job so far."

I snapped my hand back. "You don't get to do that."

"Touch you?"

"Act concerned, but also, yes, that."

"It's not an act." He shrugged and turned, carrying his plate to our table.

God, I couldn't get a proper read on him. How could he blow his kindness out of proportion - how much did a restaurant cost? - and then turn around with such chauvinist views like 'all men everywhere only care about external beauty'. Was that a generational thing? He did have like ten years on me. Maybe I shouldn't have cared. This was the third and last time I'd meet this man. Then again, I'd have to make conversation with him for the next hour or so, just to make Cordelia look good.

"Okay August Beckett, you have to answer some questions for me." I piled some pancakes onto my fruit bowl before joining him at the table. My apple juice was already waiting for me.

"Beck," he corrected me, "and only if you answer some for me."

"Fine. Truth for truth."

"Go ahead."

"Why meet me here when you know I have a boyfriend and you have no chance?"

"First of all, I reject the premise that I don't have a chance if your only reason for not going on a date with me is your relationship status," he pulled a croissant apart over his plate, "but to answer your question, I intend to get to know you, Del. You're the owner of Axent's biggest competitor. I would like to get to know you intimately, yes, but it would be a stupid business move to ignore your existence just because you rejected my advances."

Damn. That actually sounded like a logical answer. "But why-"

He interrupted me: "My turn."

"Okay." I picked up my first pancake with my hands - not a date, no audience, manners were overrated.

Beck watched me tear into the pancake, but only asked his question: "Read or watch anything good lately?"

"Really? That's your question? - Don't answer that." I caught him off just in time when his grin had widened. I wasn't wasting one of my questions on that. Oh god. I had no idea what Cordelia would read or listen to. And I had no idea what would make a good impression on Beck. Rereading Sense and Sensibility for the 100th time probably didn't. "I've been listening to this podcast on Greek mythology." That one could work. It was niche, but it wasn't too weird. "It breaks down The Odyssey and compares different interpretations and translations, including Emily Wilson's, who's the first woman to translate it into English."

"That's neither read nor watch, but I'll let it slide because it was a good answer."

"Do you really think men care more about what a woman looks like than what she has in her head?"

"I never said that." I raised my brows at him, and he sighed and leaned back in his chair. "First impressions matter, and in most social constructs, first impressions happen visually. Most people take one look at a person and can tell you whether or not they're attracted to them and would like to engage with them in a sexual context. That can be a long-term relationship or a one-night-stand. That's all. Of course, there's exceptions. There's always exceptions. If you met your boyfriend on one of those swipe-right dating apps though, I doubt he's the exception."

"You're really good at rationalizing."

"I'll give your compliments to my old therapist." Beck smiled and God, his smile was beautiful, but it disappeared as fast as it had come. He nodded at my hands wrapped around my second pancake. "Why do you hurt yourself?"

"I don't *hurt* myself."

"Del." He leaned forward, arms braced on the table, and dropped his voice. "Why do you hurt yourself?"

The only person who had ever put it that bluntly was my former therapist – back before I lost my health insurance. Defne had only voiced some concerns when she'd noticed my nervous habit, and Tabitha had suggested a number of workouts as substitute. "Please ask a different question." Cordelia didn't need that kind of weakness pinned on her.

Beck didn't move and didn't speak, his dark eyes burrowing into me. Was it getting hot in here? I pulled on the collar of my dress, aching for a little cool air. "Alright," he finally said, "you get one pass. Ideal first date?"

That was easy. And matched Cordelia's lifestyle. "Sleepover."

He choked on his croissant.

"Not like that, perv." I rolled my eyes at him. "Actual sleepover. Cute PJs, watching movies, doing face masks, consuming a copious amount of sugary snacks, talking until 3am."

"So your boyfriend is actually a girlfriend?" Asshole. I

chucked one of my strawberries at him and he barked out a loud, chesty laugh. "Sorry. Sounds cute. Your turn."

"Actually, I need a minute. Does your new restaurant happen to have any bathrooms?" He pointed over my shoulder to the door in the corner of the restaurant with the stick figures on it. "I'll be right back."

As much as I'd enjoyed tearing through those pancakes, the grease was clinging to my fingers. Just looking at the oily sheen made my spine crawl. I didn't even want to think about the stains that could leave on this $300 dress.

When I came back from washing my hands, I halted dead in my steps because the room was filled with loud moans and a woman yelling 'harder, harder, harder' at the top of her lungs. It stopped a moment later. Beck slipped his phone back into his pocket. Oh, for goodness' sake. "Were you just watching porn? In the middle of a restaurant?"

Beck raised his brows at me, then turned around pointedly. Got it. Obviously, we *were* in the middle of a restaurant but there was nobody here to judge him. "It's technically not porn," he said when I didn't sit back down.

"Technically?"

"If you must know, someone illegally obtained a recording of myself and my ex. I had to open the video to confirm its authenticity to my lawyers."

Where did you even start with that? The illegal part? The lawyers, multiple, who must have seen that video? "That was a sex tape?" I asked because my brain was still catching up with the information.

"Yes."

"Of you?"

"Yes."

He either had a great poker face or he was actually telling the truth. Giving him the benefit of the doubt, I decided to take my seat again. Apparently, men who bought restaurants on a whim also made good targets for illegal sex tapes. Scandal followed money. "It sounded like porn," I said. Astute observation, Delilah. Truly highlighting your intelligence.

"It sounded like good sex," he chuckled.

Sure. Right. Ugh. I wouldn't know anything about that. Time to make it a little less awkward. "So, is this some sort of blackmail situation? Are you going to pay the people who sent it to you?"

"No."

"Sue them?"

"No." He smirked and popped another mini donut in his mouth. I had absolutely no reason to find that one specific move so compelling that I couldn't look away from his lips. Jeez.

"Then what?" I asked, stabbing my fork into a kiwi slice, "Hire a hitman and have them taken out?"

"What does good sex sound like to you?" He asked instead of answering me. I was going to go with the hitman theory then.

"That's none of your business," I said.

"Oh, but I intend to make it my business, sweetheart." He leaned forward, elbows on the table.

Sweetheart? Nope. Big nope. "I think we're done here."

"You proposed a truth for truth deal. I answered six questions since you came back from the bathroom. You owe me six answers."

And that's why I was an English teacher, not a corporate contract negotiator. I bit the inside of my cheek before I said: "More verbal."

"Ashleigh was very verbal, but you thought she sounded like a porn star."

I narrowed my eyes at him. "That wasn't a question."

"You're catching on." He took a sip from his coffee cup, regarding me over its edge. "What does verbal mean to you?"

Okay. I could play *this* game. That was an English teacher's game. I grinned. "Verbal means relating to *or* in the form of words. It can also mean relating to a *verb*, specifically."

He laughed and tapped his temple with two fingers in a fake salute. "What does verbal mean to you in the context of good sex?"

The tension had strangely ebbed from the question. It was about sex, but it was also just a question laced with genuine curiosity. "I suppose it would be less *harder, faster, stronger* and more communicative. It's not just an act. It's an interaction."

"Hmm," he hummed, seeming to actually consider my words, "can you give me an example?"

Ha. That was a yes or no question. "No," I grinned, awfully pleased. "I don't do fake orgasms in restaurants. I'm not Meg Ryan."

"I can draw a real one from those red lips if you'd prefer that." He leaned over and dropped a hand into my lap, knuckles brushing over my naked thigh right by the hem of my dress. My skin prickled hot under his touch and my breath stuttered in my throat, but-

What. The. Heck.

"No," I gasped and clenched my thighs together to stop him before his hand could wander further. To his credit, he immediately drew his hand back and a flash of confusion furrowed his brows. "Does that usually work for you?" I asked because he seemed to think that was genuinely the move to make on me. "Did you really think I'd like that?"

"Yes."

"Did you think I'd let you touch me right here in public?"

"Yes." He sighed and pressed his lips together. "Because *that* has been going on since you heard the sex tape." He jutted his chin out and it took me a moment to follow his gaze. The deep sweetheart neckline of the dress hadn't allowed for one of my usual T-shirt bras, but I wasn't really busty enough to desperately need that support anyway. So, I'd gone braless. In this case, however, that meant the silky fabric of the dress clearly outlined the hardened peaks of my breasts.

Heat shot up my neck, burning my cheeks. "I'm leaving," I said, voice strained. I grabbed my bag and crossed my arms in front of my chest. "You're very pretty but you need to learn some manners."

This time, he didn't try to make me stay.

Victor leaned against the car in the parking lot, a pair of aviator glasses hiding his eyes, but he didn't even have to take them off for me to feel his gaze on me. "What?" I barked, angrier than he deserved. Instead of replying, he tilted his head towards the restaurant. Our table by the window technically had a seaside view, but it was also in direct line of sight from this parking spot. Probably why Victor had stayed right here. "Amazing. So you saw. Whoop-dee-doo."

"Do you want me to punch his lights out?"

I gaped at him. Those were the most words he'd ever spoken to me. The startling part was the sincerity in his voice though. I had zero doubts that he'd march in there and introduce his fist to Beck's face if I asked him to. "No," I said after imagining the satisfying crunch of Beck's nose, followed by the disaster that could turn into, "can you please just take me home?"

He nodded. "Hop in."

"Can we stop at a Dunkin' or something on the way? I'm still starving."

Victor must have pitied me, because following my order of one donut and one refresher, he bought two dozen donuts and two more refreshers, and then carried all of that into my apartment for me alongside the rest of my new outfits. He didn't even blink an eye when Fitzwilliam attacked his ankles.

And then he left. The door shut. My adventure as Cordelia

Montgomery was over. No more opulent events, overpriced clothes or confusing billionaires.

When Parker came over that night, he accepted my explanation that I'd stocked up on donuts to make up for our missed date last night, and we had a donut taste test date while some Marvel movie played in the background. Spending downtime with Parker was easy and nice and relaxed, and I didn't have to watch out for verbal traps or negotiate conversation rules. I didn't even feel bad about comparing him to Beck, because Parker was so sweet to me, he came out on top. No questions asked. And then I felt *a little* bad, because when Parker took my dress off and pushed my legs apart that night, I had zero physical reaction to his touch. I wanted to sleep with him for the sake of being close to him, but Beck's knuckles against my leg had made my skin burn hotter than Parker's hands roaming my whole body.

EIGHT

BECK

Two nights a week, Vortex was filled with the ear-piercing screeches of little girls as they barreled into each other and tried to do some damage to the punching bags that hardly swayed from their attacks. We'd had to enforce a hair tie rule though. For what these kids lacked in muscle power, they easily made up for in foul tricks.

Thankfully, Scarlett's office upstairs was soundproof.

"Looks good to me," I said after reviewing her plans for the new Vortex opening in L.A.

"You always say the same darn thing." She clicked her tongue at me and threw her inky ringlet curls back.

"You know what you're doing." Vortex was her thing as much as it was mine. We'd met ten years ago, when I'd thought sponsoring pro athletes might be fun. Scarlett was my first and last investment. Pro kickboxer, 23, at the height of her game, knocked out of the ring permanently by an injury six months after I got on her team. The other sponsors dropped her, I paid for her physical therapy and her business degree. Turned out, sponsoring worked in your favor beyond the trophies.

"I'll be flying out there tomorrow for three days," she said, "I'm staying at the Montgomery Beverly Hills if you need me."

"Seriously?"

She fluttered her fake black eyelashes at me. "They have softer towels."

"Noted." Actually noted. Scarlett could charge that shit to the company card and I didn't limit her on her business expenses. Which meant that other women with unlimited spending possibilities were also leaving their money at the Montgomery. Because of soft towels.

"Come on, I'll introduce you to Hannah. She's the new regional."

I glanced at the clock. "I don't have time for small talk, Scarlett."

"Yes, you do. Because you're a picky lil Gingersnap and if anything is wrong at *your* gym, you'll have to talk to Hannah. Not me." Scarlett shooed me out of her office, slapping her hand against my upper arm when I didn't go fast enough for her taste. I considered her one of my oldest friends, but fuck, she liked torturing me.

"Hannah!" She waved over a middle-aged woman from reception. Except, when Hannah walked over in her leopard-print leggings and a fitted tank, I realized that she was probably around my age. Mid-thirties. Her wagging salt-and-pepper ponytail just didn't really match the fresh face of freckles.

"Hi, you must be Mr. Beckett, it's so good to meet you." She flashed her pearly whites at me and stemmed her fists into her sides, power-posing.

"How are you liking the Vortex so far, Hannah?" I asked.

"It's amazing!" She bobbed up and down on her heels. "What you and Scarlett are building here is truly special. I mean, look at them." She threw an arm out and I was beginning to understand that her power-pose, might be more of a 'reign in your energy' pose.

Still, I followed suit and looked at the gym filled with girls, the smallest ones running circles around their trainers. "The special part is all Scarlett," I said. I'd just wanted a gym within walking distance to work.

"Fiddlesticks!" Scarlett slapped me in the arm again, and I glowered at her, because I might not mind when we were alone, but this was business. "You came up with girls' nights."

"I would love to talk to you about some of my ideas to make the space even more inclusive." Hannah reached out and squeezed my upper arm, scrunching her button nose at me. "Let's get together for a more private meeting some time." And *that* was why I didn't want Scarlett being overly friendly with me in front of others. "I'll see you around, Mr. Beckett." Hannah hopped back to reception, giving me about a dozen ideas how I could use that ponytail during a private meeting.

"She's cute, right?" Scarlett poked her elbow into my ribs.

"She's fired," I said and turned for the locker rooms.

"What? Are you kidding me?"

"You don't shit where you eat, Scarlett. Hire a regional manager who gets that."

Ten minutes later, I was in athletic gear and Hannah was nowhere to be seen. Instead, a lanky, toothy teenager popped up in front of me. "Sneak attack!" she yelled at the top of her lungs, swinging her gloved fist at me.

I blocked her, hit her between the shoulders and she dropped to the mats with an oomph. "Maybe don't yell *sneak attack* before getting to the actual attack."

"Good point," she grunted and jumped back to her feet like her joints were made of springs. Julian didn't like to hear it, but Brody had an actual chance at going pro. Lack of sneakiness aside, she had the stamina and speed to outmatch some of the women already in the UFC.

"Did you warm up?" I asked because despite her skill, she also had the same affinity for following a strict training regimen as any 15-year-old: zero.

"Ye-hes," she drawled, bouncing backwards on her toes to get to our station. "Can we try the flying kicks again? I'm getting really good at home."

"You won't need flying kicks," I repeated for about the 100th time. Brody had her mother's brown skin, soft features, and naturally coiled hair - currently in dozens of tiny braids and tied together at the nape of her neck - but she had inherited the Beckett genes for height. One more inch, and she'd hit the 6-foot-mark. That already made her taller than most other fighters in her age and weight class. No need to jump through the air to land a kick.

"But flying kicks are fun, uncle Auggie. It doesn't have to make sense. You gotta embrace the fun." She slung her arms around her punching bag, giving me the big brown puppy eyes she'd perfected over the years.

Unfortunately for her, I'd had to steel my defenses against that when she was nine and kept asking for kittens and bunnies. I would have filled her entire room with fluffy pets, but her father would have ripped my head off after the hamster incident of 2014. I could only deny those puppy eyes in so many ways though. "If you land a single hit to my face today, we'll do nothing but flying kicks on Thursday."

She pumped her arms up into the air, silently twirling and jumping up and down excitedly, before clearing her throat and looking at me with a stern face. "I agree to this deal, coach."

"Jab, cross, hook, upper-cut. Come on."

I didn't go easier on Brody even if she was my niece. She was a sweaty mess by the end of each training session, rubbing the fresh bruises on her arms and ribs. She usually trained with me once a week and once with a group of girls her age. The latter was less of a challenge to her, but it allowed her to practice her lifts and sprawls.

We grabbed food on the drive home and Brody scarfed down six tacos in the ten minutes it took to get from the restaurant to her house. "Hi Dad, bye Dad!" She yelled running past Julian on the front steps. He had to be tracking her with one of those apps, because he was always waiting when I brought her home.

Today, he jogged down to the car and leaned into the door that Brody had left wide open in her haste to get inside. "You messed up."

"This?" I asked, pointing at the swollen cut on my cheek bone. "That was on purpose." Halfway at least. I'd meant to let her land one hit, but that one had not been it. That kid had speed.

His eyes dropped to the fast-food wrappers on the floor of my car, nose scrunching up. When he didn't say anything about Brody's meal plan as per usual, I got a feeling that I wasn't going to like where this was going. "I'm talking about your little date."

Ah, yes. The one I had been perfectly happy to ignore for the last few days. The one I hadn't told him about yet. "I can handle the Montgomery girl."

"It looks like the company is coming out of probate sooner than we thought. Her lawyers are working on this at full steam. At this rate, she'll be the official owner of the Montgomery corporation by the end of summer." He tossed a flash drive into the passenger seat. It was usually best not to ask where or how Julian got the information he did. He was the reason, the sex tape that had come up during my date with Del, was disappearing into thin air - alongside all the online banking accounts of the person who'd sent it. The only upside to the tape had been that it had allowed me to gauge Del's physical attraction to me, even if she was too skittish to act on it.

"End of summer?" I asked. "What, like September?"

"You need to up your game."

Jesus. Engaged by Thanksgiving seemed too far in the distance now. That would mean a spring wedding at the earliest - which was way too much opportunity for her to wreck the company. "Fine. How does a Christmas wedding sound to you?"

"Music to my ears." He grinned and tapped the roof of the car.

"Get me her next appearance as soon as it pops up on your radar." I had a feeling, if I tried to stitch things up on the phone this time, Cordelia's assistant Page wouldn't be able to help me, let alone connect me to Del, because she would mysteriously be unavailable all day.

"No problem." Julian straightened and reached for the door, then bent down again. "Oh, by the way, next time you take her for smoothies, put some flaxseed in it. It apparently breaks down the hormones in contraceptive pills. In case you're aiming for a shotgun wedding." He slammed the door shut before I even had the chance to formulate a reply.

My ring finger might have had a 20-billion price tag, but we both knew what having two kids against her will had done to our mother. No amount of money could turn me into our father. Nothing was worth repeating that shit show.

NINE

Delilah

I didn't wake up today, thinking I would get poked and prodded by a dozen wet noses, but here I was. Apparently, Fitzwilliam had left a very distinct smell on my clothes. I tried to gently push back the golden retriever trying to bury its snout in my lap. "Oh god, oh god, oh god," I whined, wriggling my fingers in its face.

I'd gotten a cat for a reason.

The huge husky currently trying to paw off my shoes had tackled me into the corner of the yoga studio earlier and I'd almost started crying. These guys had way too much muscle power, and way too large teeth.

"Jesus, that's not going work, is it?" Tabitha huffed and just pushed the dogs off by their shoulders. "Are you hiding a steak in your pants?"

"I think they can smell Fitz."

"I guess that means no dog yoga video." She shrugged, glancing over her shoulder at the other women in class, who were glaring at me. Yeah, I'd hate it too if I signed up for dog yoga and all the dogs were hyperfixated on the girl with the camera.

Since getting fired, Tab had hired me to be her camerawoman every now and again. We had already tackled hot yoga, beer yoga and goat yoga. She said it kept her content dynamic, but really, it was likely just her attempt to give me money after I'd refused to accept it as a gift. "Sorry." I handed over her stupid expensive camera. I always panicked about potentially dropping and breaking it, but Tabitha handled it like she handled her phone. The cracked display was all her. "I'll wait outside for you."

"Eh, we might as well just get out." She waved me off before I could come up with some way to film the video anyway and grabbed her gym bag from the corner. "I'm starving. Let's get burgers."

"We just had breakfast," I said once we were out of the studio.

"Okay, but I don't live in the past. And in the present, I'm starving." She drummed her fingers against her bare, toned stomach. "Or maybe hot dogs. Am I craving hot dogs? Talk to me, Kevin." She glared at her stomach, which had such a mind of its own, it did deserve a name. The number of times *Kevin* had derailed our dinner plans... Unfortunately, it wasn't just cravings. Sometimes Kevin just decided he didn't like *any* food, and it all came back out.

"Sounds like Kevin wants meat and carbs," I said.

Her stomach growled in agreement. "Burritos! Amazing. Good call." She rubbed her belly button and grinned at me. "He likes you."

A young woman walked past us with a stroller and gave us a big smile that suggested she was severely misunderstanding the situation. Little did she know, we had agreed that Kevin personified looked like Stanley Tucci - not a darling baby cherub.

My phone buzzed in my pocket, and I pulled it out, only to narrow my eyes at the unknown caller ID. I'd not heard from Cordelia in a few days, and I'd saved her number, but this whole mess had gotten too complicated to reject any calls.

"Hello," I answered, nice and vague.

"Hello, Miss Edwards?" The baritone voice was vaguely familiar.

"Yes?"

"This is Principal Baker from Truman Academy."

My heart stopped. Oh god. A call. An actual call. Not an email to thank me for my time. "Hello, Mr. Baker," I squeaked and grabbed Tab's arm to haul her into the entryway of the building we were passing. I was not having this conversation while walking. No multitasking. Maximum brain capacity. "It's good to hear from you."

"I apologize for taking this long to get back to you, Miss Edwards, we had a little trouble contacting your previous school." Tabitha pulled a face as my grip on her arm tightened.

"Oh," I gasped. Oh god, oh god, oh god. Was the air around me thinning? Because I couldn't breathe, and colorful spots danced across my vision.

"Well, we finally managed, and it looks like everything is in order. I personally think you would be a great fit for the Academy, so if you're still available, I would like to invite you to a follow-up interview."

My knees gave out and I sank to the floor, pulling Tabitha with me. She crouched in front of me, eyes torn open in alarm, as tears welled up in my eyes. "That sounds great," I said, voice clogged.

"I'm glad to hear that. I will email you the details. This follow-up will be a video call, as one of our English teachers, Mr. Day, and Mrs. Gretzki from the school administration will join us, but both are enjoying their summer holidays with their families."

He chuckled. "Do you have upcoming holiday plans we should consider?"

"Nope." I pushed the word out through a blocked throat.

"Alright, I'll let you get back to your day. I look forward to talking to you again."

"Thank you. Likewise."

The second he hung up, a loud sob broke from my chest and three months' worth of anxiety spilled through my cracks. And it hurt. My chest felt like it was being pulled apart, rib by rib. I couldn't stop crying.

"What's happening, Del?" Tabitha wrapped her arms around me, her hand rubbing circles into my back.

I couldn't breathe. I was heaving air, but I couldn't- I didn't- "She did it," I sobbed.

"Who did what, honey?" Tabitha's voice had taken on an unnerving, sweet tone, and that was enough to make me feel ridiculous for breaking down in public like that, so I started laughing and the laughing turned back into sobs - and God, someone would call the cops on me in a second because I had to look deranged.

"Cordelia. Childs," I gasped through my laugh-sobs.

"This is happy tears?"

I nodded, even though I wasn't sure whether I was happy. I was every emotion I'd kept bundled up over months of putting on a brave face. Hurt. Afraid. Helpless. Hopeless. Angry. It all poured through me, and when the crying finally stopped, it felt like I had shrugged off a weighted blanket I'd kept wrapped around me since that day in Roger Childs' office.

When all the emotions had poured out, only one was left in my lightened chest. Relief.

I sighed, sagging into Tabitha's shoulder.

"Feel better, honey?" she cooed, only to turn and bark at someone to keep walking with her usual gruff voice.

Another laugh bubbled up, but this time it wasn't interrupted by sobs. I filled Tabitha in on the phone call while she used the emergency wet wipes from my bag (purple pouch) to clean up my messed-up makeup.

"Well, shit," she mumbled, dragging a soft tissue under my left eye, "who knew you just needed billionaire friends to handle your problems?"

I hitched another laugh and grimaced right after. "Stop, that hurts my throat."

"That's what she said."

I laughed again, but the laugh turned into a pained groan. I wasn't giving her any more ammunition, so I shut up and waited for her to finish cleaning me up.

I hadn't even told my mother that I'd lost my job. Now, even the weight of that omission faded into nothingness. Mom would have told me to get a different job, any job, as long as I made money - but I wasn't ready to give up on my career just because I'd slipped up once. "Hey Tabitha," I whispered, when she pocketed the dirty makeup wipes, "can you come with me to Cordelia's?"

"Why?"

"Because I want to help her."

"Are you sure?"

I nodded and let myself be pulled back to my feet. "Yeah. I think she needs a non-billionaire friend to help with her career. I want this for her, too."

"You want her to have a Menty B between a Starbucks and a Verizon?" She patted down my jeans, swatting off any dirt.

"A fair chance."

"Yes?" Victor pulled the door open but didn't move, taking up almost the entire frame.

"Do you do yoga? Because we could do some awesome couple yoga videos. I bet you can lift me with one hand," Tabitha babbled, tilting her head sideways, "and do those tattoos go everywhere?"

He turned from her to me, ignoring her questions. "I'll do it," I explained my presence on their doorstep, "Tabitha's here for emotional support."

We had to wait outside for a minute before being waved through. Cordelia bit her lip and smoothed her hands down her pale pink dress repeatedly at the sight of Tabitha in her office. "Hello." Her voice quivered, but she nodded at Victor who took that as a sign to leave us alone. "I'm Cordelia."

"Ooh." Tab swiveled left and right between us. "I get it. You're like Smurf Cordelia."

"That's Tabitha," I said. "She knows everything. I hope that's okay."

"I won't blab. Cross my heart and hope to die." Instead of crossing her chest, she held up three fingers in a scout's honor gesture, when I knew for a fact, she was neither Christian, nor had she ever been a Girl Scout.

Cordelia's hands still trembled, making me wonder if maybe I should have done this alone after all. Tabitha's presence next to me, as she shamelessly turned and twisted to take in the full modern rococo glam of Cordelia's house, calmed my own nerves though. It was a blip of normalcy in an utterly surreal situation. "I'm going to do it," I said, "I'll pretend to be you for the rest of summer."

"Really?" The glimmer of hope in her voice solidified the decision for me. I nodded. "Oh dear, I need to buy so many clothes."

Tab let out a startled sound, but I chuckled, having learned a few things about Cordelia Montgomery by now. "Did you skip five thoughts ahead again?"

"Yep." She grinned, then launched herself around her desk to hug me. Her long arms snaked around my shoulders, and I wrapped mine around her waist in return. Her back shuddered under my hands as silent sobs started rocking her body.

"Alright," Tabitha sighed, "I'll go get the makeup wipes."

TEN

BECK

THE POOL WAS PINK AND FILLED WITH BUBBLES AND NAKED women. I only stared for more than a moment because it looked like some of them were either breaking out in rashes - or the pink water was staining their tits. Either way, they were too drunk to care. I took another quick look around the rooftop, but the lounge chairs were predominantly occupied by busy couples and throuples. Back to the loft, even though the strobe lights and pulsing bodies turned my search mission into a nightmare.

Gavin Decker's birthday was the last event I'd expected Del to attend. Decker was known for his escalating parties and the fact that he sank his father's vintage Mercedes convertible in the ocean. Literally drove the thing off one of his family's yachts. Del could hardly handle a business party and now she had shown up to *this*?

I grabbed another drink at the open bar before checking the

bedrooms. Door after door, none of the scenes in and around the beds included a certain blue-eyed blonde. I'd rather not have found her snorting a line, or with some guy buried balls deep inside her, but at least then I would have found her. Maybe the only reason I'd never been with a short woman, was the fact that they were practically invisible.

The only place I hadn't breached yet was the dance floor, which was filled with people grinding their bodies against each other, eyes glazed over, hair dripping in sweat. That had never been my scene, not even in my twenties. I pushed myself through the masses, eyes raking over every blonde I came across.

My attention was snatched by a flash of gold in the corner of my eye. Jesus. How could I have missed her the last thirty minutes? Del was in the middle of the dance floor, dancing circles around an athletic girl with short brown curls. She threw her head back, laughing at something her friend said. Her sparkling high-waisted shorts revealed her legs from the very curve of her hip downwards and the matching crop top wasn't offering much coverage either. Under the strobe lights, the golden sequins of her outfit turned her into a writhing disco ball. It did nothing to distract from the way her legs shifted though. The shorts *just* covered her ass cheeks, but when she swung her hips, her thigh crease still flashed out from under the sequins.

I wasn't the only one hungrily watching every sway of her body, but the second some guy with a neck tattoo tried to get close, the brunette pushed him back and wagged her finger at him. I couldn't help but grin at his dumbfounded expression and his friends hollering at him. Blondie had brought someone to enforce her personal space.

She was mesmerizing on the dance floor, but I waited until she detached herself from her friend and angled towards the bar, before I moved in. I hadn't been the only one waiting for an opening. Neck tattoo guy jumped away from his friends to go after her.

Bouncing bodies and sweaty faces shoved themselves in front of me, slowing my steps. If this guy was one of Decker's friends, I didn't trust him alone with Del for even a minute.

By the time I made it to the bar, he had her cornered by its side. I might have come on strong at Bumble, but he took up most of the space that would have allowed her to leave. Didn't he see her hands balled into fists by her side? Hell, he probably did and didn't care. I put my drink down on some side table and flexed my fingers. Shit, I wanted to punch that lazy grin off his face. I just had the feeling Blondie wouldn't talk to me ever again if I did.

So instead, I slipped through the few inches of space Neck Tattoo had left between him and the wall, and I wrapped my arm around Del's middle. "Sorry for being late, sweetheart." I tugged her against me and pressed a kiss against the crown of her head. Even in this pit of nicotine, weed and spilled beer, her fresh, sweet jasmine scent was as strong as ever. She blinked up at me, brows quivering as her hand folded around my wrist on her stomach. The quiet relief seeping through her shoulders was enough to incite more violent thoughts as I dragged my eyes from her to Neck Tattoo and offered him my hand. "August Beckett."

"Jordan, uh, just Jordan," he said and placed his hand in mine. I squeezed it tightly enough for a bone to pop beneath my fingers. Jordan winced, his knees trembling when I finally let go. "I, uh, forgot, uh…" He walked backwards, clutching his hand to his chest, before turning on his heels and diving into the crowd of dancers.

Del turned in my arm, positioning herself between me and the bar. "That was unnecessary but thank you," she said. Despite her deeming it unnecessary, she made no move to distance herself from me. I knew well enough that *that* wasn't about me, so she had to be more rattled than she let on.

"What are you doing here?" I asked.

"I could be asking you the same thing." Her eyes raked over

me in a pointedly unimpressed curve. Yeah, I may have dropped the tie, but I was still in the same suit I'd worn to the office. Which didn't exactly fit in with the twenty-something party crowd here. To be fair, she'd come here without notice, and I'd booked it, the second Julian alerted me to the paparazzi pictures from outside. Del shook her head and closed her eyes, sagging against the bar for just a moment before putting on a big smile again. "I'm showing the world that I'm young and hot and totally extroverted."

"But you're not." Her mouth dropped open. Oh fuck. Come on. I quickly added: "Extroverted, I mean." My communication skills clearly plummeted around her. What the hell was this tiny blonde woman doing to me? I'd never had issues saying the right thing at the right time.

"Why are you talking to me, Beck?" She scrunched up her nose at me, but still didn't move an inch.

"Here." I pulled the small brown box I'd been carrying around from my jacket pocket. Not exactly how I would have wanted to present it, but fine.

"What's that?"

"An apology," I said, "I was out of line and caused you to miss dessert, when that was the very reason I meant to take you to Bumble by the Sea. It's their famous honey-lemon *blondie*."

Her lips twitched into a small smile, but she didn't reach for the box. "This is a birthday party. There's probably going to be cake."

"It won't be this good."

"Have you been saving this for six days?" Curiosity won over and she took the box, flipping the lid open. The cake bar inside didn't look like much, a blondie with some white chocolate and honey drizzled on top, but I hadn't lied when I'd said it was famous.

"No, I heard you might come here, so I picked it up on the way."

Del didn't look impressed, but she still lifted the blondie from the box and took a bite. "Oh god," she moaned as the cake melted on her tongue, revealing a core of salted caramel. Her eyelids fluttered and she held a hand up in front of her mouth. "Oh, that's good," she sighed.

I couldn't help the grin that formed on my lips at those sounds.

"Why are you looking at me like that?"

"You sound like you're having good sex," I replied, echoing our conversation from Saturday.

"This is better than sex," she said and took another bite, breath quivering as she nodded to herself.

"I'm starting to think that your sex life is lacking."

"I'm starting to think you'll have to bring the whole apology cake next time." She pointed a warning finger at me but couldn't even keep up the attitude before the cake was more important again. One last bite and she'd polished it off. "Oh god, this is amazing though. I also had like five coffees and no food today, so this is hitting all the right spots."

She was riding a full foodgasm. If I'd known that was all it took, I would have brought this cake the first night we met. "You have some honey on your lip, here let me-"

She smacked my hand out of the air. "If you touch me again, you'll have to buy me a whole apology bakery."

Not that much of a foodgasm then. "Fair enough, here." I touched the left corner of my mouth, and she mirrored the movement, brows furrowing when she didn't find any honey there. "Sorry, just kidding, here." I ran my pinky to my cupid's bow and watched her do the same. The image of her smudging lipstick embedded itself into my brain for later. More confusion rippled over her features though when she didn't find honey on her cupid's bow either. There was no honey. My move had backfired.

Still, I grinned, wanting to test just how gullible she was. "Actually, no, it's right here." My hand dropped to my chest.

Del's hand lowered two inches, then froze. She narrowed her eyes at me. Not very gullible. Instead of calling me out on my bullshit again, she tossed the empty cake box on the counter behind her before looking up at me again. This time, her eyes were widened, and she bit her full bottom lip. "Right here, yes?" She asked, her voice extra breathy as she dropped her hand to her chest and flicked her thumb over its highest point.

Fuck.

I inhaled deeply through my nose, that one move having sent a flaming bolt right down to my dick.

Blondie was feeling feisty.

I braced one hand on the bar, angling myself just enough to give us a little privacy when I moved my hand across my chest. "There's some more over here."

"Oh dear, what a mess," she breathed and dragged her fingers over rustling sequins to her other breast. Instead of flicking it again, she pushed two fingers against it, as if wiping off some honey - except, it also pushed half her breast to swell over the edge of her top.

Oh shit. My breathing shallowed. Where had she kept this playful, sexy side of her? I worked my jaw to keep my hands to myself and not crush my mouth into hers, push her up against that wall, suck those perfect dainty tits into my mouth. She knew exactly what she was doing to me, blinking up at me, all innocence and smiles.

My hand slid from my chest to my stomach. She mirrored my move, letting her fingers catch on her top, giving me just a flash of breast. "Did I get it now?" She ran her tongue over her full lower lip.

The hot pressure pooled in my hips. It wouldn't take much before she'd see exactly what this little game was doing to me.

I let my hand sink to my belt buckle and Del's eyes dropped to it. I could practically hear her thoughts whirring before her ocean eyes found mine again, and with a big grin, she slipped her hand into her shorts. Not just into the waistband either. The ripple of the sequins clearly outlined her hand traveling down her stomach and in between her legs. Her grin quivered as she let out a small gasp.

Holy fuck.

I was so hard, my dick was straining torturously against my trousers.

Who had taken Blondie and replaced her with a girl who fingered herself in a room full of strangers? I shifted closer, wanting to hear every ragged breath from that gorgeous mouth of hers.

"Tell me, Del," I whispered, bringing my lips close to her ear. Her hot breath trickled over my skin, coming in short bursts as her hand continued moving. "What does that verbal orgasm of yours sound like exactly?"

"Oh god," she gasped, sending another pulse to my hips, right before she giggled and rolled her shoulders back. "I don't actually know," she laughed. Breathing evened out instantly, she pulled her hand from her shorts and grabbed one of the napkins from the bar. She wiped her hand off unceremoniously and raised her brows at me. "I'm really good at putting on a show though. You can stop fantasizing about hooking up with me. Neither of us would enjoy that experience."

My thoughts were still clouded by all her little sounds, so realization took a second to settle in. "Did you just Meg Ryan me?"

"Yeah. Now, if you'll excuse me." She patted my shoulder and circled around me. Apparently over her original plan to get another drink, she pushed through the crowd and followed the makeshift signs towards the bathrooms, and I lost sight of her within three steps.

I flagged the bartender down for another drink as the other

meaning of her words filtered through. *I don't actually know. I'm really good at putting on a show though. Neither of us would enjoy that experience.*

Del was clearly not a virgin. At least I'd never met a virgin who fingered herself in public, which made her confession even more bewildering. If she was, indeed, freaky enough for that kind of behavior worthy of a Gavin Decker party, there was no reason for her to… She had to have… What the fuck?

I should have been thinking about how I could use this to my advantage, but every time I closed my eyes, if I so much as blinked, I saw her trembling lips and heard her little *Oh god.* I blamed my still hardened dick for the fact that I couldn't focus on anything but the mental image of how her cheeks would flush red to match her lipstick once I sank my head between those thighs. I imagined her hitching breath once I buried myself inside her and how beautifully she would fall apart riding my cock.

She had to be thoroughly underfucked, and even if I sucked at romance, *that* was something I could fix.

I had to fix something else first.

By the end of my drink, I found Neck Tattoo in the hallway to the bedrooms with a redhead hanging on his shoulder, stumbling over her own two feet. I had no doubts that could have been Del if she'd ordered a drink in front of him. I tapped him on the shoulder, and he turned, annoyance quickly replaced by recognition. "Dude, I didn't know she was your girl. It's all good."

"See, I don't think it's all good." I kissed my teeth and took another look at the girl with her glazed brown eyes and the strap of her little black dress falling off her shoulder.

"I'm just taking her to lie down. She's super drunk, man."

"I'm sure you won't mind if I lend you a hand." Before he had the chance to protest, I scooped an arm around the girl's middle and pulled her through the next bedroom door. Neck Tattoo stumbled along because the girl's arm was still hooked around his neck. "Hi, don't mind us." I gave a short nod to the two girls going at it on the dresser and directed the redhead onto the rumpled bed. She collapsed into the sheets, sighing, and her lights went out.

Neck Tattoo seemed to weigh his options, glancing between the comatose girl, the other two, and the door. I didn't have time for this bullshit.

"Girls, would you look out for her for a second? It looks like she's had too much to drink." One of them pulled her hand out from under the other's dress, glancing over, eyes falling to the lifeless body on the mattress. "I'll be right back," I promised, grabbed Neck Tattoo's collar, and hauled him into the bathroom. I shoved him forward, giving me the space to position myself between him and the door.

"Hey, what the fuck?" He clutched his hand to his chest, reminding me of the satisfying crunch of his pinky. I locked the door behind me. "Hey, yo, I'm flattered and all but that's not my thing."

"What's your thing?" I slid my jacket off my shoulders and hung it on the doorknob.

He backed up, hands raised. "Girls, man, I just play for pussy."

"Doesn't feel so good, does it?" I asked, taking a step closer to him, popping open the buttons around my wrists.

"What? Uh? What?" He backed up until his legs hit the toilet, eyes skittering left and right.

"Being boxed into a corner. Feeling like your physical choices are being stripped from you." I rolled my sleeves up.

"What do you want from me, man?" He scrambled for something to hold onto, something to swing at me. And only found a toothbrush. He actually did swing that out like a knife. I plucked it from his hand and tossed it over my shoulder.

"Kneel down."

"You want a blow job, dude? That girl out there will totally give you one. Like, she doesn't even care."

He made me sick.

"Get on your knees." He swung out a fist with all the speed and strength of an 8-year-old girl. I blocked it, twisted his arm, and brought my heel down against his knee. It cracked and he buckled to the floor with a cry. "Wasn't so hard, was it?"

"Shit, fuck, you broke my leg."

"Give me your belt."

This time, he didn't protest, fumbling to get it off. It was an old, wrecked pleather piece of shit but it would do the job. I slipped the end through the buckle, dropped the noose over his head, and yanked.

His eyes bulged and his hands flew up to his throat, feet scrambling to follow as I dragged him to the towel heater. I pulled the belt around one of the pipes. Low enough for him to breathe if he knelt very still with his ear pressed against the heater. "Have you ever heard of autoerotic asphyxiation?" I asked, crouching down to meet his panicked eyes while he gasped for air. "I'm sure you're not quite sober, so it wouldn't even be investigated beyond the toxins in your blood if you were found here. Pants down, dick out, choked by your own belt."

"Please," he gasped, one hand grasping at his new pleather necklace, the other slapping upwards against my hold on his belt.

"What's wrong? I got the distinct impression you liked to mix sex with helplessness." I pulled on the belt, knocking his head back against the heater. He squeezed his eyes shut and scratched at his neck as the air flow to his lungs died down. I waited, watched his head turn red, watched the veins bulge around the rosary tattoo on his neck. What a good and god-fearing Christian he was... I dropped the belt when the strength left his muscles. He collapsed to the floor, heaving for air, and I pulled his phone from his pocket. No screen-lock. I found his mother in his contacts listed under Mommabear. Great. She picked up on the second ring.

"Jordan? It's late."

"This isn't Jordan. I'm at a party with him. He tried to roofie and rape a young woman tonight." I put the phone on speaker and dropped it next to the coughing mess on the floor before I grabbed my jacket and walked back out to the bedroom. The other two girls had crowded around the passed-out redhead. "Can you guys make sure she gets home okay?" I pulled two hundred from my pocket and handed them to the girl who looked a little less drunk than the other one. "That should cover the Uber."

ELEVEN

Delilah

I couldn't even blame the alcohol. People pulled stupid stunts while drunk all the time. I'd only been riding a caffeine and sugar high, and I wanted to wipe that stupid smirk of Beck's stupidly perfect face. He'd smelled so good, too. Maybe his perfume was laced with pheromones because that would explain my clouded judgement. Yep. After a quick google search to legitimize my theory, I decided that Beck must have bought one of those pheromone perfumes, which actually existed, and that was the only reason I slipped my hand down my pants in a room full of strangers.

At least I hadn't felt anything besides the pulse-hammering thrill that came with doing something scandalous. And maybe a bit of an extra flush in my cheeks because of the shadows that had crept over Beck's face when he'd watched me.

Stupid, stupid, stupid.

"I know you're nervous about the interview." Parker leaned in the bathroom door while I fixed my makeup for my Zoom call. I should have been nervous about the interview, but my brain had been consumed by those ten minutes with August Beckett all weekend. Ten minutes that I definitely couldn't tell Parker about. Or anyone. Ever. "So, this is kind of bad timing."

"What's up?" I asked, selfishly hoping he had done something horrible, so I'd feel less bad.

"Could you Venmo me the cancellation fee for the restaurant the other night?"

"Oh, yeah, sure," I mumbled, putting the mascara down to fish my phone from my pocket.

"I wanted to wait until you got the job before I asked, but my mom's car broke down and I had to send her some money," he explained, words tumbling from his lips in a rush.

I couldn't be even a little mad about him bringing this up before my interview when that was the reason he needed the money. Come on. Parker was so nice, he constantly helped out his parents, even if it put a strain on his own finances. "There you go," I said once the money had gone through. I'd just pocket some extra food from the next charity dinner Cordelia would send me to.

"Thanks, you're the best." He blew me a kiss and checked his phone when it pinged with the Venmo notification. Something about that irked me. Like he didn't quite trust me to send the right amount, or wanted to double-check that the notification really was my payment. And the fact that I got irked made me feel even worse, because I knew he had his thing about money, and that was so fine. I had enough of my own anxieties to understand the constant double-checking.

I was a horrible human being. There. I was a horrible person who did horrible things and had horrible thoughts. Perfect mantra for ten minutes before a job interview, right?

"Alright, I'm going to leave you to it. You got this. Text me the minute you're finished, and I'll come running back."

"Thank you!"

My studio was too small for him to stay through the Zoom interview. It would have been too awkward, because he'd either be in the background, or I'd be sitting in front of a wall, but would be on display for him to watch me. Thankfully, he'd agreed to go get coffee, while I handled this.

And I did handle it.

The interview was amazing. Principal Baker was still as warm and welcoming as when I'd met him in person. Mr. Day and I immediately clicked because he was as much of a Jane Austen nerd as I was, and when Fitzwilliam decided to jump through the frame, that led us down a sidebar about Pride and Prejudice, because Mr. Day's dog was called Darcy. And Mrs. Gretzki, who worked on the admin side of things, was a total no-nonsense organizational genius. She was still asking me about my color-coded note-taking techniques when the scheduled hour was up.

And then I had to wait. They literally put me in the Zoom's waiting room, asking me to give them fifteen minutes to reflect.

My heart fluttered hard enough for Fitzwilliam to sit between my legs and rub his head against my calves instead of scratching them up. My nerves were so raw, even the demon child pitied me. I didn't expect them to come to a decision today, but Baker said there was only one other candidate, so they wanted to make the call as soon as possible.

Oh god, what if the Pride and Prejudice chat had derailed the interview?

What if using Notion for structuring and prioritizing my tasks was horrible because that meant it was all stored in a cloud?

"Miss Edwards?"

I blinked, seeing only Baker's face on my screen. It couldn't be good that the others had left, right? That meant he wanted to break the bad news to me without an audience. "Hello again," I said, pasting on a big smile.

"Thank you for waiting."

"Of course."

"In the name of all of us here at Truman, I would like to extend the invitation for you to join our staff in September."

I blacked out after that. I vaguely remembered smiling and laughing and thanking him, but I couldn't piece it together within twenty seconds of ending the call. I had a job. All other details just blurred.

I actually, finally, really had a job.

And my first thought was that I'd have to tell Parker in public, because I didn't want to ruin this with another celebration that came in the form of his wet mouth on me.

Horrible person with horrible thoughts.

"I'M SO PROUD OF YOU, BABE." PARKER PULLED ME CLOSER against him and I had to jut out my frappuccino-holding hand to keep from spilling it down his back. A park bench had been a great idea as an oral-sex-repellant, but it also came with its share of physical boundaries unless you were down to jump into someone's lap in public.

"Thank you," I whispered and kissed his cheek.

"I knew it was only a matter of time before someone realized how smart you were."

Yeah, it had never been about how smart I was... I forced myself to smooth my furrowed brows before pulling out of the hug, because I hadn't told Parker about Childs. Of course, he thought the problem with my months and months of unemployment lay with me and how smart I presented myself. "Thank you," I said again, unsure how else to respond.

"Del?"

My back stiffened at the sound of that voice. Parker looked up before I did, letting out a long "uuuh" sound at the sight of August Beckett. Beck wore a pair of Armani sunglasses, because of course he did, with his perfectly crisp white shirt and perfectly tailored grey trousers and perfectly shiny leather shoes. All polished six-foot-four of him the exact opposite of Parker's sweatpants and my torn mom jeans. (Zoom interviews didn't show below the waistline, and these were my most comfy jeans, ok?)

I grimaced against the sun that outlined Beck's perfectly broad shoulders. "Hi."

"Casual Monday?" He asked, eyes dropping to where my knees poked through shredded fabric.

"Something like that."

"Looks good on you." He put on that stupidly shameless grin that was apparently capable of making me lose my mind, and God, I was already getting the urge to wipe it off his face again.

Next to me, Parker straightened and cleared his throat, as annoyed by that stupid grin as I was. "Hi, I'm Parker. Del's boyfriend?!" The second half of that almost sounded like he was questioning it.

"Beck." He shook Parker's hand, and I swore Parker winced beside me at the grip. Not as hard as that drunk guy at the party, but it was still a wince. "Nice to meet you."

"Yes, nice to meet you. Who are you exactly?" Parker ran a hand through his unruly curls, but that did nothing to make him look more put together. I reached around him and ran my hand over his neck, trying to calm whatever doubts he had. Trying to show Beck that he was not derailing this.

"Do you mind if I steal your girlfriend for just a second?" Beck asked.

Asshole. I was right here. Parker was hardly my keeper.

"Actually, we were in the middle of something. I'll talk to you some other time, Beck."

"I promise, it will only take a second, hun."

Hun. As in honey. As in, I had pretended to wipe honey off my nipples in front of him less than 24 hours ago. Him and his stupid, mental word games. "Fine," I huffed and untangled myself from Parker and the bench. I shot my boyfriend a reassuring smile before walking ten feet off with Beck. "What's so important?"

"You look good in jeans, Blondie."

"Seriously? That's what you wanted to tell me?"

"Let's get dinner. Right now. There's a great Ethiopian place down the street."

I didn't understand this man. I just didn't. "You want to have dinner with us? Why?"

"No, just you. I don't give a shit about Porter," he scoffed.

"Parker."

"You're too good for him."

"Ohmygod. And let me guess, you're good enough for me? You don't even know Parker."

"It's part of my job to assess people within seconds of meeting them. I wouldn't be where I am if I couldn't. And I have assessed that he's not worth your while." He shot a pointed look over my shoulder. Great, now Parker would know we were talking about him.

"Looks like you're really bad at assessing people if you think I'm going to ditch my boyfriend to hang out with you."

"Isn't that what you're doing right now?" That grin was back, and I felt the responding heat rising to my cheeks.

"Screw you," I hissed, hating that he was right.

"I wish you would. I promise, you *would* enjoy that experience."

That was it. Oh god. Just let the ground open up and swallow me hole, because my face was burning with the blush to end all blushes. Of course, it hadn't been enough that I'd fingered myself in front of him. I'd told him that I'd never had an orgasm. "Are you following me?" I asked instead because I was not reopening that can of worms.

"Last night? Kind of. Today? No." He pointed down the path at a tall, tan, curvy woman with shiny black curls, clad in a tight denim jumpsuit that highlighted just how long her legs were. They probably reached up to my navel. Physically, she was the exact opposite of me. Despite being on the phone, her eyes were firmly trained on us. "Technically having dinner with her."

A sour taste spread in my mouth, and I crossed my arms in front my chest. "Good. Go have dinner with her," I snapped, sounding an awful lot like I was jealous.

Oh. My. God.

Could the earth hurry up with the swallowing-me-whole already?

At least he didn't point it out or make fun of me for my stupid, childish reaction. Instead, he said: "Still ready to ditch her if you say yes."

I stared up at him, feeling my nostrils flare and my pulse spike against my will. How could he- He was just so- What on earth made him think-

"Del?" Parker called from behind me, snapping me out of it. I turned to face him, knowing fully well that my face had to be the same color as his strawberry refresher. "Uh, it's just that I have work." He tapped his wrist where a watch would be if he wore a watch. I glanced back at Beck's wrist, finding a glinting gold watch with a leather strap on his arm. What the hell had I done that for? Horrible person, making horrible comparisons. Watches? Who the hell cared about watches?

"Coming!" I called and turned to Beck one last time. "Enjoy your date."

He smirked. "It's a business dinner."

"Whatever," I bit out with all the cadence of someone who was definitely, totally, absolutely unaffected by that revelation. Beck had an unnerving ability to creep under my skin. Totally not my fault, right? I breathed in deeply, filling my lungs with his citrus, woodsy smell, that *unfortunately* didn't compare at all to the sugary, flowery scents the pheromone perfumes had described. "Enjoy your business dinner."

TWELVE

Delilah

My eyes burnt, but no matter how much I blinked, the pain didn't ease up. All the bright pink in Cordelia's office didn't help. It burnt itself into my corneas. That's what I got for sleeping all of two hours.

Defne and Tabitha had insisted on celebrating my new job with me even though I had felt less than jubilant in midst of the Parker-Beck-chaos. Plus, I couldn't really go out, now that my physical appearance was tied to Cordelia - at least until I cut and dyed my hair at the end of summer. That hadn't deterred them from pumping me full of caramel fraps and dragging me to a karaoke bar, where they'd booked a private room for us. And by the third Abba song, my life had been peachy.

Except now I didn't feel like much of a dancing queen at all anymore, trying to focus my eyes on the little plastic card in my hands. "Where did you get this picture?" I asked, holding the license up to the light.

"I don't know. I just tell people what to do. I don't ask them how they do it." Cordelia shrugged as if it was totally normal that she could just get her hands on my passport picture, and put it on a fake ID.

"Wait," I scanned the details on the license again, exhausted brain goo piecing together that I wasn't just getting an ID that made me 29 instead of 27, "why are you giving me a fake ID with your name on it?"

"I would have just given you mine since we look similar enough, but I don't have a driver's license."

"This is your real address," I added, pointing at the Beacon Street address on the card.

"Real name, real date of birth, everything. Your height, obviously. In case anyone ever questions you, I suggest dropping your wallet at some point, in a restaurant, or a hotel lobby maybe."

"Makes sense." At least it sounded logical to my tired brain. I pulled out my wallet and placed the Cordelia ID in the little see-through compartment, hiding mine between old receipts and half-full loyalty cards.

"One last thing," Cordelia hummed and opened the top drawer of her desk, pulling out a set of keys with a large, gold CM keychain. "You should move in here for the next five weeks. The guest suite on the second floor has been prepared for you. Feel free to go have a look. If there's anything missing, just let Victor know and he'll sort it out for you. There's a grocery list on the fridge that the housekeeper takes care of twice a week."

I laughed. "Cordelia, I can't move into your house. I have an apartment."

"You're renting and your boyfriend lives with his brother, right?"

I wasn't even going to start discussing Parker with her. She probably knew about him the same way she could get her hands on my passport picture. "Yes."

"I can cover the two months of rent if that's what you're concerned about."

What? Pay for my rent while I was living here for free? God, I wished I had more energy for this conversation. I reached for the cup of horribly rancid tea on the desk in front of me and downed it in one swig. *Bitter caffeine save me.* "I have a life to go with that apartment," I said. "I have friends. I have a- I have a cat."

"Is the cat physically chained to your apartment?"

"No."

"Then you can move in here. No offense, but your neighborhood isn't the kind of place I would be seen in more than once. I don't need anyone tracing me there after an evening event." She placed the key on the table between us. "Pool and gym are in the basement. Breakfast is ready at 7.30, dinner at 8.00. The Wi-Fi password is on the desk, but I do ask you not to illegally stream or download anything while living here. The TV in your room is all set up and you can buy whatever you want to watch. We've had… an issue with that before. During the Game of Thrones hype."

My brain was trying to process the information as fast as it was relayed to me, but I was still stuck on *pool and gym are in the basement.*

"Victor will pick you up with the car at 9pm sharp. That should give you ample time to pack your bags. What supplies will your cat be needing?"

"What?"

She started typing something into her computer. "I'm assuming bowls for food and water, a pet bed, some toys. Does it have to be a specific brand of food?"

Too stumped to perform more than the simplest task, I just told her the two brands of food I usually got for Fitzwilliam.

"Perfect. If you want to have a look at your suite, it's all yours. Otherwise, I'll see you tonight."

"You keep saying suite…"

"Delilah." Victor materialized next to my chair, making me jump. He swept his arm out in an unmistakable get-out-of-Cordelias-face kind of gesture.

Grabbing the keys from the table, I slipped out of the office. The sweeping staircase in the entry mocked me for letting myself be pushed around like a chess piece once again. I was definitely not going to look at my *suite*. There would probably be a bed in there and then I'd collapse and never leave this place again.

"Are you ok?" Victor asked when I didn't move.

"Yeah, fine. I was out celebrating because I got the job at Truman," I sighed, rubbing my palms over my blurry eyes. "I don't know if you know, or what Cordelia has told you, because I was, I mean, before this…"

"I know," he said and one look at his face told me that he *did* know. "He's taken care of. Enjoy this. Congratulations."

My stomach churned the same way it always did when *he* was mentioned. "What do you mean? Taken care of?"

"Do you really want to know?" He cocked an eyebrow. Something in the stern set of his mouth and the way he asked that question told me that, *maybe*, I did not want to know.

"Thank you."

"I'll drive you home," he nodded at the door, and I was too exhausted to refuse his offer. I almost passed out in the backseat of the car, toppled onto my sofa the second I got home, and only woke up when Fitzwilliam jumped up on me and sank his claws into my back to demand his dinner.

I had all of one hour left to pack up my shit, so I got out my old suitcase, two blue Ikea bags, and I just started dumping stuff into them, while I called Parker and put him on speaker. "Hey babe, can this wait? My shift is over in like an hour."

"Sorry, I'll be really quick," I said while emptying my box of bras into my suitcase. "A pipe burst in the apartment above mine or something, so I have to move out for a few weeks."

"Oh shit, is your stuff okay? Do you have insurance?"

I blinked at my phone and his name on the screen. Okay, sure, I was lying to him, but his first question was about my stuff?! What about my cat? What about me? "It's fine," I huffed. I had no right to be annoyed when I was literally lying through my teeth. "I just have to stay somewhere else for a few weeks until they can get this fixed."

"Uh, are you asking if you can move in with me? Because I'd have to check with Tanner."

"No, no, don't worry." As nice as Parker was, his brother would smother you in kindness. I'd been to their place all of three times, and Tanner had doted on me like an overeager grandmother. Hand-knit socks included. I'd not gotten a second alone with Parker. "I'm staying with a friend."

"What friend?"

"You don't know her yet," I replied and tossed all the books from my TBR pile by the bed into one of the Ikea bags. Twelve books should last me for the next five weeks, right? Just to be safe, I went and pulled some of my favorite classics from my shelf, only realizing then that Parker hadn't answered in a minute or two. "Parker?"

"Is it the *friend* from yesterday?" He asked with a strange emphasis on 'friend'.

"What friend?"

"The one from the park."

I clasped a hand over my mouth to stop the gagged sound I was about to make at the thought of moving in with Beck. "I wouldn't call Beck a friend."

"I figured," he scoffed. "How did you pay your rent these last few months, Delilah?"

"What?" I grimaced at the phone. "Savings. What?"

"I saw all your shopping bags of new clothes. I know how much money you spend on those overpriced coffees."

I tried to piece together the conversation *he* was having, when I'd just been focused on my burst-pipe-lie. "What are you asking me exactly?"

"I'm asking if *he's* the reason you haven't been dead broke the last three months."

My stomach soured at the implication, and I picked up my phone, taking it off speaker. I needed to hear him say that shit directly to me. Because I was *good* with money. I didn't spend too much on coffee because I had a budget. I had savings because I'd been budgeting for years. Most of my books were secondhand, and my biggest splurge was a new Ruby Woo lipstick every couple of months. I wasn't as frugal as him, but I wasn't irresponsible. "Ask me outright. Ask what you want to know," I hissed at the phone.

Parker was silent for a moment before he let out a deep sigh. "Shit. I'm sorry, babe. I'm sorry. Forget I ever said that."

"Ask me."

"No, look, I had a really long shift. This guy got in my head."

Of course, the exhaustion was at fault. Of course, Beck was at fault. God forbid he actually owned the fact that he was so insecure about his own finances that he projected it on me. "Ask. Me."

"Does he pay for your company? Or, I don't know, like, cover your expenses?"

"You think I'm a call girl?"

"Shit, Del, I don't know, ok? You were fired from a *school*. Who gets fired from a *school*? And then you get this mysterious letter of recommendation and that guy in the park looks-" I didn't hear the rest of it, because my blood was rushing through my ears, and I just managed to hang up before turning around and diving for the toilet. I'd barely eaten all day, so I was dry-heaving bile, stomach convulsing. I'd finally found a new job despite what I'd done to Roger Childs, and he was still hanging over me, ruining a perfectly good relationship.

When I opened the door for him, Victor took one look at me, told me to wait in the car with the cat, and moved the rest of my stuff into the trunk by himself.

Three little knocks woke me the next morning. I blinked against the light streaming through milky curtains, eyes dragging over the pastel blue and gold tapestry and stucco ceiling. I'd somehow woken up in Versailles.

Someone knocked against the door again, and my eyes landed on my suitcase next to it, memory pieces clicking back into place.

"Yeah?" I croaked, pushing myself upright. Somehow, I was surrounded by all my own throw pillows, but I was wearing a summer dress as a nightgown. My packing skills had clearly tanked after that phone call.

"Good morning," Cordelia cooed, slipping through the door, cradling-

I blinked. Rubbed my eyes. Blinked again.

Fitzwilliam had turned into a purring, fuzzy ball in Cordelia's arms, letting himself be cradled like a baby for belly rubs. Belly rubs! I was barely allowed to touch his back.

"This handsome guy somehow found his way to my bedroom last night." She smiled and sat at the foot of my bed, scrunching her nose up at the lovey-dovey cat that had replaced my demon spawn overnight.

"That's Fitzwilliam," I said, "also known as Fitz, Fitzi, Demon, Satan, Ghostface, and Killer Cat."

"What?" She laughed and ruffled her hand over his head in a way that would have cost me a finger. "He's such a cutie."

I pulled the neck of my dress down, revealing the deep red marks he'd left last night when I'd forced him into his carrier. "He's a menace to society."

"Oh, come on." She sat him down on the bed, but he climbed right back into her lap, carefully pawing her arm. And I remembered the way he'd sat between my legs during those fifteen minutes of raw nerves after my second Truman interview, trying to calm me down.

"Cordelia?"

"Hmm?" She didn't even look at me, giving Fitzwilliam boop after boop on his little pink snout. He just yawned, completely unbothered.

"I'm glad he likes you. If you don't mind, I think it would be great if he could roam the whole house instead of staying cooped up with me."

"Yeah, I'd like that." A big, bright smile flashed over her lips. "Oh, also there's a package for you downstairs."

"Did you order more clothes?"

"No, all the ones I ordered for you are in your closet already." She nodded at the double doors that led to the walk-in closet. I'd explored my *suite* last night and it was rightfully called a suite. The large bedroom, overlooking the small garden and the Charles River behind it, had a huge bathroom with a clawfoot tub on one side of it, and an even bigger closet filled with shoes and purses and dresses on the other side. Right across the hall was a smaller room that had been turned into a study, a smaller bathroom, and a guest bedroom. As in: My guest suite had a guest bedroom in case I ever had people over. "I don't know what's in this package."

"I didn't order anything," I said.

"It says it's from August Beckett," she trilled and got up, Fitzwilliam jumping after her on her way to the door. "Technically addressed to me, but I figured you're the intended recipient."

"What?" I pushed myself off the way-too-comfortable

mattress, feet slapping against cold floorboards as I followed her. I caught a glance at myself in the mirror by the bathroom door though. I'd not taken my makeup off last night, and my hair was both oily around my face and a dry bird's nest atop my head. Great. And Cordelia had been her usual perfectly made-up self with her hair in a braid and a pink polka dot dress.

Shower first. Package later.

THIRTEEN

BECK

STEVE, MY DOORMAN, WAS AN ARMY VET WHO HAD BEEN TO actual war, and yet his voice quivered when he tried to announce my visitor. Del barely let him get a word out, a heated tirade in the background, clearly meant to be heard by me.

"And if he doesn't want me in his house, he can come down here, but that will turn you into a murder witness, Steve. Do you want to witness a murder, Steve?"

Steve's high-pitched "Mr. Beckett?" crackled through the intercom.

"Send her up and put her on the visitors list."

"I don't need to be on any-" Del's voice cut off as the intercom died. I unlocked the front door to my apartment, leaving it open for her before going back to the kitchen. I was in the middle of cooking dinner, and she'd find her way by herself. The layout of my place was big but not that complicated. Entryway, followed by the open concept kitchen, dining, and living space. There was a guest bathroom, office, and master bedroom. I'd looked at plenty of places before choosing this one. I didn't need a private gym or a guest bedroom or any of that shit. I had a sundeck, but I barely used it. This place had been modernized to the highest standard and was practical, and that's what had sold me on it.

The door slammed shut and Blondie marched in, shiny hair whipping through the air as she spun around until her eyes landed on me. Her brows were drawn so deep, the blues of her eyes almost looked grey. "You," she hissed, pointing a finger at me, a blue box in her hand. I'd wondered how she'd react to that.

"Hi," I said, taking a second plate from the cupboard. "I see you got my gift."

She slammed the blue box down on the breakfast counter between us hard enough for the pages of my cookbook to flutter. "This is not a gift. It's a joke and you know it is."

"No, it's not. You don't strike me as the kind of woman who would think that's funny." I glanced at the box, noting how the safety sticker was still on its side, perfectly intact.

"Exactly. You're taunting me." She walked over to the sofa and flung her bag onto it, followed by the denim jacket that covered a perfectly proper shift dress made for offices and business lunches. Whatever preppy thing she'd been to before this, she'd been carrying a vibrator around with her. The box design was subtle, but the text on it still clearly stated what was inside. The thought kicked up the corners of my mouth.

"I'm not taunting you," I said, and clicked the button on the rice cooker two seconds before the timer was up, before it could derail this conversation with its beeping. "I happen to be very sex positive. You've never had an orgasm. I know women with similar issues and air pulse vibrators have helped them. Rather than just buzzing away at your clit, these create a vacuum that-"

"I know what it does," she barked.

"Doesn't work for you?" I asked.

She hesitated a moment and I could feel her eyes traveling over me as I portioned the rice onto two plates. "No," she sighed, energy deflating. "Don't you think I've had plenty of time to explore my options?"

"Yoni eggs?"

"Yes."

"G-spot vibrators?"

"Yes. Not that I should even be talking to you about this." She hoisted herself onto a barstool and folded over, arms braced on the counter, head down. She mumbled something including the word *horrible* but most of it was muffled by her arms.

"And you're medically okay?" I asked while pouring the curry into the bowls. If her lack of sexual fulfillment was my way into the Montgomery chain, I was game.

She dragged her head up and sniffed the air instead of answering. "What are you cooking?"

I just pointed at the cookbook next to her. No change of topic on my watch. "There's no underlying medical cause for your anorgasmia?"

Her eyes snapped up from the recipe. "You know what it's called?"

"Eat." I placed a plate and spoon in front of her. "And yes, I know what it's called. Believe it or not, there's people that engage in sex beyond a quick in and out before bed."

"Like call girls," she snorted and heaped a spoonful of curry to her mouth. I watched her reaction, as the taste sank in. She let out a small sigh. Not quite a foodgasm, but I'd take it.

"You don't have to be a sex worker to understand that sex is complicated."

"You made this recipe, right? Coconut curry?" She pointed at the cookbook on the table, changing the topic again.

Fine. The fact that she hadn't gotten spooked off yet was good enough for me. I'd pick this topic back up some other time. "Yes, but I'm not particularly good at sticking to recipes," I admitted, picking up my own spoon, "I learned to cook from my grandmother and she would just switch out ingredients depending on her mood."

"I'm guessing you added peanuts, right?"

"Yes, how did you-" The words died on my tongue as I registered the blood shooting into her cheeks, her face reddening before me. And not the cute, riled up blush that tinted the tip of her nose first. Swollen, patchy redness. "You're allergic."

"I'm going to lie down. EpiPen's in a pink pouch in my bag. Jab into my thigh and hold for ten seconds, and uh… there's wet wipes for your peanut hands before you touch me." Her voice was losing air with every word as she climbed off the bar stool hands trembling.

"Shit. Shit, shit, shit." I darted around the kitchen counter, and my first instinct was to grab hold of her, but she had given me clear instructions. I grabbed her bag from the sofa. Del's breathing came in gasps as I emptied the contents of her purse on the floor. Pouches. So many damn pouches. Pink. I snatched it up and shot to her side. Her face had taken on the same shade as her red lipstick as she stretched her neck, trying to get air. Fuck. I tore through the wet wipes, knocked the damn EpiPen from its packaging, pushed her dress up and held my own breath as I jabbed it into her. She didn't even flinch as the needle went in. "You're going to be okay, sweetheart," I gasped, mentally counting down the seconds. Ten. She'd said ten. I left it for fifteen just to be sure. Then I got out my phone to call an ambulance because that's what the packaging said to do.

"No. No 911," she heaved, the first bits of lung capacity returning, glazed eyes on me.

"You need to go to the hospital."

"No." Panic crept into her voice. "Please. I'll be fine."

"Del, I'm not letting you die in my living room. You need medical attention."

Her arm jerked up and she slapped the phone from my hand, strength returning to her muscles. "If you take me to the hospital, I will kill you. I am so fucking serious, Beckett." She squeezed her eyes shut, her hand wrapping around her own throat. "Actually, I will hire someone to kill you and I will make it look like an accident."

She wasn't kidding, and I wasn't sure if this was part of the whole 'not leaving the house for 15 years' thing or if she just hated hospitals, but the idea of getting an ambulance freaked her out more than dying here. "Fine," I pushed the word through gritted teeth.

Del pushed herself up on her elbows and didn't protest when I wrapped my arm around her back to help. "I have antihistamines. I just… need five minutes." She looked down at her jittering hands.

"Blondie."

"It's just the adrenaline." She flexed her hands and looked at me with dark, wide pupils. "You might have to help me get up. I get really dizzy from the epinephrine."

"Come here," I slipped my other arm around the back of her knees and Del automatically slung hers around my shoulders, no protest as I lifted her up. Her entire body trembled against my chest. She felt small, nestled against me. Not just physically. All the fire she had stormed in here with had cooled to embers. I placed her on the sofa and scrambled together all the small bags that had been in her purse. "Which ones are the antihistamines in?"

"Pink one, too."

I just brought her the whole rainbow collection, before excusing myself for a minute and ducking into my bedroom to make a call. Isaac stepped into my apartment less than fifteen minutes later, patting me on the shoulder as he slipped past, medical bag slung over his shoulder.

"So, you must be the girl Beck tried to poison." He slipped on his doctor mask, easy smile hiding the shadows under his eyes.

"Who are you?" Del asked, pushing herself up further on the sofa.

"Dr. Hunter, Boston Memorial, but victims of attempted murder by peanut can call me Isaac."

"No, no, no." She shook her head. His joke didn't land because panic shot back into her eyes as she looked past Isaac to where I stood. "I said no 911."

"It's alright, darling. I'm not 911." He tugged on his Guns'n'Roses shirt as if to prove a point, and definitely leaned into his accent. "Just a mate of Beck's. It's alright. You're not going to the hospital."

She visibly relaxed, swallowed, nodded.

I watched as Isaac took her blood pressure, had her blow into some plastic thing to measure her breathing and checked the swelling in her throat. "I have to check her lungs," he announced and turned to look at me over his shoulder while he slung his stethoscope around his neck.

Del raised her brows at me when I didn't respond.

"What does that have to do with me?"

"I have to take my dress off," she said in a tone that implied a *'Duh!'* at the end.

"Lifting it up will be fine," Isaac quickly added. He could probably sense my pulse spike across the room. Logically, I knew he was a doctor and that came with a lot of indifference to the human body - but I'd seen him pull the stethoscope bit back in college, getting girls naked with some sleazy line about heartbeats - and *that* Isaac was on my mind, when he raised his brows at me.

"Beck, please turn around. Please. I'm tired," Blondie pleaded, chin quivering.

I was doing that to her. I was turning her into an exhausted, trembling mess, close to tears. My fucking curry and now my fucking ego. I turned around and braced my hands on the granite countertop, stone biting deep into my palm as I strained to listen like a creep. Some fucked-up part of me already considered that woman on the sofa mine. Realistically, Del was far from agreeing to marry me anytime soon, but when Isaac touched her, that fucked-up part of my brain was roaring that he was touching *my wife*.

After what felt like an eternity, Isaac finally cleared her, and I walked him to the door. A little too eager to get him out of my apartment. "Looks like you reacted quickly enough," he said, walking with me, "but you will need to keep her on close observation for at least four hours, and if her condition worsens, you have to do this again, and call me." He handed me a freshly packaged EpiPen.

"Thanks. I don't need to remind you that-"

"My lips are sealed."

"Good."

"Beck?" He turned around in the door and leaned back, voice lowered. "If this is who I think it is, take a big bag and throw out every open product in your kitchen. You don't want her cross-contaminated just because you put peanut butter on everything. One allergic shock is a good joke for the wedding vows, but two..."

"I'll see you at the Vortex tomorrow, Isaac."

He left and I went back inside to find Del sitting up on the sofa, phone in hand.

"How are you feeling?"

"Better." She put the phone down and watched me rummage through my kitchen while I dumped most of my food in the trash. "What are you doing?"

"Making sure I don't almost-kill you twice."

"Airborne isn't really a big issue for me unless we're on a plane, because they circulate the air. Just keep the curry far, far away."

"Better safe than sorry." No need to spook her with the idea of her spending a lot more time at my place in the future.

"So… you just happen to have a super hot doctor on call?"

"Excuse me?" I turned to find her grinning wide, phone pointed at me.

"That face was perfect." She giggled at her screen, but the burst of energy quickly dissipated, and she leaned back again, eyes falling shut. "Seriously though. *Doctor Hunter, Boston Memorial?*" It sounded like Del was trying for a Scottish accent, but it came out strangely Swedish.

"We went to college together."

"Really? He looks older than you."

"Is that a compliment?"

"No, just an observation. It's probably the George Clooney temples." Her phone pinged before I even had to deign that with another response for her to photograph. She opened one eye to glance at the new message. "Victor will pick me up in fifteen."

"Hell no." I dropped the family size jar of peanut butter in the trash can. "Isaac said you need to be supervised."

"Victor can do that." She clicked her tongue at me.

"I'm the one who almost killed you. I'll be the one who makes sure you don't die in your sleep."

"How romantic."

"I'm serious. Tell him to go back home and take the night off." I'd seen her driver outside Bumble by the Sea, all tattoos and muscle.

"Beck, please. I need to brush my teeth and I want my PJs, my really cuddly blanket and then watch something that requires no brain power because I've seen it a million times before."

"You're under observation for four hours. If you get worse,

you need medical attention again. You're staying here, and if anything happens, I have Isaac on speed-dial. Who would Victor call?"

She worked her jaw before sighing and turning back to her phone. "Fine."

"Give me a minute." I took the bag out to the chute and thoroughly washed my hands to make sure no peanut traces remained before I returned to Del in the living room and stretched both hands out for her. "Come on, up you go Blondie."

"Why?"

"Will you stop questioning everything I do and just trust me for once."

"I'm just inquisitive by nature."

"Uh-huh."

She slipped her hands into mine, gripping them tight enough for her knuckles to whiten as she pulled herself to her feet. She wavered slightly but didn't drop back to the sofa. "I'm good," she said before I could offer more help. She leaned on me enough for most of her weight to be on me, her feet sort of moving as an afterthought as I led her through the bedroom and into my bathroom. Her eyes roamed over the rooms, but she didn't comment on it, further proof of just how badly this had taken her out.

"Sit," I instructed, even though I was basically maneuvering her body for her anyway, as I directed her onto the small stool in the bathroom. It had come with the place, and turned out to be quite useful when your muscles needed a hot soak, but the work didn't stop, so you needed your computer on you.

Del sighed and dropped back against the towel heater, a blissful smile trembling on her lips. "I need one of these."

"Here," I broke a fresh toothbrush out of its packaging and handed it to her, spreading toothpaste onto the bristles. "Brush."

Eyes closed, back melting against the heater, Del brushed her teeth and I... watched. I wasted three minutes watching her brows pull up and her nose crinkle as she directed the toothbrush into every corner of her mouth. "You're done, come on."

I helped her up again and she braced herself on the sink while I filled my plastic cup with mouthwash and warm water for her, then held her hair back so she could rinse.

"Thanks," she mumbled once I had her sitting on my bed. "Good mouthwash to water ratio. Not too minty."

"Thanks," I chuckled and pulled out the only pair of actual PJs I owned. They still had the gift bow on them because someone must have once thought I was a flannel PJ kind of guy. "I'm assuming you can change on your own."

"Yeah, thanks."

I left her while I went to clean up the rest of the kitchen, the curry going down the garbage disposal. My appetite had left me anyway.

"Can I come in?" I rapped my knuckles against the bedroom door.

"Yep." Del sat in the same spot on the edge of the bed where I had left her, but her sensible dress had been replaced with the flannel shirt that dropped to mid-thigh for her, where a bruise was blooming around the injection site. Her dress and bra were neatly stacked beside her, and I ignored the urge to linger on the white lace. "I might need some help with these. I tried to lean forward and then the whole room started spinning." She pointed at her strappy shoes, heels digging into the dark rug before my bed.

"No more leaning forward then," I said and knelt down in front of her. Something had to be seriously wrong with me because she was a wreck after I almost killed her, but all I could think of was wrapping her naked thighs around my neck. It had to be a Pavlovian response because the only reason I'd voluntarily kneel, was making women moan at the flick of my tongue. My brain was basically hard-wired. Had to be. I folded my hand around her delicate ankle and pulled her right foot into my lap, focusing on the tiny straps instead of how my face was a mere ten inches from the space between her legs. Three clasps later, the shoe sprang free. Del winced as I slipped it off, toes curling. "What's wrong?"

"Nothing. Thank you. One down."

"You're in pain," I said and pulled her other foot into my lap, too, thumb circling over her ankle.

"It's heels, of course I am," she laughed, but the sound was cut short by a hiss when the second shoe came off.

Before I had the chance to debate with myself over it, I pushed my thumb into the arch of her foot, and she yelped. She would have kicked me in the groin, too, if I hadn't had such a tight hold on her foot. That was the only protest I got from her though, her breath hitching as I circled the ball of her foot with strong fingertips. Her eyes falling shut as I rubbed some life back into her toes. If she was aware of the small sighs of relief she was letting out whenever my fingers connected with a particularly tense spot, she didn't show it. My hands found her other foot, angling for the arch first, and this time she let out a full whimper when I pressed into her. Her hand flew up to clutch her mouth. "Shit sorry," she whispered, eyes squeezed shut.

Fuck. I had to move her feet out of my lap, or she'd figure out what those noises were doing to me real quick. "No need to apologize," I said, adjusting my position so her feet perched on my knees, several inches away from where my pants were stretched taut, "feel better?"

"Mm-hmm," she mumbled from behind her hand.

She kept quiet throughout the massage of her second foot, but her toes flexing and digging into my thighs spoke their own language. I guess if I couldn't relieve her tension with my tongue, this was a close second.

Her watery blue eyes found my gaze when I set her feet down

again. Only then did she drop her hand back onto the mattress. "Thank you," she mouthed.

"What was next on the list?" I asked, "Cuddly blanket and a comfort movie?"

"Mm-hmm."

"Scoot back."

While she nestled against the headboard, I got the soft fleece blanket from my closet, where it lived until the colder months crept in. I shook it out to spread over her, but Del caught the edge of it mid-air. "No, no, like *this*," she said, a tired smile on her lips as she corrected me by drawing the blanket around her shoulders like a cape. "Remote?" she asked and dove for the nightstand.

"Wait," I shot forward, heart leaping up my throat, but she had the drawer open before I could stop her.

"Huh," she pulled the remote out, but kept her eyes trained on the other contents of the drawer. I mentally cursed myself for choosing a nightstand specifically big enough to house that collection. "I get the handcuffs and the dildos, but what's the..." She tilted her head.

"It's an adjustable spreader bar," I said and closed the drawer without meeting her eyes, even though I felt hers on me.

"Spreader bar." She repeated the term, taste testing it, as she switched on the TV, which came to life with a chipper little jingle "Oh, like for the legs. Got it."

There went my plan to be Prince Charming about the whole orgasm thing. At least she wasn't running away screaming, although that may be down to her physical condition, not her open-mindedness to a little bondage in the sheets. "I'll take a quick shower, ok? Call me if you feel worse." I grabbed the flannel pants from the foot of the bed and a fresh t-shirt. I usually slept naked, but that probably wouldn't go over well with her. When I disappeared into the bathroom, I left the door open just a crack in case she did need medical help again. Then I took the coldest shower of my life.

By the time I got out, Del had formed a nest of blankets and pillows around her, eyes trained on a pastel-colored movie full of ruffled gowns. "Marie Antoinette?"

"Emma," she whispered, nuzzled into the fluffy blanket, and wiggled a few inches over when I climbed into bed.

"You're not one of those girls waiting for Mr. Darcy, are you?"

"No," she snorted and waved the remote at the TV, "Mr. Knightley is right there."

Mr. Knightley was, in fact, right there, flashing his ass on screen. Del neither audibly nor visibly reacted despite having just professed her preference for the man.

"Can I ask you something?"

"Sure."

"What good does a spreader bar do? Like, sexually, what do you get out of it?"

I almost choked on the air in my lungs. Okay, if *that* was where her mind went at the sight of Knightley's ass, I'd have that movie play on every screen in the house. "You could obviously tie someone's ankles to bed posts if you just wanted their legs spread, but this way, my partner stays mobile enough to try a few different positions and actively participate," I replied matter-of-factly without taking my eyes off the movie.

"Okay but I mean, wouldn't they spread their legs anyway? Why force them apart?"

"They're not *forced* apart," I said. "Consent and communication are key to any sexual practice, especially in BDSM." When she didn't react to those four intimidating letters either, I continued: "It's a form of submission. When used, the woman has to give up control to me. I decide what I want, how I want her, when, how and how often she gets to climax."

That last word finally made her flinch. Right. That. The reason she showed up here tonight in the first place. "Got it. Thanks," she said, sounding a lot more clipped.

"What's Parker doing to help you with that?"

"I don't want to talk about that right now."

"Does he know?"

A beat of silence passed. "No," she admitted quietly, eyes locked to the screen. "I've gotten pretty good at faking it over the years."

"How many?"

"How many orgasms I've faked?"

"How many men have you slept with, without them doing anything about *your* pleasure?"

"It's not like that. I do find it quite pleasurable. It's nice."

"Number."

"I feel like the first boy I slept with doesn't count. We were both fifteen and didn't know what we were doing, so embarrassed we didn't speak again afterwards. But I told both my exes after a while. The first one got so in his head about it, he couldn't get it up anymore. And the second one tried so hard, he had stress dreams about it, so I just ended up faking it again for his benefit. When I met Parker, I figured he was better off ignorant."

Four. I did count the first one because I had a feeling *he* did get off. Four assholes too consumed by their own dicks to make their girlfriend come.

"I can hear you thinking, you know?" She pushed herself up from the pillows, clutching her blanket cape around her shoulders, hair standing off around her head.

"What am I thinking?"

"That they're all idiots and you could definitely make me orgasm if you had the chance."

I smirked and smoothed out the knot above her ear. "Something like that."

"I've heard all that before. My sexual inexperience is not a challenge for you to prove your manliness through. It's not a competition."

"I know."

"Do you? Because sleeping with someone is about connecting with a person I care about, not about getting pounded into oblivion by whoever fucks the hardest."

"I understand that climaxing isn't the only good thing about sex, Blondie. I just think the person you care about should care enough about you to make sure you experience the rush of an orgasm every now and again."

"I don't even know why I'm talking to you about this," she huffed and dropped back into her mountain of pillows. Some of them had shifted though and half her head was now resting on my stomach, her hair splaying out like rays of sun against my dark shirt.

"Hey Blondie?" I asked a while later when Knightley and Emma were having it out under some flowery tree like that wasn't a hay fever nightmare.

"Hmm?"

"Sorry for poisoning you."

"I've had worse nights," she sighed, voice small and tired. She wrestled one of the blankets from her nest over us to cover my legs and most of her, adding to the cape she was still snuggled into.

"My abs do make a pretty good pillow," I chuckled.

She poked her fingers out from her cocoon and reached up to pat my stomach. One, two, three times her fingertips drummed against it. She made no further comment before her hand retracted back into the covers, like a little hermit crab. I had to tell myself that she was just grogged out on antihistamines, because otherwise that would have been the cutest lil shit I'd ever seen.

FOURTEEN

Delilah

Beck's bedroom was predictably boring. If you googled *modern industrial bedroom*, you would find a picture of this place, and just accept it as some interior designer's show room. Huge metal bed frame with random modern art hanging above it, one exposed concrete wall, and a mixture of wooden and slate grey accents. I doubted he'd even picked the two plants framing his floor-to-ceiling windows himself. No pictures, no souvenirs. The only remotely personal item was the book on his nightstand, which vaguely looked like a thriller - but it was in Spanish, and my Spanish skills started with 'Hola' and ended with 'Gracias.'

I glanced into his closet, while pulling my dress back on, but that was equally-predictably filled with neat rows of suits and button-downs. My color-coding heart did give a little flutter though because everything was arranged perfectly from lightest to darkest color.

The only thing his bathroom cabinet revealed was that he used a Christian Dior cologne, not some sketchy pheromone perfume from the internet. Which meant my brain short-circuiting around him was all on me. Cool.

Maybe I should have felt a little bad for snooping, but the man had given me an anaphylactic shock and the best foot massage of my life last night, so I felt like I deserved some insights.

Eventually, I followed a promising smell back to the other side of the penthouse and found Beck in the kitchen again. His kitchen was huge. The entirety of my apartment could fit into it. I didn't even know what half the appliances in here were. Beck's suit jacket hung off one of the bar stools, but even buttoned up with a black tie around his neck, he looked more at ease in a kitchen than I'd ever been. "Hi," I said after feeling a little creepy for staring.

He looked up from the laptop propped open on the counter. For the first time since meeting him, the way his eyes travelled down my body didn't set my skin on fire. It felt more like he was checking that no limbs had fallen off. "Good morning," he said once he was satisfied with my state of four-limbedness.

"Did you make breakfast?" I asked, trying to catch a glance at the pan on the stove.

"I got bagels on my run and made some eggs. Did you want anything else?"

"I was in the mood for a PB&J actually." I grinned and fluttered my lashes at him.

"Very funny." He rolled his eyes at me, but I swore I saw some muscle in his back unclench. I'd had my fair share of allergic reactions over the years and had quickly picked up on the fact that the people around you struggled more with your near-death-experience than you did yourself. Three years ago, Defne had spent two days crying after seeing me go down. The cupcakes at the charity bake sale she'd been part of had just been incorrectly labelled. Human error. It happened.

I climbed onto one of the barstools, stomach rumbling at the spread before me. Beck had decked the breakfast bar with fresh fruit, juice and smoothie options, three different kinds of cream cheese and a whole bowl of different bagels. "How long have you been up?"

"Five."

"Why?"

"Because I get up at five every day."

"But why?"

"Ah, that inquisitive nature of yours." He set down a plate of scrambled eggs for me. "I go for a run and take a shower. I check the news and my emails. Sometimes I have to take international calls, sometimes to make breakfast. And usually, I'm in the office by 7.30."

We both glanced at the clock on the wall creeping towards eight o'clock. "You didn't have to wait for me."

"I wanted to make sure you survived the night."

"Yep, still alive. You should go to work."

"I'm *at* work." He nodded at his laptop, and as if on cue held up his index finger for me before tapping the AirPod lodged in one ear. "It sounds to me like there's a management problem, not a distribution problem, so I'm more inclined to make changes to the team structure."

Oh, he was actually at work. On a call. I'd never felt less productive than when I scooped some eggs into my mouth. I suppressed the sigh that tried to break free. Why did my scrambled eggs never taste like that? Like sunshine and blue skies? I had no idea about spices and herbs, but these eggs tasted like you were soaking up summer mornings.

"Let me cook dinner for you," he said after clicking his earbud again.

I snorted. "No thanks."

"Let me cook dinner for you. No peanuts."

Yeah, because that was the only reason I'd say no. "I have plans."

"I didn't say when."

"I'll have plans then, too. Because I have a boyfriend and I have a cat and I have to make sure the whole Montgomery family business stays afloat and *you*, Beck, don't fit into my life."

"See, I think I do." He leaned against the counter, grinning at me with that stupid mischievous spark in the corners of his lips.

I narrowed my eyes at him, curiosity winning out. "How so?"

"Because you probably don't talk to anyone the way you talk to me. Because you don't like me enough to care about my opinion, which makes me the perfect person to talk to about orgasms and sex toys and your Jane Austen crush and the fact that you want white ducks at your wedding."

"I never said I want white ducks at my wedding."

"You did. After Emma and Clueless, you made me put on the Notebook even though you were basically sleeping. And you shot up straight in bed at the lake scene to tell me you needed white ducks at your wedding. And when I asked who you were marrying, you said Mr. Knightley but - and I quote - the hot Emma Approved version."

Well, that explained my dream about walking down the aisle of an old English church in a feathered gown. Before I had the chance to answer, Beck was back on his call. "If you're just going back and forth on this, I have another important meeting to get to. Send me the solution you agree on by ten or I'm dropping the whole division." He clicked his AirPod off and tossed it on the keyboard before walking over to me and bracing his hands on the counter. "So, dinner on Friday?"

"Why are you still talking to me about this? Didn't you just say you have another important meeting to get to?"

"I blocked an hour between eight and nine. Figured you'd be awake by then."

"Oh." *I* was the important meeting. I cleared my throat, suddenly way too aware of my bare face, and my hand-brushed hair, and the ungodly amount of cream cheese I'd heaped onto my bagel. "Welcome to my meeting. Hi."

"Hi," he chuckled, "dinner on Friday?"

"No."

"You're making this really hard for me."

"Well, no, I do actually have plans on Friday. My friend has a small scene in a new Netflix show that drops on Friday. It's her first proper, paid acting gig, so my friends are coming over for a watch party."

"Saturday?"

"I can do Saturday," I said. Wait. Had I just agreed to let him cook me dinner? I'd gotten too caught up in the back and forth of the negotiation.

"It's a date."

"Not a date!" Ohmygod. Maybe he had some pheromone shampoo? I'd have to check his bathroom next time I was- Nope. No. Hell no. I was never ever setting a foot in his bedroom or bathroom again. What was wrong with me?

My ringtone chimed up and I hadn't even clocked my phone by the time Beck unplugged it from an outlet in the kitchen and handed it over. Parker's name and goofy grin lit up the screen. For once, my shoulders stiffened at the sight of his caller ID, and I clicked him away. "You charged my phone," I said even though I could practically hear Beck's very loud thoughts filling the kitchen.

"Same charger as the Bluetooth speaker," he replied.

We looked at each other, the unasked question crackling in the air between us like a game of who-blinks-first. The thing was that I couldn't talk to Tab or Defne about the argument we'd gotten into without admitting to them that Parker wasn't completely off about Beck, without sharing what had happened at Gavin Decker's birthday party. I wasn't ready to tackle all their questions about that.

"If I tell you, you can't be all Beck about it." I pointed my fork at him.

"What does that mean?"

"You have to be objective, or at least a little unbiased. No smug replies."

"I can't be unbiased when it comes to you, Blondie." I glared at him, and he held up his hands in defeat. "But I can reign it in."

"He accused me of cheating on him. He thinks I'm sleeping with you in exchange for business favors." I managed to slip in the *business* at the last second when I meant to say *financial*. But Cordelia Montgomery didn't need financial favors.

"Leave him."

"Beck!"

"This is me being objective. I'm well aware of the role our meeting in the park must have played in this, however, I can take myself out of the equation and still see the issue."

"Enlighten me because I don't know what to think anymore. Obviously, I didn't tell him about the party thing, but I guess that does border on cheating." I sighed and put my fork down, rubbing the bridge of my nose as the whole stupid discussion replayed in my head. "But I don't even know where that accusation came from."

"Whatever you've recently achieved - don't tell me or we'll go to jail for insider trading - he doesn't think you're smart enough or skilled enough to have achieved it on your own. Which is the first strike. He should be supportive of you." Well, that wasn't too far off from what I'd pieced together. Parker didn't think I was financially responsible. "That leads us to me, or any other businessman you could have come into contact with. If we ignore Parker's inferiority complex, because many people deal with that, he still assumed that our business arrangement could only work if you jumped into bed with me. Which tells me exactly what value he sees in you. Second strike. And then you said he *accused* you, which leads me to believe this wasn't a healthy conversation. Third strike." He leaned back.

"When you say it like that, it sounds so simple. Ugh." I grabbed one of the two fresh smoothies he'd set out, needing something to soothe the sharp sting that had welled up in my throat.

"Wait, this one." He snatched the Nutribullet from my hand and replaced it with the other - almost identical one, minus some dark flecks. "Yours is without flaxseed."

"Isn't that supposed to be good for you?"

"Are you on the pill?"

"Yeah?" I furrowed my brows at him.

"Flaxseed can mess with that, so unless you're trying to trap your catch of a boyfriend with a baby…"

"Good to know," I mumbled, even though Parker always insisted on a condom anyway. We both had clean bills of health, but he'd insisted. I knew it was responsible, and it only made things a little more uncomfortable for me, but on the back of this conversation his reasoning left a bitter taste in my mouth. He wanted to wait until I had a proper job with proper health insurance again. At the time, it had sounded like the right call, the responsible call. But shouldn't his reason at least have included my health instead of my health insurance? Or maybe that was just his way of expressing his concern for my health? Why couldn't people just say what they mean?

"Hey," Beck pulled me out of my thought spiral. "Now, if you asked me to be smug about the situation, I'd say Parker knows his beautiful girlfriend is way out of his league and seeing her with a handsome man who's clearly a better match for her, pushed all his buttons."

A small laugh bubbled from my throat. "Good thing you're not smug, Casanova."

"Me?" He grinned. "Never."

FIFTEEN

Delilah

"That means red is Gavin?"

"Blue is Gavin," I groaned, retracing the big fat blue G at the top of the page, only to look up and see Tabitha grinning at me.

"You make it so easy." She poked her tongue out and snatched the legal pad out from under my pen. "Thank you. Love you."

"Have we settled it yet?" Defne asked as she carried a tray with three champagne flutes into the TV room - two filled with bubbly, one with apple juice. "Who gets Sundays?"

"Charlie," Tab and I answered in unison. She turned the legal pad around for Defne to admire my color-coded schedule. She tapped her pen at the paper, explaining: "Charlie gets Sundays because he never works Mondays, so that leaves room for wakeup sex. We put Gavin on Tuesdays. Wednesdays are for admin stuff." She shot me a sharp glance, because I'd made her schedule one sexless day. "Thursday nights are still reserved for Aiden, and then

Friday and Saturday are all you guys or going out or spontaneous Tinder hookups."

"I'm so flattered that you made time for us." Defne laughed and let herself fall into the fluffy pink sofa. The thing basically filled Cordelia's entire TV room. Four people could probably stretch out on it without ever touching.

"What can I say? Men want me." Tab wiggled her brows at Defne. She wasn't lying, as proven by the fact that I had taken her to a party thrown by Gavin Decker, a notoriously single millionaire, and she walked out of there adding him to her roster of men. At least focusing on her guy problems let me ignore mine for a while.

"Are you guys ready?" Defne grabbed the remote and queued up her big debut on Netflix, but before she could click play, she was interrupted by the doorbell. We all looked at each other, then at the empty hallway.

Cordelia had agreed to my friends coming over as long as she could stay upstairs with Fitzwilliam, and I'd text her when they were gone. And Victor had the night off and had headed out an hour ago. I shuffled off the sofa because that only left me to open the door.

"What are you doing here?" I asked at the sight of Beck and his dark sunglasses, dipped in the warm glow of the setting sun, his suit jacket slung over his shoulder.

"You invited me to a party," he replied, cocking one brow, "hello, by the way."

I crossed my arms over my chest, not budging from my spot in the door. "I didn't invite you. It's not a party. It's a TV night. With my girlfriends."

"I guess I'm going back home. Too bad about the honey-lemon blondies." He held up a large takeaway box with Bumble by the Sea's logo on its side.

Damn him.

It would basically be a crime to let him walk away with those. I mean, it would have been inhumane to deprive Tab and Defne of the chance to try the famous cake bars. At least that's what I told myself when I opened the door wider. "Fine. God. You're annoying."

He stopped in the doorframe, close enough for me to inhale his rich, fresh scent. Something about the way he looked down at me, when I couldn't see his eyes behind those glasses, made my insides clench up. "Am I getting under your skin, sweetheart?"

"No," I grinned up at him, "but if I'm ever single again, do you think I could get Dr. Hunter's number?"

Beck closed the distance between us in a flash. I barely managed to shuffle backwards, my shoulders hitting the door. Those few inches between us were reduced to a breath as he leaned down, one arm braced above me. His stubble grazed over my cheek and my inhale caught in my throat. With his voice dropped low, he rasped a single word into my ear: "No."

An involuntary shudder rippled down my spine, but before I had time to process, Beck had stepped inside, leaving me dazed and breathless at the door.

What the hell?

I shut the door and dashed past Beck, not even looking at him because even though my friends were all caught up on the peanut curry night, I didn't trust them not to lose their shit.

"Okay, so I may have mentioned tonight to Beck, and he's here and he brought cake, so be nice," I whispered, getting the words out as fast as possible. Four eyes were on me, then swung up to the person who'd stepped into the TV room behind me.

"Oh fuck, you *are* hotter in person," Tabitha exclaimed, heavily implying that I had not only shown her pictures of him but also told her that he was way better looking IRL. Which I had. But he didn't need to know that.

"That's Tabitha," I said, ignoring the hot blush spreading up my neck, "and that's Defne, tonight's guest of honor."

"Congratulations." Beck offered her a polite but warm smile that was so different from the cheeky grin he usually spared for me, I stared at him just to make sure he was the same person.

"How old are you again?" Tabitha narrowed her eyes at him as he placed the box of blondies on the sofa table.

"38," he replied.

"That's nothing," Defne tsk-ed.

"That's a significant gap." Tabitha scratched her chin and picked up her phone. "How long since you made that '30 under 30' list?"

"12 years," he replied, taking a seat with plenty of space between himself and Tab.

I sprinted to the kitchen to get him a drink, too, and came back to find Tabitha asking him about the kind of women he'd dated 12 years ago.

"Stop pestering him and put on the show, would you?" I settled in between the two of them and patted his knee in consolidation.

"On it," Defne chirped.

"Hey Del, what were you doing 12 years ago?" Tabitha asked, completely ignoring the fact that I'd told her to be nice.

"That's irrelevant. You said nothing when I befriended my old neighbor, Mrs. Hutch. She had already buried two husbands by the time I was born."

"You've never shared a bed with Mrs. Hutch."

"You don't know my life." I grabbed one of the blondies from the box and put it right in front of her mouth. "Eat that."

She scrunched up her nose but took the cake from me.

"Mrs. Hutch was kinda cute when she was young though," Defne sighed. "Alrighty, okay, before I hit play, it's just a teeny tiny scene in episode two. The water was really cold, and the swimsuit was very white and very wet. Tabitha you better be a real gentleman about it."

"Me?" she scoffed, mouth full, "There's a geriatric stranger right over there."

Defne shrugged with a saccharine smile, then hit play. The show was some college drama about affairs and lies and possibly murder, Riverdale-levels of unrealistic, but just as addictive. The second Defne's long black hair swooshed over the screen as she whipped it, emerging from the pool, Tabitha and I broke out in cheers loud enough for us to miss Defne's first line of dialog. We had to rewind and watch again. Even though that was clearly our sweet little Defne on screen, it was also not. *That* Defne was a total minx, winking at her hot swim coach, shooting him a cheeky grin over her shoulder.

The second the show cut back to the main couple, Tabitha pressed rewind again.

We watched the whole scene like five times until we had dissected the way the camera panned over Defne's curves, the way they had smudged her makeup, the way her co-star's head tilted and every syllable from her lips.

Defne was beaming, hiding her big grin behind pulled-up knees.

"What did you think?" I turned to Beck who hadn't said anything the entire time.

"This isn't really my thing."

"Sopranos guy, huh?" Tabitha mumbled.

"Okay, but what did you *think*?"

Beck scratched the space between his brows with his thumb before turning to look at me. "That it was unrealistic for a college-level competitive swimmer to be training in a bathing suit clearly designed for parties in Ibiza."

"I think realism went out the window when the first episode opened on a dorm room-based escort service. This is the kind of show best enjoyed when you stop thinking too much about how much sense it makes and start thinking about who should date. Or who would make the most interesting bad guy."

He raised a brow at me. "Coming from the queen of questioning everything."

"This is different. This is just indulging in silly fun."

"And hot people," Tabitha chimed in while three of said hot actors were ramping up to a threesome on-screen. "Watching hot people be hot is also part of it."

"Refills?" Beck asked and stood up, collecting the empty champagne flutes from the table. Defne held her still half-full glass up in response, but Tabitha and I both agreed. Beck had barely made it out the door when Tab elbowed me in the ribs.

"What?" I hissed.

"Go after him," she whispered and behind her Defne made a shooing motion with her hands.

"What is happening? You've been giving him shit since he walked in."

"Yeah. Someone has to. He's still hot and rich and joining girls' night just to spend time with you."

"Do I need to remind you that I'm in a relationship?"

She rolled her eyes at me. "I'm not telling you to get married. I'm telling you to get railed."

"I don't think Parker will mind a break-up via text," Defne said with an angelic smile.

"Ohmygod."

"Go, go, go." Tabitha shoved both hands into my side, pushing me off the sofa.

"Do you want me to text Parker?" Defne giggled.

"You guys better enjoy all the comforts of this house because this is the first and last time I'm having you over. You're insufferable." Despite my words, I didn't even try to sit back down, tiptoeing towards the kitchen instead. Beck had the champagne bottle in one hand and his phone in the other, typing away while refilling Tabitha's drink. "Work?" I asked, picking up the glass with the red lip stick stain that had already been topped up with juice.

"My brother, actually." He slipped the phone back in his pocket. "Do you mind?" He pointed at the bar cart by the dining table.

"Go ahead." I figured Cordelia wouldn't mind. "Older or younger?"

"Older," Beck said, pulling a small crystal tumbler from the cart and filling it with a golden liquid, "Julian's Axent's CTO."

"So it *was* work."

"No," he chuckled, "but it looks like I'll have to take a rain check on dinner tomorrow."

"Wow, you practically begged me to have dinner with you for weeks and now you're canceling?"

Beck took a sip of his drink and regarded me over the rim of his cup. "I don't beg, Blondie."

"You sounded pretty desperate to me."

"What are you doing here?" He crossed the room, putting his drink down on the counter.

"I live here," I replied, blinking, watching him take the champagne flute from my hand and placing it on the counter next.

"Why did you follow me to the kitchen?" Hand splayed out, his fingertips connected with my stomach, pushing me backwards.

"Tabitha thought you might need help with the drinks." My breath hitched in my throat as my back connected with the fridge. He'd caged me in for the second time tonight and my pulse hiked up faster than it had the first time. "What are you doing exactly?"

"Does it bother you that I'm nine years older than you?"

Nine older than Cordelia. Eleven older than Delilah. Technically. "Like I said, I don't particularly care how old the people I befriend are."

His hand slipped in under my oversized shirt, fingertips resting against my abdomen. God, his hand was big, all splayed out over my stomach. "What about the men you're with?"

"Beck."

"Tell me to stop." His hand slid further up, skimming the underside of my ribcage.

"Stop," I breathed.

Immediately his hand dropped out from under my shirt, and he fell a step back, darkened eyes on me as he jutted his chin as if to say *See?*

"I googled you," I said.

"I figured as much, considering Tabitha's '30 under 30' research."

"Your ex was in your own age range, so I just need to know whether you're going through a midlife crisis trying to hook up with someone younger, whether you are viewing me as a weird challenge because of my name, or whether you're actually interested in *me*. And if you are interested in me, whether that's purely sexual or also emotional."

"Do you ever stop thinking this much?"

"No."

"Not even during sex?"

"No."

"I think we just found your problem, Blondie."

"If you're going to tell me to just 'let it go', I'll-"

"No, if you're overthinking everything, you need to work through your thought process and rationalize."

"What do you mean?"

"May I?" He raised his hand in the air between us, similar to how he had just touched me. I nodded, and he stepped forward again, his hand above my shirt, fingers dipping into my belly. "What are you thinking?"

"That you haven't answered my question."

"I know that you're too young for me. I wanted to meet you because of your name, but I am genuinely interested in you. Mainly sexual, mixed with some curiosity. What else?"

"That I had a lot of cake."

"Why are you thinking about cake when I touch you?"

"Because you're touching my stomach and if you press any harder, I don't think you'll have any interest in me at all anymore…"

"I can be careful." His hand slipped in under my shirt again, but his touch rested much lighter now. "Thoughts?"

"You adjusted your pressure."

"Yes. I told you: consent and communication."

"But that was about sex."

"This is about sex."

"What if someone comes in?"

"Who would come in?"

"Tabitha or Defne, or what if Victor comes home early?"

"Your friends sent you in here, right?"

"Yeah, and Tabitha did imply that I should hook up with you, so they would probably not come looking. And if Victor came home, the intercom system would beep when he unlocked the door, so it's unlikely he'd be able to surprise us."

"There you go, you're getting the hang of it." His hand slid up, past my ribs, the tips of his fingers grazing the underside of my breasts. I sucked in a sharp breath. "Thoughts?"

"I have a boyfriend, and this *is* sexual, and I'm not a cheater. We should stop. I know we should stop. But God, you are so pretty, and your hand is really big actually, and I don't know why that is in any way relevant, but that's what I'm thinking. And does the fact that I don't actually want you to stop mean that I want to break up with my boyfriend? Because I like him. He's nice and he's so good to his parents, and I don't want to hurt him. And your hand is so close to my breasts. Like so close. And if I'd known you'd show up, I'd have worn a bra and I bet my free-floating boobs encouraged you to touch me like this."

"Alright, let's break this down," he said, shuffling closer until one of his knees was between mine, my thighs clenching in response. "I've been wanting to touch you like this since I first laid eyes on you. I noticed you weren't wearing a bra, but it didn't *encourage* my actions. Your state of undress was not for my benefit, and I'm capable of distinguishing between a woman who shakes her tits because she wants me to touch her and a woman whose tits shake because she's in comfort clothes."

I swallowed. My tongue felt like sandpaper in my throat.

"Whether you have a boyfriend or not is irrelevant to me, and it's irrelevant to how you want to be touched. A social contract does not define your physical needs."

"That sounds like a fancy way of saying you don't believe in monogamy."

"I don't."

"See, that makes us very incompatible because I'm a picket fence kind of woman. And Parker is a picket fence kind of man. So that would work much better for everyone."

"Do you want to stay in a relationship with Parker and buy a picket fence house with him?"

"No," I said. The truth of that one word sank through me like a stone tossed into a lake. I had somehow expected to skip over the water, but when it did sink, I wasn't even surprised. All stones sank; some just skipped a little further.

"Do you want me to keep touching you?" Beck asked, only his thumb traveling along the curve of my breast.

"Yes, but-" The second the *but* was over my lips, his hand stilled. He was really good at this whole consent thing. "But I need to break up with Parker first. I *do* think it's relevant."

He pulled his hand back, my skin immediately too cold without his touch. "Go get your phone."

"He deserves to be broken up with in person."

"He deserves to be broken up with once his girlfriend realizes he's not the right man for her, instead of being strung along."

I narrowed my eyes at him. "Do you actually believe that or are you just saying that for personal gain?"

"Both."

"Well, at least you're honest." I sighed and walked back to the living room, where I'd left my phone on the coffee table. What was I even doing? Should I be clearing this with Cordelia? If I was hooking up with someone who thought, I was her?

"Hey, did you- oh, I think we're going to go," Tabitha said, pushing to her feet.

"What? The episode isn't over yet?!" Defne protested.

"Yeah. Stay. Watch the show." I waved for her to sit back down.

"Thanks," Defne chirped. Tabitha kicked Defne's foot, causing her to look up, eyes widening when she spotted me. "Oh. Never mind."

"What?"

"You look a little flushed," Defne whispered as she ducked past me.

"Have fun." Tabitha winked at me.

They shouted their goodbyes towards the kitchen as they huddled down the doorway, whispering and giggling. Well, at least I knew what they thought of Beck. "Traitors," I hissed. A glance at my reflection in my dark phone screen confirmed Defne's words though. My cheeks had gone bright red, and my hair stood up in the back of my head from leaning against the fridge.

I shook my head. No matter what happened with Beck, I had no doubts about Parker's future in my life. He picked up on the third ring.

"Hey babe, I'm so glad you called. I'm so sorry for-"

I didn't let him finish. "I'm breaking up with you."

"Wait, no, I'm apologizing."

"Don't bother. I doubt you'd do it right."

"I'm sorry for hurting your feelings, Delilah. Please, let's talk about this."

"Like I said, you didn't do it right." I sighed. Sorry for hurting my feelings, but not sorry for making assumptions, for pinning his insecurities on me. "If you left anything at my place, I'll mail it over." I hung up before he could say anything else and closed my eyes for a moment. He made that so much easier than I'd anticipated.

When I turned around, Beck leaned in the doorway, one hand braced along its top. His eyes lazily traveled down my body, and the sliver of guilt I felt over breaking up with Parker on the phone vanished. One second of Beck looking at me like he didn't know where to touch me first as soon as he had permission, and I was over my breakup. If that wasn't telling.

I dropped the phone on the sofa and shrugged. Might as well embrace being a horrible person who did horrible things, since I spent the summer being a different person anyway.

"Do you want me to keep touching you?" He repeated his question from the kitchen, but it held a lot more weight now.

"Yes." My voice came out smaller than I meant for it to.

"Take your clothes off."

"You just want me to get naked?" I stemmed my arms into my sides. "That's a little unfair. What about you?"

"You want me to touch you. I want to touch you. That premise doesn't require me to take my clothes off."

"What if I want to touch you?"

"You're not ready for that. Now," he crossed his arms in front of his chest, dropping sideways against the doorframe, "take your clothes off."

I rolled my eyes but pulled my shirt over my head, throwing it on the sofa. "Is this what you want?" I asked, opening my arms.

To be fair, my boobs weren't that much to look at anyway. When he didn't reply and just let his gaze roam over my bare skin, I sighed and shimmied out of my leggings and panties in one fell swoop. I tossed them onto the sofa, too. And then I just stood there. Naked. In the middle of the living room. "This feels weird."

"You're so fucking beautiful, Blondie."

"Okay then." I cleared my throat. Flexed my toes. Pursed my lips. And counted the spotlights on the ceiling. Eight.

"Look at me." So demanding. I ran a hand over the back of my neck and forced myself to meet his burning gaze. "I said, you're fucking beautiful."

"Thanks."

He finally walked over, but he didn't touch me yet. He stopped just short of our chests colliding with every inhale. "Just to reiterate, you say stop, I stop. I remove my hands from your body. Full stop."

I nodded.

"Do you need any other safe words?"

"I don't know."

"The most basic ones are *wait*, useful if you need a moment to adjust but don't want to stop overall, and then *slower* which is self-explanatory."

"Alright, let's go with those. *Stop. Wait. Slower.*" I nodded. "Okay."

Beck leaned in, hands barely grazing my waist as his hot mouth claimed the nape of my neck, stubble brushing over my sensitive skin. What was it with men wanting to drape their spit all over you? "What are you thinking now?"

"That your lips are warm but also that I can feel your saliva on my neck and that's wet and not *sexy*."

"No problem." He reached up to wipe the spot he just kissed, only to kiss it again, mouth closed. "Better?"

"Thank you," my voice cracked. Fuck. Why did my voice

crack? So not sexy. I just didn't know how many times I'd mentioned getting icky from wet kisses to the men I'd been with, and none of them had even tried that. They'd thought I was a little funny, a little peculiar, chuckled and shook their heads. Just one wipe. One adjustment to accommodate my sensory needs. "Sorry, that sounded pathetic."

"You don't have to apologize for the feelings you have or the sounds you make while I touch you," he said and slid his knuckles up and down my sides, letting my skin warm to his touch.

"I think I need you to go wash your hands," I whispered, words tumbling from my mouth when he passed my hip bones. "I just- you were outside and then you came in and you handled everyone's glasses, and even the idea of your hand between my legs-" I shuddered.

"I just did."

"You did?"

He smiled and held up the back of his hand under my nose. Sure enough, the faint scent of almond soap stuck to his skin. "I figured that might be on your mind."

"Really?"

"You washed your hands in the middle of brunch. And at Decker's party, you went straight for the bathrooms after you touched yourself. I figured."

"Thank you. That's really thoughtful."

"Put your hands on my shoulders."

I did.

"Good. Feet apart." He tipped his foot against the inside of my ankles, and I inched my foot to the side.

"What if this doesn't work either?" I asked. "No matter what you try?"

"Define work."

"Orgasm."

"I don't think you'll orgasm tonight."

"I thought that was the whole point?"

"No, the point is for you to practice being comfortable in your own head during sex." One of his hands slipped into the warming space between my thighs, my breath hitching as his thumb brushed over my clit, sparks shooting through my stomach. Despite my physical reaction to his touch though, I couldn't help thinking how absurd it was to just stand here, naked, with his fingers sliding into my folds like he- "Tell me what you're thinking."

"Are you supposed to do that? Shouldn't you be touching my breasts first? Or kissing me? Any kind of foreplay? That's- oh god," I squeezed my eyes as his stroking intensified, my insides tightening at the pressure building under his touch, wet heat blooming between my legs. "I feel my body reacting to your touch, but you're just standing in this living room fingering me like that's the most normal thing to do and *oh*." Beck slipped one finger into me, barely down to the first knuckle, but I clenched up so hard, he couldn't go much further. "You're inside of me. Your body is literally inside my body. This is happening. I just- I want-" My nails dug into the fabric of his shirt.

"What do you want, Del?"

"Keep going."

He pushed the rest of his finger into me, pulling a loud gasp from my throat because, as assessed in the kitchen, he had big hands. My walls ached around him, physically trying to accommodate what my brain didn't want them to.

"I bet you have a big dick," I winced.

"At least that's a more sexual thought."

"Oh, this is still very much anxiety because if your finger is-" I yelped as he curled said finger, finding a spot inside me that sent an electric spark through my nerves. "We are *so* not having sex, like ever. Because neither of us will find my thoughts very interesting when it's just about how much pain I'm in."

"Are you in pain right now?" he asked, moving his finger back and forth at a languid pace.

"A little discomfort. I mean, I know intellectually that vaginas can stretch a lot, but I usually need a lot of pre-" He slid his finger out and added a second one, and this time, a sharp pain jostled through me, wrenching a gargled noise from my lips, followed by "Wait."

He stilled, two fingers half buried inside of me. I closed my eyes and let my forehead drop against his shoulder. His other hand wandered up my spine until he could cup the back of my neck, thumb massaging strong circles into the tense muscles there. It did nothing to relax the muscles between my thighs though. I had literally just broken up with Parker on the phone, so I could do this. And yet, here I was again. Same old Delilah, unable to do the most humane thing any human had ever done without switching her brain off. Wanted to have a bit of casual sex, then couldn't.

"Talk to me," he murmured, lips brushing over my temple.

"I can't," I murmured, voice clogged.

His hand slipped out from between my legs and came up to tilt my chin so I could look at him. I could smell my own arousal on his touch, and another pang of guilt marred my insides. Because I was so obviously physically attracted to him and I. Just. Couldn't.

He tilted his face until his eyes found mine. "This is not a failure, Del."

"Of course, it is. I'm clearly into you - and then I can't even relax enough to enjoy this."

He leaned down, his lips tracing the curve of my cheekbone, stubble brushing over my skin. At the same time, his hand slipped back down, curving to my backside instead. He grabbed my ass at the same time as kissing the hollow beneath my ear, and I melted into him, the rich fabrics of his clothes so soft against all my naked skin. "Do you enjoy this?" he asked, voice husky when his mouth travelled lower, leaving a scalding path down my neck and to my collar bone.

"Yeah." I swallowed.

"Come here."

Beck directed us onto the sofa and pulled me into his lap with firm but gentle hands, until I had one knee braced on either side of his hips. He leaned back, deep into the cushions, widening the gap between his chest and mine. Like this, with my legs spread around him, he had a full view of my swollen sex. "Is this uncomfortable to you in any way?"

"No."

"Being naked, sitting on me like you're about to ride my cock?"

I rolled my eyes at him. "Just because you spell it out, doesn't make it uncomfortable."

"Alright, I need you to think about the next question. Don't answer the first thing that comes to your mind, just sit with the thought for a moment. Do you *want* to have sex - or do you want to want it?"

Despite my first instinct to answer, I allowed the question to unfold in my mind. The problem wasn't that I didn't want to have sex - I was just so tired of feeling like I was doing it wrong because I couldn't climax. If I could somehow leave my prefrontal cortex at the door and just lose myself in the physical sensation? I'd pay any sum for that. "I want to, I just-" Before I could get another word out, he kissed my neck again, took my hand and directed it to his crotch, where a thick hardness was pushing against his trousers.

"Ignore your anxieties. Just the idea of me inside you."

Ignoring the fact that what I was feeling had absolutely no chance of ever fitting inside me? Ignoring that my core was already clenching shut because I was going to be in pain if he ever tried to push himself into me? Ignoring that I'd lie there like a starfish, worrying about whether the pain could lead to lasting medical issues? Just Beck's hands on me and his skin under my nails and our bodies moving together? "Without the anxiety? I'd want that. A lot."

"Good. That's settled."

"What is?"

He smiled, hands wandering over my thighs. "Everything considered, we had to clear up the basics. Asexuality or compulsory heterosexuality."

I blinked. I'd been over my situation with my exes, with my OBGYN, and even with my old therapist. "Nobody's ever brought that up."

"Very few people think about sex and sexuality in more complicated terms than missionary or doggy style, straight or gay."

"But you do?"

"You saw my nightstand. That's just the easy-to-reach-for part of my collection."

"Should I start reading 50 Shades of Grey for research?"

"No." He chuckled. "Don't worry. I don't have a red room of pain. Besides, that would make terrible research. I can recommend much better books if you do want to familiarize yourself with the topic."

"BDSM?"

"Sexual behavioral theories. Sexuality. Safe sex. Kinks." He repositioned us, allowing me to slide deeper into his lap until his erection pressed hard against my center, and his face was only a few inches from mine. "Terms like BDSM have become sensationalized by clutch-your-pearls kind of people. Those of us in the community usually have a nuanced understanding of our sexuality, physical and emotional boundaries, and the boundaries of others. Knowledge is power. Even in the bedroom, sweetheart."

I chuckled. "Are you going to make me study for sex?"

"Sounds like that's something you haven't tried before."

"Not unless you count Buzzfeed's 9 tips to spice up your sex life."

"Do I even want to know?"

"One of them was having sex in public, as if that wouldn't get people arrested. Or worse, filmed or photographed for the world to see. And if it's in nature, you have to start thinking about insects, allergies, rashes from poisonous plants..." The smirk on his lips widened as my list grew. "You've had sex in public before, haven't you?"

"Yes."

"Where?"

"A bathroom, a changing room, a plane, a beach, a jacuzzi..." He thought for a moment. "And I once got a blow job in the American Wing at the Met. Not a lot of foot traffic at the colonial furniture collection."

"You can write a whole listicle for Buzzfeed about that. Wow." I grabbed my shirt from the back of the sofa and threw it back over my shoulders, Beck watching me with a grin. "Any places you haven't done it yet?"

"A car, actually." I raised a brow at him, because that seemed like the easiest and safest place to have public sex in. I had a friend in high school who lost her virginity in a car. That's how normal it was. "I'm saving that one for you."

"Oh, that is so not happening," I laughed.

"No poisonous plants, no allergies, the interior can be sanitized, tinted windows for privacy."

"The windshield isn't tinted."

"I was thinking about the back of a limo."

"And have the driver hear everything? Hell no."

"We'll see." He smirked. "Monday morning, my place."

"I'm not having sex in your car, and definitely not on a Monday morning."

He reached up and pushed my hair behind my ears. "You have a date with my books. Non-fiction. I have a couple that might help you."

"Can I use highlighter in them?" I asked.

"Sure."

"Write in the margins? With pencil, of course."

"You can do whatever you want as long as you don't dog-ear them."

"Beck," I gasped, "I would never!"

SIXTEEN

BECK

I TAPPED THE SCREEN AND FLIPPED THROUGH TO THE NEXT PAGE, where I crossed out another useless passage. My lawyers had drawn up a first draft for a prenup, but it was littered with useless paragraphs about international private properties, cars and taking potential future children to live abroad. It was lacking the corporate solutions we needed in place.

They'd clearly not done enough research on Cordelia Montgomery if they thought my ski chalet in Switzerland would be of any interest to her. She may feel pressured to put on appearances at a few events right now, but everyone knew that she wasn't doing it because she wanted to.

I typed out a quick email to let the legal team know they'd fucked up and told them to hire a marital law specialist. We'd need one to push the merger through anyway. Might as well keep one on the team instead of hiring an outside attorney.

"So? The girl?" Julian asked, snapping his laptop shut and shooting a glance out the window. Our private jet was slowly descending, clouds and blue skies replaced by fields and winding roads.

I'd looked at the files on the flash drive. The proceedings behind the scenes were moving faster than we'd expected. Mostly thanks to Gregory Montgomery being incredibly by-the-book. Not a single cent out of place in his company. Not a noteworthy extramarital affair, not even after his wife's death, which meant no illegitimate offspring to challenge Cordelia's claim on the company. The only reason things had stalled in the first place was a claim raised by three senior members of the company, trying to declare Cordelia mentally unfit to accept her inheritance. Except now Blondie was out there flaunting that dazzling smile. And mysteriously all three of those Montgomery employees had left their positions over the last few weeks. Officially, they were citing personal matters and health concerns. Unofficially, not hard to guess why they no longer had a future at that company.

"We can discuss that on Monday," I replied, "it's a business matter."

"The Montgomery merger is huge. If you pull this off, it would be the biggest milestone of our lives. We should-"

"I know how important it is, asshole. Which is why I'm not discussing it here. Not now." Maybe it was hypocritical of me to throw that at him when I'd just sent an email about the very same topic to our lawyers. Then again, our lawyers didn't drag me across the country first thing on a Saturday morning. Actually, our lawyers probably would have objected to us flying out to Raleigh. But Georgia Beckett didn't take 'no' for an answer, and Julian wouldn't even try to refuse her. He had yet to recognize that life was easier without her in it.

"At least tell me if you got her to dump that boy yet."

I rolled my eyes at him and watched the city come into view outside the window. "Yes."

"Okay, see? That's progress. I can work with progress." His chipper grin only soured my mood more. While I could easily ignore him on the flight, being crammed into a rental car for two hours made it a lot harder.

"Any idea what she wants?" I asked before he could keep needling me about my impending engagement.

"I know as much as you do." I doubted that since he was the one still in contact with our mother. "Just don't mention her yoga classes to her. They hired a new instructor and she's on a war path."

Which meant the instructor would likely be fired by the end of the month. As a bartender-turned-trophy wife, Georgia had always felt like a small fish among sharks when navigating social circles. In prison? Georgia was the shark. Not that you could really call her lodgings a prison. She was in a minimum-security facility lovingly nicknamed 'Camp Cupcake' where the inmates lived in group cottages, could spend their time freely on the grounds, and had a shit ton of recreational activities to partake in. Like yoga classes. Julian had pulled the strings to get her relocated there from state prison within her first year of incarceration.

On our way from the airport, he filled me in on the latest Camp Cupcake news, as if our mother's personal vendetta against her snoring bunk buddy was in any way relevant to me. I hadn't spoken to Georgia in almost two years, when she'd been hospitalized with pneumonia, and before that it had been three years. Whatever emails she sent were automatically directed into my spam folder.

The visitation center was as inviting as a three-star-hotel lobby. Comfortable enough to spend one or two hours in, if need be, with low sofas and a couple of tables with chairs, all bolted to the floor, but not a place you wanted to stay longer than necessary.

Georgia Beckett looked like someone costuming in prison uniform. Her hair was in a neatly cropped brown pixie cut and by the look of her full lips and wrinkle-free eyes, her last 'medical leave' had involved more Botox than usual for a root canal.

"My boys!" She fell around us in a hug that lasted the exact predeterminate five seconds before falling back and running her fingers through my hair, fixing a strand that was certainly not out of place. I wasn't dumb enough to come here giving her any kind of ammunition. "Look at you Augustus. I keep forgetting how tall you are. You have to come visit more often."

"Beck," I replied.

Her faux warm smile dropped instantly. "I named you Augustus when they cut you out of my flesh, and that's your name until the day I die." Not legally, not anymore, but that hardly mattered to Georgia.

"Hello mother," Julian said and pressed a quick kiss to her cheek before settling on one of the sofas. I took the seat next to him and watched Georgia sink into the armchair across from us with all the grace of a snake. Almost 70, seventeen years in prison, and she had not lost a drop of composure.

She folded her hands in her lap, all business. *Here we go.* "We need to discuss Cordelia Montgomery."

Oh, for fuck's sake. I turned to Julian. Mr. *I know as much as you do*. "Did the two of you conspire against me?"

"I didn't say a word." He held up his hands in defeat but didn't even try to hide the dirty smirk on his lips.

"He didn't have to. I keep up with the news." Sure, and who chose and paid for the gossip magazines and society pages she got in the mail?

"Is this why you wanted us to come?" I asked, staying on track rather than picking a useless fight.

"Yes." Georgia leaned forward, elbows on her knees, narrowed eyes on me. "It's a brilliant move in theory, but you're aging out of being a desirable bachelor and she's too rich to be complacent arm candy. What's your play?"

Jesus fuck. This woman couldn't let go of her manipulations even thousands of miles and many years out of my life. "I can handle her."

"Three strategies. Go." Three simple words and I was thrown back to long nights at the dinner table, when Georgia made us go over international politics, historical wars, chess games and celebrity PR campaigns. Anything that required any sort of strategy. We wouldn't go to bed until we came up with three satisfactory strategies each. The number of nights I slept with my head smacked against the mahogany tabletop probably matched the number of nights I spent in my bed.

"Pregnancy and shotgun wedding," Julian said, repeating the same *strategy* he'd mentioned to me a while back.

If Georgia had personal feeling on the matter, she pushed them aside. "Contraceptives?"

"Flaxseed or a little food poisoning to make her throw up the pill."

"Jesus," I muttered.

"Yes, good thinking." My mother pointed at me as if I'd just thrown in a valid argument, and I shouldn't have felt proud like a fucking fifth grader getting a gold star, but old habits died hard. "Is she religious enough to go through with it? Abortion?"

"She's not the type to get an abortion," Julian scoffed.

"You would be surprised how many women get an abortion every day, Julius. There's no *type*." She pursed her lips and Julian slid an entire inch lower in his seat.

"Del wants the whole goddamn picket fence dream," I supplied. Maybe I didn't want to play this game anymore 30 years later, but this was what I was trained to do. I knew how to play. I knew how to win. I may have spent many nights at the kitchen table, but Julian had spent more. "You don't need three strategies.

You need one strategy. Sternberg's triangular theory of love proposes three major objectives."

Mom folded her hands under her chin, listening.

"First, passion. She has sexual hang-ups, but she's attracted to me, so even if she doesn't see a romantic future for us yet, that's my way in. No pun intended. I've made first progress on this, but trust me, I'm not getting her pregnant anytime soon. However, she's still a romantic at heart, so I doubt she'll be able to keep sex and love separate for long." I pinched the bridge of my nose.

"Keep going." Mom's words were an order - not an encouragement.

"Secondly, commitment. She clearly has clinical anxiety, so I will be her reliable source of comfort. This is the part that will likely take the most time. She already trusts me to a certain degree, but I need to solidify myself as someone she can depend on. As *the* someone she can *always* depend on. If I'm the only person who can offer her peace of mind, that makes me the perfect person to spend the rest of her life with."

Mom shook her head, and my stomach sank at the cool disapproval in her eyes. Just like it had always done. "That's too vague. Define your goals, Augustus."

"Anticipate her needs, remove stressors, offer emotional and physical comfort during and after stressful situations."

"What's your third objective?" she asked, no beat wasted.

"Intimacy."

"You already mentioned sex," my brother piped up.

"Hush, Julius."

"Intimately knowing someone is not the same as having sex with someone, idiot," I shot him a look over my shoulder, but looked back at Mom to explain, "It's about knowing their comfort movies and their guilty pleasure foods. Getting them to open up about their family and their childhood trauma and their hopes and dreams and shit."

She clicked her tongue. "Language."

"And how exactly are you going to do that?" Julian asked.

"Would it surprise you to find out that many women are capable of having actual conversations?"

He chuckled bitterly. "Fair enough, I suppose if she's not letting you fuck her, that's the way to go."

"She told me about her picket-fence dreams before I finger-fucked her in the living room, if you must know."

Mom snapped her fingers in both of our faces. "Enough, boys."

"He wanted to know. You wanted to know." I was steamrolling through this, no thoughts, just the need to prove that I knew what I was talking about. "Want me to tell you how she sat on my lap and held my cock in her hands? Is that strategy breakdown enough for you?"

"Fine. I get it," Julian groaned.

"No, please, let me indulge you with details of the sounds she made when I hit her G-spot."

The slap snapped my head around. The sharp sting of my mother's hand burned on my cheek as I blinked. A prison guard materialized next to us before I'd even processed that my mother had just slapped me. "I think it's time to go, Mrs. Beckett," the guard said, brows raised.

"I agree," Georgia huffed and pointed her bony index finger at Julian and me, "you two are brothers first. Treat each other with respect."

"Yes, mother," both of us replied in unison to the same line we'd heard all our lives. *Brothers first.* The words hung in the air as Georgia Beckett was led back out of the visitation center.

Even though a wide grin tugged at Julian's lips, I was the one who had pushed these details. For what? Proving in front of my incarcerated mother that I knew what I was doing even if Julian thought his strategies were better? I fell back in my seat and watched a woman hug her kids at the far end of the room, all of them beaming. The universe was really rubbing it in today, huh?

"Good to go?" Julian asked after a few minutes of sitting in silence.

"Yeah." I stood and cast one last glance at the family that was playing some board game in the corner, actually enjoying each other's company. Georgia had come up with many games over the years. But even if you won, afterwards you always felt like you'd lost *something*.

SEVENTEEN

BECK

I opened my door to reveal a tiny woman with a huge blue and pink backpack that jingled and rustled thanks to all the straps and keychains on it. Del was in yoga pants and a crop top, and looked younger without her usual red lipstick. It made sense. With the red, she had the whole blonde bombshell association going for her. Without it, and dressed like this, she looked like a wide-eyed Scandinavian graduate, ready to backpack the world. "I'm sorry, you must have the wrong address. The dorm for Swedish exchange students is two blocks south."

"Very funny, Mr. Beckett." She rolled her eyes at me, soft pink lips pulling into a small smile.

I grimaced. "Mmh no, don't call me that when you look like this."

"Like wha- ew, you're gross."

"I told you *not* to call me that." I shrugged and opened the door for her to shuffle in. Some men might have been into that kind of power play. While I didn't mind that there was basically a decade between us, I didn't need to fetishize it. "Not my thing."

"You made the connection in the first place."

"That's just because I have a dirty mind."

"Exactly. Now." She dumped the bag on my sofa and pulled out a pastel project book, and pastel pens and page flags to match. "Show me the books."

"Wow, you're a geek."

"Yep." She jutted her chin out and grinned widely. "Books!"

Her enthusiasm was too cute considering the fact that she wasn't here to borrow books on princesses or unicorns or whatever else matched her pastel stationery. I showed her down the hallway and opened the door to my office for her. "All yours."

"Hmpf." She furrowed her brows, looking over the shelves lining the walls, and clicked her tongue when she took in the sleek glass desk in the middle of the room. "This is not an inviting library."

"It's an office, not a library."

"How many books do you own?"

I had a vague sense that I was answering a trick question when I said: "Must be around 2000 now." At least the bookcases had been advertised to hold 200 each.

"Well, you need only 1000 books to qualify as a library, Mr. Be- Becks? Becky? B?"

"Beck."

"And a library must be inviting. It should be begging you to make yourself comfortable and stay for hours."

"Or you just take a book from *the office* and read it on the sofa."

"Hold please." She pushed her stack of pink and blue and orange stationery into my hands and disappeared down the hallway, returning a minute later with my entire bedding piled high in her arms.

"That belongs in the bedroom."

"Don't you have work or something?" Del scrunched her nose at me and nodded at my desk.

"That's why I suggested you read in the living room."

"Good thing I'm a quiet reader." She grinned and spread the thick fleece blanket on the floor like a picnic cloth, arranging pillows against the bookcases to create a reading nook for herself, before stretching her hands out for her study supplies. I handed them over and watched her arrange them, color-coded along the edge of the blanket. While I wasn't keen on having my apartment rearranged, I wasn't opposed to having Del make herself comfortable in my office.

"That shelf," I said and pointed at the one opposite my desk. It was the safest placement in case of video calls. You didn't want screenshots blown up to reveal books like Tantric Massage 101 or Advanced Japanese Bondage.

"Any pointers?"

"Follow your gut." I had a meeting, but it was the one I'd promised Julian about a certain person in attendance right now, so I dropped into my chair and typed out a quick message to let him know she'd be able to hear me, and waited for him to react with a thumbs up before I picked up my headphones and jumped on the video call.

"You had a girl over and that's the reason you didn't show up at the office today? Very unprofessional of you."

"Do you need me to run you through the whole strategy again or do you think I might have it handled?" I raised my brows at him, almost daring him to question me again. If nothing else, Georgia's seal of approval of my approach, should have shut down his doubts. Del shot a quick look over her shoulder, but returned to browsing the shelves when she registered that I was on a call.

"I'm not asking if she sucked your dick for breakfast, idiot."

Del couldn't hear him but that didn't stop the muscle in my jaw from twitching at his words. "It was more of a last-minute arrangement."

"Hmm, just make sure she's not friendzoning you, Mr. Intimacy."

"That's currently no concern," I replied, shooting a look over the screen of my laptop. Blondie was pulling out a large coffee table photography book, featuring close-ups of people wrapped in ropes, and raised her brows at the cover.

"What's that smirk for? Is she twerking naked on the other side of the screen?"

"Trust the strategy," I reminded him, "When the deal goes through, you'll need to meet face to face with the stakeholders too and potentially maintain that relationship for many years. You don't want to get sidetracked by acquisition details, do you?"

"Alright, alright, no more discussing your future wife's ass, got it."

On command, my eyes dropped to Del's ass, clad in tight black leggings that left little to the imagination, not even the line of her cheeky slip. "I'm still brainstorming how we'll facilitate a growth shift on the third objective without coming on too strong."

"Take her to Cannes. Showing off your yacht always works, right?"

He wasn't wrong about the principal. The yacht had little to do with it, but an international holiday would have been a good bonding experience. "Probably not with this account," I said, dragging my eyes from Del's ass to the book on body modifications in her hands. "They're not projecting any interest in international expansion."

"Oh yeah, I almost forgot. Cordelia Montgomery leaving her house is one thing, but leaving the country?"

"Any further word from Georgia?" I asked, letting Julian know that I was done talking about the merger.

"No. She called yesterday, but Brody took the call and spent all fifteen minutes waffling about some boyband announcing their breakup. She was crying into her breakfast this morning because they had a hit song about French toast and now, she won't ever be able to eat French toast again. Or something."

I didn't like the idea that Georgia might sink her claws into Brody, but to her credit, she had spent the last fifteen years playing a perfectly loving grandmother who just happened to be in prison. A few years ago, Brody had claimed that Georgia was *badass* but from all she'd told me, Georgia had only ever listened to her and encouraged her to do whatever the hell she wanted. I was fairly certain that was one of the reasons Julian allowed Brody to get into the ring rather than sticking her with *appropriate* piano and tennis lessons.

"Maybe Georgia should spend her time and energy on facilitating that reunion rather than interfering with my schedule."

"Could you imagine? Our mother, the boyband manager."

Del yelped, and I glanced up to find her with her hand clutched over her mouth, eyebrows knitted together. "Sorry," she whispered and pulled up her shoulders.

Julian was going on about something, but I didn't hear him, cocking my head to see what caused the bright pink blush on Del's cheeks.

She turned the book around.

Ah.

It was called Milkmaid Diaries.

A Dutch pornstar's autobiography chronicled through cumshot selfies.

Nothing like a close-up of a labia covered in five men's semen to drive home the point that this was not the cozy library Del wanted it to be.

"...and then everyone died."

I raised my brows at Julian, who was possibly the only person at Axent with the balls to call me out when I stopped listening. Although to be fair most people just talked to hear their own voice anyway. "Care to explain?"

"No, you go back to eye fuck- I mean giving your girl the attention she deserves. The Montgomery account takes top priority."

"I'll see you Thursday at the latest."

"Have fun."

I closed the window and dropped the earbuds, but when I checked on Del again, she had settled down on the floor with four piles of books neatly stacked, a color-matched set of highlighters, gel pens and sticky notes on each stack.

"You have a system, Blondie?" I asked.

"Personal accounts, essays, biographies," she explained, slapping her hand on the first stack. "Biology and psychology and sexology and everything else that sounded vaguely like science." She slapped the second stack. "Guidebooks on how to have sex in all the different ways." She drummed her fingers against the third stack, and finally touched the furthest stack with the tip of her cozy-socked toes. "Photography to look at when the text starts blurring in front of my eyes, but I figure I can compile some notes on aesthetics. - I was considering a fifth category for a historical approach, which is really interesting as well but..." She shrugged and looked at me, eyes so big they looked like frosted lakes. "This is going to sound silly, but I only have four colors. I'd rather have four truly relevant categories than have five categories, but the color-coding is off on one of them."

"You need a fifth highlighter color?"

"Yes, but no, you don't understand, it's a whole system. And I don't do neon."

I opened the top drawer on my desk and pulled out a muted

red highlighter, a pad of red sticky notes and a red gel pen. All usually reserved for when people fucked up and I had to correct their fuck-ups. "Does this work?"

She scrunched up her nose, eyes flitting to her four stacks. I double-checked her setup and realized why she was hesitant. I opened the second drawer and pulled out a small booklet of page flags that included red ones. "How about now?"

She bit her lip to stop a stupid big grin from breaking through. "Thank you, thank you, thank you." She nodded and got up again snatching the stationery from my desk, doing a giddy little dance as she clutched them to her chest and wiggled back to the shelf to pull the historical category. I'd never seen anyone that excited to annotate books about the history of vibrators.

To her credit, she *was* a quiet reader, but her very presence proved to be a distraction. I sent a few emails, then looked up to watch her lie on her stomach, feet kicking, tapping her pen against her lips while she made her way through *Milkmaid*. Every couple of pages, she stuck a page flag to a paragraph and scribbled a few lines into her notebook. By the time lunch rolled around, I had gotten as much done as I otherwise would have in an hour. And while I usually didn't take a break unless a lunch meeting was required, I had no intention of letting Del starve.

I closed my laptop and eyed her playing with the blue pearl on her necklace, waiting until she turned the page. "Has all that studying made you hungry yet?"

"Hmm?" She whipped her head up, finger on the page to remember her place. She blinked, trying to focus her eyes on the clock above the door. "Oh. I guess I could eat." She unfolded the dust cover of the book to tuck the flap around the pages she'd already read, bookmarking her spot.

"What are you in the mood for?" I asked, reaching out a hand for her. She took it, letting herself be pulled up, grimacing at being pulled out of the position she'd been stuck in for hours.

"Oh, I brought snacks."

"I have a fully stocked kitchen. No peanuts."

"I'm just here for your books. I don't expect you to play host or anything."

"It's food, not a monogrammed set of towels." *Just here for your books.* Maybe I did have to revisit the friendzoning situation Julian mentioned.

She pulled two containers of purple Tupperware from her backpack, shaking them like maracas as she followed me to the kitchen. "Microwave?"

"You are not eating microwaved food on my watch." Okay, so I wouldn't win her over with my charm, but *please*, standards.

"Fine. I'll eat it cold then," she huffed and climbed onto one of the barstools.

I blinked at the food she brought when she popped the lids off. "Absolutely not." I grabbed one of her boxes, ignoring her yelp of protest. "Fruit, yes. Mini pancakes, no."

"First of all, you don't tell me what to eat. That's abusive. Second of all, those aren't mini pancakes, they're Poffertjes, a Dutch delicacy."

"My place, my rules. You're here to work, so you need brain food. A pancake by any other name is still as unhealthy."

"You can't just misquote Shakespeare at me to prove a point."

"Pancakes are comfort food. You can have these back when you're done working." I closed the box of tiny pancakes and shelved it in the fridge, pulling out fresh vegetables and diced teriyaki chicken I'd prepared last night.

"I don't like tomatoes," Del interjected as she watched me cut up the veggies.

"More for me."

"What are you making?"

"Lunch wraps."

Her stomach gurgled in response, and even though her cheeks

flamed red, she still sounded playful when she said: "Sounds like you better hurry up." She popped one of her grapes through full lips and I almost lost a finger while chopping cucumber. Fuck. I needed to get laid if this was all it took to distract me.

Del spent the rest of the afternoon with her nose buried in the books and jumped up when her phone buzzed at precisely 5pm.

I spent that evening at Clandestine, the kind of club people spent 10k a month to be anonymous members of, but I couldn't find the distraction I was looking for. Every woman I met was too tall, too brunette, too eager. Usually my M.O. - beautiful, self-aware, out for just sex - but all I kept thinking about was a certain short blonde and her stationery happy dance.

Del was back in my apartment the next morning, carrying pillows and blankets from the bedroom to the office and settling in for the day. It was a little easier ignoring her presence in the slouchy floor-length t-shirt dress she wore, at least until she flopped over and put her legs up against the bookshelves, the dress pooling around her hips, baring every inch of milky white leg. No idea what happened in that 11am meeting, but I would be able to draw every dip of her legs from memory.

We ordered sushi for lunch, during which she mostly rambled down the contents of her research. I'd read every book on my shelves, but I didn't stop her from recounting her findings. She was excited about this. I wasn't going to dim her enthusiasm. And when I lost track of time discussing erogenous zones, I told myself that engaging with her genuine curiosity wasn't endearing or intoxicating – just beneficial. This was a long con. At least I wouldn't be stuck in a sexless marriage. That was all.

There would be no marriage and no merger if I couldn't hold it together in actual business meetings though, so I worked from the kitchen for the rest of the day.

EIGHTEEN

Delilah

Beck welcomed me back on Tuesday, ordered sushi for lunch and Starbucks in the afternoon, pulling a face when I spelled out my drink choice for him. It was all sugar and milk and ice - perfect for hot summer days - and had very little semblance to his simple black coffee with a dash of milk.

On Wednesday, Steve, the doorman, handed me a key and a note the moment I set foot in the building. Apparently, Beck had to work at the office, but he gave me free reign over his apartment and his library. I smirked at the word *library* on the heavy linen paper. Damn right, it was.

Stepping into Beck's apartment without him there felt an awful lot like being in a school on a Saturday. Same walls, same floors, same furniture, but with a touch of eeriness. When I walked into the library, however, it was exactly as inviting as I'd left it. Pillows, blankets, books. He'd told me he'd take care of it when

I'd started shuffling my stuff around last night. Apparently, he hadn't. Had he slept without blankets or pillows? Unless of course, he hadn't slept in his own apartment at all. He could have gone out last night. The thought plummeted through me, stomach sinking at the thought. We weren't dating. We weren't even… anything. He could sleep wherever and with whoever he wanted. Maybe a cool, experienced woman who didn't go through anxiety spirals when sex was on the table.

I sighed and dropped my backpack by the door, sinking into my plush corner. I reached for my current book but stopped with my hand mid-air. My nest was *not* exactly as I'd left it.

A familiar blue box sat on top of the stack of sexual guidebooks and self-help instructions with a color-matched sticky note on it. Forget the vibrator. The fact that he'd used a pastel green sticky note for the pastel-green-marked stack of books that thematically matched the idea of using a vibrator? He got it. It took me a moment to blink through the sheer color-coding joy and read the note he'd left.

To study or to practice that is the question.

Another badly butchered Shakespeare quote. I sighed and set the box aside. Just because I had spent two days hyperfocusing on sex books, didn't mean the vibrator was magically going to work now. Maybe some other day, when I had a better understanding of the whole mind-body-balance during sex. Today, I had a book on achieving mind-blowing orgasms on the TBR. It was one of the first ones I'd grabbed, obviously, but a cursory glance at the index had confirmed that I had been lacking some base knowledge. I settled in my corner with the book and wrote the title down in my notebook.

I just couldn't focus.

If a vibrator had eyes - this one was staring at me.

With every single page I turned, that box's presence burrowed into me, until my brain was unable to compute the words on the page in front of me. Groaning, I snapped the book shut and narrowed my eyes at the sex toy. "What the hell do you want from me?" I huffed. This was how far I'd fallen. Talking to a vibrator.

NINETEEN

BECK

I HAD TRIED AND FAILED TO LEAVE EARLY. I'D MEANT TO HEAD home in time to see Blondie off, but the servers had gone down at the office - and I'd had to stay until all systems were back up. Not that I could do much, but I couldn't be seen breezing off while everyone else was in panic mode.

It was pitch-black outside by the time I made it home. The apartment was dark and quiet, but I still checked the office for any sign of her presence. None. I flicked the lights on to find her corner tidied up again, books stacked in a row, no blankets, or pillows even though I'd left them out for her.

My attention snagged on the blue box on my desk and the red sticky note on it. I picked it up, but the message was short and clear.

No.

Well, it had merely been a suggestion. I'd figured she might get a little inspired by her reading materials.

I was going to put the box back in my nightstand where it had been living for a while, but as I walked into the bedroom, the light caught at just the right angle on the box to show the thin cut along the plastic seal.

She didn't.

I flipped the box open. No hygiene seal, no instructions booklet, and while the vibrator was in the box, it was upside-down.

My brain short-circuited as the other meaning of *No* filtered through. No, it hadn't worked. Which would mean she had tried. Here. Sometime while I was at the goddamn office, Del had fucked herself in my apartment. Where? On the sofa? On the floor of the office? My desk chair? My bed? The thought of her body writhing against my furniture spiked my pulse in an entirely unhealthy way and sent heat shooting to my hips.

I pulled her contact up on my phone, fully aware that she could be fast asleep already and typed out the question:

BECK:

Where?

The reply came almost immediately:

BLONDIE:

At home :) watching Little Women.

Of course, she had no fucking clue what I meant. I swallowed and tossed the vibrator on the bed, loosening my belt buckle as I typed it out more clearly:

BECK:

Where in my apartment did you practice?

Three dots appeared on screen, then disappeared again. I

peeled out of my clothes and was stark naked by the time she'd finally replied.

BLONDIE:
> Bed… but don't worry I put down a large towel and took it with me to wash. You'll get it back spotless.

Spotless. Fuck. Had she been wet enough to spot the towel? Drenching it with her sweet juice before she got all in her head again?

I dropped into my bed, which had started smelling like jasmine and amber after the first day she'd claimed my pillows, but I swore the scent was stronger now. And as I curled my hand around my cock, imagining her face pressed into my pillows, her hips arching off my mattress, I typed out one last text.

BECK:
> Next time I'll help.

TWENTY

Delilah

On Thursday morning at 3am, I got another glimpse at why Cordelia Montgomery hadn't been seen outside her house in 15 years. Or rather, I got an audible reminder. The screams had me shooting out of bed and into the hallway, swinging the first vase I could grab. I followed the sound upstairs, where Victor stopped me with one hand raised to his lips to motion for me to stay quiet, the other hand outstretched for the vase. He was clad in a simple black shirt and a pair of loose gray sweatpants, ready to spring into action even in his sleep.

I handed the vase over, my eyes fixed on the door behind him. Cordelia's screams raised the hairs on my neck, but they died down after a minute or so.

"Waking her during a nightmare would just cause a panic attack," he spoke in a low voice, shelving the vase in a nearby bookcase. "And please, Delilah, don't hit intruders with 200-year-old delicate antiques. I can arm you with an adequate golf club."

"I…" I was too stunned to form a coherent sentence, still watching the door, as if the screams might start again. "Does that happen a lot?"

"No," Victor sighed, "not anymore. This was the first one in over a year."

The handle of the bedroom door turned, lock clicking open, and Cordelia stepped out, hair rustled, nightshirt twisted around her waist, a soft smile forming on her lips when she spotted Victor. Her shoulders stiffened when her eyes fell on me. "Did I wake you?"

I waved her off. "I was barely sleeping." At least that was true. I'd stared at Beck's last text until the phone fell out of my hands, and even then, I was still tossing and turning, dreaming up snippets of his hands on me mixed with the pictures from his books. Stress dreams, not wet dreams.

"I'm sorry," she breathed, shoulders falling inwards, "I promise this won't happen again."

"For what it's worth, Delilah was ready to defend your honor with the Fontainebleau vase," Victor said, a chuckle lilting his words. It was the closest I'd ever seen him come to joking.

Cordelia only needed a split second to locate the vase, the smile from before returning to her lips. "I never much liked that thing anyway."

Victor clicked his tongue in disapproval. Who knew he was the one appreciating all the floral European decor?

"Anyone else feel like ice cream?" Cordelia asked and leaned back into her room, grabbing a silky robe that billowed out behind her when she slid past me down the stairs.

Victor made an *after you* gesture, and I wordlessly followed my hostess. "I'll be there in a second," I said and dipped into my own suite. I grabbed a wooly knit cardigan and my phone. Ice cream at 3am meant I was definitely not going to be ready for another study session at 8 o'clock. I unlocked my phone and hesitated. Beck's last message was only four words but to me, it took up the entire screen.

> BECK:
> Next time I'll help.

I was fully aware of how stupid it had been to take that damn vibrator to his bedroom, but it had also been… strangely erotic. To be engulfed in his scent, knowing I was doing something taboo, spurred on by the breathing exercise I had just read about. At least right up until I started worrying about potential housekeepers and security cameras, and my risqué bubble had burst.

I sighed and shoved the memory down.

> DEL:
> Something came up. Won't be able to make it today. Sorry <3

The message looked like a lame follow-up to his offer of help. If you could call it that. It felt more like a promise. And something inside me stirred at the thought of anyone, let alone *him,* using a toy on me. I'd never done that. It seemed like a waste of everyone's time, considering the toys didn't even work when I was alone, and I would likely end up faking it again, just to break the awkwardness of neither party getting anything out of the experience. But something about the way Beck had phrased his questions…

Where?
Where in my apartment did you practice?
Next time I'll help.

He called it 'practice'. He knew that I hadn't just masturbated in his bed for the kick of it – I'd also failed at climaxing yet again, and he… He wanted to *help.*

"Rocky road or mint chocolate chip?" Cordelia's voice echoing from the stairs ripped me from my thoughts.

I'd been biting my lip so hard it hurt when I opened my mouth. "Mint chocolate!" I left the phone on the nightstand and followed the sound of voices and clanking spoons to the kitchen.

Cordelia and Victor were already at the dinner table. Victor had a bowl with a small dollop of green ice cream in front of him, while Cordelia was pouring rainbow sprinkles over a mountain of rocky road, whipped cream, and gummy bears. That monstrosity looked like it would provide a three-day sugar high.

"I'm sorry for waking you up," Cordelia said as I took the chair next to her, where another *normal* portion of mint chocolate chip ice cream was set out. "I know that's not normal. I know I'm crazy."

"You're not crazy unless you're talking about that ice cream," I replied. Victor chuckled but Cordelia poked her tongue out at him. He smirked a strangely upside-down grin I hadn't seen on him before and returned to eating his ice cream. It felt like a way too intimate moment. A little private exchange that wasn't to be seen by anyone who knew Victor's usually stoic exterior.

"I think," I started, then decided to rephrase my thoughts to center Cordelia rather than my perception of her. "Your mother was shot. You were there and you were very young. That kind of trauma rewires your brain. It's unrealistic for people to expect you to go out much after that in the first place. And it's unfair of people to expect you to return to what they think of as *normal* at all, no matter how much time passes. You don't need to conform to anyone's idea of a *normal* life as long as you find happiness and safety in your way of living."

"You almost sound like my therapist." She shoved a huge spoonful of ice cream and sprinkles in her mouth.

I sighed and stared at my ice cream, then decided *fuck it* and drowned it in whipped cream, too. "We all have our funky little brain issues to deal with."

"Funky little brain issues, I like that," Cordelia said through a held-up hand, not even having swallowed yet. Victor grimaced at her full mouth but didn't say anything.

"I'll also take neurospicy."

"Yeah," she giggled, "that sounds better than rattling down the whole list of acronyms. ADHD, PTSD, SAD. I'm working on collecting the whole neurospicy alphabet."

I nodded. "GAD and autistic for me."

"I had a feeling."

"Same."

We smiled at each other over our ice cream bowls. There really was a neurodivergent radar. I didn't know how to explain it, but you somehow gravitated towards each other. Apparently, some studies showed that neurotypicals thought something was 'different' about neurodivergent people within two minutes of meeting them, without being able to put a finger on what it was. Thankfully, that same instinct worked the other way around, too.

"Well, I also want to be a good teacher. And good teachers understand that every person has different needs."

"I think you'll be a great teacher."

"Thank you," I laughed, "and I think you'll be great at bossing people around from your home."

"Look, I know my mother's death was very public. She was shot. I was standing right next to her. That's the story, right?" Cordelia pushed a red gummy bear around the mountain of whipped cream, but her eyes were on the kitchen window - not that there was anything but pitch-black outside.

"Cordelia," Victor said in a tone I couldn't quite place.

She nodded and gave him a small smile before fully turning in her chair, facing me. "She was shot, but the story doesn't end there. I was grabbed and pulled into a van. The kidnappers apparently thought that killing my mother would make my father realize they wouldn't hesitate to shoot me too if he didn't hand over the 20 million they demanded as ransom." She grimaced but didn't pause long enough for me to ask questions. "I sat tied up in some windowless room for three days, a bottle of water and a cheeseburger to tide me over, before they got me out of there. My father spent those three days negotiating them down to four million. I'm not saying this for you to pity me, but I think you deserve the full truth, considering you are one half of me now."

"God." I breathed. I couldn't even imagine the pain and fear she must have gone through in those three days. No wonder she didn't want to go back out there. And to think her father could have shortened that time. The Montgomerys were billionaires. With a B. That sixteen-million-difference was nothing at their level of wealth. "Your dad sounds like an ass."

Cordelia let out a loud cackle. "Oh, he was. Hope he rots in hell."

Victor let out a vague harumph of agreement while scratching the last bits of ice cream from his bowl.

"I think my dad would have loved you," I said.

"What was he like before he got sick?"

I didn't even bother asking how she knew he got sick. I had come to terms with the fact that Cordelia had sleuthed through my life before allowing me into hers. Knowing what she'd been through, I could hardly hold it against her. "He worked at the Sallow candy factory." I pointed my spoon at her mountain of sugar. "He considered himself Willy Wonka. He didn't make the candy, but he always said that Willy Wonka had the Oompa Loompas do that anyway. He was in packaging. Or as he put it, he was the one who made sure kids got excited even just holding a bar of chocolate in the candy aisle. He loved the simplicity of it. Candy makes people happy."

"I bet your house was *the* place to be trick-or-treating on

Halloween." Cordelia added another heaping of rainbow sprinkles to her bowl. God, Dad would have really loved her. He'd have clutched his chest, wheezing with laughter before copying her ice cream composition for himself. Just to try. He'd have stared at it for ten minutes before eating, and he would have spent the next five days dissecting how the colors and textures worked together.

"It was." I nodded and scooped down some ice cream. I wasn't religious and didn't believe in the afterlife or ghosts or anything, but if there was a way for Dad to watch, I really hoped he did. Just because he'd get such a good laugh out of Cordelia's recipe.

TWENTY-ONE

BECK

BLONDIE:

Did you know that people are hornier in summer than in winter?

BECK:

Yes

BLONDIE:

Apparently a mix of the extra Vitamin D and dopamine from the sun, and all the exposed skin releasing pheromones.

BECK:

We should test your theory on my sun deck.

BLONDIE:

It's not my theory, it's science.

She didn't even react to my come on. You'd think after trying to get herself off in my bed, she would have been a little flirty. Except, when she texted me, it was links to articles about hormones and studies on the germs exchanged during oral sex. She'd gone into deep research mode - and today she hadn't even shown, after I'd clearly signaled that I wanted to try a more hands-on approach.

She'd been quivering around my fingers last Friday and now she shot me down again and again. What the fuck was I supposed to do with that?

BECK:
Call it a scientific experiment then.

BLONDIE:
I don't need to experiment to know that this heatwave is just making me sweaty and lazy.

Another knock-out.

"Who could possibly be more important than me, huh?" Brody's cushioned glove knocked into my side as she tried to angle over my shoulder and catch a glimpse at my texts.

"It's just work," I said.

"Uh-huh *Blondie* sure sounds a lot like work."

I slipped my phone back into my pocket and narrowed my eyes at her, then at the ring, where two teen girls were dancing around each other instead of landing hits. "Shouldn't you be getting the shit kicked out of you right now?"

"Next one," she replied, jumping up and down, keeping her muscles warm, "they had to let Felicity go first because she needs to be home by nine or her mom will freak out again."

Sports for teen girls was very different from sports for adults. Parental curfews mattered more than skill. "You need a pep talk?"

Brody jumped from side to side, pumping her arms. "I need you to tell me who Blondie is. Am I finally getting an aunt?"

I didn't point out to her that she technically had an aunt, because her late mother's sister was an old hag. She hated Julian for getting Brody's mom pregnant and hated Brody for being born. Which had led to her mother's death. Eclampsia. Preventable but not uncommon. "We'll see," I said, and Brody almost stumbled forward in the middle of a jump, scrambling to turn to me.

"Wait, what the fuck?"

I raised my brows at her choice of words, but I knew better than to stop a teenager from cursing. "I thought we were getting somewhere but she canceled on me today. Your father thinks she's friendzoning me."

Brody rolled her eyes at me. "The friendzone is a patriarchal concept invented by men incapable of seeing women as anything but servants or sexual partners."

The bell rang in the ring, fight over. "You're up," I said, pointing at the corner she'd have to fight from. If this had been an official fight, I would have been in coach mode, but since this was just a friendly competition, I was allowed some blonde distraction.

"Give me three minutes," Brody said, shoving her mouth guard in.

She only needed two. She polished that other girl off without letting her get a single hit in. The sense of pride that swelled in my chest diminished when she stopped in front of me and nailed me with an icy glare though. "So? Are you a patriarchal asshole who only wants to use this girl for sex - who gets mad when she values your companionship over your penis?"

Brody may have inherited her mother's soft face, but that attitude of hers was all Julian. "I'm not discussing my sex life with you, Brody," I said while helping her out of her gloves. "You and your father are way too nosy."

"You come to *my* fight and spend the entire time looking at your phone. I deserve an explanation that doesn't involve the word friendzone." She grabbed her water bottle but kept her eyes trained on me, brows raised, waiting for an answer while she drank.

I huffed an exasperated sigh. The CIA should employ teenage girls. If anyone could torture information out of you, it was them. "If you liked a boy, how would you signal that to him?"

"Depends on the context." She shrugged and chugged more water from her bottle even though her brow was barely crested in sweat.

"Explain." I had stooped so low as to ask my teenage niece for dating advice. Great.

"If we went out on a date, absolutely dress up. I'd want to look my best, look cute, snap a couple pics with him and take some videos. We could totally match our fits for the aesthetic. And he could be all 'look at my hot girlfriend' you know?" The word *hot* didn't compute in relation to my niece, but I understood the basic gist of what she was saying. Going out equaled being seen - even digitally - which equaled getting dressed up.

"What about... study dates?"

"School, library or at home?"

Part of me was curious why the location seemed to matter, but that wasn't the point. "At my place."

"Hmm." She weighed her head back and forth. "I'd dress casual but cute. I feel like if I dressed up too much, I'd signal that I was just there for a quick stop between more important plans. If I'm legit just coming to *study*, I'm in the most comfortable shit, loose shirt, stretchy pants, mismatched socks. But if it's a study *date*, I'd still do my hair cute, wear some skintight yoga pants, maybe a little crop top moment with a dainty necklace. Comfortable but I have a great body and am not afraid to show it, right? I might slide a little closer, let my arm brush his, tell him he smelled nice. Stuff like that."

I blinked at her. She had described the outfit Del had shown up in on Monday. Down to the fucking necklace. There was no arm-touching when you sat eight feet apart though. "I see."

"So?"

"So, what?"

"What did she *signal*?"

"Yoga pants."

"Good for you, uncle Auggie." She punched my upper arm with more force than necessary, and I hated to admit that it hurt enough to bruise the next day. "And good for me. I'm in desperate need of a cool aunt who doesn't turn green when I use the word penis."

I didn't tell her that the woman in question might turn bright red instead.

TWENTY-TWO

Delilah

Beck was at the office again on Friday, making this the second day we didn't see each other after the whole vibrator incident. I went to his place with the best intentions of burrowing myself in his books, but yesterday's heat was still simmering in the streets and his penthouse was mostly south-facing windows. By 11am, the relentless sunlight had brought the sweltering temperatures inside. I tried adjusting the thermostat, but it was on a timer and no matter how many buttons I pressed, it just beeped angrily at me and flashed a big red light. Asshole.

There was no way Beck didn't have AC, but there was every way he didn't switch it on unless he was actually at home, considering most of his time was spent out and about.

Fine. I could get some cool relief in other ways. I yanked the freezer door open, a wave of cool air hitting my damp skin. Thank God. I sighed and turned, trying to get that 360-degree popsicle treatment, but the problem with freezers was that there was no air blast. The cold barely penetrated past my clothes. I'd taken my pants off for far more scandalous reasons in here the other day, so I had less inhibitions as I yanked up the hem of my shirt. Immediately the cool air sank through my belly, deep into my nerves, soothing my discomfort. "Oh, come on," I groaned as I tried to peel my soaked t-shirt over my neck, but it was stuck somewhere between my bra and my elbows, too wet to slide off, "for goodness' sake."

"Need help?"

The low rumbling voice made me scream and jump.

I hadn't even heard him come in.

He was supposed to be at the office.

And I was currently stuck in front of his freezer with my pink Taylor Swift shirt covering my face but not my chest.

"I'm good," I squeaked, turning in the direction his voice had come from, only to collide with a hard, warm wall. I yelped again. Damn, his steps were silent.

"I'm guessing you're the one who entered the security code wrong three times and tripped the silent alarm?"

"Security code?" I asked and tensed when his hands slid up my sides to hook in under my shirt. Oh god. That thing was so sweaty. He'd have my smelly, hot sweat all over his hands.

"Did you touch the keypad by the door?" he asked.

My face fell at the exact moment he freed my head from its fabric prison. "Sorry," I breathed, looking up into a pair of dark storm gray eyes, ringed in perfect black lashes, that pierced down into me with enough intensity to cool every blood cell that had been boiling five minutes ago. He lifted my shirt higher, palms sliding over my arms and elbows and just when I was supposed to be free, a sharp pain shot through my wrists as they were yanked together by a twist of fabric. I hissed, eyes snapping up to where Beck had tied my hands together and still held them above my head. "I was looking for the thermostat," I said as if *that* was important when he had me pinned in place like that, but my brain was still playing catch-up. "What are you doing exactly?" My voice hitched in my throat, as the anxiety started to trickle in.

"Tying up the intruder who broke into my house," he replied, the corner of his mouth quirking up. One hand still on bound hands, the other on my waist, he pushed me back a step, hooking the shirt around the top of the refrigerator handle. My back pressed against the cool edge of the freezer, cold coating my damp skin on one side, while his hand seared my waist on the other. He had me tied up. His words finally clicked. My shirt had become a handcuff and I was in a bra and bike shorts, and he was standing over me, eyes drinking in my body so shamelessly, every muscle in my stomach tightened. "I'm glad I didn't send building security to check the alarm."

"I haven't really gotten to the roleplay section of my research yet," my voice trembled, "and I don't think we should try that because if I were an intruder and you tied me up, does that mean we were waiting for the police? Would I only do you sexual favors in hopes of being let go to avoid jail? And why did I break in in the first place? Am I stealing for self-preservation? What's my backsto-ah." He shoved something hard and cold into my mouth and closed his hand over it. So even though my first instinct was to spit it back out, I couldn't. Alarm spiked through me, immediately replaced by just one thought: *Cold*.

"Suck," Beck growled.

I had to. There was nothing I could do but swirl the ice cubes around on my tongue, hoping they would dissolve faster, hoping the cold would ease up, instead it seeped through my gums and numbed the insides of my cheeks.

I stared up at him, drawing ragged air through my nose as I tried to breathe through the cold.

"Did you know the human body is not equipped to deal with

the sudden onset of cold? You can ward off a panic attack with a single ice cube to the wrist, because your survival instincts will overpower your brain."

I whimpered under his hand because the ice cubes had barely melted, and my mouth was just *cold* to a point my temples began aching and goose bumps raced down my neck.

A single other sensation broke through the frosted haze: His knuckles grazing down my stomach, hard against my soft flesh.

"Do you need me to stop?" he asked.

His question swam through my mind as I swallowed melted water. It ran an icy path from my throat down to the pit of my stomach.

"Do you need me to stop?" he asked again, knuckles trailing up and down the dip of my belly. I shook my head, and squeezed my eyes shut against the ice cubes hitting my teeth.

"Stomp your foot if you want to stop, understand?"

Stomp my foot? I furrowed my brows trying to find the synapses in my brain that controlled my feet. I flexed my toes, testing. Okay, okay. Stomping. I could stomp. I nodded and winced when more ice water trickled down my throat.

Beck's hand slid into my pants and my eyes flew open. His eyes were on me, black pupils bleeding into dark irises, watching my face as he unceremoniously slid a finger into me. My muscles tensed and my instinct to squeak was cut short by my tongue inadvertently pushing the ice cubes against the roof of my mouth. The brain freeze drowned any other sensation.

The moment the cold fog cleared a little, my hips jerked, low pressure building between my legs. Beck's finger pumped in and out, his thumb rubbing my clit. I wasn't even sure when he'd started that. Fuck. My waist tilted for him, each thrust pulling against my restraints, fabric digging into my wrists. The pain barely registered against the heat pooling for him.

He pushed a second finger into me, stretching me. My walls

ached, struggling to accommodate the new thrusts but before I could dwell on the pain, I clamped my mouth shut tighter, the shrinking ice cubes biting into my gums. *Cold.*

Between the fire building under his touch and the frozen thoughts, I felt *it.* The low hum of promise. The climb before the roller coaster dropped you over the edge. I'd been this close before. It was always the edge, never the drop.

"Let it go."

Of course, he made a fucking Frozen reference in the middle of fingering me against his freezer, ice cubes in my mouth.

I stiffened as the clarity of that thought broke through and swallowed. Water. Not ice cubes. My eyes flew up to my favorite t-shirt, all stretched out and twisted and ruined. He had me tied to his kitchen, mouth clamped shut, fingering me against his fucking freezer, and I was supposed to *let it go*?!

I stomped my foot. Hard.

Beck stopped mid-thrust, hand falling off my mouth immediately. I gasped for air as he freed his other hand from the entanglement of my underwear and bike shorts. Before I could even get a word out, my hands fell to my sides, my shirt in his hands. My arms were numb and tingling, fingers burning as blood rushed back into them. I stared at my wrists and the fabric lines etched deep into my skin. It looked more painful than it had felt.

"What happened?" Beck asked after a moment when I still didn't look up. His voice was way gentler than I deserved.

"The ice cubes melted," I replied, throat raw from the cold. "Sorry."

"Why are you apologizing?"

I dragged my eyes up to meet his. He leaned against the inside of his freezer door, top buttons of his white shirt undone, and sleeves rolled up, but otherwise still dressed for business. He'd really just come home from the office. "Because I couldn't do it."

"Do what?"

"Stop acting stupid," I huffed and snatched my shirt from his hands, "it doesn't suit you." The shirt went on easier than it had come off but that was mostly due to the fact that it was about twice as wide as it had been three ice cubes ago.

"I'm not acting stupid. I'm genuinely curious why you're apologizing to me for not climaxing. Aren't you the same woman who told me sex wasn't just about coming?"

"Yeah, when you're *with* someone. This? Here? It's literally about figuring out how to make me come. And you tried something. And it didn't work. So, yes, I'm sorry. I'm sorry that your efforts were in vain."

A dark expression ghosted over his face, there and gone in an instant. "Blondie, this? Here?" Beck fisted the front of my shirt and pulled me aside. He threw the freezer door shut, then pushed me up against it, knee wedged between my thighs. "We're practicing because when I fuck you, I want you screaming in pleasure. Real pleasure. And we'll practice again and again and again, until your overactive brain is completely shut-up and the only thing left on your mind is my name. Your first climax will only be the beginning of *this*. Understood?"

I swallowed. *Your first climax will only be the beginning of this.* All the air had suddenly left my lungs.

"Understood?" he repeated, closing his hand around my chin in an iron grip that sent a hot shiver rippling down my spine.

"Yes," I croaked.

"One more thing," he bent down, lips ghosting over my cheek bone, and continued with his voice dropped to a low growl, "if you ever touch yourself in my place again, I will tie you to my headboard and spank that tight ass until you're begging me to fuck you."

I winced at the sheer word choice but couldn't ignore the moisture gathering between my legs. "Beck?

"Hmm?"

"You ruined my favorite shirt."

Beck let go of my shirt and looked down at the deformed, stretched-out mess he left behind. He sighed and pressed a quick kiss to my temple before he disappeared from the kitchen. Hopefully to fix the AC.

Despite having just had some icy refreshments - involuntarily - my throat felt like sandpaper. And by the time I'd downed a glass of water that cleared my head, and had wandered back to the library, Beck found me, a bundle of fabric in his hands. He placed it on the shelves before his fingers found the hem of my shirt. I let him peel me out of it again, barely a moment to think about how he kept seeing a whole lot of my skin and I had yet to see his, before he opened the fresh white button-down for me to slip into. It swallowed me, the crisp fabric loose and surprisingly breathable.

"Thanks," I sighed and rolled up the sleeves to my elbows.

"I'll take care of this," he said, throwing my pink shirt over his shoulder.

"Don't throw it out. I'd rather have it stretched-out than not at all."

"You'll get it back as good as new."

"Do you have a fashion fixer on call or something?"

"Or something." He smirked.

A soft tickle of cold air curled around my neck and my head whipped up, trying to find the fans for the AC. Unseen and unheard.

"Where's your phone?" he asked, but I didn't need to answer because he had already picked it up from my study corner. "Unlock."

"Why?" I asked but tapped in my code. There were some incriminating texts between Cordelia and me on there, but Beck didn't seem like the kind of man who would snoop through my phone.

"I'll log you into my home systems. No more tripped alarms. You can start the AC 30 minutes before you get here, play music, start the coffee maker, run a bath..."

Of course, he didn't have a thermostat on his wall like a normal person. "Thanks. Wait. Run a bath?"

"Perfect to loosen muscles after a long workout." A grin tugged on his lips, and I had a feeling he wasn't referring to the gym. He handed my phone back, opened on an app that showed a plethora of functions grouped by rooms. Sure enough, the bathroom showed bath settings for temperature, jacuzzi air streams and even for adding bath oils. Imagine all those winter nights after trudging through the snow, and the bath was already waiting for you?! My idea of a dream house had just shifted - Cordelia's interior designer, but Beck's tech features.

TWENTY-THREE

BECK

"This is just soap," Isaac muttered, reading through the list of ingredients of a *rejuvenating* hand wash.

"Don't let anyone hear you or you'll get us kicked out."

Between the socialites and influencers, the Kit by Kristin Carter launch wasn't my scene, but I went wherever Blondie went. Julian had pulled the guest list from the event planner's cloud and Cordelia Montgomery had RSVP'd yes to her invite. It wasn't a bad business move. A new luxury skincare line aimed at women too old to ignore their wrinkles, but young enough to care about name-dropping Boston's version of Kim Kardashian, Kristin Carter, on Instagram. If they managed to get Kit into the bathrooms at Montgomery, or worked out an exclusive line for the Montgomery On The Go online shop, Del would be the perfect face for that collaboration. She'd made sure of that by popping up all over social media in her tiny gold outfit at Decker's birthday. Even without her own profile, she'd posed for plenty of pictures with those that wanted to be seen with the elusive Cordelia Montgomery.

"It's an actual crime to charge more than three quid for this." Isaac uncapped the bottle and took a sniff, recoiling instantly. "It's an actual crime to charge for this. Period."

"Why did you want to come again?"

"Because I'm getting a kick out of seeing you suck at something."

"I don't suck at anything."

"You suck at courting fair lady Cordelia." He grinned. "I'm a doctor, so you can trust me when I tell you that the way to a woman's heart is not through her cervix." I hadn't even told him about the little freezer moment.

"Why don't you leave fair lady Cordelia to me?"

"Because your idea of a romantic gesture is buying someone a vibrator."

"Vibrators can be romantic." Del piped up behind Isaac, who whirred around, soap still in hand.

"I'll take this." Defne plucked the bottle from his fingers and let it disappear in a huge shoulder bag that seemed a little too bulky for a casual chic event like this.

"You shouldn't use that to rejuvenate anything," Isaac said.

"I'm not." She blinked at him and shouldered her bag higher. "I don't know what you're talking about."

"Beck, you know Defne. Defne, this is… Isaac, right?"

"Dr. Isaac Hunter, enchanté." He bowed his head and kissed Defne's hand, and the poor girl erupted in giggles, her long, sleek black hair dropping like a curtain in front of her face.

"Jesus fucking Christ," I muttered, and Del whacked her pale-yellow clutch against my upper arm. It complimented the daisy-print crop top and skirt combination that bared a sliver of midriff, just wide enough to tempt me to run a finger along.

"Found another one," Del said, picking the hand wash out of my gift bag and handing it to Defne.

"That was mine," I said, less bothered than intrigued.

"We'll put your name on the donation receipt," Del replied, grinning.

"Do you know what's so great about the Kit rejuvenating hand wash?" Defne asked, holding the bottle up with a pearly white grin as if she was presenting it on a late night shopping channel. "The bottle is worth more than its content. It's sturdy." She rapped her knuckles against the plastic. "Spill proof." She turned the bottle upside down and squeezed. "And reusable." She twisted the lid off and on again.

"I don't follow," Isaac said.

"Do you know how many homeless women get sick due to infections caused by inadequate access to hygiene products during their period?"

"I do," Isaac said, causing Defne to falter in her speech.

"Well, we're dropping these off at a shelter afterwards. Everyone here can buy their own soap."

"You could also just donate money," Isaac said.

"That's not the point," Del replied, shaking her head.

"It's also not half as much fun," I said, a small grin unfolding on my lips, "don't you want to be a little more like Robin Hood? Steal from the rich and give to the poor?"

Isaac scoffed. "You're *the rich*."

"And my soap has already been stolen. How many have you got so far?" I nodded at Defne's bag.

"Around 15," Del said.

"That won't do. There have to be at least 100 people here."

"Alright," Isaac clapped his hands, "First of all, we'll need a second bag. Then we divide and conquer." He shot me a pointed look over the girls' heads. Divide and conquer had been our play when we'd wing-manned each other through college, one of us voluntarily entertaining the best friend or sister of the girl the other one wanted some quality time with.

"I'll just use this." Del emptied his gift bag on the table, face cream, face masks and whatnot spilling out.

"No offense, but you two are probably recognized less than us, so I suggest you hit the tables where people have left their gift bags out, and we'll go socialize." I put a hand between Del's shoulders, and she leaned into it just enough for her earlier words to echo in my thoughts. *Vibrators can be romantic.* "We'll meet back here in an hour."

Half an hour later, we had shaken many hands, asked about many summer vacations, and Del had accepted many business cards. Even if she had no noteworthy experience with these social gatherings, her easy smile and genuine interest in people's children and dogs charmed the pants off anyone we met.

"How are you doing?" I asked after TV host Marc Trenton said his goodbyes and left us on the far end of the rooftop terrace, his soap now in Del's bag.

"Amazing. Look at this." She held the bag open. "That's got to be at least another ten."

"No, Blondie, how are *you* doing?"

She blinked at me, a pink blush creeping up her cheeks. "Are you asking whether or not I've- because I haven't, but I don't think we should be discussing this here," she whispered.

"Del." I loosened the bag from her grasp and placed it aside. The skin of her right hand was creamy white, without any fingernail marks etched into it.

"What?"

"How. Are. You. I'm trying to make conversation. What's

been going on in your life since Friday? Did you go out? How did you spend your Saturday?"

"Oh."

"Am I doing this wrong?"

"No, I just didn't expect that." She shrugged. "Uh, well... Defne's been staying with me this weekend because her roommate's a dick. We've just been hanging out, watching movies, reading books, coming up with mermaid personas while swimming in the pool. Normal stuff."

"I have so many questions."

"Do you want me to tell you about my mermaid?" Her eyes glinted with excitement.

"First, I need you to tell me why you read books when your friend is visiting."

"Because we both like reading. What kind of question is that? You read a lot. You should know."

"I read when I'm alone."

"That's only half as much fun. She reads really smutty books about bikers and the mafia and whatnot, and I read my historical romances full of ball gowns and elaborate engagements, and then we read each other the best passages. Which, in Defne's case, will be like *Jax and Teague ripped my clothes off and we had a really hot threesome, and I came five times*, and in my case it's a full-page description of the flowers blooming on Prince Edward Island in spring, including their distinctive scents and what they mean in the language of flowers. We get the best of both worlds without actually reading a whole book in a different genre."

"Maybe you should study some of *those* books."

She rolled her eyes at me. "Can I tell you about my mermaid yet?"

"Sure."

"Okay, so, basically, I came up with these two underwater kingdoms that have been at odds for centuries and Defne's mermaid is the princess of one kingdom, and my mermaid is the princess of the other, and they befriend each other despite their differences. My mermaid is called Sirena. That will be important later." She delved deep into the backstory of her mermaid, the history of their kingdoms, the conflict between Sirena and her parents, the romance between Sirena and a soldier from the enemy kingdom. At some point, I managed to snatch two glasses from a server's tray, and Del paused in her elaborate story just long enough for a 'Thank you!' and a sip before detailing how the magical abilities of the princesses complemented each other in the good and the bad. "...so we come full-circle, back to the cave where they met."

"You should write that down," I said.

"What?"

"The book."

"It's not a book. It's just... make believe. Did you never play mermaid in the pool? Or, I don't know, Aquaman?" She poked a finger into my biceps.

I ignored her attempt to turn the conversation on me and plucked her hand from my arm, keeping hold of it. Her fingers folded around mine, barely able to close around two of them. "It sounds like you came up with a whole book about your mermaid," I said.

"Shit," she hissed, and I realized why she'd taken my hand. My watch. "We're late. We were supposed to meet Defne and Isaac ten minutes ago."

"It's fine. I texted Isaac."

"You did? When?" She dropped my hand like hot coal.

"Around the time Sirena found the melody stone in Cerulean's hideout." She stilled, even her breathing shallowing out. "What? Did I say her name wrong?"

"No, not at all." Her voice was blocked, and she cleared her throat before continuing: "You actually listened to all that?"

"Of course, it's a good story. Interesting world, engaging main characters, a moral conflict, action, romance, and just a hint of tragedy. You should write it down. It sounds exactly like the books Brody, my 15-year-old-niece, can't get enough of."

"You're not being sarcastic, are you? In a *silly books for silly girls* kind of way."

"No. Brody is actually very smart. Mostly because she reads smart books for smart girls written by smart women."

"Maybe. Someday."

"Why not today?"

"It takes a lot of time, and it would be a passion project, not a stable career path. And then what if I suck? What if people don't like it? What if I spend all this time and energy on a book only for people to tear it apart because at its core it's very cutesy and predictable. Because I'm not the kind of person who enjoys books that reinvent the wheel, you know? I like cutesy and predictable because the world is unpredictable enough. I mean, there's war out there. And nuclear weapons. And sharks."

"Hey, breathe. Del. Breathe. Think." I hooked my finger into the waistline of her skirt and pulled her against me, her chest colliding with mine, air whooshing into her lungs as it did. She'd clearly thought about this herself - and had tricked herself into believing all these doubts filling her brain. "If you pick up a new skill, how do you get better at it?"

"Practice."

"Okay. That means, the only way to make sure you don't suck, is to practice. Which means you need to start writing. Next," I slipped my hand out of her skirt and to her back, resting it there with my fingertips grazing the sliver of naked skin, "are the books you enjoy reading cutesy and predictable?"

"Yes."

"And are you the only person in the world who reads them? Or is there an audience for these books?"

"No, there's others who read them."

I brushed the hair from her face but allowed my touch to linger, thumb brushing over her cheekbone. "What was the other thing? It takes time. It's a passion project. Sweetheart, time passes anyway, you might as well spend it on something you're passionate about."

She scrunched her nose at me, but that little feistiness didn't match the way she tilted her face to lean into my hand. "You and your rational brain," she mumbled.

"Where did you keep all that creative energy hidden the last few weeks?"

"I don't hide it." Her chin dipped down. "It just takes a while to come out around new people. Mermaids and water nymphs going to a ball in Atlantis? That's not really small talk."

This wasn't the same as talking to me about sex. Sex was a taboo topic in a polite society, but almost everyone talked about it and did it behind closed doors. This was more personal. Something intrinsically hers.

"I hated reading as a kid. I wasn't good at it either. I took forever to get through a single page. Loved sports though. But in the Beckett family, sport was an acceptable past time, not something to waste your life on," I admitted, to offer truth for truth, create some sort of bonding experience, but the words came easier than I expected. "My brother was good at numbers and tech, so I had to cover the other side of the business. People, culture, politics. I quickly figured out that I could take the dust jackets off the books I was supposed to read and slide them over the books I liked more though. And then I grew to love those books because they were my own thing."

She smiled and blinked up at me, lids fluttering against the bright sun. "What kind of books were you hiding?"

"Whatever I could get my hands on. Narnia from the school

library. A spy thriller borrowed from our doorman. Some raunchy historical romance I stole from our maid's bedroom."

"Can I hug you?"

"You want to hug me?"

"I do." Her voice wavered and she pulled her shoulders up, self-consciousness sneaking in.

"Alright."

Del bit her lip and raised her hands and for a moment it looked like she wasn't quite sure where to put them, but then she slid them around my waist. With her arms slung around my middle, she sank into me. Her soft body molded with mine and I let my own arms fold around her.

She closed her eyes, ear against my chest, and I wondered if she could hear how my heart slowed as I held her. There was no urgency and no demand in her embrace. I'd never felt touch-starved before, but I didn't remember the last time I'd really been hugged. Not just as a quick greeting, or in a way that involved more tongue and less clothes, but just hugged for the sake of hugging. The warmth and calm in that one touch radiated through me. Maybe I hadn't been starving, but I sure felt like I'd been malnutritional.

"You smell so nice," she mumbled against my shirt.

I tried to push down the laugh rumbling through me, but my chest still shook, making her prop her chin against my sternum to shoot me a quizzical glance. I could hardly tell her that my teenage niece's dating advice was far more accurate than I would have expected. "Sorry," I whispered, "have I already told you that you look breathtaking today?"

She swallowed, inhaled, and opened her mouth to respond but our moment was cut short, when Isaac cleared his throat. "Sorry to interrupt, but uhm, Defne got caught with her bag. She's not on the guest list, so they are about to call the police if you…"

"Shit. I'm coming." Del ripped out of the hug, grabbed the bag with the soap bottles and sprinted towards the exit.

I followed them wordlessly. The names Cordelia Montgomery and August Beckett were more than enough to get Defne off the hook with just a warning from the event planners, but I had a feeling we'd just gotten ourselves blacklisted from any future Kristin Carter endeavors.

TWENTY-FOUR

Delilah

My new schedule was too easy to get used to. I spent the days at Beck's and the nights going to dinners and events with people who pretended they'd been close to Cordelia for years - and didn't blink an eye when I didn't reciprocate their familiarity. I shot a few texts here and there to Cordelia. I had to confirm a few details when people asked about her father or the business, but I usually managed to avoid hard conversations with a smile and a swift change in topic, usually a compliment. Thankfully, I'd become very good at complimenting people over the years. When I didn't know what else to talk about, I just praised their clothes, their car, or – heck – even their curtains. Sometimes Beck was there, sometimes he wasn't, but he rarely left my side when he was, easily falling into any conversation.

Monday morning of my fourth official week as Cordelia Montgomery, I showed up at Beck's with my backpack again, and he let me hole up in the library while he took Zoom meetings at the dinner table. I reassured him that he could just work in the library, but he mumbled something about legal and data privacy or whatnot. I nodded like I understood. Not that I could actually do anything with what I heard in his meetings about mergers, expansions and KPIs even if I had understood. But no matter what he worked on, or where he worked from, the corner across from his desk had become *my* spot. The blankets and pillows still arranged exactly like I'd left them. - No idea how he slept.

When I tiptoed past him during a meeting to grab a drink from his fridge, I swore I could feel his eyes burn the back of my neck. He hadn't brought up the *thing* from the other Friday. The thing where he had tied me up against the fridge and gagged me with ice cubes. But when I tossed the fridge shut and looked over, Beck was nodding at his screen.

He had no meetings on Tuesday, which meant I got him to myself. Nope. I scratched that thought the second it popped up. It just meant that I got to- with him there- and his forehead crinkle-just- Tuesday was good.

By Wednesday, my eyes had grown a little weary of reading about sperm, squirting and sex swings. So, for my breaks, I brought more recreational reading material, and whenever I got to a great passage, I read it for Beck, so he could comprehend the joy of reading vicariously through someone else. My phone chirped, cutting me off in the middle of a swoon-worthy engagement speech. I glanced down, expecting a message from Tab or Defne who had been bugging me about getting to the part where Beck had promised to practically help with my research. But I wasn't intent on throwing myself at him. I wasn't quite ready for the disappointment if that wouldn't work either.

Instead of more advice on which position we should try first, I found a message from Cordelia:

> C:
>
> Can you please stay at your own place tonight? Need the house. Thank you!

Theoretically, yes. Practically, the keys to my apartment sat on my nightstand at Cordelia's house because I didn't want to risk dropping two sets of keys and having to explain that.

"Everything okay?"

I could probably get a room at the Montgomery, right? I wasn't sure if they would recognize me. Especially considering I didn't look like the Cordelia from the opening party today, with my hair in a bun, wearing a loose T-shirt dress. But I still had the license with Cordelia's name on it. That should work, right? Oh god, I couldn't afford a broom closet there if they asked me to pay.

"Yeah, I'm good. My evening plans just changed."

"Does that mean I get to finally show you how the vibrator works?"

"No," I scoffed even though I could hear Tabitha scold me for refusing, "get your mind out of the gutter."

"Stop pinching your hand. What's happening?"

I looked down to where my thumb dug into the back of my right hand. Huh. Hadn't even noticed that. I shook both hands out and shot Beck a smile that hopefully looked lighter than it felt. "I could tell you, but don't you want me to be a little mysterious to keep you on your toes?"

"No, I want to know everything about you."

"Oh, okay." That statement landed like a sucker punch, when the reason I couldn't tell him what was happening, was the fact that I was lying to him backwards and forwards. He didn't even know my name. "My- So you- Okay, well-"

He got out of his chair and crouched down in front of me. "What can I do?"

Four simple words that loosened the knot in my chest. He

didn't ask for an explanation. He just offered help. "How do I get a room at my own hotel?"

"You have your assistant call the front desk."

"Okay. Okay." I didn't have an assistant. Cordelia had made up her own assistant, Page, when she'd been in touch with Beck. Cordelia probably had an actual assistant that I wasn't aware of… I could just call Cordelia and ask her to set me up with a room, right? I should just tell her that I had to get my keys. What on earth could she need the house for? Oh god, what if she had a date over? You didn't have to leave your house for Tinder. I couldn't interrupt her if she was in the middle of getting hot and heavy with a Tinder date.

"Do you need a place to stay tonight?" Beck's question ripped me from my thoughts. Of course, I did. Otherwise, I wouldn't have asked how to get a hotel room. But admitting it out loud would just open the floor for more questions. I couldn't lie like that. Oh god, why had I ever agreed to this whole stupid arrangement? I was not cut-out for a double life. I would make a horrible spy. "Del," Beck lifted my chin up with the tip of his finger and forced me to look at him. His dark eyes burrowed into me, and I was sure he could see the truth right there, inscribed on my retinas. "You don't have to tell me why. It's a yes or no question. Do you need a place to stay tonight?"

I nodded.

"Do you want me to arrange a hotel room, or do you want to stay here?"

"I can't stay."

"Why not?" He furrowed his brows, seeming actually oblivious.

"You don't have a guest room."

He cocked his head to the side like he was looking at an alien. "You've stayed in my bed before."

"I was on so many antihistamines, I was basically high." Or

drunk. Or something. Both groggy and unable to sleep due to the adrenaline pumping through my bloodstream. I'd seen literal shackles in his nightstand and had shrugged off the possibility that he might be an unhinged axe murderer, because I'd been so desperate to just lie down. "That night hardly counts."

"What are you worried about?"

"Sex," I said because he was clearly not an axe murderer.

"Off the table unless you ask me for it. What else?"

"Being a nuisance."

"I don't tolerate nuisances. If I didn't want you in my space, you wouldn't be in my space. Anything else?"

He was rationalizing again. I blinked at him. His gray eyes were unwavering as he waited for my answer, ready to talk through every racing thought in my brain. Even though none of this was about sex. Or orgasms. This was just me and my overactive mind. "Don't you have plans? A business dinner? Or a date? I don't want you to cancel your plans for me, so you should go, but I would feel uncomfortable staying here without you."

"Actually," Beck said, "I do have plans tonight but you're welcome to join me."

"OH GOD, IT'S DRIPPING. IT'S DRIPPING." I SCOOPED MY FINGER along Beck's neck to stop the gloopy face mask from running into the collar of his shirt. He'd taken off his tie and loosened his collar, but it was still a crisp white shirt vs. a neon blue gel.

"You get it?" he asked and lifted his chin to give me better access.

"I think I used too much. Oh no, no, no." Now that he tilted his head back, it was dripping down his hairline. Those tiny blue micro-beads couldn't be good for his hair. One hand still on his neck, I tried to scoop the gel mask from his hair back to his face with the spatula that had come with The Kit. "Shit."

"Blondie, this was supposed to be relaxing," he chuckled, throat vibrating against my fingers.

"I am very relaxed," I protested, voice shrill.

"I think the face mask is a bust. Let's just skip to the next step." He pulled the towel from the back of the sofa and wiped his face off. I stood between his knees, bent over him to spread the mask evenly - but had clearly failed. I sighed and wiped my sticky fingers on the towel he offered.

"I'm sorry," I mumbled. I wasn't 100% sold on this being his predetermined evening plan, but since he had zero blemishes on that perfectly sculpted face, he might actually spend every Wednesday night going through elaborate skincare routines. How would I know? I had no idea how people kept up with these routines. I used a whopping combination of micellar water and SPF.

"Let's see," his hand dove into the gift bag in his lap and he pulled out another very beige, very minimalist container. "Nutrient-rich face cream for a daily glow-boost."

"Do you mind if I just use my hands? I don't think that spatula is working for me."

"Go for it. Boost my glow by any means necessary." He grinned and tilted his head back again, eyes closed.

"No pressure," I laughed. I liked this playful side of him. The calculated, rational Beck was comforting in contrast to the flock of hummingbirds in my chest, but this relaxed version felt like a glimpse at something he didn't let the world see. "You actually have really nice skin."

"Thank you."

I dipped my fingers into the smooth surface of the face cream, testing a tiny amount for its consistency between my fingertips before even getting near his face this time. "Here we go," I whispered before I brought my hand against his face. I smoothed the cream over the bridge of his nose and along the curve under his eyes, his breathing even while I held mine. My face hovered inches above his as I drew meticulous borders around his hairline. I stopped after my hand sloped down his sharp cheekbones. "What do I do with the beard?"

"You can put some on it," he said, voice lowered, "it's short enough."

I dipped my fingers back into the lotion, hoping I was getting the right amount to not ruin his beard, but those doubts vanished the second I touched his face again and he let out a low hum. My insides tightened at that one sound. And my mind immediately conjured up visions of what that rough stubble would feel like grazing against other parts of my body. How I would touch him to hear that hum again. God, I needed to get a grip. Because speaking from experience, reality didn't live up to the images in my head.

"All done." I cleared my suddenly clogged throat and leaned back. His skin had already absorbed most of the moisturizer, leaving a thin sheen behind that only highlighted his unfair bone structure.

"Your turn."

I climbed sideways onto the sofa, so he could just turn around to me instead of bending down. If he had to fold all that height down, he would have probably toppled right on top of me. On second thought, maybe I should have chanced that. *Nope.* Just here for his bed, grateful for shelter, nothing more. "You're the lucky winner of a deep tissue detox." He smirked as he read the back of the tube he just pulled out. The gift bag wandered to the floor and Beck hoisted himself around. He popped the lid off the detox and a splotch of green goo splashed into his palm.

"Oh, definitely not. That looks like it will toxify my skin rather than detox it."

"Come here." He chuckled and squeezed more of the glibbery, Shrek-colored slime from the tube.

"I don't think so." I physically recoiled when flecks of dark green started rising to the surface.

"Come here, woman," he said, still grinning, except this time he tossed the tube aside and grabbed the back of my knee. With one quick pull, he drew me against him, my legs awkwardly folded over his lap, and my breath blubbered from my lungs. We'd had plenty of physical contact before, but that one jolt, that one hint at how much muscle strength he was hiding under those suits of his, sent a wave of heat to my cheeks. "Close your eyes for me."

"You're so demanding," I muttered, "where are your manners?"

"Close your eyes, please."

I smiled at his correction and let my eyes fall shut. I flinched when the first dollop of cold gel met my cheek, but despite what it looked like, it actually smelled amazing, like rain and flowers. Beck only used one finger, tracing the dips and curves of my face. I could have spent hours losing myself in the light pressure, and the cool product mixed with the warmth of his touch. By the fourth time his fingertip circled over my chin, however, I was a little too aware of the clock ticking in the background somewhere.

"How do I look?" I asked.

Beck pulled his hand away and I immediately regretted asking. "Sweetheart, I wish I could tell you that you're breathtaking, but you look like you face-planted in a bowl of pesto."

My eyes flew open, and I laughed because he grimaced so hard at the rest of the green goo he was wiping on the towel. "We should work on your complimenting skills."

"Alright, how is this?" Before I had time to protest, his hands were on my waist, and he hauled me into his lap. I let out a loud squeal that did nothing to deter him. I barely managed to grab his shirt in both fists to keep myself steady while he positioned my legs on either side of him like I weighed nothing. "Look at me," he said once I was settled, then added: "Please."

"What are you doing?" I met his charcoal eyes even though the sharp focus in them made me want to look away. I didn't think I'd ever been looked at with that much intensity.

"Hmm." His chest rumbled under my hands. "When you concentrate really hard to make sure your highlighter is a straight a line as possible, you purse your lips, and it puts the cutest dimple in your chin. Right here." He tapped the tip of his finger against the center of my chin. "You try to put on a poker face but when you're ever so slightly shocked by something, you swallow so hard, your throat hitches and I can't help but stare at that gorgeous, graceful neck and think about all the ways I can cause that reaction." His finger slid down my neck until it rested in the hollow of my collarbone. "And despite how fast your thoughts might be spinning and your heart might be beating," he flattened his palm against my sternum, where he had to feel my accelerating heartbeat, "you're a fucking firecracker, Blondie, and that big, beautiful brain of yours has no reason to make you feel small."

"I would like to retract my previous statement," I said, voice suddenly hoarse, "Your complimenting skills exceed expectations."

One corner of his mouth quirked up. "Do I get a gold star for that?"

"How is this?" I asked, mirroring his words, and lay my hand over the one he still had on my chest. "If I could write the beauty of your eyes, And in fresh numbers number all your graces, The age to come would say 'This poet lies; Such heavenly touches never touched earthly faces.'"

"Are you really complimenting me in Shakespeare?"

Oh. Shit. "Ohmygod. I'm so sorry. You're gorgeous but that was so cheesy. So cheesy." I pushed myself off his chest, desperate to put distance between us. What was I thinking? Following his trifecta of personalized compliments with Shakespeare? Shakespeare!

"Stop, stop, stop, hey. Come here." He pulled me back to him. Closing his arms around my waist, he locked me against him. My chest quivered against his through panicked breaths. "Tell me again."

"Are you mocking me?" Oh great, my voice cracked, and my eyes were starting to burn. Because nothing screamed *romantically incompetent* quite like whipping out the Bard and then breaking into tears.

"No. I'm sorry. My question came out wrong. I really didn't mean to make you feel bad. I was caught off guard, in the best way, by you effortlessly reciting poetry like that." He loosened one hand from my midsection and drew a slow circle between my shoulders with his fingertips. My stupid body betrayed me by shuddering under his soft caress. "Was it actually Shakespeare?"

"Yes. Sonnet 17."

"Can I please hear it again?"

He sounded genuine, but I hesitated, waiting for a grin or a raised brow, or any other sign that he was joking. None came. I took a deep breath and let the anxiety simmer down on the exhale. "If I could write the beauty of your eyes," I started and let my hands fold around his face, my thumbs smoothing over his temples, "And in fresh numbers number all your graces, The age to come would say 'This poet lies; Such heavenly touches never touched earthly faces.'" Each word calmed my nerves, because even if quoting Shakespeare was cheesy, each word rang true. Beck was indescribably, breathtakingly beautiful.

"Thank you," he whispered and tilted his head just to press a kiss to the inside of my wrist. His lips were so soft. I wanted to-

Before I could talk myself out of it again, I leaned in, my breath catching as my nose brushed against his, but just when I thought he'd close the last whisper of distance between us, Beck tilted his head down. Chin against his chest. He didn't even look at me.

"Ohmygod." I scrambled out of his lap, and he didn't try to stop me this time. "I'm so sorry."

"Sorry. Shit. Del, wait." He reached his hand out for mine, but I jerked back.

Shame and heat crawled up my neck until my whole face was on fire. "No, oh god, I feel so stupid. I read that entirely wrong." What had I done? I was so stupid. I was ruining this thing. We'd gotten so comfortable around each other, and I... I just... I had to put some distance between us. Physical distance.

"Don't feel bad. This was on me. Stay here. Please." He rose from the sofa, following me as I inched backwards.

"No. I have to wash the mask off. I'm so sorry. I've read about the whole *no kissing* thing. It's a thing. I get it. Kissing is too romantic. Sex is sex." I turned and rushed towards his bedroom. "Don't worry about it!" I tried to sound lighthearted, but even I could hear the telltale squeak of panic in my voice.

He followed me, and even though he probably could have easily caught up, he didn't try to get in my way as I beelined through his apartment. I closed the bathroom door and turned on the faucet to drown out the sound of my panicked breathing. I could still hear Beck groan "Fuck!" on the other side of the door though.

When I got out of the bathroom, the flannel pajama top he'd offered me a few weeks ago waited neatly folded on the bed. I quickly slipped into it, then got to work on his bed. Clearly, Tabitha and Defne had been totally wrong. Throwing myself at Beck was not the way to go. He'd told me that he didn't do monogamy. He'd told me his interest in me was sexual.

I used all the pillows and blankets I could find to erect the highest pillow wall anyone had ever seen. At least his king size bed still left enough room for both of us to stretch out on either side - even if we'd sleep on the bare mattress without any cushion or cover.

Beck had been friendly, not romantic, ever since I rejected him at brunch. Sexual, sure, but not romantic. I'd dared him to compliment me and then got swept up in the moment. God, I was so stupid. What was I thinking?

I couldn't even date him. I'd start my job at Truman in a few weeks and this version of me would cease to exist.

I flopped down in bed and stared at the ceiling. I'd never been this casually intimate with anyone. What did that even make us? Friends with benefits? The term felt strange considering Beck and I hadn't really started out as friends. Fuck buddies? Not likely since there was a definitive lack of fucking. Summer fling? Sounded too romantic.

Summer study buddies with benefits?
Sex tutorship?
A liaison?

TWENTY-FIVE

BECK

My hard-on was throbbing when I woke up. Fuck. It was almost painful. I'd not woken up with that much white-hot pressure in my dick since I was a pimply pubescent teen. I blinked down and quickly figured out what the hell was going on. Del was sprawled on top of me. She'd slung an arm and leg over me, her head on my chest. Her flannel shirt had ridden up, exposing her flimsy lilac panties. My dick jerked at the sight of those two little dimples right above her panty line. Jesus. She'd slotted over me with my hard-on right in her thigh crease. So much for the pillow wall.

At least I was still on my side of the bed. Even if I'd promised her sex was off the table, I could hardly control how my body reacted to her climbing me like a monkey.

She shifted, mumbling incoherently, and her hip rubbed over me. She was fucking dry humping me. And I was about to explode right here. And then it wouldn't matter whose side of the bed we were on.

Not even getting into the mess that I'd caused last night. I'd been drawn to those full lips since the first night we met, and then I turned my head away when I finally had the chance to claim them.

Somehow, I managed to slide out from under Del, earning nothing but a few annoyed moans before she hugged my pillow instead of my chest and fell silent again. I hit the shower and shot a load down the drain within a few strokes to my dick, pressing my mouth into my shoulder to keep the noise down. A fucked-up part of me wished she would have walked in right then. At least she would have seen what she was doing to me.

When I walked out in my bathrobe, Del sat in the middle of the bed. Her hair stood off in all directions and she was rubbing her eyes. "I had the weirdest dream," she mumbled, voice still croaky. Fuck that was cute. I almost regretted not watching her wake up. Jesus fuck. What the hell was wrong with me?

"What did you dream about?" I asked, grabbing fresh underwear from my dresser.

"I was free climbing this huge mountain." That tracked. "But then this flock of birds surrounded me, and I had to hold on for dear life. Except then it wasn't birds anymore, it was flying fish. And when I fell, it was only like three feet into the ocean." She crinkled her nose and blinked at me. "Did you shower?"

"I did. I put out a fresh set of towels if you want to go next. Unless you'd rather stay dry considering you went for a swim in your dream."

"Thanks." She detangled herself from the blanket and crawled out of bed. Her muscles weren't quite back to their normal energy yet, every step a little groggy and slow. "Sorry for destroying the pillow wall. I didn't punch or kick you, did I?"

"Not that I'm aware of." Technically not a lie.

"I'm a horrible sleeper." She began making the bed, eyes half-closed, operating on muscle memory. "So many weird dreams. And sometimes I wake up with my feet on the pillow." She froze. Turned to me. Turned back to the bed. "Pillows."

"Are you having a stroke?"

"Library, pillows." She pointed at the door, then at the bed. "Bedroom, pillows."

"Yes, I own many pillows." I hadn't. Not until Del had clouded my thoughts with images of her writhing in my bed when I left her alone in the apartment. It had seemed like a good idea at the time. In case she ever wanted to revisit the vibrator, she wouldn't have to carry my whole bedding from room to room to be comfortable.

"Good. Next time, I'll build the pillow wall even higher." She grabbed her neatly folded stack of clothes and headed for the bathroom.

"Don't bother," I said, "I actually quite enjoyed getting climbed like a mountain."

She turned in the door, cheeks instantly turning pink. "I didn't."

"Purple lace." I grinned and dropped my eyes to her hips. "Maybe next time you can dream about horseback riding. I feel like the up and down would do more for me than just climbing upwards."

"I'm going to take a shower and if you ever mention this again, my next dream will be about strangulation. I can't be charged if I do it in my sleep, right?"

"Don't tempt me with a good time," I grinned.

"You- wha-" Her mouth dropped open. "Seriously?"

"Sometimes." I shrugged.

"Huh." Her brows danced through a row of thoughts and emotions as she closed the door to the bathroom, but all I felt was relief easing through my chest. I'd clearly hurt her last night when

I botched the kiss, but Blondie was still curious enough about sex not to bolt.

Kissing is too romantic. Sex is sex.

I couldn't have her thinking that this was just about sex for me. I had to show her that this thing between us went beyond helping her through all the anxieties that kept her from climaxing.

Dumb mistakes called for drastic measures.

"I can't go in there with you," Del said as she got out of the car and blinked up at the Axent HQ on the other side of the street. "It's okay that we hang out, but I can't risk rumors of any business deals between us."

"Don't worry." I placed my hands on her shoulders and turned her 180 degrees. "We're going in there."

"A gym?" She tilted her head back and grimaced at me. "Sorry to break it to you, but I burn all my calories by stress-pacing."

I pressed my lips into a tight smile to stop myself from suggesting some calorie-burning exercises that could make her uncomfortable. I'd pieced together that she wasn't the athletic type. Her body was all soft dips and smooth curves. Even when she'd clung to me while dreaming, her muscle definition was basically non-existent. "Don't worry," I said instead of telling her what the perfect curve of her thigh had done to me that morning, because this wasn't about sex, "I'm not going to make you get in the ring."

"In the ring?"

I opened the door to the Vortex for her. The screeches of two dozen girls crashed over us the second we stepped inside. The young woman at the counter looked up, spotted me, and just gave a small wave before turning back to the computer she was working on.

"Michelle," I greeted her, and her head snapped up again, confused. "Could you unlock the shop for us?"

"Oh. Uh. Sure, Mr. Beckett." She pulled a huge key chain from her pocket to unlock the glass door behind the reception area. I hit a light switch, and the small shop stacked with workout gear came to life.

"I need more information," Del whispered as I directed her forward and angled for the women's section. She narrowed her eyes at a pair of boxing gloves and kneaded her hands in front of her. Uncomfortable, but not trying to ground herself yet. At least that's what I figured the pinching was for. Trying to keep herself in the moment rather than losing herself in her thoughts.

"You can't wear your regular shoes in the gym," I explained, "the dirt and gravel mess up the equipment."

"Oh, okay. You just want me to pick out shoes? I can do that." She slipped past me to where boxes of trainers were lined up.

A few minutes later, Del had settled on a purple pair of running shoes and a rainbow set of sports socks to go with them. I'd also thrown a tie-dye blue yoga set into the mix because her eyes kept flicking to it. We left all the tags with Michelle at reception, and I told her to put it on my account. Del protested for all of ten seconds until I told her that I could send her the invoice if she insisted. I wouldn't, but I didn't want to derail the evening by discussing financial principles, sexism, and social conventions - all of which were probably racing through her thoughts.

Brody barreled towards us the second we stepped out from the changing rooms. My niece wrapped Del in a tight hug before she could have even realized what was happening. "I can't believe you're actually real," Brody squealed, tightening her arms enough to make Del gasp for air.

"Brody," I sighed, "this is Cordelia Montgomery."

"Call me Del," she huffed when Brody loosened her grip.

"Del, that's my niece, Brody."

"He usually calls you Blondie, not Del." Brody pointed at me, grinning her troublemaker grin.

"I know," Del shot me a look over her shoulder, a mix of amusement and surprise in her smile, before turning back to Brody, "He's impervious to manners."

"*Impervious*. Big word. Amazing." Brody clapped her hands together. "You'll be perfect."

"What?" Del laughed but Brody turned on her heels and waved us toward her spot at the back of the gym.

"To Brody my life is just a casting show to find the perfect aunt," I explained with my voice lowered, one hand on the small of her back as I directed her forward. "She'll interrogate you all night."

"Can't wait," Blondie muttered under her breath.

Del offered to film Brody's training session, and I lost both of them the second Brody pressed her phone into Del's hands. Her phone case was covered in stickers, and one of them was a quote from some costume drama about a viscountess in desperate need of a husband. Which both of them were apparently obsessed with. Brody got all of three kicks in before she turned back to Del. "Okay, but don't you think Charles would be a much better fit for Minnie? Henry is so boring."

Del laughed and lowered the phone camera. "It's different in the books, Brody. I promise you; Henry is actually *not* boring."

"Fine. Fine. Give me, please." Brody plopped down on the floor and stretched her hand out for her phone. "Downloading right now. If they're not as good as you say, I will sue you."

"Oh, wait." Del's hand flew out and she snatched the phone back from Brody fast enough to make me think she might have a future in boxing after all. Her wide eyes flew to me. "Uh. Is she… allowed?"

"Is she allowed to read?" I asked, leaning against the wall, since I was clearly not doing a lot of coaching today.

"Grown-up books, for *adults*," Del added.

"Oh my god. I'll survive a few sex scenes." Brody grabbed the phone again and Del shot me a panicked look. "I have the internet and I have a girlfriend."

"You have a girlfriend?" I asked. This was the first time I was hearing about this. Not the *girl*- part. Brody had never been very covert about her bisexuality, considering how hard she'd been swooning over both leads in that Miraculous Ladybug cartoon. After I tracked that, and she brought up topics like dating and marriage, I'd just made sure to use non-gendered terms. It had never been a point of contention. The girl*friend*-part was new though.

Brody shrugged and smiled up at Del. "FYI Uncle Auggie's sex talk was way more efficient than my dad's ramblings about bees and flowers. You're in good hands."

"Uncle Auggie?" Del grinned and raised her brows at me.

I shook my head before she could get any ideas.

"Yeah, so, it's fine." Brody tapped away on her screen. "I'm not a virgin. I can read sex scenes."

My pulse spiked. "You're not-" I cut myself off, turned around, and headed straight for the water cooler. Brody's giggles erupted behind me. If she was planning on giving me a heart-attack, she was doing a good job.

Last year, after Julian had called me at 10pm one night, uncharacteristically lost for words after a disastrous discussion about pollen and bees technically representing artificial insemination between two flowers, when you considered the process, I had scraped together a fact-based sex talk. Brody had hated the idea, but I had put my coach face on, and had talked her through it like I talked her through fights. It had been informative. Not... I didn't need to know whether... Jesus.

I threw back a cup of cold water like a shot, and narrowed my eyes at Del nodding and smiling at something Brody was saying.

Bringing Del to girls' night was supposed to show her that I wanted her in my life, not just my bed. I hadn't considered that Brody's enthusiasm about the woman in my life could be the bigger issue. If Brody needed a woman to talk to, about girlfriends and sex, then this might not only be overwhelming for Del, but it would also mess with Brody if I fucked this up.

"What did you do?" Isaac leaned against the water cooler.

"Excuse me?"

"Do you know how many single mothers I've seen throw themselves at you over the last few years? And what did you tell me, time and again? *You don't shit where you eat, Isaac.*" His American accent was good, but he dropped his voice low enough to sound like a bad Darth Vader.

"Are you trying to impersonate me?"

"Why did you bring Del?" He pulled a cup from the water cooler and twisted it in his hands. He wasn't even close to breaking out in a sweat and needing refreshments. In fact, he looked like he'd just walked in.

"What the hell are you doing here? It's girls' night." Most members would have been turned away at the door. Maybe I should have a talk with Michelle about what privileges she afforded Isaac just because he usually came here with me.

Isaac pointed at Gabriella, one of the kids' coaches, with long dark curls and an hourglass body. "I don't really care *where* I eat as long as it's her." She looked up as if she'd heard him and gave him a flirty wave over her shoulder.

"There are children around," I dead panned. Not that it seemed to matter. Because the very child I was here for was apparently sexually active. Fucking hell.

"I can wait. They'll all be gone in two hours and then Gabby can show me the staff changing rooms." He wiggled his brows, but his grin died when I didn't react. "So, it's that bad, huh?"

"She wanted to kiss me," I admitted.

"That's great. Good job, mate."

"I pulled away."

"Are you daft?" Isaac whirled around. If I needed a reminder of how bad this was, Isaac turning his back on the woman he was planning to fuck tonight, would be a massive, red, flashing sign. "That's not how you get a woman to fall in love with you."

"And you'd know about that how?" It was a cheap, deflective blow since he had never shown an interest in romantic attachments.

To his credit, Isaac knew me well enough not to take the bait. "Are you having second thoughts? You can call the whole thing off, you know."

"It was a slip-up," I said because I couldn't tell him what I'd realized last night. Not without sounding absolutely pathetic. Every good strategy required some sort of sacrifice. You lost one fight to win the war. You sacrificed your personal life to further your career. To get the Montgomery merger, I'd agree to marry Cordelia. I accepted that trade-off. I just hadn't considered the next step. To make Del fall in love with me, I'd have to... Yeah, fuck. Turned out Sternberg's triangular theory of falling in love worked in both directions. And if I kissed Blondie, I'd be sealing a trade deal I wasn't ready to make.

TWENTY-SIX

BECK

Del snapped her book shut and groaned, pulling me from the report on this year's summer bookings in Southern Europe. Her frown etched deep wrinkles into her forehead. "I am dealing with a conundrum," she declared and repositioned herself to face me.

"About," I tilted my head to read the spine of her current read, "the sexual liberation movement of the sixties?"

"Sort of."

"Alright, let's hear it." I closed my laptop and leaned forward on my elbows.

"I'm all for women doing whatever they want with their bodies," she tapped her fingers against the book, "but Brody mentioned something to me, when you were off having your little water cooler talk with Isaac, and she's still very much a girl, not a grown woman. I think I should talk to her mom."

I already didn't like where this was going. "Brody's mom died a long time ago. It's just Julian taking care of her. If you think you need to talk to a parent, it would be him."

"Oh god, I'm so sorry." She pushed herself upright. "What happened?"

"Childbirth. Eclampsia. It's preventable if you know what to look out for but they were first-time parents without much of a support network. The doctor they'd been seeing was on holiday when she went into labor too early. Everything that could have gone wrong in the delivery room, did go wrong."

"Shit. I'm sorry," she fell silent and looked at the book again, "you or Julian should talk to her about the risk of sending explicit pictures to her girlfriend. I tried to, but she said the app she uses doesn't allow screenshots. All you need is an iPad or a second phone to take a picture of your screen though."

Oh, fucking hell Brody. "Tell me, she didn't."

Del pulled her shoulders up, face still scrunched up. "You can't yell at her or she'll lock up. Just stay calm. If she listened to your talk about safe sex, she'll listen to you about this, too.

"Jesus," I groaned and pulled my phone out to text Julian.

"What are you doing?"

"Having my brother scrub Brody's cloud."

"Beck, stop." She pushed herself off the floor and slapped the book against the desk. "She can handle that herself."

"Brody might not have realized it yet, sweetheart, but she's bound to be one of the richest women in the country one day. She'll inherit Julian's share of Axent. And her mother's family runs a huge donut imperium, of which she will own 50% one day. We can't risk pictures like that falling into the wrong hands.

"Beck." Del held her hand out expectantly and after a moment I placed my phone in her palm. She clicked the button to lock the screen, then placed it back in front of me. "Explain that to her.

She's old enough to understand that her actions will have consequences. If you go behind her back, she won't learn."

The irony of Del lecturing me about going behind Brody's back hit me in the gut. What if I'd been upfront? What if I'd proposed a marriage of convenience? Would I still have gotten all this time with Del? Would she have agreed to it? Would the Montgomery's lawyers have shut down the idea even if she had? It didn't matter now. "Fine," I breathed. "I'll talk to Brody."

"Julian can still scrub her cloud like a week later, just to make sure."

"Trust is good, but control is better?"

"Something like that." She nodded and returned to her corner, folding her legs beneath her, and I made a mental note to get her some proper floor cushions. Maybe one of those fluffy yoga pillows. Del flipped through her notebook until she found a blank page and pulled a different book from one of her color-coded stacks.

"How's the research going?" I pushed out of my chair, not feeling like facing 137 pages of revenue breakdowns anymore.

"Do you want to have a look?" She scooted sideways to let me take the spot next to her. Between the stacks, the shelves and the pillows, I barely had enough room to fold my legs in. I definitely had to get her something more comfortable than that.

Del handed over her notebook and I flipped through dozens of pages of very neat handwriting, lists, dates, chapter summaries. "These are very comprehensive but there's nothing about you in them."

"It's research, not a diary," she grumbled.

"But the research is meant to fit your needs. Do you have any sexual fantasies that you researched? Did any of these practices intrigue you?"

She shrugged.

"Any sex dreams?" I asked.

"More like stress dreams about sex," she snorted and held her hand out for the notebook.

Ignoring her silent demand, I flipped to the sixth and last tab in her notebook. A category yet unused. I also grabbed the black gel pen because that seemed to be the only one she considered neutral enough to use throughout all her notes, no matter the color-coding. "Give me a detailed outline of your sexual history." I wanted to hear about other men fucking her about as much as I wanted a root canal treatment, but that hardly mattered.

"Lost my virginity at 15." She hummed a little thinking sound and tilted her head back, eyes wandering over the ceiling as if her sexual past was outlined there. "But then didn't have sex again until I was 20 and in my first real relationship."

I wrote down her timeline, my cursive looking like chicken-scratch after her tidy notes. "What about those 5 years in between?"

She pulled her shoulders up. "My first time sucked, so I wasn't desperate to try getting naked again. I just figured I'd have better sex when the right guy came along."

"Alright, what was your first boyfriend's name?"

"That's irrelevant."

"Not to me."

She crinkled her nose and nudged me with her elbow. "I won't let you cyberstalk him."

By the time we were finished outlining her sexual history, the positions she'd tried, the four models of vibrators and dildos she'd experimented with and the short list of places she'd had sex in (bed, sofa, shower), I was piecing together why she hadn't shown up on Thursday. Despite how willingly she let me touch her, my promise to help next time she used the vibrator was already pushing against the boundaries of the safe and familiar for her. She could count the times she'd been eaten out on one hand for fuck's sake. Although that might be coming down to her aversion to saliva on her skin. The fact that she herself wasn't sure, simply meant we'd have to experiment. I could think of worse things to spend my time on.

I glanced over the edge of the notepad at the stacks of books. "I'm taking you out tomorrow."

"I'm not going on a date with you," she laughed and grabbed her water bottle.

Maybe I should have seen that as more of a red flag. Especially after I fucked up that kiss. If she still refused to be seen together in public but allowed me to push my fingers into her behind closed doors, this was teetering too close to casual.

"I'm talking about a sex club, Blondie," I said.

She spluttered water back into her bottle. "What?"

"Theory is good, but I think it's time you get a more personal sense of what makes people lose themselves in ecstasy. Because this," I flipped back through her notes to where she had drawn very detailed genitals including a dozen labels with all the corresponding medical terms, "won't get you off."

"I can't go to a sex club." She snatched her notebook out of my hands and closed it, barring me from looking at her diagrams. "Just to clarify, I'm not judging you. I'm approaching all of this," she waved at the books, "with curiosity, not judgement. But, Beck, you and I are in a minority when it comes to that kind of attitude. I can't risk anyone seeing me at a sex club."

"It's the kind of club that prides itself on discretion. It's more likely you'll be the one recognizing some politician with a squeaky-clean image while he gets his cock sucked by a girl in a dog mask."

She paled and shook her head. "I don't think so."

"I'm picking you up tomorrow at nine."

TWENTY-SEVEN

Delilah

I WAS GOING TO A *SEX CLUB*.

I was going to a sex club.

I'd sent a desperate message to the GC after leaving Beck's that night, asking how one could get out of going to a sex club with a man that had fingered you twice.

The responses had been predictably on Beck's side.

• frap sluts •

TABITHA:
loving this freaky new version of you

DEFNE:
Bring condoms! And dental dams! Be safe!

TABITHA:
now I want to go to a sex club

TABITHA:
would it be weird if I showed up at the same one?

DEFNE:
Bring lube, too! Just in case.

And when I'd asked them what the hell one was supposed to wear to a sex club, since I was apparently not getting out of this, their responses had boiled down to *leather* or *nothing*. So half an hour before Beck was supposed to pick me up, I still stood in front of the mirror, trying to wiggle my black denim shorts in a way that was less Girl Scout and more Daisy Duke.

I didn't pay attention when the doorbell rang, since I still had time, and my bralette made the shorts look even worse. This was more volleyball on the beach than it was... well, I still didn't know how people actually dressed at a sex club. The knock on my door had me yelp and jump, scrambling for my cardigan. "Hold on!" I didn't bother with the buttons, pulling the cardigan tight around my middle and folding an arm over it instead. "Yeah?" I opened the door just to see Victor raise his brows at me and tap his foot against the floor.

"I'm in the middle of getting dressed," I hissed.

"Beckett is here," he explained and nodded at the stairwell, jaw twitching.

"He's early," I protested as if that could fix it.

"I know." He pressed his lips together. Right. Fuck. Where was Cordelia? If she was downstairs, Beck was one wrong door away from blowing this up. No wonder Victor seemed fidgety.

"Okay, uhm, send him up. I'll keep him in here and we'll be gone by nine, promise. I just need to finish getting dressed."

"Nine." Victor nodded, turned and jogged back down the stairs, obviously eager to get the untimely visitor out of the way.

A moment later, Beck appeared in his stead. His black hair wasn't as neatly styled away from his face as usual, and his crisp light shirt had been replaced by a tight-fitted black one, sleeves rolled up, top buttons popped open, revealing a triangle of tan skin. And instead of suit pants, he wore jeans. Jeans. Black jeans that looked unfairly good on his long legs. "Are you checking me out, Blondie?"

"Get in here," I hissed. The second he was within reach of the door I grabbed his arm and pulled him into my room, slamming the door shut behind him.

"Wow, you're very eager. Maybe we don't need to go to Clandestine after all."

"Shut up. You're early."

His eyes travelled down my body and he squinted at the loose legs of my shorts before he held up a sleek white bag with golden handles. "I had a feeling you might need a dress."

"You bought me a dress?" I lifted the bag from his hand and walked over to my bed to dig through the crinkly tissue paper. What I pulled out was hardly a dress. It was a thin, black, shiny pleather tube with two golden zippers. One in the front. One in the back. Practical for easy access. Not that you needed it. The dress was short enough to be considered a top. "You bought me a sex club dress." I turned around to find him running his finger over the books scattered on my window seat. God, his ass looked good in jeans. Whoa. Hold on. Delilah. *Focus*.

"Any good?" He held up a copy of a war journalist's autobiography, wiping away any thoughts of his butt. Not the book I'd expected him to pick up considering The History of Pornography was right next to it. Then again, I'd only browsed one of his many bookcases.

"Yeah, it's really good. It's honest and shocking but so bleak," I replied, "I cried like three times."

"Mind if I borrow it?"

"No, go ahead."

"You can't wear underwear with that," he said, pointing at the dress while pocketing the book. Jeez. That man and his topic changes.

"I won't fit into that," I replied, holding the dress up against my body. It was half my size.

"It's stretchy. Go on." He nodded at the open door to my bathroom.

"Why are you allowed to go fully dressed?" I asked, narrowing my eyes at him.

"I'm taking my shirt off when we get there."

"Oh."

"Go." He laughed and pointed at the bathroom again. At least he didn't expect me to get naked in front of him. Grumbling, I trotted to the bathroom, testing the pleather's stretch between my hands. Okay, he wasn't entirely wrong about that.

I tried the dress on with underwear first, but I figured out what Beck meant within ten seconds of zipping it up and turning in front of the mirror. The dress molded against my body, and it pulled on my underwear with every tiny movement. The friction on my waistband was the worst, like someone trying to saw me in half with a piece of elastic. I sighed, peeled the dress off, tossed my underwear in the hamper, and tried again.

The second time, the dress fit so much better. And even though it barely covered my ass, it didn't move an inch, no matter how I bent or turned. It had glued itself to my skin. That also meant every dip from my breasts down my belly button to my hips was clearly visible through the fabric, but that was kind of the point, right?

Was I hot?

I'd always considered myself on the cute side, but this dress made me look like I actually had curves. I sucked in a deep breath, watching the ripple of my stomach under the pleather. Part of me had expected a wave of anxiety and self-consciousness to wash over me, but I liked what I saw in the mirror.

I stepped out of the bathroom, arms open in a 'here I am' kind of gesture, only to falter in my steps. Because Beck was in my bed. He was propped up against the headboard, swallowed by the 10 throw pillows I'd brought from home, using my blue axolotl plushie to prop up the book he was reading. He was a streak of blackness against all my pastel and my stomach flipped because of how much space he took up in a queen sized bed.

He looked up from the book and his brows jumped up. "Fuck," he mumbled as his eyes raked down my body. I swore he had to have Clark Kent laser eyes because my skin was heating fast under his charcoal gaze.

"Good to go?" I asked.

"Sure, but I might have to bring your stuffed animal along or Yelchin out there is going to get a good look at what you're doing to me."

"What? Yelchin?" I furrowed my brows. "Victor?" What was it with men and calling each other by their last names? "Doing what?"

Beck tossed the axolotl aside and I understood. As tight as his jeans were, they left very little to the imagination now that he was sporting a semi. I quickly tipped my head back, blinking at the ceiling, pretending that I had not just gotten a very good idea of the exact shape and size of his penis. I'd felt it before, but that was nothing against being confronted with the actual sight.

"At least throw on a jacket, so I don't have to punch him if your tits in that dress get him hard, too."

"Yep, I can do that," I squeaked, still looking at the ceiling as I turned towards my wardrobe. I didn't lower my eyes until he was out of my line of sight and I could grab the thin kimono-style jacket that Cordelia had insisted I get for mild summer evenings. It reached down to my knees, so as long as I kept the belt wrapped tight, it covered more skin than the dress did.

We didn't even cross Victor's path on our way out, and were greeted by Beck's driver, Fred, on the street. I climbed into the limo in front of Beck, still refusing to glance in his direction.

"You can look at me again," he said when the car stopped, "although you might not like it in there if that's how you react to every erection."

"You had an erection *in my bed*." I glared at him, but then Fred pulled the door open for us. We got out in front of a nondescript building in town. A few people stood outside with drinks and cigarettes, but otherwise it didn't resemble a club. At least not from the outside. Beck scanned a key fob at the entrance and punched in a four digit code. The door swung open to reveal a lavish, modern foyer with two girls taking the coats from a couple that had walked in before us, and four refrigerator-sized bouncers positioned in the corners.

Beck grinned down at me as he started unbuttoning his shirt. "Well, now we can call it even for you masturbating in *my* bed."

Coherent thought left me, because Beck was shrugging out of his shirt and his body had to have been sculpted by Michelangelo himself. The way his shoulder muscles sloped down from his neck, the way his stomach was clearly outlined without him flexing, and his arms... God, I wanted to wrap my hands around that dip of his biceps.

"Miss?" My head snapped up. One of the girls held out a hand for me and it took me a moment to realize she was already holding Beck's shirt.

"Sorry," I mumbled and pulled the Kimono off, heat shooting to my face. I felt Beck's eyes on me and didn't have to look up to know the huge grin he was sporting right now. The girl scanned his key fob again, then sauntered off towards a backroom. Props to her for not ogling the customers, even when they looked like Roman statues. She had better composure than me.

Beck placed a hand on my shoulder and gently directed me towards a table with three boxes full of colorful ribbons. "Look, things in there can get a little intense. You know your safe words, right?"

"*Stop, wait, slower?*"

"Good. Don't hesitate to use them at *any* point." He picked one of the ribbons from the box and placed my right hand on his chest. I was lightest-shade-of-concealer pale, but I hadn't considered the contrast to his olive complexion until now. I had to look like a ghost next to him. "I don't care if we walk two steps in there and you call tonight off. It's not for everyone. You say stop, we stop."

"What are the colors for?" I asked, looking back and forth between the boxes of ribbons and the red one he was tying fast around my wrist.

"Red means nobody touches you. Nobody tries to fuck you. You're here with one person and that person is the only one who comes near you." A low warning carried in his voice, and I couldn't help but wonder if that was for my benefit - or directed at me. Nobody but him was allowed to touch me.

"Blue and green?"

"Blue means consent check. The person is open to sex, but they have ground rules in place. Usually along the lines of no anal, no sex with the opposite gender, no sex without condom. It's the most common one you'll see in there," he slipped his fingers through mine, and pulled me forward into a long hallway, "and green means free use."

"Free use?"

"If you walk in there with a green band, it means anyone can fuck you however they please. You wouldn't get further than two steps into the room before someone would have you pinned to the nearest sofa, fucking your ass while someone else pushed their balls in your mouth. Anything goes."

I was beginning to understand that he wasn't being graphic to be crude. He was being graphic because he was describing sex in its rawest form. No emotional attachment, just bodies coming together in certain ways. It mirrored the descriptions in many of his books. "That sounds exhausting."

He chuckled. "Probably."

At the end of the hall, a heavy door, followed by a set of velvet curtains, finally led us into the belly of Clandestine. It was both exactly and nothing like what I expected from a sex club. There were a lot of genitals and there were a lot of leather and latex clothes, but it wasn't one huge orgy. It was a modern, dimly lit club with colorful lights, with a dance floor and a bar, and the actual sex part was… no, okay, just as I thought it was tamer than I'd expected, my eyes landed on a very public blow job. "You're not wearing a color," I said, pulling my eyes from the man getting sucked off on a leather armchair, a blue ribbon tied around his neck.

Beck pulled me deeper into the club but looked back over his shoulder at me with a glint of amusement in his eyes.

"What did I say?"

"Nothing," he smiled, "I don't need a color."

"Why not?"

"Sweetheart, I'm the guy who fucks the girl with the ribbon."

My stomach fluttered, but I inhaled deeply to keep the nerves calm. He didn't mean me. We hadn't even discussed having sex. He was just speaking in generalized terms. "So it's a dominance thing?"

"That simplifies it, but yes."

I furrowed my brows at my own ribbon. "I could be dominant."

"You're wearing ballet flats to a sex club."

"I could be dominant with a preference for comfortable footwear."

He turned around and I barely had a second to react before his hands were around my waist and he pushed me back, lifted me up. A glass shattered somewhere behind me as he sat me on the bar, and I yelped as he pushed my knees apart, positioning himself between them, one hand on the inside of my thigh. My pulse hammered loud in my ears, drowning out the music and the people around me.

"Ballet flats," he said again, grinning.

"You're an ass," I grumbled, pushing his hand out from under my skirt. He rested his hands lazily on my hips instead, glancing past me to nod at the bartender. Maybe I should have felt more self-conscious about sitting on the bar with Beck between my thighs, especially when I wasn't wearing underwear, but this gave me an unobstructed view over the main floor of the club. There were several archways leading out of this room, neon signs above them labeling them The Island, The Rainbow, The Loft and The Dungeon. The first three were definitely more ambiguous than the last one. One last archway had a less fancy neon sign above it to show people the way to the toilets. My eyes roamed over the far end of the room, where platforms, about the same height as the bar, offered people the chance to pole dance. Or, in the case of that one woman, hold herself upside-down on that pole while another girl ate her out. The stamina and stomach muscles that had to require...

"Here." Beck handed me a tall glass filled with something pink, and adorned with cocktail cherries and pineapple slices.

"Thanks." I took a sip to test the drink first, then gulped down more of it when I realized it was nothing but cranberry juice. He knew I didn't drink, although I hadn't explicitly explained to him that it was because alcohol was *not* great when you had anxiety. Neither was coffee, but a girl could only make limited sacrifices.

"Thank god, a pretty face." A man with a big smile and shaggy brown curls stopped at the bar. He gave Beck one of those manly shoulder-claps before motioning for the bartender. Where Beck was all hard lines and shadows, this guy radiated soft comfort, but they had to be around the same age.

"Harlan," Beck said by way of greeting, turning slightly in a way that let him drape an arm over my lap where the skirt had ridden up. "No Scarlett tonight?"

Harlan made some non-committal noise, handing the bartender a fifty before turning to face Beck. "She's at the glory holes fulfilling some cumslut fantasy she's been on for weeks. I'm picking her up in an hour or so."

The club lights caught on the gold ring around his finger. Assuming Scarlett wore the twin band, that meant his wife was somewhere in this club, having sex with other men, while Harlan was getting a drink.

"And who's this lovely, young lady?" he asked, stretching a hand out for me. If he noticed Beck's jaw clenching, he didn't show it.

Red means nobody touches you. I hesitated but shook Harlan's hand. Surely introductions weren't covered by ribbon color, right? "I'm Del, nice to meet you."

Harlan's eyes dropped to the streak of crimson around my wrist as he shook my hand, and a wide grin shot over his features. "I'll be damned, August Beckett brought a red ribbon girl." He laughed and clapped Beck on the shoulder again. "It's good to meet you, Del. How does a girl like you end up in a place like this with someone like Beck?"

The implication wasn't lost on me. I was the younger woman with the ballet flats. Beck was a regular at a sex club. I smiled sweetly. "I once fingered myself at a party in front of him and he has been awfully determined to fuck me ever since. I'm not sure *this* will work though. He promised me people writhing in ecstasy, but all I see are middle aged men with bald spots trying to get their dicks wet."

Harlan choked on his drink and a small smile passed over Beck's lips. There and gone in an instant. "That mouth of yours," Beck said, shaking his head at me. "Excuse us, Harlan, I think I have to show my guest the rainbow rooms."

Harlan spluttered something into his drink as Beck lifted me off the bar, tugging my dress into place in one fluid motion before pulling me deeper into Clandestine.

"Friend of yours?" I asked once we were out of earshot.

"His wife is. Harlan's okay as long as he's sober. One drink and he thinks he's awfully funny and charming." He walked us through the Rainbow archway into a hallway of doors, each flashing a red light, until he found one with a green light. "In here," he said, boxing me through the door. The room was barely a room. It was the size of a broom closet. Black walls, illuminated by a dim pink light. With Beck behind me, there was hardly enough room to turn. The lock clicked shut once we were inside. "What is this?"

"What does red mean, Blondie?"

"Huh?" I meant to face him, but Beck took a step forward, colliding with my back, caging me between his body and the wall. I flattened my palms against the cold concrete, too aware of how small this space was.

"Who's allowed to touch you tonight?" he asked, his voice gruff against my ear as he leaned into me. His hands were on my dress, pulling it up to bunch around my waist. My bared lower half was backed into him, his thigh pressing hard against me.

"Is this about the handshake?" I asked, voice barely more than a breath.

For a moment all heat of his body left me. Then his hand

connected with my ass in a sharp slap, pain shooting through my flesh. I let out a pierced cry and barely caught my breath before another slap shattered against my other cheek. This time, the heat of the pain shot straight to the space between my legs. Oh God. My muscles pulsed, aching for more. I'd never gotten turned on this fast.

"Who's allowed to touch you tonight, Del?" Beck asked again, aligning his body with mine. The denim of his jeans was too rough against my sore skin, and I whimpered on impact.

"You," I replied, voice clogged, "just you."

"That's right," he rasped and slipped a hand around me and between my legs. I squirmed as his finger slipped into me easily, heat prickling low in my stomach. "Two slaps and you're already soaking wet for me."

Two slaps. I'd let him *slap* me. I'd let him lay a hand on me for shaking another man's hand. And he was right, it had made me wet. Despite the last weeks of research, knowing something so violent could *theoretically* be a turn-on, and *experiencing* it, were two entirely different things and my heart started hammering too fast and my breathing shallowed, black dots dancing in front of my eyes.

"Look at me, look at me." Somehow, I'd gotten turned around and Beck's eyes were frantically searching mine as he clutched my face in both hands. "There you are. What's happening?"

"Anxiety," I mouthed, his face swimming before my eyes.

"Tell me what you're thinking, sweetheart," he whispered, smoothing my hair away from my face.

"You were right."

"I often am, but I need you to elaborate. And breathe, Del, breathe."

I inhaled deeply. Once. Twice. The air cleared some of the jitters. "Just now," I stammered, "you *hurt* me, and I liked it." He didn't get it. I saw it in his eyes. This was so normal to him. He lived in a world where people were okay with being tied up and gagged and slapped before being fucked. "I know that's the whole point, right? I've read your books, but they're *your* books. Why do *I* get turned on from being slapped? I mean, that's violent. That's- that's- it makes no sense."

He hummed a low note, understanding dawning on his features. "Does the *why* matter? If you tell me, you want me to spank your ass until it's raw, I will. If you tell me to choke you, I will wrap my hand around your throat and squeeze. If you tell me to lay you on a bed of rose petals and make sweet love to you, I will. And if you tell me that the one thing that turns you on is getting fucked in a burning building, I will lay the world to ashes just to please you."

I took a stuttering breath, then another, blinking up at him. The conviction in his eyes charged the space between us. "I am scared," I whispered, afraid the truth behind these three words would shatter if I spoke them too loudly.

"Of what?"

"I'm scared of figuring out that the things that turn me on are things I logically shouldn't be turned on by. Like getting spanked. What if the reason I've not had an orgasm is that I... you know... am too different."

"First of all, there's no such thing as too different. There are so many kinks in the world, sweetheart, and plenty of people who enjoy them. Second of all, if you have a partner you trust, you should be able to experiment with them. They shouldn't make you feel weird about the things you want to try. Because third and last, as long as it's consensual, sex doesn't have to be logical. It just has to feel good."

I winced even though I knew his words were right. I just didn't like illogical. I could work with the experimentation part though. Experiments led to results. So even if the experiment seemed illogical itself, the outcome could be life-changing, right? That's how an old Petri dish led to Penicillin after all. "Actually… there's one thing I might want to try." He just raised his brows, so I told him.

"I don't think that's a good idea. At least not here."

"Oh." So much for experimenting.

"I have a lot of self-restraint, but nine square feet would be pushing my limits, Blondie."

So when he said *here* did he mean *in here*? "What about out there?"

"Will you spread your legs for me?"

"I'm not having sex with you out there."

"I never said anything about sex."

His words replayed in my head. Spread my legs for him. Well, I'd just done that at the bar without much of a second thought, so that wasn't an outrageous request. "Okay."

Five minutes later, I leaned against the cushions of an *island*.

The island room was dark, dotted with round beds, draped in gossamer curtains. There were lights right above the islands, but the rest of the room was covered in shadows. Watchers stayed anonymous, while the people occupying the beds barely registered anyone outside their gauzy private island. Only half the beds were taken, the room filled with soft moans and quiet nondescript background music.

I sat pushed against the pillows on the bed, dress pushed up to my hips, legs spread just enough for Beck to have an unobstructed view. Even if someone watched us, there were enough cushions to keep my privacy intact.

Beck's eyes were hard-fixed on the space between my legs as he unbuckled his belt. My mouth ran dry as I got an unobstructed view of the sculpted V that pointed right down at his - he pulled his pants down and I gasped. I felt the shock in every muscle of my body, and Beck smirked, eyes unrelenting on my pussy. Yeah, that part was also very tightly clenched, because Beck was *big*. I'd felt his girth through his pants and had gotten an idea of his size in my bedroom, but he wasn't just thick, he was almost as long as my forearm - and there was no fucking way that I would ever, *ever* have sex with him.

"Is this what you had in mind?" he asked, placing his clothes aside before crawling towards me and curling his fingers around my calves.

I'd asked to see him naked and turned-on, to even the playing field, and he'd delivered.

"Yep," I squeaked as he tugged on my legs, pulling me down the cushions until my knees framed his hips.

"Let's get you out of this," he said, unzipping my dress. The stretchy fabric snatched open instantly, baring me for the whole island room. So much for privacy. My nipples had already hardened, and enough moisture glistened between my legs to announce to the whole world that I wanted August Beckett. And I didn't care if they saw. I just- "Beck, wait."

His hands stilled on my thighs, and he raised his brows at me, actual confusion wrinkling his forehead. "Just watch." He waited a moment to see if I'd say anything else before his hands came back to my knees and pushed them wide. I was spread out before him, but instead of touching me, Beck started touching himself - and it was the hottest thing I'd ever seen. His eyes were trained on me, raking over my face, my chest, my sex, but he was fisting his cock, panting, pre-cum leaking down his length.

"Del," he moaned my name, and it sent a spark down my spine.

"Keep going," I whispered, shifting a little, seeking any kind of friction. I hadn't considered that I could enjoy seeing a man touch himself, but there was something about the way the vein in his neck pulsed, and his dark eyes roamed over my body.

Beck leaned above me, his free hand gripping mine, pressing it deep into the pillows as his hips bucked in rhythm with the pumps of his hands. My thighs were brushing against his, but his body still hovered well above mine. That didn't stop the moisture dripping from his tip to my stomach. "That's so hot," I gasped, my forehead against his as I looked down to watch.

He came over me, moaning, painting me in white ribbons of cum from my tits to my clit.

When the shivers that rocked his body subsided, he leaned back on his heels and offered me a lopsided smile. He trailed lazy fingers down my stomach through the mess he'd left there, swirling his cum on my skin.

"Fuck, I'll never get this image out of my head, Blondie. You're so fucking gorgeous, covered in my cum." I swallowed, his words sending a small tremor through my body. He smirked. "You like that?" he asked, still husky. "Me telling you how good you look after I marked you?"

My stomach clenched and I nodded.

Apparently, I did like that.

"Hmm," he hummed, "how about how good you look with my cum inside of you?" Two of his fingers coated in his own cum dipped into me.

"Beck," I gasped, bucking under him but he pulled his hand back before I had a chance to even consider whether I wanted him to touch me like that. In here.

He smirked and cocked his head, admiring the view once more. "I can't wait to fill that gorgeous pussy with a whole load, Blondie. You'll have my cum trickling down your thighs for days."

My breath stuttered from my lungs. I wanted that. I wanted him to follow up on that promise, and I wasn't sure how to tell him.

He left a kiss on the inside of my thigh and draped my hand with the ribbon over my chest - clearly visible to anyone - before he disappeared to get some things to clean up. He'd left me burning though, and something bold festered in my bones, something that told me it was okay to lie in a room full of strangers, covered in a man's cum, and *like* it. My hand slipped through his slick juices and into my own folds. I started playing with my clit, dipping one finger, then two fingers into myself, feeling my moisture mix with the traces of his cum. I thrust them in and out, finding the spot that made my muscles clench.

And just when I felt a low pressure building in my core, someone coughed and all I could think about were germs. How many people in here were breathing and sniffling and coughing their sinus infections right my way?

TWENTY-EIGHT

BECK

If i'd thought it had been glorious to see Del lie spread out, dazed and glowing with heated cheeks, covered in my cum - that was nothing against seeing her writhe on the mattress, playing with herself, playing with my cum. She was breathing hard, her legs twitching, and I mentally cheered her on, but the moment passed, and her limbs dropped back to the island as if nothing had happened.

I slipped back through the flimsy curtain before the self-doubt could fester in her mind. "What are the chances you'll let me eat that pussy right now?" I asked, putting on a wide grin because I knew the chances were next to zero, but I wanted to pull her from the depth of her thoughts.

To my surprise, she hesitated before shaking her head. "Not tonight."

"Fair enough. We'll just have to come back tomorrow," I said, wiping the traces of my orgasm from her skin with a wet wipe.

Twenty minutes later, we were in my car, on our way back to my place, her head leaning against my shoulder. "What happened after I left you on that island?" I asked, watching the buildings zip past in the dark.

"You saw?"

"Yeah. You were mesmerizing."

She sighed. "It felt... free. Everyone there liked sex. Nobody was going to judge me for wanting to touch myself with your cum on my hands. The further we get from the club, the sillier it feels, but in that moment, I just wanted-"

"You don't have to feel ashamed for what you want, Del. It's not silly."

"It doesn't make sense. I hate wet kisses on my skin. But I wanted to have traces of you inside of me. Not on me. In me. I don't know. It sounds stupid."

"Come here." I pulled her into my lap, opened that silk jacket and shoved her dress up to her waist, her bare ass resting against my legs, her pink pussy opened wide and still glistening. I sucked two of my fingers into my own mouth and released them covered in a thin sheen of spit. "Ride my hand."

"What?" She looked down at my hand in the space between us, chest trembling. "Just like that?"

"Just like that." I widened my knees to spread her legs further and positioned my fingers at her entrance, barely opening her up. She let out a small gasp and gripped my shoulders for support. "Ride."

"Your driver," she protested, tilting her hips ever so slightly to slide onto my hand a little, desire already winning against her doubts.

"Can't hear past the sound-proof partition," I explained anyway.

Her lips fell open in wonder and pleasure as she took my fingers down to the knuckle, then started rolling her hips back again. Her eyes dropped to where our bodies connected, my fingers glistening before she pushed herself onto them again. Once she'd tested out how to tilt her hips, I met her accelerating movements, each thrust growing faster, more desperate.

"Beck, I can't," she whimpered and stopped moving mid-thrust, grasping at my shirt.

"Talk to me."

"We're in a car. There's people outside. I don't know what to do with my hands." She winced, squeezing around my fingers as the thoughts started clouding her mind.

"Tinted windows. Nobody can see. - Put one hand in my hair, one on the handle above the door," I said, calmly. She did. Earning herself enough leverage to pull herself up and fuck my hand harder than before. "Good job, sweetheart."

"Oh god," she moaned, rocking against me.

"That's it. You've got it. You're so fucking gorgeous with your pussy all covered in my spit and cum. You're all mine, Blondie."

"Oh god, oh god." Her breathing grew frantic, her hips tilting faster, and I curled my fingers into her. She cried out as I hit her G-spot.

"Such a good little cunt, look at your sweet pussy milking my fingers." I hadn't imagined the ripples in her muscles when I'd told her how good she looked covered in my cum, lying on the island. Every dirty praise, she lapped up like water in the desert.

"Beck, Beck," she gasped my name, voice growing smaller with each thrust.

"Good girl, keep going. You're doing such a good job."

God, she was so fucking beautiful, and she unraveled in my lap with a series of high-pitched moans, fisting my hair, tears rolling down her cheeks, before collapsing against my chest, sobs rocking through her. I waited until her pussy stopped quivering before I pulled my fingers out and started rubbing her back instead.

She stilled after a few moments and stayed curled in my lap, face buried in my shirt.

I didn't expect her to be ecstatic after her first orgasm. Not with all the mental blocks that had kept her from it. But I expected… something. Instead, once we got out of the car at my place, she went through the motions of coming home without a word or look in my direction. She was damn near catatonic as I boxed us into the shower and washed the night from her skin and hair, then toweled her down and sat her down on the edge of my bed. It wasn't until I pulled a shirt over her head that she even seemed to blink.

Fuck. Had I broken Blondie?

"This isn't my shirt," she said, voice small.

"Sure, it is. I told you I'd take care of it."

She furrowed her brows in a deep frown and bent her spine, rolled her neck, shaking her head. "Mh-mm, no." She contorted herself to reach behind her and pull on the neckline of the pink shirt that was an exact carbon copy of the one I'd ruined by tying her to my refrigerator with it. "I cut out my tags."

No point in lying even though I could have slapped myself for such a silly oversight. "I'll cut them, hold on. I'm afraid yours was stretched beyond repair."

"It's a limited edition from a couple of years ago."

"I know," I chuckled. A limited-edition Taylor Swift shirt was not as hard to procure as the tone of her voice made it seem. "Don't worry, it's practically brand new. You're the first one to wear it."

"How did you get it?" she asked as I brushed wet strands from her neck to access the scratchy little tag in the shirt.

"I bought it."

"People have offered me their first born for that shirt."

"Don't worry, my future children are safe." I threw the tag out and switched off the overhead lights, crawling into bed next to her. "Come here, Del."

I was not the kind of man you got into bed with to cuddle, but this was well underway to being the third night that Del spent in my bed just to sleep. She picked out her favorite pillow with deliberate fingers and wedged it between her head and the mattress, leaving ten inches of space between every part of her and every part of me.

"Are you alright?" I asked after a moment of watching her stare into space.

"No," she huffed.

"Are you hurt?"

"What. The. Fuck." She threw her arms out, slapping my chest involuntarily, but that was all the prompting she needed. "How fucking selfish has everyone in my life been to tell me that it was okay if I just enjoyed having sex for the companionship? This is what I've been missing all these years? Is this what it's like to come every single time? Because if so, I demand my money back for all the nights I have just laid in bed while some asshole came inside me without caring about whether or not I was getting off. I'm not hurt, but my pride sure is. Although I guess I must have been a damn good actress for anyone thinking that my fake orgasms were close to the real thing. So, I guess I can take pride in knowing that I can, in fact, beat Meg Ryan in that Oscar category. What the fuck, Beck?"

She blinked at me, cheeks glowing red with anger. There she was. Little firecracker. "Oh, don't look at me." I turned to my side to face her. "I've been wanting to make you come since our first dinner together."

"And we didn't even have sex. I mean, it was sex, but it wasn't *sex*. Why have I been wasting my time on penises when I just needed two fingers? Do you know how disgusting it is to have some guy pant and drool all over your neck while his dick goes limp inside of you? And you just have to lie there like *oh yes, that was so good, you rocked my fucking world*?"

I chuckled. "I can't say that I have personal experience with that." Under different circumstances the idea of anyone's dick inside her would have pulled a much different reaction from me, but not when she was yelling at me about how getting finger fucked in my limo was better than any cock she'd ever had.

She sucked in a deep breath, ready for the next cascade of words, but the tension rippled from her body in a whooshing exhale. "I need my notebook."

"Your notebook?"

"I need to write down what happened tonight, what worked for me and what didn't, while it's still fresh in my mind." She shot up in bed, but I grabbed her wrist before she could leave.

"I'll remind you tomorrow. Come here." I pulled her to me, tucking her against my side. Her leg fell over mine, her bare lower half pressing against me. My cock jerked in response, ready to claim her right then and there, but I resigned myself to running my thumb over the curve of her lower lip, full and warm. Even with the red lipstick washed off, it was still tempting as fuck. Her pulse hammered in her neck as she watched me, mouth slack, ready to let me claim it. Fuck, the things I wanted to do to that mouth. But I knew that if I kissed her, I'd be making a deal I couldn't back out of, and she wasn't ready for what that entailed. "You just had your first orgasm."

"I did," her voice trembled, a fraction of what it was ten seconds ago, realization flashing through her eyes.

"When I said that your first climax would only be the beginning of this, I meant it. We're just getting started."

She swallowed, lips closing around the tip of my thumb for merely a split second, but long enough to shoot another spark of heat straight to my hips.

"I trust you."

Those were the wrong fucking words. Whatever tension had been building inside me deflated at the sight of those big ocean eyes and the sound of those three damn words. I leaned in to press a kiss to her forehead, schooling my face before it could betray me. "Get some sleep. It'll be the last night you spend in this bed without begging me to fuck you."

She snickered but just buried her face against my chest. Despite the tornado of emotions from before, her breathing evened out within two minutes. And for the first time since I rearranged the place cards at the Truman Academy charity dinner, so I could sit next to Cordelia Montgomery, I wondered what the fuck I was doing.

TWENTY-NINE

Delilah

"How long have you been working for Cordelia?" I asked, watching Victor dice the bell pepper impossibly small. I'd sat next to Cordelia through enough dinners to know that she hated any trace of vegetable - except potatoes - in her food and would stop eating at even a hint of onion. How many vitamins did he smuggle into her diet like this?

"Five years," Victor answered without looking up.

"And before that?" I asked, stealing a slice of cucumber from one of his cutting boards.

"I worked for my family."

Getting information from him felt like squeezing the last bits of toothpaste from an already empty tube. Considering he'd probably run a full background check on me - or had at least read the results of one - this relationship was a little unbalanced. And for some reason, this morning seemed like the perfect opportunity to rectify that. Definitely not just to keep me from texting Beck. He had work to do. Important business-y work. And he had ordered me to take a day off studying - even though I'd told him one orgasm wasn't going to prove anything, especially since we'd tried to practice in bed all Sunday and I hadn't even gotten close. Taking a break was not the way to go if you asked me, but it was his apartment and if he didn't want me coming over, I could hardly argue. We'd agreed to go to the annual fundraiser for the Museum of fine Arts together tonight though. I just had to kill a few hours until then.

So. I would study Victor instead of books. I narrowed my eyes at his perpetual scowl. Fine. Quick fire round it was. "How old are you again?"

"33." Only four years older than Cordelia.

"Are you from Boston?"

"Yes."

"Married?"

"No."

"Kids?"

"No."

"College?"

"No."

"Kissed Cordelia?"

"Yes." His knife came down in a hard chop and stayed down, as his quick reply registered. His eyes flicked up, his face drawn into a sharper frown than usual. Under different circumstances that face, when he was holding a sharp knife, could have made me nervous. But I doubted he'd stab me over tricking him into admitting a kiss.

"Are you two together?" I continued my questioning, pasting on a saccharine smile.

"No," he huffed and continued chopping. "Enough prying."

"Oh come on. It was just getting interesting." He had probably spoken a total of 100 words to me over the last couple of weeks, despite the fact that he kept driving me to dinners and luncheons and Beck's place. But if you multiplied that by 5 years, him and Cordelia must have had a few noteworthy conversations.

"Why don't I start interrogating you?" He asked, his voice sharper than his knife. "Starting with your reasons for going to Clandestine with August Beckett."

My stomach soured. That club was supposed to be a secret. Beck had said that they prided themselves on discretion. "I don't know what you're talking about."

"Delilah, you are out there wearing Cordelia's name tag. I know where you go, who you talk to, and who takes you to sex clubs. Clandestine's walls may be impenetrable - pun intended - so I don't know what went down inside, but if I was able to find out you went there in the first place, others can easily do the same."

"I- That's-" Shit, shit, shit, shitty shit.

"For some reason, Cordelia doesn't mind you spending all this time with Beckett, and she thinks Clandestine's discreet enough. But if I get even a whiff of a scandal because of your actions-"

"Oh, leave her alone, Victor." Cordelia waltzed into the kitchen in a pink tweed dress, Fitzwilliam traipsing behind her like a shadow, and leveled an icy glare on him. "Even if someone found out Cordelia Montgomery went to a sex club, we'd spin it in our favor."

"Cordelia, I'm so sorry," I said.

"Listen, Del, I'm not worried about sex scandals. You're out there to make me look good. The world seems to think that I'm weak and incapable just because I don't like leaving my property. So, actually, I think going to a sex club could easily be spun into an amazing narrative. I'd just get Refinery29 or InStyle on the line and give an interview about how empowering it is to claim your space in the boardroom *and* the bedroom."

Victor let out a sound that couldn't be described as anything but a growl. Cordelia didn't even look at him. Instead, she took my hands in hers, pulling my full attention to her. "Are you being safe?" she asked.

"Uh…" Not the conversation I saw myself having ten minutes ago. "I'm on the pill."

"That's not enough. Condoms?"

"I, uh, Cordelia, that's…"

"You can put them on the shopping list if you want. Just put down which brand and size to get and we'll keep you in stock." She waved a hand in the general direction of the refrigerator, where the shopping list was pinned. "A pregnancy scandal wouldn't be quite as easy to get out of."

"I don't need- we- we haven't even…" I shook my head.

"Oh." Surprise lit Cordelia's features. "Wait, so what exactly do you do all day with him?"

"Did you think I was going to his house 8 hours a day to have sex?" I gaped at her.

"Well, I figured some eating and cuddling was involved, too, in between, to refuel, but…" She shrugged.

"I read," I squeaked. Not necessarily the full truth, but the core truth.

"You? Read?" She asked, the corners of her mouth twitching as if she'd just found an onion in her chicken soup.

"He has over 2000 books."

"Huh. You read." She cut a glance at Victor, but I couldn't understand the quiet conversation that played out between them. Maybe that was why he didn't like to talk. He and Cordelia were telepathically linked. "Is he seeing anyone else?" she asked after a moment, turning back to me.

I wanted to laugh at the question, but it made sense. It made too much sense. If he wasn't sleeping with me, he'd likely have someone else tending to his needs. And if he had someone else, then I was putting Cordelia in a position of being labelled The

Other Woman. "I don't know," I answered truthfully. We spent a lot of time together, but there were many nights for him to go out, date, meet women at Clandestine.

"Ask him, would you?" She clicked her tongue.

"Okay." She stared pointedly at me. "Right now?"

"You have his number, don't you?"

THIRTY

BECK

There was nothing as excruciating as board meetings - except board meetings on a Monday morning - except board meetings on a Monday morning after I'd spent a perfectly good Sunday, staying in bed with Del.

I'd wanted to recreate the limo experience for her, and I got plenty of moans out of her, but she kept cycling through everything that happened on Saturday night in her mind. Instead of climaxing, she'd started rambling about the statistical probability of all the events that led up to her orgasm. At that point, I got her notebook and pens from the library and sat down with her to methodically write it all out. She even had me describe how, when I fingered her, whether I thrust from my wrist or my shoulder. And to demonstrate what she meant, she gave me a hand job, alternating between jerking me off with wrist- and shoulder-based pumps.

Following that kind of Sunday with a Monday morning surrounded by a bunch of old men who wanted to rule the world? Fuck no. They wanted to micro-manage every business decision, ignoring the fact that all their ideas were stuck on 20th century standards that would generate no fucking money. I was merely here, so they'd feel like they were important. Axent wasn't going to use any of their ideas, but I had to sit here and listen and nod, because it was their assets tied up in my family's business. At least the Montgomery merger would be big enough to get rid of some of them though.

Steven Richards was going on and on about how TikTok was doomed and would never generate leads, when our budget hotel chain, Jewel, had soared in profits *three years ago* when we handed our social media assistants a couple of phones, sent them on a trip around the world in Jewel hotels and told them to put it all on TikTok. They had mostly shit-posted, but their series about judging the breakfast buffets based on how hangover-friendly they were, while actually hungover, had done better than any professionally produced commercial video.

A message popped up in the corner of my screen, and for once I was glad to be sitting at the head of the table. Sitting there, people could usually tell immediately when I stopped listening - but at least nobody could see my screen.

> BLONDIE:
>
> I need to ask you something and I need you to just tell me outright without reading too much into this, because I know you said you don't believe in monogamy and that's okay: are we seeing other people?

The blood roared in my ears at those last five words, much louder than I wanted to admit. Just because I planned to put a ring on that hand for business purposes, didn't mean I wanted to think about my future wife getting dicked down by any other men. I didn't believe in monogamy. But when she'd come apart in my lap, that was *mine*. Her trembling lips and glossed over eyes and the way her cheeks flamed hot, that was *mine*.

Instead of telling her all that, and scaring her off with the possessive streak that had gripped me, I typed out a response that put the ball in her court.

BECK:
Do you want to see other people?

Three dots appeared on screen then disappeared again. They came back, they disappeared. This went on for five minutes as she kept overthinking her response. Five minutes during which I heard not a single word spoken in that boardroom.

The reply that followed wasn't quite what I'd anticipated.

BLONDIE:
Have you slept with anyone since the night of the watch party?

The night she broke up with her boyfriend. The night she let me touch her for the first time. The night I'd left her house with an erection hard enough to hurt and had fucked the first woman I'd laid eyes on at Clandestine.

BECK:
Once.

The next reply came much swifter than the previous one.

BLONDIE:
I'd prefer if you didn't.

BECK:
What about you?

BLONDIE:
good one

BECK:

I'm not just talking about sex.

BLONDIE:

ok

Another message popped up, but before I had the chance to read it, my laptop was snapped shut. I was going to kill the fucker who- Julian grinned at me, the only person left in the room. "And how's the Montgomery account doing?"

"You can wipe that grin off your face." I rolled my eyes at him and shoved out of my chair. "Or you can try putting a ring on her finger yourself."

We'd obviously had that discussion, but I was the obvious candidate. No children and 4 years younger than him. "You're so touchy these days," he mused.

"You never had any interest in how I handled my dating life, excuse me for finding it hard to fess up now just because there's billions at play." I cut him a sidelong glance. "It's progressing across all three categories. If it wasn't, I'd let you know."

He chuckled and typed something on his phone. "I think it's time Del met your family. Let her experience the full Beckett charm. Show her that you're seriously *committed*."

"Absolutely not." Julian saw Del as a walking gold coin, and I had just gotten to a solid stage with her literally five fucking minutes ago. No fucking around. Just her and me. He'd not screw that up for us. "You have no idea how to handle her."

"Bring her to barbecue night," he said, unfazed. "How many drinks and baby pictures of Brody do you think it would take for her to catch baby fever?"

Again, with his bullshit pregnancy strategy. My phone buzzed in my pocket, and I pulled it out, more than happy for the excuse to ignore my brother - except, the text was from Brody.

> BRODY:
> omg are you srsly bringing Blondie over?

"That's a cheap trick," I huffed, frowning at Julian.

"Can't back out now or Brody won't let you hear the end of it. Don't worry, I'll be my most charming self."

"Beck, I need five minutes of your time." Jonas, Axent's CFO sidled up to me at the end of the day as I beelined for the elevator. Despite being a head shorter than me, he didn't struggle to keep my pace.

"I'm on my way out. This will have to wait until tomorrow," I replied. I wasn't postponing my evening plans with Del for yet another discussion about the tax cuts we were angling for in the UK. They'd exited the EU. That meant we could get away with a few paragraph adjustments here and there before starting construction on the new Axent in Newcastle. He could take it up with legal if he was pressed for time.

"I checked with your assistant. You're all booked for tomorrow." He stepped into the elevator with me and glared at a young man in a pinstripe suit. "Get out," he barked. "This is a private conversation."

"I, uh, yes, of course Mr. Young. Mr. Beckett." He nodded at both of us and dashed out of the elevator, shooting a confused look around. He'd probably never even been on the exec floor.

Once the doors closed, I raised my brows at Jonas. I wouldn't question him in front of some assistant, but this wasn't his usual attitude. "Bad mood?"

He ran a hand through his hair. "Our numbers don't add up."

That got me to turn my full attention on him. Even before asking for details, I knew that whatever he'd tell me in the next 60 seconds would ruin my night. "What do you mean, they don't add up?"

"I mean," he whispered as if anyone could overhear us in this whirring metal cage, "there's a hole in the boat and I can't patch it up until I find it."

"How much?"

"Enough for me to come to you instead of handling it myself."

Shit. "How did nobody notice until now? This couldn't have happened over night."

"Because we had to do the numbers by hand the other day, when the servers were down."

And here I thought we'd gotten through that day without hiccups. Actually, I'd forgotten most of that day, favoring the memory of coming home to learn Del had used my bed to her advantage. "What are you saying exactly?"

"The numbers add up in the system. Not on paper."

The elevator stopped and opened its doors to the grand lobby, where all foot traffic led in one direction: out. I worked my jaw and hit the button for the 20th floor again. "Show me."

Once upstairs, I motioned for Jonas to give me a minute while I dialed Del's number and slipped into an empty conference room. She picked up in a heartbeat. "I'm afraid Del can't come to the phone right now, she's dead."

"Oh no." I chuckled, wishing I could see her bright smile instead of facing a mountain of paperwork. "That's horrific. She was so young. How did she die?"

"She was too overwhelmed by the sheer number of shoes in her closet."

"The white ones, with the round buckle."

She tsk-ed at me and I knew the exact eye roll that went with that sound. "You don't even know what I'm wearing."

"No, but your ass looks great when you wear them." I grinned and narrowed my eyes at the view from the window. The general direction was correct, but there were miles and hundreds of buildings between us.

"Wow. Okay, Casanova, lucky you, I was planning on wearing a white jumpsuit, so they could actually work. They're damn uncomfortable though, so if I wear them, you better be prepared for another foot rub in exchange."

Might as well rip the band-aid off. "I won't make it tonight. I'm stuck at the office."

"Oh. Okay."

"I'm sorry." I meant it, too. I had no doubts that she would have looked amazing, or that she would have let me take off far more than her heels later tonight.

"It's okay." Her voice didn't sound like it was okay. "But then I won't wear the white shoes."

"I can send Fred if you need a ride."

"It's fine. Victor should be able to drive me."

"I can hear your brain churning through the phone."

"The Kit event was so much easier with you there," she said, voice small. "You're really good at striking up conversations."

"Del, I promise you, everyone thought you were charming." If only she could have seen herself from the outside, seen how everyone she talked to had been genuinely laughing and smiling between all the fake niceties of that event. "It didn't have anything to do with me."

"I'm good once people spill the beans about their lives, but you're the bean can opener, slicing through the cold, hard exterior before we get to the good part."

That had to be the strangest compliment I'd ever gotten. "Do you want to know my two best tricks for this kind of networking?"

"Yes," she mumbled, "please."

"First, you ask people about the day of the week or even the month. Just say something like 'Wow can you believe it's already August?' or 'What a week and it's only Monday, right?' and they'll steer the conversation to talk about their business plans, family vacation or whatever they actually have on their mind. And then, if they give clipped answers or you just want them to keep talking, you stay silent. You smile and you nod like you expect more, all your attention on them. People hate awkward silence, and they'll fill it as long as you keep looking at them."

"That sounds fake."

"Consider it your sociological experiment for the night. And Del? The red block heels with the big bow."

"How do you know my shoes better than I do?"

"I remember everything you wear." Especially since Brody had let me in on the whole secret code of women's outfits.

"You almost had me thinking you have a foot fetish. Which would be fine. By the way. No kink-shaming."

Jonas rapped a knuckle against the glass door of the conference room, brows raised. If he was rushing me, it had to be bad. Fucking hell. I raised a finger at him to get one more moment.

"Kink-shaming? Picked up a new term, Blondie?"

"Yep," she chirped, and I wished I'd had the time to go through some of the weirdest kinks out there, just to see which ones would make her blush and stumble over her words.

"I have to go," I said instead.

"Ugh, okay, I should finish getting ready."

"I'll see you tomorrow."

"Don't work too late."

THIRTY-ONE

Delilah

I sat in the back of Beck's limo and picked at the loose thread at the hem of my pink summer dress. Cordelia may have ordered my whole summer wardrobe online, but the designer label in the back made it pretty clear that this dress should not be coming apart at the seams. Beck's hand closed over mine, stilling my fingers before I could rip the fabric.

"Sorry," I whispered, slipping my hands out from under his and flattening them against my stomach instead, forcing my breathing to even out. I'd gotten better at the whole event scene, but this was different. This was family.

"Say the word and we turn around right now."

"I'm good. I'm good. I'm a social fucking butterfly," I muttered under my breath.

He chuckled and braced his hand on my knee, rubbing soothing circles into my skin. I glanced up from his hand on my naked leg, his profile outlined against the car window. The last time we'd been in this backseat, he had shattered my concept of human touch, and it was entirely unfair that he could look so absolutely at ease here. "Thoughts?" he prompted.

"Just remembering the last time we were in this car together."

"Care for round two?"

"Nope."

He raised his brows at me, hand lightly squeezing my knee, "Might help you relax."

"Have you met me?"

"Fair enough." He chuckled. "I just think it's cruel that you waltz around in that pretty little sundress, and I don't get to hike up that skirt and suck your clit until my name is the only thing left in that big brain of yours."

"You're being overly confident." I shook my head, unable to stop the grin from forming on my lips. "Besides, on an analytical level, I don't think stimulating my clitoris would get you anywhere. Nothing has ever gotten me as close as your or my fingers inside of me, so I'm assuming most of the nerves I derive pleasure from are engaged during penetration." He was looking at me with an unreadable expression. "What?"

"I just realized that I'm dating a total nerd."

"We're not dating, but I'll take that as a compliment. Nerds are cool."

"Well, if you're just using me for nerdy sex, I probably shouldn't introduce you to my brother."

"Do you actually want to take me out?"

"I *just* took you out."

"On a real date. That was a sex club," I protested, just as the car door was opened. If Fred had heard me, he knew better than to react, but my cheeks still flamed red hot. No matter how easy it was to talk to Beck about sex, I couldn't ignore that it still felt wrong the second someone else was within earshot.

Beck draped an arm around my shoulder and leaned down. At first, I thought he wanted to press an encouraging kiss to the top of my head, but instead his voice brushed over my ear in a low hum: "Consider yourself wearing a red ribbon in my brother's company." The growl of a warning rumbled under his words, and my breath hitched in my throat at the reminder of what the red ribbon meant and what it entailed. "If he touches a single hair on your body," Beck couldn't finish his sentence because the door flew open, and a bouncing ball of a girl jumped out.

At least Beck's warning hadn't extended to the whole household, because Brody wrapped me in a tight hug before I even had a chance to side-step her. She was almost as tall as Beck and had the muscles of a pro athlete, rendering breathing impossible. "I'm so glad you've not dumped him yet," she squealed.

"Yet?" Beck asked.

"She's clearly out of your league." Brody leaned back. Her toothy grin immediately made her look her age despite all that muscle mass.

"Clearly," I agreed and shot Beck a smile.

Brody led us down the hallway and through the tastefully bright and modern living room. I barely took anything in, stuck on the last few minutes of conversation, first in the car, then with Brody. Did Beck actually want to take me on a date? Was that why he had brought me here? His niece already thought we were together. But despite everything, we hadn't kissed. He hadn't shown any interest in romance. But you didn't introduce your fuck buddy to your family, did you?

We followed Brody to the deck behind the house. The low sunlight dipped the entire wooden patio into a warm glow that perfectly matched the smell of smoke and grilled meat.

"I was beginning to think you'd stand us up!" Beck's brother looked so much like him, my spine stiffened at the sight. Just as tall, just as tan, same dark hair and dark eyes. Beck was a few years younger but the only detail that betrayed the age difference was the sprinkling of white hairs on his brother's head. Where Beck sported a well-trimmed stubble, Julian was clean shaven.

He set down the barbecue thongs and walked over, a pearly white smile splitting his face. "You must be Cordelia, I'm Julian," he stretched his hand out for me, and I instinctively shrank against Beck's side.

"Hi," I gasped, mentally replaying the memory of sharp pain shooting through my flesh just because I'd shaken another man's hand. "Nice to meet you."

To his credit, Julian dropped his hand without dropping his smile. "First things first, do you eat meat?" Up close, he looked even more eerily like Beck, except Beck's nose was just crooked enough to add a little spice to his features and Julian's was straight as an arrow, ripped straight from the pages of a fashion magazine.

"I do," I replied, glancing past him to the smoking grill station, "as long as it doesn't look remotely like an animal."

"What does that mean?"

"Chicken nugget, yes, chicken wings, no." He furrowed his brows at me, clearly confused by the logic, but I just shrugged. I couldn't help the fact that I liked chicken nuggets too much to ever become vegetarian. I could at least avoid having to pick at bones.

"She's allergic to peanuts, and no tomatoes," Beck said, the first words he'd spoken since stepping outside.

"Well, I'm not roasting peanuts today, so you don't have to worry."

I was covering my second mini burger in ketchup and mayo when Brody knocked her foot against mine under the table to get my attention. "Is it true that you haven't left your house in 15 years?"

"Brody," Julian chastised without looking up from his own plate.

"What? It says so on Google." Brody waved her phone through the air, having ignored her father's no-phones-at-the-table rule for the last thirty minutes.

"Don't trust everything you read on the internet. I've been out. Just not a lot." Ha. Vague enough. Maybe I could get through the evening without having to outright lie to her. As much as I could tell myself that it didn't matter with Beck, lying to a kid felt wrong. How did parents ever keep up the tooth fairy scheme?

"It also says you gambled away your whole family fortune and you're seducing Uncle Auggie to get his money."

"Where does it say that?" Beck plucked the phone from her hands, but I recognized her grin while he was still scrolling. Apparently the Becketts had the same evil twinkle in the left corner of their mouths when they tried to get a rise out of you.

"At first, I was only in it for the money, and I was going to leave him high and dry," I mused, "but it turns out he's really good in bed."

Brody screeched with laughter, while both men at the table paled. If I knew anything about teens, it was that you had to meet them at eye level. If she could joke about me seducing her uncle, so could I. "Ohmygod," she gasped, "no, but- no but seriously, what happened here? You're way different than Ashleigh. She was such a grade-A-bitch."

"Language," Beck hissed, at the same time that Julian moaned: "Manners."

"Ashleigh?" I asked after a moment of nobody else speaking up.

"My ex," Beck supplied, "the one you googled and considered age appropriate." Oh right. It wasn't lost on me that he didn't defend her against Brody's insult.

"How long were you together?" I stabbed my fork into a baby potato.

"Too long," Brody moaned, but stiffened at a stern look from her father.

"Two years," Beck supplied, his hand finding the spot where my chair ended and gave way to my bare back. His fingertips grazed up and down my spine. "It was mutually beneficial until it wasn't."

"That sounds more like a business agreement than a relationship."

A tired smile played over his lips. There was probably more to their story than he was willing to discuss in front of Brody, but he just shrugged and said: "Sometimes they go hand in hand."

"Spoken like a true romantic," Julian teased, "the true formula for love: passion, commitment and board room meetings."

Beck's hand stilled for just a heartbeat, and I wouldn't have noticed if Julian didn't sport the exact same lopsided grin as Brody had earlier. "Are you seeing anyone?" I asked, more than happy to stop talking about Beck's ex.

"No," Julian shook his head and directed a more genuine smile at Brody, "I already have my hands full with this one."

"Please." His daughter let out a gagging sound and tossed her braids over her shoulder. "You're a textbook commitment-phobe."

"I'm sorry," he laughed, "do you *want* a stepmother?"

"You don't have to get married right away, Dad. You could start dating though."

"Brody, you know-"

"Yes, yes, nobody will ever compare to my mother. I know." She rolled her eyes. "I just think you need someone to keep you busy when I go off to college."

"Do you already have plans?" I cut in, since it sounded like I had brought up a discussion they'd had before, "For college?"

Brody shook her head at the same time that Julian replied: "Harvard. It's a Beckett tradition at this point."

I was beginning to see why Brody hadn't clicked with her

father's talk about the birds and the bees. Julian was so much stiffer than Beck, so even if he meant well, he'd always clash with a free-spirited teen like Brody. They probably had a couple of difficult years ahead of them. "Does that mean you went to Harvard, too?" I asked and bumped my knee into Beck's. His hand dropped under the table, easily catching my leg. Fingers wrapped around the inside of my thigh, he held it in place, lodged against his own leg.

"I did," he said, thumb circling over my knee, "business and law."

"Business *and* law? And you call *me* a nerd?"

Brody snorted a laugh, but Beck just grinned at me. "I never said I wasn't one."

"You have too much muscle mass to be a nerd."

"The brain is a muscle."

"It's not. That saying is commonly misunderstood. The brain is an organ, but you should exercise it like a muscle."

"See?" He leaned over and pressed a quick kiss to my temple, stubble barely grazing my skin. "You still get to be the bigger nerd."

That was very much a semi-public display of affection. Actual affection, not desire like at Clandestine. Somewhere in the background Brody squealed, but my focus was solely on Beck whose eyes crinkled in the corners and who kicked his chin up in a quiet challenge. Oh, he knew exactly what he'd done.

I just didn't know what it meant yet.

Julian's hug lingered long after the car door fell shut behind us, silence swelling in the back of the limo on the way home. The muscle in Beck's jaw ticked and he tapped a single finger against the leather seat. It felt like a countdown to the explosion I knew was coming. When we got into the elevator of his building and the number on the display kept climbing, I couldn't take the cold shoulder anymore. "It was just a hug."

"Inside, Del," he thundered the second the elevator stopped on his floor.

"I don't understand why you're so upset."

He opened the door to his apartment, only to throw it shut behind us, hard enough for the lock to rattle. "I told you not to let him touch you."

"What would you have me do? Shove him off me? He's your brother."

"You have no idea what he is." He charged towards the bedroom, and I had little choice but to follow him, since he was so not getting out of this discussion.

"*What* he is?" I shook my head. "Is this about Ashleigh? Did something happen?"

"I don't give a fuck about her. This is about you. About his stupid ploy to get you into his house, and him putting his fucking hands on you."

"I don't understand the problem." I kicked my shoes off, not caring where they landed. "It was one hug."

Beck grew eerily still, his breathing flattened, and his gaze hardened on me. It felt like being watched by a lion just before the kill. "Take your dress off," he growled after a beat of silence.

"No." Was he serious? That was *so* not the mood right now.

"Take. Your. Dress. Off."

"No."

"Do you want to know the truth?" He stalked closer, step by step reminding me of the towering height he had on me.

"Yes," I breathed.

"Julian thinks you're a joke." The words stung like a slap across my cheek. "Every smile he gave you tonight was followed by a side eye at me. Every little joke you shared with Brody, he grimaced the second you weren't looking. He had made his mind up about you long before ever meeting you, taunting me, needling me for information he could use to ridicule you. Young, naive, sheltered. Just another woman that should do her hair, open her legs, and stand behind her man. And he had no right to touch you." He snarled the last few words.

My eyes watered at the thought of that man making fun of me, and of the things I shared with Beck in private. I'd never been good at reading the subtext of a conversation. I'd been the butt of the joke too many times throughout my school years. I thought I'd put all that behind me. "What did you tell him about me?" My voice waivered.

"I told him fucking nothing." He cupped my face in his hands and ran his thumbs over my jaw and cheekbones, his touch too soft paired with his rough tone.

"Do *you* think I'm a joke?" I'd accused him of taunting me once, of making fun of me by sending me a vibrator, but he'd spent the last few weeks finding ways to slip under my skin. Maybe I shouldn't have let him. It only took one glance at his luxury, minimalist apartment, and his custom-tailored suits to track that we weren't actually occupying the same universe. I was okay with being different. I was *not* okay with being looked down upon.

"No, and it doesn't matter what Julian thinks. You're not a joke." His reply came swift and stern, and his eyes softened for a moment before turning back to steel. He leaned down, ghosting his lips over the corner of my mouth, warm and soft. "You're mine." His tender kisses travelled down my neck, and I broke out in goosebumps. "Every hitched breath, every racing thought, every inch of skin, is mine. Now take off that dress, so I can remind you of who gets to touch you." He left a last kiss on my collar bone before leaning back and waiting.

I may not have tracked Julian's intentions, but Beck had

always told me outright what he wanted. He'd told me he prioritized consent and communication before he'd ever touched me. And I believed him. Even now. He was waiting for me to take off my dress, so he could touch me. God, I wanted him to touch me. To make me forget this whole stupid, two-sided afternoon. I wanted something simple, straight-forward. His touch. My body's response. I unbuttoned my dress and let it fall to the floor.

For a moment, I just stood in front of him in nothing but a silky pair of white panties, and his eyes drank in every inch of exposed skin. Beck pulled his hands off me and straightened to his full height. "Get on the bed and face the headboard."

My stomach clenched at his tone, but I didn't protest. This was so easy. He told me what he wanted. I did it. And something inside me buzzed at how easy it was. I didn't have to worry about signals crossing or misunderstanding him.

I had just knelt down between the pillows, when Beck came back from his chest of drawers with a piece of thick, black rope. He tied it around my hands, yanking my wrists together. I winced, prompting a "Too tight?" from him, but I shook my head because the burn was just enough to overpower the quietest of my anxieties. I didn't even have to worry about what to do with my hands. He tied them to the top of his headboard, and I glanced down, realizing I had no way of lying down on the mattress. My breathing fluttered, realizing I also had no way of turning to him.

Beck climbed onto bed behind me, pushing his body against mine, the stark outline of his growing erection hard against the curve of my ass. "What do you say if you need me to stop?"

"I say stop, you stop," I whispered, the anticipation racing through my blood.

"Good."

His warmth ebbed from my back and then his hand was in the hem of my underwear and with a sharp yank, he pulled it tight into my crease, exposing my cheeks. "Your ass is so fucking beautiful," he rasped, fingers digging into my flesh, pulling my cheeks apart, pushing a thumb into the dip of my panties where they covered my entrance. He knew I'd never even experimented with anal, and that little bit of pressure already set off a spark in my belly. "Tell me who gets to touch your ass, Del."

"You," I replied, already breathless.

My answer was followed by a sharp slap to my left cheek while his thumb still pressed against me. The pain burned and radiated over my skin, the heat rippling out like an earthquake.

"Who gets to touch your ass?" he asked, thumb pushing aside my panties and dipping in. I whimpered at the unfamiliar sensation that made my toes curl.

"You," I gasped.

Another slap to my ass followed. The heat shot straight to my core, moisture pooling between my legs. "Who gets to touch your ass?" he asked again and pushed his thumb down to the hilt, a different sharp pain wrangling a cry from my lips.

"You," I whimpered, "just you."

"That's right," he brushed a soothing hand over my pulsing cheek and rasped: "*Just* me."

He repositioned himself behind me, his finger leaving me aching just before one of his hands reached around and he pinched one of my nipples. No caress, no foreplay. I cried in time with a slap to my other ass cheek. "Who do your tits belong to?"

I knew he wanted me to say they were his, but they weren't. They were mine. I still belonged to me. My body belonged to me. If he wanted me to say that he was the one who got to touch them, fine, but *belong* was the wrong- His hand came down so hard on my ass, I lost my balance. Pain shot down my arms where the restraints kept me upright, and a hot ache pulsed in my hips. "Who do your tits belong to?" he asked again, finding my other nipple, and squeezing it between his fingers, the blinding mix of pleasure and pain clouding over all rational thought.

"You," I panted, "just you."

I scrambled to regain my hold, get back to my knees, but before I could, a hard jerk on my hips ripped the fabric of my panties. "Look at you, dripping wet, so fucking beautiful." Beck's hands closed around my waist, and he pulled me back until my arms were fully extended, my bare ass pulled deep into his lap, legs spread so wide, my hips ached.

I barely existed outside my body, being strained in all the right ways, caught between the heat of pain and the heat of arousal. Beck slipped his hand between my legs, parting me and running a languid finger through my folds. Just enough to wrangle a moan from me before his touch disappeared again. Fuck. Not seeing him was screwing with my head. Not seeing what he was doing. "You taste so fucking good, Del," he breathed. "Who gets to taste this sweet pussy?"

Was he really licking my juices off his finger? My pussy clenched, more heat flooding through it as the realization sank in. "You," I whispered, the word swimming somewhere along my last coherent thoughts.

The next slap landed right between my legs, a violent pain shooting up my spine, quickly followed by another one, and another one. I bucked and screamed in pain, but by the time my voice died, the pulsing burn on my clit was morphing into a deep-rooted, warm pressure. I was barely aware of two of Beck's fingers slipping into me at first, but he stretched my walls with merciless rhythm, plunging them deep and hard. The slick sound mixed with the loud ragged breaths I was heaving as I pushed against him and swayed, needing... something. Wanting. Feeling. Just feeling. His hands on my body were all that mattered. But then his fingers left me, and I was suddenly too cold and too empty. "Who gets to taste your sweet pussy, Del?"

"You," my voice was hoarse from screaming, "just you."

"That's my girl," he rasped and yanked my hips back again,

my arms crying at being pulled taut, but a different sensation pierced through. Him. He was hot and solid, sliding his tip up and down my fold, thick enough to part me wide without even entering me. "Last question, sweetheart. Who gets to fuck that beautiful tight pussy of yours?" He positioned himself at my entrance, both hands on my core to work me open.

I let out a strangled sound, somewhere between pleasure and protest. "Please," I whimpered.

I earned myself another slap on the ass for that answer, but that barely broke through all the other beautiful, terrible pain. "Who gets to fuck you, Blondie?"

"Just you," I whispered, dooming myself.

He pushed himself into me inch by inch, my moans turning to sobs as I was stretched beyond comfort. Yet I arched into him, wanting, needing to be unequivocally his. His hips snapped forward as he buried himself in me, and I dissolved crying his name and jerking around him. The orgasm washed over me and drowned me, filling my lungs and blurring my vision.

My arms fell from the headboard, but there was barely enough strength in them to hold me up. Dazed and aching, tremors still rocking through my body, I tried and failed to help as Beck turned me around and lowered me into the pillows, then sank back into me. I shuddered, stomach tightening. I'd never felt this full. "God," I gasped, as some light broke through my cloudy thoughts. Each deep thrust drew a strangled noise from me. "Beck."

"You're doing so well, sweetheart, taking my cock like that," he purred and leaned down, lips tracing the curve of my jaw.

Some feeling returned to my arms and hands, and I wanted to hold him, all of him, bring our bodies as close as physically possible. I pushed one hand into his hair grasped at his shoulder with the other.

His dark eyes found mine through the haze. "You're all mine," he rasped, lips ghosting over mine, before melting into me with a kiss. Our first kiss. God, our timeline was so messed up, but he was such a good kisser, I didn't dwell on it. His lips were strong but soft, and his tongue teased mine without haste.

His pace picked up as the kiss deepened. The sharp ache of adjusting to his size ebbed and was replaced by the dull pain of the depth of him as he thrust into me harder, as if each push of his hip laid a claim to my body.

I moaned his name into our kiss as I dropped over the edge of another orgasm, quivering under him. I was still shaking when a deep moan rumbled from his throat. The tension snapped from his body, and he spilled himself in me with one last thrust.

While my body had dissolved beyond repair, Beck was on his feet within a few minutes, disappearing into the bathroom and returning with a warm washcloth. I hissed under his touch but every inch he cleaned, he adorned with a soft kiss afterwards. And each kiss was followed by praise, softly whispered against my body, telling me how soft my skin was, how beautiful my breasts, how good I tasted. The words lulled my mind into the same warm bliss the rest of me had already sunken into.

My eyes had fallen shut, a deep exhaustion rooting in my bones, by the time he crawled back into bed with me and pulled me against him. He tucked my body into the curve of his and trailed kisses along my shoulder. A sweet humming melody filled the room, and I chuckled at how cheesy he was. Humming after sex.

"Good song," I mumbled, tongue heavy.

"Good night," he whispered back.

THIRTY-TWO

BECK

I fucked up.

THIRTY-THREE

BECK

I panicked for a brief moment when Del wasn't in bed the next morning, tossing the covers back as if her small frame had disappeared into the folds of my sheets.

The clanking crash of pans and pots betrayed her before I got the chance to consider just how much I'd fucked up the day before.

I found her in the kitchen, wrapped in my bathrobe, fishing eggshells from a bowl that looked about as appetizing as cat vomit. Cooking skills aside, she seemed okay. Her eyes seemed bright as ever and a soft warmth tinged her cheeks. The girl I'd broken and stitched back together last night was gone.

"I'm making breakfast." She beamed as she spotted me walking into the kitchen.

"What are we having?" I asked and stepped around her to peer at the recipe on her phone, my arms coiling around her waist on their own accord. When I'd said she was mine, I'd meant it. I'd claimed her and my body knew instinctively that meant I wanted her near me, pressed against me, wanted as much of her as I could get.

"Frittata," she replied with a thick fake Italian accent that sounded eerily French.

I eyed the bowl that spotted at least two more shards of eggshell that I could see and the mess on the counter next to her. Points for trying. I grazed my teeth over the back of her neck. "I had a different breakfast in mind," I whispered and slipped a hand into the bathrobe to cup one of her perfect handfuls of chest, but Del froze under my touch, even her breathing pausing for a few heartbeats. I pulled my hand back as if her skin had burned me.

"I'm sorry," she whispered and turned around, her lips quivering under a forced smile. "I'm okay."

"Are you?" I asked and pulled her hands into the space between us, the bruises around her wrists blooming dark blue against her cream skin. A primal part of me loved seeing them because if I took her to a place like Clandestine, she'd not even need a red fucking ribbon anymore. Those would show everyone that she was all mine. But I was plenty aware of the pain that followed the ecstasy.

"I'll be okay," she sighed.

"Tell me where you're hurt."

She gasped a gurgled sound between a laugh and a sob, and a single tear rolled down her cheek. Fuuuuck. "No, I'm sorry. I promise I'm fine. I don't regret a single second from last night." She hiccupped. "Just not used to it."

I brushed her hair out of her face, tilting her chin up with the touch of my index finger. "How many times must I tell you not to apologize?"

"I don't want you to think that I didn't-" She hiccupped again, nose taking on a traitorous red tint.

"Come here," I sighed and wrapped my hand around hers, careful not to touch her wrist. I grabbed the first aid kit from its spot on the wall and pulled her to the breakfast counter. Bathrobe untied and slipped off her shoulders, I assessed the damage.

I'd done a lot fucking worse before but considering this was the first time Del had even let me fuck her beyond fingering, I'd overdone it. It had been Julian's fucking wink over her shoulder as he hugged her goodbye that had triggered the most possessive parts of me. I pushed the image aside and focused on the bruising that marred her body. Her wrists were the worst, closely followed by the dark hand-shaped shadows on her thighs and ass. Even her breasts had some minor yellowing marks. As much as I admired her soft, milky skin, it also seemed prone to bruising. "Can you sit?"

She shook her head.

"Just your ass?"

She shook her head again.

Shit.

I vividly remembered the primal scream she'd let out when I'd spanked her pussy. It had been fucking wild, but of course it had left its mark. "You don't have to pretend you're okay," I said and popped the first aid kit open on one of the barstools, "you're physically hurt."

"Isn't that just what happens when you have sex like this?"

I tilted my head from side because it was that simple, but it also wasn't, and I wasn't sure how much she'd read up on the things that happened after the orgasm. "Now comes the part called aftercare," I explained as I spread cooling gel around her wrists and wrapped them in bandages, "because the pain you enjoyed last night might now be a whole lot to deal with. Physically and emotionally."

"Mostly physically," she sighed and closed her eyes when I let go of her wrists and spread some of the gel on the fingertip-sized splotches across her chest.

"Mostly but not totally?" I asked, guilt sinking through my chest. Maybe I should have talked her through it more. Should have taken more time. Three dozen books, and one night at a sex club didn't make her any more sexually experienced.

Her shoulders eased as the cooling gel soaked into her skin. I knelt and continued spreading it along her thighs where I'd held her wide open for me last night even when her legs had started shaking and jerking against me. Twice.

"At Clandestine, I shook Harlan's hand even after you told me the rule. I understand that." Her voice was barely a whisper, but my head snapped up at the trembling breath wrecking her body. "Yesterday, your brother hugged me. You inflicted pain on me because of *his* actions. Not mine. I mean, I can't deny that I got pleasure out of it. I'm just trying to understand how that's a fair concept."

"You equate pain with punishment," I summarized and gently turned her hips, so I could spread the gel along her back. I traced a kiss along the edge of the bruise where her thigh curved into her ass.

"Isn't that what spanking is? The whole thing about acting like a brat and getting punished for it in the bedroom?"

"For some people," I rose back to my feet and wiped the rest of the gel off on a dish towel.

"Not for you?"

"I thought I told you what I was doing." I raised my brows at her and shook two Advil from their bottle. I picked up her hand with careful fingers, dropping the pills into her palm. "Did I say anything along the lines of *This is what you get for letting another man touch you? You have been a naughty girl and I have to teach you some manners? This will make you think twice before disobeying me again?*" My voice had taken a gruff edge and Del shrank under the words, her hand curling into a tight fist around the two little pills.

"No," she said after a moment of contemplation.

I got a small bottle of orange juice and an ice pack from the fridge, and handed her the former while wrapping the latter in paper towels. "For me, it's not about punishment or discipline. I don't care for women acting like brats to get a rise out of me." I waited until she had taken the Advil then claimed her mouth in a kiss. She gave it willingly, melting into me. I locked her against me by the neck before I slipped the ice pack between her legs. She hissed and shoved both fists against my chest but deflated within the same moment as the cold comfort seeped through her skin. "It'll help with the swelling," I whispered against the corner of her mouth, holding the ice pack in place. She closed her eyes and folded into me, face buried in the crook of my collar while I held her, thumb tracing up and down the back of her neck. "For me, it's making you feel with every fiber of your being, that you're mine. Every muscle spasm, every sound, everything you feel, is because of me. I'm the one who touches you. I'm the one who knows every dip and curve of your body. I'm the one who gets to make you come."

A little laugh trembled through her torso. "The only one who can, statistically speaking."

"You must be feeling better if you're bringing statistics into this."

"What can I say? I'm a nerd." She shifted and it was impossible to miss the twitch around the ice pack, but she pushed through the pain, propping her chin up against my chest and blinking up at me. "Statistically speaking, what percentage of your sex life requires medical attention afterwards?" She held up her bandaged wrists in case I didn't get what she was saying.

I got what she was saying, but I'd clearly underestimated her readiness before.

When I didn't answer right away, her hands slid up to cup my jawline. "Curiosity, not judgment," she reminded me.

"Blondie, I'm not worried, you'll judge me. I'm worried that you'll be scared off."

"Well, statistically speaking, 100% of my orgasms happened on the nights that you spanked me, so I might be more aligned with you than you think."

I barked a laugh. "Alright, statistically speaking? When I'm single, 100% of my sex life requires intensive aftercare. I usually frequent Clandestine because the women there either have partners or a good enough understanding of their own needs to not require my attention the next morning." Her eyes flashed but before the anxiety could weasel its way into her thoughts, I slipped my arm around her waist. "This doesn't happen often, but when I agree to an exclusive arrangement with a woman," I looked at her pointedly, "a 100% rate isn't feasible. I would estimate 70% of the time, you'll be perfectly fine, like when I tied you to the fridge with your shirt." Her thighs clenched around the ice pack at the memory. "25% of the time, you'll walk away with some bruises and a bandage here and there." I tilted my head to press a kiss to the inside of her wrist, causing another jerk around my hand. I was beginning to think those might not *just* be painful for her, but if I acted on it, her soreness would outweigh any pleasure.

"And the other 5?" she asked, breathlessly.

"Hmm…" I smirked because her big eyes were so eager for more information. "I won't just fuck you. I will wreck you. I'll drive you to the point of passing out, caught between pain and pleasure. You'll scream so loud, you'll lose your voice. And when you think I'm done with you, I'll start all over again. Your body will break in ways you didn't know were possible and you're going to beg me for more." With every word her thighs squeezed my hand harder and when I was finished, her throat bobbed.

"Well," she breathed, "we'll see about that. You owe me a proper date first."

THIRTY-FOUR

Delilah

I SLEPT ON MY STOMACH FOR TWO NIGHTS AFTER MY STAY AT Beck's.

On the first day, Victor caught a glimpse at my wrist bandage slipping out from the slouchy hoodie I'd thrown on after coming home. He cocked his chin in a silent question, eyes sharp enough that I had no doubt he'd rain hell on anyone who dared to lay a hand on Cordelia - even fake Cordelia. I shook my head and smiled at him, and that was that.

I wasn't entirely sure what to do with myself. My research project had come to a somewhat surprising and abrupt end. I wouldn't mourn the descriptions of foot jobs and diaper fetishes, but I'd grown used to curling up in Beck's library. Spending hours upon hours with him, surrounded by books. It would be weird if I kept taking up all his time though…

Cordelia spent most of her time holed up in her office these days and spared me only vague greetings in the hallway. When I poked my head through the door a few days later, she was digging her nails into her cheeks, frowning at her screen. "You wanted to talk?"

She'd sent me a calendar ping. Not even a text. "Yes!" Her head snapped up. Her nails had left crescent indents on her face. "You. Lavender Room. Tonight."

I blinked at her. "I'll need more detail than that."

"Right. Right." She shook her head and raked her fingers through her bangs while she scanned the mess on her desk, shooing Fitzwilliam aside from where he'd been snoring on a stack of papers. That traitor didn't scratch her, snap at her fingers or do so much as hiss. He just moved aside and curled up on a stack of mail instead. Safe to say, my cat had switched sides.

"I can organize that for you, you know?" I pointed at the paper mess on her desk. "Get you on a filing system."

"This is perfectly organized. Ha!" She grinned and snatched up a thick linen card. The swirling font on it glistened purple as the light hit it. "Cordelia Montgomery has been invited to join the Marigold Club."

I took the card from her, brows furrowed. "I'm still going to need more details than that."

"The Marigold Club is, ah, how do I say this? It's where rich women go to 'drink tea'," she made some air quotes with perfectly manicured fingers, "which is just code for gossip, make backroom deals and ogle the servers - who usually work there for no more than a year before being snatched up by modeling agencies." She rolled her eyes. "But. It's highly exclusive. They only invite 3 new members a year and most of them are legacies. So, I need you to accept this in person tonight, so I get access to the members only website and network. Those are worth so much more than hot servers and high tea."

"That's amazing. Congratulations on the invitation!" I read

through the swirly text. High tea at 9pm. That seemed late for tea and scones, but who was I to tell these high society ladies when to sip their Earl Grey.

"This is all you. I don't know how you managed to get on Scarlett Ashton's radar, but I'm glad you did."

"Who?"

"She's on the membership committee. Marilyn Sterling handles legacies, Poppy Wellington looks into member referrals, and Scarlett finds brand new candidates since she herself married into old money when she got hitched to Harlan Ashton."

The name clicked into place, and I bit my tongue before the words *Cumslut Scarlett* crossed it. "I haven't met her, but I've met her husband." I didn't say that she was a friend of Beck's. I'd rather have Cordelia thinking that all it took to be accepted to these circles was leaving her house every now and again. That felt like less of a slap in the face than leaving the house, going to sex clubs, and sleeping with the right men.

"Amazing." Cordelia clapped her hands together. "I'm loving this energy."

"Cocktail attire for a tea party?" I flipped the card over, trying to find any more details on what I could expect tonight.

Cordelia shrugged and turned back to her screen, hammering away at her keyboard again. Alright, guess I was dismissed. Ten minutes later, I had pulled every dress from my closet and sat on the floor staring at my phone.

• frap sluts •

DEL:
Where do I find a long-sleeved cocktail dress?

TABITHA:
Asos?

DEFNE:

EthicalOnlineShops.PDF

DEL:

By tonight

TABITHA:

-shrug emoji-

DEFNE:

Long-sleeved in July? Idk Macy's?

TABITHA:

It's way too hot for long sleeves.

Right... I hadn't caught them up on the most recent details of the Beck situation yet. I clicked on the button that started a video call on the GC. Tab picked up immediately. She had her headphones on, the phone angled at her face from below as she huffed and swayed from side to side, sweat dripping down her face. Somewhere in the background the Peloton instructor yelled at her. It took Defne a moment longer to pick up. When she did, she was pushing a white veil from her face. "Uh, anything you want to tell us Defne?"

"Oh, yes, I booked that commercial for that new jewelry brand. Or rebrand? I don't know. Just getting fitted for the wedding scene."

Being friends with a budding actress/model sure sobered one's perception of Hollywood glamour. Then again, jobs around here were limited, and she couldn't move to New York until she finished grad school. "What's up?" Tabitha asked.

I took a deep breath then shared the details of why exactly I needed a dress that covered my thighs and wrists. Not the Julian of it all, but the rest... Defne's eyes had grown to the size of saucers while Tabitha huffed faster, paddling harder into her workout.

"I can't say I'm surprised," Tabitha huffed through her workout, "he looks like he fucks."

"I'm more surprised by Del," Defne said.

"What do you mean he looks like he fucks?" I asked.

"I mean... there's people you sleep with and there's people you fuck. You usually pick men you sleep with. August Beckett looks like he fucks."

"And you can tell just by looking at them?"

"Yep," Defne chirped.

"Yeah," Tabitha bit out through clenched teeth.

"Neither of you felt like you should share this information with me? Like three boyfriends into me complaining about my sex life?"

"Delilah, you don't look like you fuck," Tabitha laughed, and groaned as the instructor yelled a loud 'release' in the background and she leaned back, her pace slowing.

I opened my mouth, then closed it again, because I couldn't argue with her on that front. Ballet flats and all.

"Back to the fashion issue at hand," Defne said, "how bad is it?"

I raised my unbandaged wrist to the camera. The twin cuffs of bruises had subsided from dark blue to purple and green, but they were still too starkly contrasted against my pale skin to cover them with a bit of makeup.

"Oh, that's not bad at all, darling, I can take care of that for you." An older woman with cherry red curls piled into a beehive popped up behind Defne.

"Defne," I hissed.

"I told you, I'm at work!"

"I have seen and heard so much more scandalous things, honey." The woman tsked at me. "I have the perfect dress for you. Size four?"

"Yes."

Two hours later, Defne, still wrapped in layers of white tulle, watched me as the owner of the bridal shop, Janice, stitched the sleeves in place. "See? No problem at all."

I looked at myself in the mirror. The dress was creamy white and draped around my body in a fluid curve down to my knees. The sleeves were soft translucent taffeta, flowing with every move, down to my wrists, where they were secured with four inches of the same cream fabric that hugged my body. It was the cocktail version of a dress made for a Greek goddess.

"You're a genius," I sighed, waving my arms around. She had tightened the cuffs half an inch, so the fabric barely slipped. If I moved carefully, nobody would even get a glimpse at the bruises.

"Hold on." She waddled away and came back with a massive golden can of hairspray. She undid the small gold buttons around my cuff, sprayed my wrist in sticky hair product, and refastened the buttons, then did the same on the other side. "Works better than any double-sided tape."

I'd not even considered double-sided tape, but Janice made it sound like it should have been obvious.

"You look amazing," Defne sighed, her voice sounding clogged.

I turned to find her rubbing a tissue around her nose. "Are you crying?"

"You're going to make such a beautiful bride someday."

"Oh my god," I laughed and rolled my eyes at her, "you're the one in a veil right now."

"Yes, but this is fake." I gave her a pointed stare, and she just shrugged. To be fair, this couldn't be easy for her. She'd broken off her engagement the day before her wedding last year. I thought she'd moved on but putting on a wedding dress had to be *a lot*. "You have a boyfriend that you can marry someday," she sniffled.

"I don't have a boyfriend. We're just..." I wasn't even sure what we were. This relationship was all over the place, but at least the limbo allowed me to pretend it didn't matter that Beck didn't even know my name.

"Uh-huh, sure," she said in a tone of *you tell yourself that.* "Because August Beckett is the kind of man who takes just any girl home to meet his family."

"Oh, shut up."

"I'm putting a pair of extra buttons and a small sewing kit in the box, just in case one pops off your sleeve," Janice said, waving a small envelope at me before putting it in the big pink dress box. "And *you* have to take off that dress now." She leveled her eyes on Defne.

"But I feel so pretty," she whined, smoothing her hands down the structured corset.

I should have charged the dress to Cordelia. She wouldn't even notice the $1200 missing from her accounts, whereas my savings were now nonexistent until I got paid for the Elie Saab dress - because apparently bank transfers of $10,000 or more could take forever to process. Not the kind of money I usually received, so it had been flagged by the bank, and not come through yet. It was just that Cordelia had outfitted me in plenty of dresses. I could hardly ask her to buy me more just because my sex life had taken a surprising turn. At least Janice reassured me that if I brought it back flawless, she could give me a partial refund. Not full because of the alterations she'd made, but I'd take a $600 refund over no refund at all.

THIRTY-FIVE

BECK

I DROPPED THE PRINCESS CUT DIAMOND BACK ON THE VELVET pouch. It still caught the light and scattered rainbow sparks across my desk, including the revised prenup Axent's lawyers had drawn up. That damn diamond was mocking me. Even if I didn't touch it, those flecks of colorful light would remind me of its presence. I hated that thing. Just because Julian had the platinum band removed, didn't mean it wasn't the same diamond my father had used to keep my mother on a leash. She'd signed a prenup, too. One that guaranteed she'd end up with nothing but the fucking ring if she walked. Not even the right to see her children. Not because our father wanted us, but because he wanted to make sure she stayed.

My phone buzzed before I could ride too far on that train of thought. Del's name lit up the screen alongside a selfie she took of us the other day. She sat in the front, I sat at my desk in the background. Snapped just to prove to her friends that she was really here in a fully clothed co-working capacity.

"You're calling late." I picked up the call and slid a paper over the diamond. I didn't want that thing bringing any of its bad luck into my relationship.

Wait, *relationship*?

"So, hi," Del said, sounding out of breath.

"Hi," I said, "are you okay? Is this a booty call?"

"Uh…"

"Del?"

"Hi," she said again, erupting in giggles.

"What's up?" Was she out? There were some noises in the background, but it didn't sound like a party or a bar.

"Hi means hi. The hi in the hi."

She wasn't making any sense and the breathiness of her voice set my teeth on edge. "Blondie, where are you?"

"No-ooh, Beck, high. The tea. Is high tea. Ssh." She erupted in another fit of giggles.

Oh, for fuck's sake. *High* Tea. I'd heard plenty of stories from Scarlett. Even though, technically, the club members weren't supposed to share details of their events with outsiders. "You're at the Marigold?"

"I didn't say that. I'm not. Uuuh I'm… at the… Dlogiram."

"That's just Marigold backwards."

"Oh," she choked on her laugh, "mirror."

"I'm picking you up in twenty." I was out of my chair in a flash. Del didn't so much as sip champagne, and she had gone to High Tea. And from the sounds of it, she hadn't known how high the uppity ladies at the Marigold liked to drink their tea. "How much cake did you eat?"

"You need lipstick."

"I need lipstick?" I asked, engaging her nonsensical thought process if it meant keeping her on the line, while I took the stairs down to the garage. The elevator would have cut off our call.

"As a disguise."

"Why do I need a disguise?"

"Because it's for women. Or naked."

"Naked?" My steps faltered.

"The men are naked."

I ignored the thundering beat behind my temples at the thought of her surrounded by a bunch of naked men. She wasn't anywhere sleazy. Just somewhere women with too much money wanted to feel a little scandalized. Those naked men were either servers or dancers. I doubted Del got too cozy with any of them. "Don't worry, I have my lipstick and my high heels in the trunk."

"Good."

"Keep talking," I ordered as I got in the car and connected my phone to the Bluetooth.

"I don't want to go home."

"You're not staying at the Marigold," I replied and wove my car out of the garage and onto the street.

"Noooo, I don't want to go home home home. *Home*." She giggled again, a squeaky snort escaping. "Humhumhum."

"You can stay at my place," I replied.

"No."

"Del-"

"You said your bed is only for sex."

I had said something along those lines, and she seemed to be one of those people who got extremely literal when tripping. So instead of arguing about my bed's purpose, I just said: "You can sleep on the sofa."

"Okay. Wait. Cake."

"No, hey, Del, no more cake."

"But it's chocolate."

God, she needed it spelled out for her. "Pot brownies, sweetheart. It's pot brownies."

"Cupcakes!" she squeaked before the line went dead. Fuck. She was going to be the death of me. I pushed the gas pedal down harder and wove the car through the streets of Boston like I was gunning to make the Grand Prix.

The Marigold was a good 30 minutes outside the city. I made it in 22 minutes. 22 minutes of being unable to get Del back on the line. From the outside the Marigold looked like a small, luxury country club and spa. Nothing to raise your brows at. If you ignored the fact that the women in there either ran the east coast or were married to men that did. I threatened at least three people, that I didn't want to make enemies of, to get in, but the thought of Del in that shark tank, tripping, surrounded by men who liked to be ogled at by women all day... Only one of them had to figure out that he could make millions off a sex tape with a rich girl while she was wasted.

Scarlett stopped me with her arms crossed in front of her chest when I finally reached the doors of the Lavender Room. "I don't even want to know how you got in," she snapped her fingers, "but you can march that pretty ass right back out."

"Where is she?" I snarled.

Scarlett rolled her eyes at me, unimpressed. "She's a grown woman. Let her have some fun." Scarlett was 6ft tall, wore 5-inch stiletto heels, and her nails were sharpened to points that could slash throats. It may have scared off lesser men, and while I usually admired her ability to stand her ground, she'd be about as difficult to get out of the way as a twig if she wasn't careful.

"Scar, I swear to god," I breathed.

"Try me."

"Stockholm, 2019. Axent Grand."

Hurt flashed across her features for a moment before she jutted her chin out. "That would hurt you just as much as it would hurt me."

"Would it? Tell me, when did Harlan agree to open your marriage? Two years ago?"

"You have a girl in there, who doesn't seem like she would date a man who blackmails his friends. Are you willing to chance that?"

I pulled out my phone and had the video on my screen within ten seconds, turning it around for Scarlett to see. Her taped moans filled the hallway outside the Lavender Room, and the blood drained from her face. Yeah, getting fucked by a stranger in a closed hotel bar was fun right until you realized that there were security cameras.

"You delete every copy of that video," she hissed.

"The second I have her out of here safe and sound."

"Fine." She stepped aside. "You better put a ring on her finger if you're ready to ruin *my* marriage for her."

"That's the plan."

Del was draped over her chair, chin resting on its back, eyes closed, shoveling vanilla ice cream into her mouth. Her dress was soaked through up to her waist and pushed up enough to expose the bruises on her thighs, but nobody was lucid enough to register them. Her naked feet tapped against the marble floors with a rhythm only she could hear. "What happened to your dress, sweetheart?" I asked, crouching down in front of her.

Her eyes flew open. "Hi."

"Hi."

"It's high-high tea," she whispered, chin not lifting from where it rested.

"Where are your shoes?" I asked, running a hand over her cold ankle.

"Oh!" She beamed up and jerked around, spoon pointing at the glass doors at the other end of the room. "There's a fountain."

That would also explain the state of her dress. "Alright. Come on, you promised me a sleepover on my sofa."

Her forehead wrinkled as she tried to piece together the fragments of our conversation from before. "You're not naked."

"Yeah, they let me in fully clothed." I chuckled and pulled her off the chair, fixing her dress around her thighs. We'd have to keep that thing around. It tightly hugged her ass, highlighting that gorgeous waist to hip ratio.

"Do you want ice cream?" she asked, twisting in my arms, and picking up another bowl off the table. "It's so tasty."

"That's not a good idea." I eyed the sprinkles that topped off the half-melted vanilla sundae – less of the chocolate, more of the cannabis variety.

A few minutes later, Del was sitting in the passenger seat of my car, and I pulled the seat belt around her while she ran a fingertip up and down the curve of my ear. "I have a secret," she whispered.

"I have many," I replied. One less now that I'd delete Scarlett's video off the cloud.

"I have two secrets." Her hand slid from my ear to my hair. I should have just gotten into the driver's seat and taken her home, but her eyes and hands on me were paralyzing in an excruciatingly delicious way.

"Anything I should know about?"

"No, no, he won't bother me anymore. He's been taken care of."

Her words dropped into the silence of the car like a man falling in a hushed ring, the thud of his body echoing for a moment before the roar of the crowd started. The roar being the rush of blood in my ears.

"Who?" My voice could have sliced steel. Who had bothered her to a point of it being kept secret and how had he been taken care of? Considering that Yelchin, that incapable joke of a bodyguard, was nowhere to be seen, while Del was soaked through, barefoot and high, surrounded by strangers. What exactly was his idea of *taking care* of someone?

Del furrowed her brow and the soft haze behind her eyes tipped. "Tag," she whispered.

"Tag? Who is Tag?"

"Tag," she hissed, more fervent, pulling her hands off me and grasping her neck. "Tag!" She scratched at the high neckline of her dress, nails digging into the fabric. Her breathing grew panicked as she tried to claw her way out of the collar, and it didn't click until fabric ripped. Tag. So much for keeping that dress around.

"Hold on, hold on," I pushed her forward and unzipped the back of her dress. The culprit was a thin black piece of scratchy fabric that I tore out with a single yank. A bigger paper tag slipped out of the dress, still attached to the fabric one. If you asked me, $1200 was too cheap for a dress this devastating. But with her aversion to any tags in her clothes, this seemed like an unlikely oversight.

She sagged back, sighing in relief, eyes fluttering shut, and I slipped the tags into my pocket before getting in the driver's seat.

A few minutes later, Del snapped upright, gasping: "You're driving."

"I prioritized speed over comfort tonight."

"Look at all those lights." Her hand snapped for the dashboard, and I gently pushed it back into her lap before she could put on the warning signal.

"Hey, look at those lights," I pointed towards the window and had her distracted for the rest of the ride with that, my thoughts spinning back to her words. *He won't bother me anymore. He won't bother me anymore. He won't bother me anymore.*

I put Del to bed.

I kicked the shit out of the punching bag on my sun deck for twenty minutes.

Then I picked up my phone.

BECK:
I need you to find someone.

It was past midnight, but the reply came immediately.

JULIAN:
Who?

THIRTY-SIX

Delilah

"So, I don't remember the full extent of how I ended up here. Were you driving?" I leaned in the doorframe and narrowed my eyes at Beck. He sat at his dining table, laptop and papers in front of him, a full breakfast spread on the other side of the table. My stomach gurgled in protest just at the thought of having to digest solid foods right now.

"I was," he replied and closed his laptop to look at me.

"Were you wearing lipstick?"

"No but you were trying to get me to. You thought that would help me blend in at the Marigold." A smile flashed over his lips.

"Ah yes," I nodded, "all that separates you from the prim and proper ladies at the Marigold Club is a bit of makeup."

"You need to drink a lot today." Mr. Change-the-Topic reached over and pushed a bottle of water across the table. "Stay hydrated, flush the systems."

"Thanks." I finally pushed myself out of the doorframe and walked over, the hardwood floors warm against my naked feet. I hadn't been able to find my dress, but I was sporting my old Taylor Swift shirt - the one so deformed it almost reached my knees now. My memories may have been patchy, but it didn't take much to piece together that he had taken care of me last night. And was still doing so now. "I've been high before, you know?"

"Really?" Actual surprise quirked his brow. "A prim and proper lady like yourself?"

"Defne wanted to try microdosing last year after breaking up with her fiancé, widen our horizons, and find answers to our troubles in the universe. She wasn't great at mathing out the micro- in microdosing though."

"And? Did your horizons widen?"

"I was convinced I was in a musical episode on TV and could only communicate through song, Tabitha spent half her monthly income on cheese and Defne was mainly crying in the bathtub in her wedding dress."

"How did the three of you meet?"

"Uh," my lips twitched at the memory, "in a bathroom."

"What is it with girls and bathrooms?"

Good question. I'd met Cordelia in one, too. There was nothing quite as bonding as a bathroom breakdown. "I was throwing up. My hair was longer then, and Defne took pity on me and braided it to keep it vomit-free. Tabitha was technically just vaping by the window, but she shared her gum with me when I was done. And the rest is history."

"What made you sick?"

"Those were the days I still got drunk on overpriced gin tonics." I shrugged and sipped on the water, which felt ten times better than any gin tonic, cooling my throat and flushing my mouth.

"I like your hair this short."

"Thanks," I chuckled, "do you have a Tabitha and Defne?"

"No," he said, "I have an Isaac, and I have Julian."

"Your brother?" I asked, because the other day it hadn't seemed like the two of them were the best of buddies.

"Yes. He's a dick but I know that I can trust him with my life. He's also the only person who understands what it means to be raised by Georgia Beckett."

"You've never mentioned your parents."

"Neither have you," he said and got out of his chair, leaning against his floor-to-ceiling windows instead, before he continued: "Georgia was always obsessed with power. I'm fairly certain it's because she never felt like she had any, grew up poor, married rich but turned out he was a tyrannical control-freak who knew every step she made, every person she talked to, every dollar she spent. The only power she ever really had was over her sons, so she named them after Roman emperors, Julius and Augustus, and made sure they learned to take what they want, without remorse for who might get hurt in the process. The Becketts against the world until the Becketts were on top of the world."

The bitterness in his voice cracked my chest wide open. I couldn't imagine that kind of dysfunctional family. My mom and I weren't super close, but there were no remarkable reasons for that. I'd just always been closer to Dad because we'd been so similar. Beck's family situation was way more complicated than that. "I'm sorry."

"Don't be. If it wasn't for Georgia's high expectations, I wouldn't be where I am today. I could have done without the whole murder thing, but you know as well as I that you can't choose your parents."

"Murder?" The water bottle slipped from my hand, and I barely caught it before it could flood the whole table.

He turned and looked at me and I got a strange feeling that I should have googled him more intensively. "You don't know?"

"No."

"Georgia killed my father around 15 years ago," he said with all the emotion of someone telling you that the sky was blue due to the particles in the air fracturing sunlight by color and blue happened to be the most visible. "She decided she'd had enough and would rather spend the rest of her life in prison than spend another moment shackled to that man. She could have easily paid for a hit or mixed up his heart medicine. I heard her mutter *'One day, I'll blow his brains out.'* so often growing up, I didn't think she'd go through with it."

"Oh god, Beck, I'm so sorry." That kind of tragedy had to leave a deep mark. Even if he'd been all grown-up when it happened. I stepped around the table, ready to give him a hug, but he waved me off.

"I've had time to cope. I just thought you would have run a full background check on me before ever setting foot in my place. Anyway, enough of that. I've been thinking about our date."

I'd get whiplash from his topic changes, but I was the last to protest when the topic of dead parents became too much to handle. I inhaled deeply, mentally saving all the information about his family, then letting my thoughts turn to our date on the exhale. "Any grand plans?"

"I'm guessing you won't let me whisk you off to London?"

"No."

"New York?" Beck walked towards me, not stopping until he was so close, I was forced to tilt my head back to look at him.

"No, sorry," I said. Even though New York was more doable, I'd rather not be crossing state lines with a fake ID. "How about we stay within like a 50-mile radius? I'm sure there's some good restaurants around here."

"You wanted a date, not a dinner." His hands folded around my neck, thumbs pressing in just enough for my pulse to spike, not enough for it to affect my breathing. "Anyone can buy you dinner, Blondie."

Translation: if I was going on a date with *him,* I'd know it. "Alright, no dinner. I guess you can take me on a carriage ride and sweep me off my feet."

"I'm not Prince Charming, sweetheart," he rasped before kissing me. My mouth parted for him on impact, allowing his tongue to sweep in. As he did, his pressure around my neck increased, air flow restricting. My eyes flew open as my body screamed for air, pulse rushing, muscles tensing, and then air rushed back into my lungs. I gasped but before I had a chance to take a full breath, his mouth was back on mine and my veins were thrumming with adrenaline. The shock that rippled through my body had set off a bright spark in my gut.

"Beck," his name was a plea on my lips.

"Your bath is ready."

"What?"

He pulled his phone from his pocket to show me the app that controlled his smart home features and the green markers next to the bathtub functions. "Best hangover cure. Breakfast will still be here by the time you get out."

Thoughts still blurring from the feel of his hands wrapped around my throat, I trotted to the bathroom and got in the bath on autopilot. I let the warm water and bubbles engulf me, and played with the settings for the lights and the massage jets. The best one was the jet that pushed deep into the tense muscles of my lower back. That tension had to come from weeks of sitting on the floor, hunched over books. Thinking about those books led to thinking about Beck's hands pressing into my flesh, and if I just shifted a little... If I got on my knees and held myself up by the edge of the tub... I let out a loud gasp as I found the angle that put the pressure right on my center. My body tensed as I allowed myself to mentally relive that moment over and over again, replaying the feel of his fingers tightening around my neck.

Kneeling like this, my chest hovered above water and as the cool air curled around my wet breasts, their peaks hardened. I reached down between my legs, opening myself for the airstream to hit my pressure points. My stomach tensed and my toes curled and even though I pressed my lips together, a sound of pleasure still vibrated through my throat.

My breathing grew ragged as I pushed myself closer to the stream, bubbles shooting at just- I just- I wan-

Wait, could you get a UTI from having air and soap water blasted at you?

My hand trembled. My fingers lost their grip. The airstream lost the right angle. Oh, for fuck's sake, could a girl not-

"-growth until 2025." The bathroom door swung open to reveal Beck, on his phone. I froze under his gaze as it traveled down my body, along where my hand disappeared under the bubbles, to the stream of water clearly gushing through the gap between my legs. Understanding passed his features. "We're not pushing our OKRs for any reason, Jonas," he said to the other person on the phone, but the tilt of his chin was clearly meant for me.

No judgement, just interest in my progress.

I shook my head.

Beck crossed the distance to the tub in three long strides. Phone between his ear and his shoulder, he rolled up the sleeves of his shirt, the veins outlined under his tan skin. Without taking his eyes off me, Beck lowered himself next to the tub until he was on my eye level. "Need I remind you that last year you were the one who recommended we switch to a new system? If said system is malfunctioning, that's your head on the line." Despite his harsh words to whoever was on the phone, when he slipped his hand into the water, his touch was gentle as his fingers traced up the inside of my thigh until they found my own hand still resting aimlessly between my legs. His eyes softened for a moment when he smiled at me and slipped his hand under mine.

My muscles twitched as he parted me again, and with his palm on my pelvic bone, pushed my hips back in line with the jet's stream. The pressure picked up exactly where it had left off. I grasped Beck's wrist underwater and suppressed the hitched sound trying to escape.

He'd know, right? He'd know if I was putting my health at risk in his tub, and he'd not encourage that, right? But why on earth was he on a call? He couldn't expect me to get anywhere, knowing that he was doing *business* while his hand was between my legs.

"We wouldn't be on this call if I wasn't ready to compromise," he said and pushed his palm down to maneuver my hips against the nozzle, where the jets sprouted with full intensity. I moaned at the sudden burst against my clit, then froze under Beck's raised brows. Shit.

We should stop. This wasn't going to end well for him. I'd be too loud and then I wouldn't even come, *all build-up no reward*. But his call would be ruined orgasm or not. I moved to get off the nozzle, but instead of letting me go, Beck pushed his thumb hard against my clit. I toppled forward and sank my teeth into his shoulder, my sounds stifled by muscle and expensive cotton. Cotton that brushed against my hardened nipples, sending a different wave of pleasure to my core.

"Trust me," he still sounded so calm on the phone while he wreaked havoc on me with his thumb, "I'd rather lose out on 5% this year than spend the next twenty dealing with more policy-pushers who think-" I didn't hear the rest of his words as the blinding rush of pleasure crashed over me, the taste of his shirt on my tongue and the hard water relentless against my clit. I bucked against him and clawed at the arm and shoulder that held me in place until the quivers stopped rocking through my body. I slumped forward, out of breath. My aimless fingers slapped at the control panel on the wall to switch off the bubbles. Instead, Beck reached around me and pressed the button that turned on *all* the jets.

I winced at the sudden pressure needling into me on all sides when every inch of my skin was on high alert to every touch.

"Who makes you come, Blondie?" Beck asked, and a shiver rolled down my spine at the tone of his voice. Guess the phone call was over.

I tried to lean back, but he still had one hand between my legs, and the other had come around the back of my neck in a hard grip. I was locked in place, riding his arm, my face pressed into his shirt. "Just you," I whispered, voice muffled by his shoulder.

"Didn't I tell you *not* to touch yourself when you're here?"

"You did."

"And? Did you touch yourself?"

"Yes."

"Do you need a reminder of who gets to touch you?"

His words resparked the fire that had just died down, but with it came a twinge of pain. The burning token of his last *reminder* still under my skin. "Wait," I breathed and tapped the hold he had on my neck. Beck loosened his grip, allowing me to lean back. I blinked as the rest of the bathroom came back into view, his phone discarded on the floor, a small puddle of soapy water beside it, Beck's charcoal eyes on me, waiting for me. Communication. "I don't... You said..." The words died on my tongue. I tried to think a straight line through the haze in my head, coming up with nothing but jumbled phrases.

"I said," Beck picked up one of my hands, whispering a soft kiss to the inside of my wrist, "if you touched yourself at my place again, I would tie you to my headboard."

"Yes."

"I said," he placed my hand down on the edge of the tub and picked up the other one, mirroring the soft kiss, "that I would spank your ass until you begged me to fuck you."

I nodded and watched him arrange my second hand a precise shoulder-length from the other. "I can't do that again," I said. "Not yet."

"Don't worry." He reached around me and lifted me to my knees in one quick move, placing me sideways in the tub to face him. "There's so many ways I can show you that you're mine to touch." His mouth came down on mine in a hungry kiss while he pulled my thighs apart, opening me for the symphony of jets. I whimpered into the kiss when one of them hit my throbbing bundle of nerves, but then Beck's hand was on my throat again, squeezing hard enough for the sound to die. That one move sent an electric shock through my system, every other sensation suddenly multiplied tenfold as my brain tried to catch up with the panic gripping my body. When he leaned out of the kiss and his hand dropped, I was gasping for air, lungs aching, and if I just reached down, I was sure it would take no more than twenty seconds for me to come again.

"Keep your hands on the bathtub," he said and stood, "only tap my thigh if you need me to stop."

Before I could formulate the question, he freed his thick, pulsing erection. He was already glistening with pre-cum. And when he grabbed my chin and pushed his thumb against my bottom lip, my mouth fell open readily. "Look at that pretty mouth, so eager to please." His thumb dipped past my lips pressing down my tongue. His taste and strength mingled in my mouth and stole the breath from my lungs. "When you're choking on my cock, what's that going to remind you of, Blondie?"

He removed his finger to let me answer. "That you're the only one who gets to touch me," I gasped, "that I'm yours."

"That's right," he said, positioning his tip on my lips, his delicious salty taste making me heady, "and I'm the only one who gets to fuck that mouth of yours." He slammed his cock past my lips so hard tears sprung to my eyes. He fisted my hair, locking me in place, but he didn't move, giving me a moment to adjust, temper my breathing, relax my throat around his girth. I blinked up at him, almost surprised to find nothing but warmth in his eyes. His thumb caressed down the side of my face, soothing the sharp pain in my jaw. "You're so fucking beautiful," he breathed, chest rising and falling hard, as he pulled his cock back an inch. "Now open wide, so you can take the rest of me."

Open wide? Wider? Rest of him? My mouth was already-fuck. He snapped his hips forward, pushing himself deeper into me. I couldn't breathe and I couldn't swallow, and I struggled against his grip on me, scalp burning, and then he pulled back, granting me relief and air for just a second. He thrust forward again. Pain shot through my neck and my jaw before he pulled out. He kept repeating, each violent thrust coming faster and harder.

"That's it, you're taking me so well." Tears welled over my lashes as I squeezed my eyes shut. Beck suddenly paused, pulling back slowly. "Look at me," he rasped. I blinked up at him through the tears and winced when he pulled out. My lips trembled but I swallowed his taste, my jaw easing at the moment of respite. He glanced down at me with so much affection, my insides tensed as he brushed the tears off my cheeks.

"I'm good," I croaked, my throat rough, "just not the kind of blow job I'm used to."

"I told you. I take what I want." His thumb grazed down my cheek and into my mouth, the taste of my own tears mixing with his arousal on my tongue. "And you are *mine*."

Those four little letters sent a warm tremor through me. My lips closed around his thumb, and I sucked it with hollowed cheeks the way I would have sucked him if I had initiated a blow job. I let my tongue curl around his finger. Beck's eyes darkened, and the muscle in his jaw ticked. In response, my walls pulsed, just knowing I could push him off balance with the flick of my tongue.

"I'm not done with you yet," he growled and pressed his thumb down, wrenching my mouth open again. "Eyes on me."

I kept my gaze locked on his when he filled my mouth again.

He didn't ease me into it this time, pushing fast and deep. He was *fucking* my mouth so hard it hurt. I let the pain flow through me, the heat cursing down my neck and into my veins. I lost my whole body in it. Every cell was buzzing, every muscle twitching against his thrusts. And oh god, the jets were still shooting streams straight at me. I pushed my hips against the side of the tub, finding a nozzle to hit my clit, and with my entire body caught on the verge, I came again, moaning with his cock on my tongue and my eyes on his.

"Fuck," he gasped and spilled himself in my mouth. My knuckles turned white on the edge of the tub, as I struggled to breathe through my orgasm and his cum down my throat. With one deep thrust, he released the last of it before pulling out. Gasping and struggling for air, I fell back, blinking through the haze to see him bent down and leaning onto the tub, breathing just as hard, forehead beaded in sweat.

I swallowed the taste of him but wiped the mess around my mouth and chin off with bathwater, a big grin stealing onto my lips. "I'm going to need a shower after this bath," I said, voice scratched up. I reached behind me and switched off the bubbles, the water calming around me within seconds.

"Jesus fuck, Del," Beck gasped, a hint of laughter creeping in as he slumped down next to the tub and pulled me forward for a soft kiss. "I have to be honest, I thought you'd tap out, and then you just go and come with my cock in your mouth."

"I've always been a fast learner," I grinned, "besides, I just did that thing I read about, where you try to channel the pain through your whole body instead of concentrating on its source. Safe to say, it worked."

"You're such a nerd," he chuckled and dropped his forehead against mine, "but I'm sorry to say, your breakfast eggs are probably cold now."

"Well, I already had a hot breakfast…"

THIRTY-SEVEN

BECK

"The ownership transition is going to be finalized in two weeks, Beck," Julian reminded me like a relentless calendar app pop-up.

"Don't worry, we'll be as good as engaged by then." No need to tell him that Del refused to acknowledge that we were even dating. I should have just taken her to dinner instead of promising her some grand evening. At least then she couldn't avoid the fact that we were a thing anymore. It would have been the sensible solution, but my choices concerning her made less and less sense by the day.

"I don't understand your problem with just knocking her up." He leaned back in his chair and pulled an orange pill bottle from his desk drawers. I didn't even want to know what that was. I shot him a withering glare, but he just responded with a shrug. "That would make things so much easier. I doubt she'd say no if there was a baby in the picture."

"She'll say yes."

"I should help things along."

He opened his laptop.

I snapped it shut.

"Julius," I warned him, his birth name slipping out in a tone eerily similar to Georgia's. Our mother had named us Julius and Augustus, and we'd both legally changed the names the week after she killed our father. One less reminder of her obsession with power. Not that it wasn't ingrained in us.

He held up his hands, capitulating. "Show me real progress by the end of the week or I'll go digging."

"Don't you have more useful things to do? Did you find out who's been troubling Del?"

"There are no traces of blackmail." He shrugged. "No remarkable assets shifting."

Blackmail was usually where things started. Every year, some new asshole cropped up, thinking they could make money or climb the social ladder by holding something over your head. But blackmail wasn't where these things ended. And I doubted the ghostly look on Del's face had been down to some asshole trying to get rich quick. "Dig deeper."

"Not to point out the obvious, but maybe just ask her. If this is something that could endanger the merger, we should know."

The merger was the last thing on my mind when her words still echoed in my ears. *He won't bother me anymore.* The hollow note in her voice so similar to my own when I'd announced our father's passing to the public. Couldn't even feign mourning that bastard. "She doesn't even remember telling me."

"Then get her high again." He pulled another pill bottle from his desk with a huge grin, placing it next to the first.

"You realize you're not above the company's drug policy, right?"

"I have prescriptions." He shrugged. "I could hack Cordelia's emails if you think that would help. But it'll take some time to make sure it won't come up if the Axent-Montgomery merger is ever investigated."

"Fucking hell." I rubbed my eyes and waved him off. Within ten minutes he'd suggested impregnating and drugging Del, as well as some light privacy infringement via cybercrimes. All in the name of business. I could get on board with hijacking a company from the inside out, but if there were lines in the sand, Julian was the guy who paved over the whole goddamn beach and erected another Axent Grand with ocean view VIP suites. "Just keep digging. There has to be some sort of paper trail."

"I FOUND THE MONEY." JONAS WALTZED INTO MY OFFICE HOURS later, like I didn't have an assistant meant to keep anyone without a scheduled meeting far away from me. I glanced at Clarice's empty desk outside, then dragged my eyes back to Jonas.

"The money you lost?" I asked, wondering if he really wanted me to congratulate him on doing the bare minimum.

"400 acres in the South Pacific." He tossed an open folder onto the desk in front of me. A bird's eye picture of a lush green island, with a cluster of buildings in its center, was clipped to a stack of papers. The neat rows of dark green plants left little doubt about it being used as a plantation. "That's what 120 million gets you."

"Are you telling me we're bankrolling a weed farm off the books?" Ignoring the principle of the situation, there had to be cheaper ways to grow a drug that was legal in many parts of the country now.

"Yes and no."

"Explain."

"It's not ours. The money was funneled from Axent, split into around a dozen shell companies all over the world. Twelve little companies, each worth 10 million, none of them directly tied to us anymore. Then another company, called Cryptiq Estates, bought said shell companies for pennies on the dollar, dissolved them, and bought that island. With our money."

With every twist in that story, a dull pulse grew stronger behind my temples. *Thump, thump, thump.* We had found each and every leak in our books. Not how they'd gotten there, not where they'd gone, but we'd found the holes. They had been strategically poked, needle thin, money trickling from a restaurant here and a beach resort there. If only one had been discovered, it would have looked like a single shady manager pocketing some revenue. All 49 leaks, however, added up to 120 million in damages. Which meant we had a problem in the C-suite, or on the board.

"Do you come offering a solution, or is your letter of resignation in here somewhere?" I snapped the folder shut and raised my brows at Jonas, who finally had the good sense to look a little frazzled. I may have been making the executive decisions around here, but Jonas had spent the last seven years becoming an essential gear in the Axent machine. We wouldn't have made it through the pandemic without his understanding of international finance laws. But every gear was replaceable if it wore out over time.

"I want an outside consultant on this," he said.

"No."

"Look at that first page again. Look at the name."

My nostrils flared, but I reopened the folder. A bitter taste filled my mouth when I found the line that named the island's owner. Just one name. No first name. "Yelchin."

"You know who that is?" Jonas asked.

"Yes."

"Someone here hitched their wagon to the wrong horse, and I'm not poking that beast."

Nobody in their right mind would poke that beast. Even the feds had given up years ago. *Thump, thump, thump.* The beating grew louder, hammering in my ears. "Il ne faut pas réveiller le chat qui dort." The words rushed out of me in a low growl.

"Excuse me?"

"Call him." I pulled my wallet out and slipped a business card out from behind my Amex. "Tell him I'm cashing in my favor."

Jonas picked up the card and blinked. "I don't think your doctor will be able to help us with this."

"Trust me."

"Beck, if I'm getting myself into the cross hairs, you have to tell me. I'm taking full responsibility, and I'm going down with this ship if I have to, but I'd prefer to get my family on a lifeboat first."

"Nobody is going down." I snapped the folder shut again and slid it back across the desk. "Destroy this. Call Isaac. It's time for him to put his diplomatic connections to good use."

I had already rocked the boat with Scarlett to get Del out of the Marigold, but apparently, I was dead set on destroying all my friendships. I could have found a different way out of this, given time and resources, one that didn't require Isaac to become the man he never wanted to be, but I didn't have time. Not when Del was living under the same roof as Victor Yelchin. I didn't need to know *how* he was connected to all of this, to figure out that the consequences for Blondie could be catastrophic if he so much as suspected we were looking into him. If this had landed on my desk weeks ago, I wouldn't have trusted a word out of Del's mouth, figuring they worked together to target me just like I had targeted her. She just wasn't that good an actress.

Grinding my molars together, I pulled my phone out and opened the text chain with Del. I'd have to get her out of that house before Isaac had the chance to set things in motion with his family.

THIRTY-EIGHT

Delilah

"Your mail," Victor dropped a stack of envelopes and leaflets at the foot of my bed, all addressed to my studio, which he frequently checked on. This had become routine since I wasn't supposed to go home.

"Thank you." I grabbed the large, bulky envelope sticking out from the rest. It had the Truman Academy crest on it. I'd signed the work contract digitally, so this had to be my onboarding package. My badge, my map of the school, and whatever else the HR department of one of the country's most prestigious schools whipped up. I clutched the envelope - and I didn't want to open it. I should have been tearing through the paper, studying every detail of my schedule, starting a new project book for the school year, picking out my highlighters and ordering new sticky notes.

"Everything alright?" Victor asked, his lime green eyes burrowing into me.

"Yeah," I exhaled and turned the envelope around to show him, "it's work."

"Hmm." He nodded and turned, no comment or opinion. "Cordelia wants to talk to you before you go."

"Thanks." I dropped the letter back onto the pile and turned my attention back to the weekender I'd been in the middle of packing. I'd deal with my new future on Monday. For now, I could focus on rolling my clothes and sorting them into neat packing cubes.

Beck had convinced me to widen my travel radius to 85 miles, so he could take me to Cape Cod for the weekend. It was at least within state lines, and he'd promised his house there was on mainland. While Martha's Vineyard might have sounded nice, I wouldn't have crossed any open water with a fake ID either.

When I was finished packing, I left my bag at the foot of the stairs and checked on Cordelia in her office.

"How could you be so fucking careless?" Cordelia's voice was barely raised, but this was the first time I'd heard her curse, and I flinched back.

"What does it matter?" I asked, waving the printed article through the air. Apparently, someone had snapped a picture of me carrying a huge white bag out of the wedding dress shop, where I'd gotten my high tea outfit. Between being seen with Beck at multiple events and these pictures, rumors were brewing, but they were just that. Rumors. "There's no ring on my finger. There's no wedding announcement. I'll just let people know that I was there for a friend and the rumors will die."

"I don't have friends!"

Cordelia's reply hung in the air between us. Four words that had nothing to do with the article. A pained confession too thick for the few minutes we had before Beck would show up to whisk me off for a few days.

"You have me," I said, trying to keep my voice calm, "I actually consider us friends."

"You're basically my employee."

I tried not to let the words sting because she was right, but she was also unaware of how much that didn't matter. "So is Victor."

"Yes, he is. And both of you should remember that."

"I'm sorry," I sighed, "I'm sorry that I went into a bridal shop. I will do whatever you need me to do to fix this, and then I'll be out of your hair in like two weeks."

"Being perceived as Beck's girlfriend is fine, Delilah, but you can't go around making it seem like there's a marriage on the horizon. A marriage is a contract, and a contract has business repercussions. Why don't you get that?"

"I'm sorry," I said again. "I'll take Victor to an event next week if you want. Make it look like I'm totally over Beck."

"No," Cordelia huffed, "we'll get through the next two weeks."

I sighed and rubbed my hands over my eyes. "Speaking of, could you please make an appointment with whatever hairdresser you deem discreet enough? Ginger hair, bangs, and a pair of costume glasses, and nobody will ever see this version of Cordelia Montgomery again."

"Del, it's-" She cut herself off, then picked her phone up. "I've already booked the appointment for you. August 26th, the day after the White Ball. It's a Saturday, and I blocked out the whole afternoon in case the color doesn't take. You'll still have all Sunday to move back home. Forwarding it now."

The date burned itself into my mind. August 26th. Sixteen days before I stopped being Cordelia Montgomery. Under different circumstances, I would have asked more about the White Ball, but all I could think was that two weeks with Beck were both too long, because *every minute* spent with him would make it harder to detach myself, and not long enough, because I wanted to spend an *infinity of minutes* with him.

"If the two of you are done, Mr. Beckett's car just pulled up." Victor announced from the doorway.

"*Mister* Beckett?" I grimaced at him. He'd never called him that. Was he getting sick?

"How long have you been standing there?" Cordelia asked.

"Only a few minutes, Miss Cordelia."

"What? *Miss* Co- oh." I shut up before I got sucked into an argument about appropriate employer-employee relationships. Thankfully, the doorbell saved me from the electric stare-off between them. "I got it."

Beck was a vision of summer chic, in light gray chinos, an Armani belt and a white shirt with the top buttons undone and the sleeves rolled up to reveal his wired forearms. It was the most casual outfit I'd ever seen him in. In public, at least. (Not counting his sex club jeans.) And he still looked like he belonged on the cover of GQ, leaning against a sleek, dark blue car like that. So pretty, the discussion I'd just had with Cordelia vanished from my mind.

"Are you driving?" I asked by way of greeting.

"Unless you want to."

I faltered in my steps and gave the car another once over. "Would you actually let me drive your Porsche?"

"Do you know how to drive a stick without getting in an accident?" He popped the trunk and took the CM-monogrammed leather bag from my hands.

"I do."

"Go for it, Charlie." He tossed the key through the air.

I barely caught it. "Charlie?"

"Top Gun reference."

"I'm too young to get that reference." I grinned and wiggled my brows at him, but he just rolled his eyes, a small smile on his lips. I got in the driver's seat, where my feet didn't even come close to the pedals. It took me a few minutes to adjust everything to my height, but once I had it, the car slid through the streets as smooth as butter in a hot pan. "Holy shit," I breathed once we got out of the city and onto the MA-3 and the car straight-up purred under my feet.

"I didn't know I was dating a Formula One driver," Beck chuckled.

"I wish," I grinned, curving the car around the slow snails on the road, "my dad used to take me driving."

"Really?" Beck asked, and the surprise in his voice hit me like a bucket of cold water.

"Uh..." Somehow, I doubted that Montgomery senior had taken Cordelia anywhere at all. Fuck it. Two weeks. It didn't goddamn matter anymore whether it all added up. "Yeah. He had an old Mustang that he tinkered with whenever he had to get out of his head. Then took me driving whenever I had to get out of mine. I was 13 and giving Lewis Hamilton a run for his money."

"What happened to the car?"

"It's collecting dust. I considered taking it, but I've not been able to look at it since he got sick." My dad got sick a few years before Cordelia's but that hardly mattered in the grand scheme of the Cordelias. A dead father was a dead father, right?

"I'm sorry, Blondie."

"Don't be. I'll get it fixed up someday, but I'll just borrow your car for now whenever I want to go for a ride." I ran my hands over the smooth leather of the steering wheel.

"I'll get you your own and we'll go for a race."

"You make your little jokes," I clicked my tongue at him, "but you would have your ass handed to you if you raced me."

"Oh, I wasn't joking. I see you shaving minutes off the GPS estimate, sweetheart."

I laughed, my eyes skipping from the street to the GPS for just a moment. "If you're getting me a Porsche, it better be Porsche-red."

"Consider it done." He pulled his phone out and started typing something.

"Wait what?"

"Eyes on the road," he said in that tone that made my thighs clench and my tongue run dry.

"Don't buy me a car," I protested when I found my voice again.

"Too late." He chuckled.

"How can it be too late? It's been 60 seconds."

"I have a guy."

"You have a Porsche guy?"

"More a… vehicle guy." He reached over, slipping one hand into the back of my neck and I had to bite my lip to keep my attention on the road. "Bikes, cars, boats. I tell him what I need, and he gets it for me."

"You don't need another Porsche," I said, the argumentative parts of my brain weakened by his fingertips running along the nape of my neck.

"I do, so I can give it to you and race you."

"Well, you better keep the receipt because-"

"There. Done. It'll be waiting for you once we get back." He placed his phone in the bluetooth holder and put on a playlist of summer oldies. Mr. Blue Sky filled the car, the cheerful melody making it impossible to keep the smile off my face.

"You're incorrigible."

THIRTY-NINE

BECK

"Don't get me wrong, but this isn't what I expected."

"I know." Which was exactly why I'd brought her here and not to the villa on the Amalfi coast. "This is the house my grandfather bought when Axent took off."

She ran her hand over the weathered metal plaque on the gate to the front yard. Swirling letters proclaimed the house to be *Casa de Camila*. "Was Camila your grandmother?"

"Yes." I tried to see the house through her eyes, not those of a boy who spent his favorite summers here. I spared no expense to keep the small cottage in top shape, gardening, housekeeping, maintenance… and years ago, my father had bought all the land behind it to ensure it would always be a beachfront property, but it was always going to be just a yellow two-bedroom bungalow with less square footage than my living room. I hadn't even changed the bright blue window shutters or expanded the patio behind the house, although both would have made sense.

"Can we go inside?"

"No, you saw it, now we can turn around and go check into the Nantucket Montgomery Inn." She spun around, brows drawn so deep, her glare could have pierced armor. "Kidding," I added and grabbed our bags from the trunk. Julian hadn't blinked twice at signing his half of the cottage over to me since it was a residential area and he laughed at the profit margin of tearing down the cottage to build a mansion to sell.

Del ran careful fingertips over the tall lavender trailing up to the house, eyes wandering over the plants, then the carved woodwork of the patio, before finally landing on the large C etched into the door. "I gather your grandfather really loved your grandma."

I unlocked the door and motioned for her to go in first. "If he didn't, I wouldn't be here today."

Inside, a vague scent of fresh linen lingered, thanks to the housekeeper who had readied the place for us. The layout was modest, with the master bedroom and bathroom on one side of the entry, the kids' room on the other side, and the living room and kitchen at the backend of the house, with large windows granting a look at the beach.

"I hate to break it to you, but a lot of lineages are born from sex, not love."

"That's not what I meant," I placed our bags on the master bed, feeling her eyes trained on my back. "They lived in Boston, but neither of them wanted more than this." I twirled my finger to indicate the house. "A small house, kids…" I gestured to the room on the opposite side of the hall, where two twin beds were neatly made, "and a restaurant to call their own. But my grandmother was unhappy in the city. No matter how well she dressed, how successful the restaurant was, how well-mannered and eloquent she was, she was still a Mexican woman in 1950s Boston. Even on a good day, people would still make fun of the way she spoke, so my grandfather sold the restaurant, and asked my grandmother for one more year." I slipped my hand around Del's and pulled her down the hallway to the living room, where a hand-painted business sign hung on the wall above the sofa. "And he opened the first Axent Luxe. A luxury lounge for the richest people of the city, including three exclusive hotel rooms that were only rented to members, not the public. Everyone who's anyone wanted a key to the Axent lounge. And all because my grandfather swore nobody would ever make fun of my grandmother's accent again."

"Hmm." She tilted her head, regarding the old Axent Luxe sign with its swirling 50s font.

"What are you thinking?"

She opened her mouth, then closed it again, and turned to face me. "I need you to be honest with me."

"Okay."

"Is this your move? Do you bring girls here and sweep them off their feet with some love story? Because that's a really good story and I'll be extremely cross with you if you're just making that up to get in my pants."

"I've already been in your pants, Blondie." I shook my head at her and turned her by the shoulders to the wall behind her, to the framed black and white picture of my grandparents kissing under the Axent Luxe sign. "Camila and Frederick Beckett."

Her features softened and she leaned in to inspect the picture closer. "They look so happy."

"They were. Madly in love their whole lives."

"Lucky." She sighed. "Very few people have that. I'm glad they got their happy end."

"Luck and a lot of work. They made many compromises throughout their lives, adjusted expectations. Having only one child instead of two. Having a vacation home on the beach instead of living there full-time…"

Del straightened, eyes wandering over the rest of the pictures on the wall. "Is this you?" She pointed at a picture of me on a boat when I was around 24. One of the last additions my grandmother put up.

"Yes."

"You were around my age in this, weren't you?"

"A little younger, but not far off."

"I would have never gone out with you at that age."

"No?"

"If this was your dating app picture, I'd expect you to tell me about your media start-up, your podcast and Elon Musk's latest 'stroke of genius' within the first 5 messages." She giggled to herself, tapping the glass of the frame. "But now I know what Tabitha meant when she said you look like you fuck."

"I do what?"

"This guy looks like he sleeps with women." Del grinned and patted the frame like the head of a puppy, then turned to me and pointed her finger up and down my body. "But all grown-up? This guy looks like he fucks."

"I feel like I should give Tabitha a call."

"Defne agrees with her. Apparently, it's a thing."

"How attached are you to your friends?"

"How attached are you to your genitals?"

"Fair enough."

We finished the tour of the house with a quick glance into the kitchen, just big enough for one counter with all the essential appliances and a small table with four mismatched chairs. The backdoor led from the kitchen to the back porch. There was still a whole lot of beach between the house and the waterfront, but at least the ocean was in view. It would be even closer for the morning high tide.

I'd thought Del's presence was intoxicating when we were cooped up in my library, but that turned out to be nothing against

Del on a beach. She kicked her shoes off after a few steps off the patio, started running - and I had no chance of keeping up for the rest of the afternoon. She charged into the ocean and ran back out squealing when a wave chased after her. She collected a dozen identical shells and gave each one a name, placing them in my palms - and I learned the hard way, after dropping Wallabee in the water, that she would mourn the loss of a single shell for at least 15 minutes. So I pocketed them all. She told me about not being diagnosed with anxiety until she was 21, and autistic at 22, because her father had been convinced overthinking every minuscule detail was normal. Turned out, he was also autistic and had anxiety. And she told me about adopting her cat shortly afterwards as emotional support - only to be given the least affectionate, grumpy cat in the world, who hissed at her if she tried to pet him.

We bought snacks and drinks in town and sat on the porch swing, and I told her about going to boarding school in England for two years, and the year I studied in France and started writing poetry, convinced that would get me laid. I told her about my father micro-managing every aspect of his life, but not giving a shit about his sons until they were 16, old enough to have a 'sensible' conversation with.

She asked to try a drag from the Cohiba I'd brought but dissolved into a coughing fit and chugged her grape juice like cheap beer to chase the taste. Chocolate and coffee according to cigar lovers. Wet leather and moldy driftwood according to her.

She spent 20 minutes in the bathroom brushing her teeth when the juice didn't help.

"Not a bad first date," she sighed and dropped into the pillows face-down. She wore the soft Afghan blanket from the living room around her shoulders, covering the short, silky nightgown that had given me half a heart attack five minutes earlier.

I eyed the heap of crochet, skin and blonde hair in bed next to me. This was good. Not how I'd expected it to go, but everything considered, there could be worse things than spending the rest of my life with a girl whose company I actually enjoyed. "Are you still alive, Blondie?"

She made a non-committal sound.

"I need to ask you something," I said, trying to get a rise out of her. She just turned her head, blinking at me through a curtain of blonde hair. "The wedding dress shop?"

She groaned and rolled over, folding herself into the Afghan like a burrito, glowering at me. "What?"

"Anything you want to tell me?"

"I needed a dress for High Tea, and I had to buy it discreetly, because it had to be fitted to hide my bruised wrists." She rushed the words out in a tone that suggested I wasn't the only one who had asked about those pictures. "Defne knows the owner. That's all."

"Defne knows the owner?"

"Yes. That's all. Don't worry, I'm not dragging you to the altar."

"Del, the owner is the one who tipped off the press."

"What?"

"Janice Terry. She made the call at some point while you were in the shop. That's how the photographer knew where you were."

"Ohmygod." She pulled the Afghan up over her head.

"Hey," I leaned over and slipped a finger into the blanket, pulling it down just enough to kiss her. "For what it's worth, when I get married, I won't need dragging. I'll be the one waiting at the altar."

"What?" She blew strands of hair from her face, wriggling for a better view. "You said that you don't do monogamy."

Pointing out that plenty of marriages were non-monogamous probably wouldn't help. Not that I'd even been tempted by anyone since Del had started rearranging my bookshelves. Even before that, the only woman I'd been with in weeks had been nothing but a quick release after Blondie had gotten my systems going. "Yeah, but I also used to look like someone who sleeps with women, and now I look like I fuck. People change."

She snorted a laugh. "Okay, you almost had me."

Goddammit. I reached over and pulled her to me by the back of her neck, wrangling a choked squeal from her lips at the sudden roughness of my touch, and I kissed her long and hard enough for desperate gasps to sneak in between our lips. She tried to untangle herself and reach for me, but her hands were caught in the loose yarn of the Afghan, sparking around a dozen ideas of how I could make this cocoon work for me. For now, I leaned back and held her with my hand around her throat, forcing her chin up to meet my gaze. "I told you, Blondie. You're *mine*. I don't care how we got here or if you need a ring or anything else as a reminder of that, but that won't change. Ever."

Her pulse was hammering fast under my hand and her lips trembled as she looked up at me with those ocean eyes. "I'm sorry."

"For what?"

"I..." She swallowed, throat bobbing under my touch, then tapped my wrist. "Please stop. I'm too tired for any *reminders* tonight. Sorry."

I pulled my hand off her and cursed myself for my fucking choice of words. Del turned over, hiking the blanket higher again, driving home the point that I was not to touch her tonight. At least not like that.

I switched the lights off and stared at the ceiling, a throbbing crescendo behind my temples as I listened to her breathing even out.

It shouldn't have bothered me that her mind had gone there, when I'd just told her- Merger aside, I couldn't help but- I mean- *Fuck.*

The lingering pressure in my head evaporated the next morning at the sight of Del in a pale blue triangle bikini that left very little to the imagination. Her nose had taken on a sun-kissed tint from the day before, but that was all the color on her face. No signature red lipstick or winged eyeliner. She'd not even bothered with her hair, throwing it all into a clip at the back of her head.

I leaned in the hallway, watching her zoom through the living room and back to the kitchen, back and forth, while she filled the basket that usually housed a bunch of old boating magazines, muttering instructions to herself.

"Sunglasses, sunglasses, sunglasses." She touched the top of her head - no sunglasses - and scanned the living room before her eyes finally found me. "Hi." Her face lit up and whatever ache I'd felt in my temples last night, plummeted to my chest. "Wanna come swimming with me?"

"Breakfast?" I had plans to show her how to make a *good* frittata with less eggshells and sugar.

"Already packed." She pointed at her basket, and rolled her eyes at me because I must have looked skeptical. "Fruit, cheese, bread, juice. I washed the fruit but everything else is exactly as bought."

"You didn't wash the fruit with soap water, did you?"

"Ohmygod, you're uninvited. I'm going alone."

"I'll change. Give me a minute."

Weeks of unrelenting sunshine had warmed the shallow beach waters. It made wading in easy, but Del stopped just when it hit her waist, pulling her shoulders up. "It's too deep. I can't. I'll just stay here."

"This is the part of going swimming, where you actually have to swim."

"But there's crabs and jellyfish and those big round fish that sting you and you die. Or what if there's sharks? I read about shark attacks around the Cape."

Despite my first instinct being to tell her that she wouldn't be attacked by a shark, I knew that would do nothing to reassure her. "If you get attacked by a shark, you pee at it and you whack it in the nose."

"Are you serious?"

"Yes, human urine and a punch in the nose, best shark deterrents."

"I just…"

"Come here," I sighed and lowered myself in front of her, back turned towards her. She climbed on without questioning, wrapping her arms around my neck and her knees around my waist. Tension burrowed through my hips at how her body pressed against mine. "See? Not so bad," I said after walking far enough for me to keep both of us afloat, a few feet between me and the sea floor.

"I never swam in the ocean before." Her words were a quiet admission by my ear.

"Never?"

She shook her head. "Tried many times, but never made it further than up to my belly button."

I reached up and pulled her around to face me. I held her steady by the waist, but her fingernails still dug deep into my forearms, her lips trembling as she looked down at the chasm of dark water between us. "How are you feeling?"

"Very close to having a panic attack." She hiccupped a nervous laugh. "Please don't let go."

"I won't."

"How are you so calm right now?"

"I don't know," I replied honestly because I didn't fully comprehend how her brain kept trying to convince her that the worst-case scenario was always the most likely one. "I don't worry as much."

"I worry all the time. I can't eat food beyond the expiration date, hate going into basements, don't do heights. I even break down in tears at the dentist." Her breath stuttered. "Ironic, isn't it? The girl with the mermaid story can't even go in the ocean."

"You're already in the ocean," I said.

"I am," she breathed, brows crinkling, eyes locked to the water. We stayed like this, bobbing in place, the current pushing us closer to shore, then pulling us back again, until her grasp on my arms eased up and she blinked and looked up, finding my eyes. "You're a very patient man, August Beckett."

"Hmmm..." I'd been called many things, but patient wasn't one of them. A cynical part of me wanted to claim that I was just working a long con, but a more integral part that was growing louder by the day was very aware of the fact that I wanted to be there for every new *first* in her life, no matter how long she took to work up to them. "Only when I want to be."

"I think you're nicer than you want to admit."

"Blondie, I'm not nice."

"Agree to disagree." She slid her hands up my arms and pulled herself closer by my shoulders, legs mingling between mine. "Good thing I have a soft spot for nice boys with private libraries." She smiled and leaned in for a kiss and before our lips could meet, I snatched her bottom lip between my teeth and bit down at the same time as grabbing her ass and squeezing hard. She let out a high-pitched squeal, eyes widening.

"Call me nice boy one more time," I warned, voice dropped to gravel as I maneuvered us closer to the shore to where I could stand but she couldn't.

"I mean..." Her chest trembled against mine. "You already know that all of that works for me. That means you're literally trying to prove that you aren't nice by providing me with a good time."

Two precise tugs and the strings of her bikini top came loose. I pulled it off her and balled it in my fist. Del gasped and immediately pushed herself against me, eyes darting left and right. Her soft curves pressed against my chest, and heat that had nothing to do with the summer sun simmered beneath my skin. "How about now?" I asked and pushed my hand into the tight space between our bodies. My thumb brushing over her nipple, playing with it, flicking it, rolling it under my finger, I watched her face tighten.

"This is a private beach, right?" she asked, voice shaking.

"Theoretically," I said and pulled my hand back, "but plenty of people pass by, running, walking their dogs…"

"Beck."

As soon as my name was over her lips, I pulled on the strings of her bikini bottoms and yanked them off her. She squealed and tried to hold onto them by clenching her thighs, but I already had them in my fist. "Still think I'm a nice boy?"

"This isn't funny," she breathed.

"I know. What was it? Get arrested? Get photographed or filmed? All the nature going everywhere?" I quoted her anxieties over public sex as we finally reached a spot in the water where she could stand. I angled her so at least her back was to the shore.

"Beck."

"Put your hands together." I pulled them from my shoulders. After shooting a quick look to the empty beach behind her, she folded her hands in front of her chest, and I tied them together with the strings of her bikini top, securing the fabric triangles over her fingers. "Do you want to guess why I'm so patient with you, Blondie?" I picked her up by the waist and, with no way to use her hands for support, she immediately wrapped her legs around my middle as I started walking towards the beach. "I'll give you a hint: It's not because I'm nice."

"Because you *like*-like me?"

"*Like*-like you? Sweetheart, this isn't 7th grade."

She tensed when we got far enough out of the water for me to be carrying her full weight, water dripping from her naked body. "I'm patient with you because you keep pushing your own boundaries and it's brave and it's fucking breathtaking."

"I don't," she laughed, but her breath hitched when I laid her down on her back at the very edge of where the ocean leapt at the shore. Her shoulders rested on soft, warm sand while waves nipped at her feet. She wriggled her head in the sand. "You're giving me too much credit."

"Am I?" I pushed her knees apart, flattening them against the wet sand. She squirmed, arms jerking against their restraints. "So, do you want me to stop?" Her eyes were on me as I leaned back to admire the view of her opened wide for me, her muscles twitching in anticipation and her wet skin glistening in the sun.

"No," she breathed, still racking her neck, and it took me a moment to locate the source of her discomfort. I reached for the clip and her hair fell free the next second. She dropped her head back with a sigh of relief. "Thanks."

"Oh, this is going to be useful." I tested the claw clip a few times, her eyes growing wide. There were a lot of fun things one could do with clamps, but the hooks on this one seemed just a tad too pointy to be used on skin in a spur of the moment situation. So instead, I yanked up her bound hands, and clipped them in place above her head. She tried to move them and hissed when the restraints tugged on her hair. "Are we pushing past your comfort zone yet?"

"Beck, I swear to God." She huffed and tried to turn hands and head to get another look at the rest of the beach.

Well, that was no reply at all, but as she lay before me, goosebumps started breaking out on her flesh and it was the hottest fucking thing I'd ever seen. I dropped two fingers into the dip of her collar bone and dragged them down her body, between her breasts and down the slope of her navel. Her spine arched, body desperate to meet my touch. I stopped just above her pelvic bone, removing my fingers, and she whimpered, hips bucking in protest. I pushed her jerking legs back down into the sand, keeping her wide enough to see the sweet arousal gathering around her opening. "Look at how wet you're getting for me, Blondie, and I've barely touched you."

"Beck, please." The ocean pushed a bigger wave to the shore, the water lapping up to Del's hips and she gasped, her whole body shivering. "The longer you wait, the more likely someone's going to see."

"From where I'm sitting, it looks like you quite enjoy being seen." I grinned and bit my lower lip, because her nipples were peaking into the air, and she was breathing harder by the second. If she was going to come just from being spread out, that would be my crowning achievement.

"Only by you." She jerked her knees up and I pushed them back down, except this time, I slid my hands down to her center and pushed my thumbs into her slick lips, parting them for an unobstructed view of her swollen clit. She moaned, pushing herself against me, but I just held her open, no friction, no release.

"You're doing good, sweetheart."

"I'm not doing anything," she whined, twitching, her moisture dripping down her sweet pussy.

"Agree to disagree." My cock was painfully strained inside my wet trunks, but fucking her now would defeat its purpose because *I* didn't care about who saw me. In fact, I would have fucked Del on the main stage of Clandestine just to show everyone that she was mine.

"Beck, please," she tried to lift her head, and jerked back with a frustrated groan when her binds kept her movements restrained. So fucking hot. All mine to play with.

"What do you want from me, Del?"

"Please touch me," she whined.

"I am touching you." I grinned and pulled her apart a little wider. Her core throbbed for me, but Del's moans were growing impatient.

"Please," she begged, "just…need…"

"Do you want me to make you come?"

"Yes, please," she whimpered.

"I have one condition."

"Fine."

"You haven't even heard it yet."

"I don't care. Just. Please. Touch me."

"Blondie, I'm going to eat your pussy like it's my last meal, but when you come, I want you to be loud."

"What?"

"Moan. Scream my name. Curse heaven and earth. I don't give a shit. I want you to come as loud as you can."

"Fine."

The second the word was out of her mouth, I leaned down and dipped my tongue into her. She moaned my name, hips bucking, while I savored her sweet and salty taste. Between the fruit she'd been eating and the ocean water still clinging to her skin, her pussy was intoxicating. And I drank her up like she was my only relief in the desert. Every long and languid stroke of my tongue had her back arching as she moaned. When I flicked her clit, she cried out. And when I thrust my tongue into her, she pleaded my name like a prayer.

"Beck, oh god, Beck, hold on, someone's coming." Her voice was breathless, and her legs jerked around me. "Someone's coming."

I glanced up and followed her gaze. Someone was coming, but they were barely an ant on the horizon. "Looks like *you* should come a little faster." I grinned and lowered my head again. Except this time, when I pushed in, her reaction was strangled. "I told you to be loud."

"I can't. Please. Beck. They'll hear."

"The alternative is, I just lean back," I did as I said, "and we wait, and they can find you tied up, spread wide open, with that sweet pussy glistening so beautifully."

She jerked and winced against her restraints once again. "Oh, for fuck's sake. Fine. Fine. Just. Please keep going."

"That's my girl." I dipped my head back in between her legs and she moaned with pleasure when I sucked and teased her clit. I glanced sideways at the jogger who was close enough to make out their red windbreaker. Since I had no intention of traumatizing Del, I decided to mix in a little pain with her pleasure - that always seemed to work. I pulled her clit in between my teeth, nipping at her nerves, at the same time that I pushed three fingers into her pulsing opening. More than she'd ever taken before. She cried out loud enough for the whole neighborhood to hear, shuddering and convulsing around my fingers, and falling still after a few more thrusts.

Her body was still pulsing with aftershocks when I scooped her up and sat her on our blanket. I released the claw clip and wrapped her in a large towel, just moments before the runner went past.

I still had my eyes on the guy, making sure he wasn't lurking, when Del erupted in giggles. "I can't believe we did that."

She held her hands out to me, eyes glassy, but a content smile between her flushed cheeks. I loosened her bikini top from her hands, and she shook them out before dropping on her back, arms outstretched on either side. The towel still pooled around her waist, but she was baring her chest to the world. Free. Beautiful. "Are you still going to pretend sex in public isn't your thing or can we agree that you have an exhibitionist side?"

Another bout of cute giggles erupted, her chest trembling.

"Maybe. Seriously." She snapped back up and clasped my face in her hands. "That was thrilling. I have never smoked a cigarette in my life, but I would even take another drag from your disgusting cigar right now. I feel like this is the kind of orgasm that warrants a cigarette after."

"I can't offer a cigarette, but I saw that you packed some cookies."

"Good enough. I'll take it."

Just this morning I'd thought that the fresh-faced, bikini-clad, summer-morning-Del was my favorite version of her, but I changed my mind. This, tousled hair, glowing cheeks, towel wrapped around her hips and not a care in the world who might see her tits while she scraped the milk cream off her Oreo? This version was a thousand times better.

FORTY

Delilah

"So Camila is the one who taught you to cook?"

"Yes," he replied and pointed at a metal nutcracker contraption thingy hanging on the wall behind me. I twisted around where I sat on the counter and handed it to him. He squeezed a small white nubby vegetable through it. A split second later, the scent of garlic filled the kitchen. Huh. I'd never seen fresh garlic, apparently. "It was, just like reading, a way for me to get away from my mother's idea of what I should be doing for a while. Georgia never dared to go up against my abuela. That wasn't a fight she could have won." He shot me a smile that hinted at just how much he'd admired his grandmother.

My mom had moved back to Hartford to be closer to her mother after my dad's death, but to me grandma had always been just a relative you saw for birthdays and holidays. "Why did you keep up with it?"

"Cooking? Because it tastes better than takeout. Here, try." He held a spoon of Bolognese sauce up to my mouth.

"I already know you're a great cook," I said but tried the sauce anyway, since he'd even adapted the recipe to work without wine. It was the perfect mixture of sweet tomatoes and hearty beef and I nodded enthusiastically. "Mmh. Mh-hmm."

He beamed and stole a quick kiss from my closed lips. God, he was so cute when I approved of his cooking. All proud of himself for a job well done.

"You're going to ruin my taste buds. How am I ever going to be content with a cheap hot dog from a street cart again?"

"You should never have been in the first place." He chuckled and put a lid on the sauce, before stepping into the space between my knees. "But if this means those taste buds are all mine to please, I'll take it."

"You're so possessive."

"You have no idea." He claimed my mouth in a lip-bruising kiss that gave me a very good idea of it though. He only stopped when the little egg-shaped timer beeped to remind us that the pasta was ready, leaving me breathless and flushed while he finished prepping dinner.

I sank back in my chair after eating enough spaghetti Bolognese to put me in a food coma. Maybe I should have thought that through, considering my bodycon dress now made me look 5 months pregnant, and I was unable to move, but any plans I had to look sexy or do anything sexy had dissipated by my second plate.

"Wait here," Beck said and disappeared into the house, leaving me alone on the patio with the flickering candles and the ocean waves crashing in the distance. This had to be the best first date I'd ever been taken on. Before the small twinge of guilt in the back of my mind could spiral out of control, Beck stepped back onto the porch, holding a matte black box with a red bow on it. "I figured you might like this better than flowers or chocolates."

"You didn't have to get me anything."

"If I'd known I'd buy you a Porsche, I might not have splurged on this." I shot him a glare, because I was so not accepting a Porsche from him, but he just grinned and placed the box in front of me. "Open it."

I pulled off the thick silk ribbon, draped it around my neck like a scarf, and flipped the lid open. Nestled in crinkly tissue paper sat a blue, leather-bound journal. A golden clam shell was etched into its cover, along with a swirly font proclaiming *Sirena's Story*. "What?"

"Now you have somewhere to practice your writing."

"I-"

"Just take a look before you say anything."

I lifted it out of the box, the leather smooth against my fingertips. "It has gold edges," I gasped, running my pinky along its sides.

"Yeah, since gold seems to come up again and again, between the melody stone and Lyra's necklace and the memory spell, I figured that was quite fitting."

I couldn't even start processing the fact that he had put that much thought into getting me a notebook, because my eyes landed on the small booklet that had been hidden in the box under the journal. "Wait. Wait. Are those- Did you get me personalized page flags?"

"For each character and each setting," he leaned over and tapped the different symbols printed onto the color-coded sticky notes. "I don't know if that makes sense, but I asked both Defne and Brody, and this is the system they agreed on. If you want different ones-" I didn't let him finish, my mouth on his stifling the rest of his reply.

"This is the best thing I have ever received in my entire life," I squealed through a clogged throat as tears started springing to my eyes.

"Just FYI, you'll have a lot of those page flags. Turns out, you can't just have them made in packs of ten."

"Beck, I lov-" no, no, no, no, *no*. *No*. "I love *it*. Thank you."

Kissing him again, I rose to my feet and took my gift with one hand, and took him by the other, leading him back to the bedroom to thank him properly. My gift on the nightstand, I sank to my knees and smiled up at him and said: "Eyes on me."

He let me start my way, testing his little reactions to my fingers, my lips, and my tongue, but when I grazed my teeth over his head, Beck groaned and snapped forward. He grabbed my hair in two fists and took his pleasure from my mouth. His way.

Afterwards, I cleaned myself up in the bathroom and slipped on my nightgown, only to find Beck lying in bed completely naked. He was the textbook definition of gorgeous, all lean muscles and olive skin, tanned from two days in the sun. "Are you trying to seduce me, Beck?" I laughed, arms crossed over my chest.

"I'm the picture of innocence."

"Uh-huh."

"Come here," he grinned, that damn twinkle in the corner of his mouth.

"Not with you looking at me like that."

"Like what?"

"Like you want to leave a permanent mark on my body."

Beck groaned and pulled a pillow over his face. I used that chance to climb over him and lie flat against his chest, soaking up his warmth and his intoxicating, fresh smell. "Next time," I promised and whispered a kiss against his sternum. "When you haven't fed me four pounds of pasta."

"I can go slow," he promised, his hands folding around my back.

"Would you even enjoy that? *Vanilla* sex?"

"Trust me, I will enjoy fucking you in each and every way."

"Hey, Beck?" I pushed myself up, the inkling of an idea forming. "You say stop, I stop."

"What are you talking about?" He raised his brows but let me direct his hands up to the headboard. I grabbed the ribbon from my gift box on the nightstand. This bed frame wasn't quite as ideal as Beck's metal one at home, but I still managed to weave the red silk through the gaps in the wooden slabs and tie it around his wrists. "And what exactly do you think you're doing?"

"I thought you knew what a red ribbon means."

"That's not how it works, Blondie."

"Isn't it?" I smiled sweetly and pulled my nightgown off, before sliding down in his lap until my bare hips moved over his. He reacted instantly, a thick bulging pressure against my middle. Beck's arms jerked against the ribbon, and he let out a long huff. "What does the red ribbon mean, Beck?"

"It means, you're the only one who touches me." His voice sounded like the growl of a caged tiger ready to pounce.

I gyrated my hips over him, pulling a deep groan from his chest. "Who gets to fuck you, Beck?"

"You do."

"Excuse me?" I reached around and gave his thigh a light slap, earning myself a low growl and a jerk of his hips hard enough to make me wince.

"Just you."

"See, I know how this works." I lifted myself just enough to position him inside my fold and let him slide back and forth. The traction sent a shiver down my spine and had his hips snapping up, pushing harder against me. I had to steady myself with both hands on his chest. Even tied up, the force of his body was enough to wreck my balance. "Who gets to ride your cock?"

"Just. You. Do." Each word was a promise for retribution, but I was having way too much fun to worry about what Delilah of the future might end up regretting.

I slid up his length, until his tip was just at my entrance, and when his hips writhed dangerously, desperate to thrust upwards, I slipped one hand around his throat and squeezed. He made a surprised, strangled sound. The second his lips parted, I slipped two fingers past them. "Suck," I commanded, my voice much stronger than I would have thought possible. Beck obliged, his tongue and lips lapping at my fingers. I pulled them out a moment later and brought them between my legs, using the moisture to guide his tip into me.

"Fuck, Del," he gasped, throwing his head back, headboard creaking against the strength of his arms.

Pushing my hands against his chest and my knees into the mattress, I tried to lower myself against the strain of his size, but my walls barely managed to stretch around him. I'd only gotten two inches, when my insides seized up against the sharp pain. I couldn't do this. It was one thing to have him thrust into me, because he was in control then, and I didn't have to worry about doing anything wrong. What was I thinking, trying to handle this on my own? I couldn't even relax my goddamn vaginal muscles enough to take him in.

"You're the only one who gets to tie me up," he panted. "Just you."

"Beck, I don't- I just need a second."

"You'll never see me in a red ribbon again, so you better make the most of this," he huffed, shooting me a big grin.

"You talk a whole lot for someone who's tied down."

"Should have gagged me."

I gasped out a laugh and, in that moment, I relaxed enough to let him slide deeper. My eyes fluttered shut and I pulled up again, easing him out, before sinking down, another inch more than before. I did that until I had him inside me, buried to the hilt, feeling like I was about to burst from fullness, my entire abdomen tense under the aching pressure.

"Beck," I whimpered, lips trembling.

"I know, sweetheart," he breathed, chest heaving, "take what you want."

I stemmed myself up, barely an inch, before sinking back down slowly. For a few minutes, the room was filled with nothing but the sounds of our labored breathing and the slickness of his cock being taken in by my warmth. Until my inner walls had adapted to his size, and I could move a little more freely, a low hum thrumming up in my stomach.

"You're so goddamn beautiful, fucking yourself on my cock. This is-" His arms jerked, and he let out a string of curses when he was reminded, once again, that he couldn't reach for me.

An unfamiliar, bubbly pleasure prickled in my chest. He was so beautiful, and I had him all to myself. "You're mine," I whispered, "all mine."

"I sure am," he responded.

"All of you." My fingernails scraped over his chest as I tried to hold on with my faster pace, tried to keep myself steady when shivers started washing down my spine. My whole body felt like it was pulsing with the erratic rhythm of my heart. This was different from all the times I'd had sex just to show affection. Somehow, right here, every part of me aligned, heart and body and soul, and it was all for him, or with him, or because of him.

"Just yours, Del," he hissed, his words barely piercing through my heated haze, and I came apart on him. The orgasm crashed over me, and I cried his name, nails digging into his skin. Until I collapsed on his chest, panting, when my muscles no longer supported my weight.

A strong hand wrapped around the back of my head, pulling my face up for a long, languid kiss that I was happy to melt into. It wasn't until he rolled us over and gave a slow, leisurely thrust that my eyes flew open. "What?" I gasped and looked up to where he had one hand hooked into the headboard, but the ribbon was gone.

"You tied it with a bow, Blondie," he chuckled, "we'll have to get you a book on the art of tying knots."

He could have gotten himself out of that the entire time. The realization washed over me with another shiver. Beck had given his precious control to me because he wanted to. He'd given himself to me. "Mine," I whispered again, warmth bursting in my chest, and I pulled him to me for a kiss filled with that word. *Mine. Mine. Mine.* "Don't pull out. I want you to come inside of me."

A deep hum rumbled through Beck's chest, but he just replied to my words with a single deep thrust.

We hardly slept that night.

When I blinked against the sun the next morning, Beck's body curved around mine, his chest against my back. Our intertwined hands rested on my stomach and our wrists were still tied together with that ribbon. Just a bow. Not a knot.

"I MEAN, YOU'RE A VERY BUSY MAN. YOU COULD BE WRITING emails while I drive and we'd be home faster, so you would be back to your beloved computer," I argued, frowning at Beck's hands on the steering wheel. The only upside to him driving was the prime view of his flexing forearms.

"You lost."

"Your hands are bigger."

"Scissors beat paper, it doesn't matter how big the scissors are."

"Fine," I grumbled. "How about a trade?"

He opened his mouth and then closed it again, shooting me a look from the corner of his eyes. Ever the negotiator. "What's your proposal?"

"If you let me drive, I'll go down on you at the next rest stop." I was only half-kidding.

He barked a loud laugh. "You're leaning into the exhibitionist kink now, huh?"

"The next stop is coming up in ten miles," I said, pointing at the street sign we whizzed past.

"Counteroffer: I go down on you at that rest stop, and then I'll drive you home."

"We're negotiating for the driver's seat, not the sex."

"Shame."

"Besides, I don't want your mouth down there, when I'm still... you know..." I gestured at the towel between me and the fine Italian leather seat. The thing not a single book in Beck's library had prepared me for: a lot of great sex led to a lot of great orgasms, but if you didn't use condoms and you fell asleep instead of properly taking care of *it*, gravity would do the job for you the next morning.

"Leaking cum?" he asked, not a note of attribution in those words. "Shouldn't that be my concern, since it's *my* mouth coming in contact with *my* cum?"

"Two miles," I said instead of answering him.

"Counteroffer," he said again, "I let you drive, and you let me take you to New York next month."

My mood plummeted. "No."

"We go to the big Barnes & Noble. You buy every single book you want."

"First of all, we would go to The Strand. Shop indie. Second of all, no."

"I'm offering to buy you books *and* let you drive. Do you really want to spend the rest of your life within a 50-mile radius of Boston?"

"Doesn't even matter." I sank back in my seat, my hands wrapping around each other in my lap. My thumb itched to dig into my skin, to stop my thoughts from plummeting down the hole that was the inevitable finish line of this. Cordelia Montgomery would vanish from public life. I'd stop seeing Beck. There was no next month for us. Cape Cod had been a blip. Two days of forgetting the outside world existed. But it did, and we were getting closer to Boston and our lives by the second.

"Of course, it matters. What do you want, Del?"

"No," I mumbled, "we just passed the rest stop where we could have switched seats. You can just keep driving."

I didn't even see the other car bulleting towards us. More than anything, I heard the crash. The crunch of metal folding in. The high pitch of glass shattering. Bones cracking. And then everything went silent.

FORTY-ONE

BECK

I COULD HAVE ONLY BEEN KNOCKED OUT FOR A SECOND, BECAUSE the airbag was still deflating when I opened my eyes. The adrenaline was pumping through my veins, clearing my thoughts as I assessed the damage to my body (glass shards jutting from my left arm and a throbbing head), then assessed the situation. The car had flipped onto the driver's side, but it looked like it had been run off the road. Good. No risk of other cars crashing into mine. The windshield was gone, replaced by dry grass and undergrowth. I could crawl out of there if I got myself out of my seatbelt. I reached out, and it released with a snap, dropping me an inch to the ground, into a sea of shards. I didn't even register the glass cutting through my clothes, because as I pushed myself upright, my eyes caught on a wave of blonde hair streaked with crimson.

Because I hadn't been alone in the car.

Moments from before the accident flashed through my mind. Big blue eyes turning from mischief to ice. Smile faltering.

I stared at her for a split-second, suspended above me by her seatbelt, blood cresting her brow and trickling from the corner of her mouth. Not moving. Not waking.

"I'm going to take you to New York, to London, to Paris." The words rushed out of me like a bargain, and I pushed myself up against her. I tried to hold her head up and steady her neck with my shoulders as I fumbled for the seatbelt, but it was fucking stuck. I clicked and clicked the damn button, but it didn't come loose. "You better be listening, Blondie, because you're not winning this argument by default, hear me?"

She didn't respond.

I kicked the seatbelt. It snapped open, and her limp body collapsed onto me. I cradled her face against my chest with my bleeding arm and used the good one for leverage against the roof of the car. "I've got you. I've got you. I've got you." I kept mumbling the same words over and over, dragging us backwards through the shattered windshield. Once outside, I could see the dark fumes rising from the car, and my instincts screamed at me to put as much distance between us and the vehicle as possible. As soon as we were a couple feet away, I laid the lifeless body down in the grass. Her right arm was bent at an unnatural angle, but that was the least of my worries.

She was so pale.

Pale skin. Pale hair. Pale blue dress. And all the blood contrasting against that. Soaking into her hair from the cut on her forehead and into her dress from where a piece of glass jutted from her ribs. Ribs that weren't fucking moving.

"Counteroffer, Delilah, if you wake up right now, I'll dress up as Mr. Knightley for the wedding," I promised. I smoothed her wet hair from her face and tipped her head back before I lowered my ear to her nose. Her breathing was slow and shallow, but it was there. "That's my girl," I sighed and tried to find a pulse on her neck but came up blank. It had to be so weak. Fuck. "Just hang on, sweetheart."

For the first time, I looked up. We'd toppled down the steep ditch, the street at least 20 feet above us. An older woman stood at the side of the road, phone by her ear. She waved at me when she saw me looking. I'd take that as a sign that she'd called 911. Except she didn't stop waving and my gaze followed her pointed fingers to the other car.

Right. We hadn't just toppled over out of the blue.

The wreckage of a silver car was smoking and creaking several feet away.

My attention fell back to the only woman I never wanted to leave - and who would never let me hear the end of it, if I didn't leave her right now to see if anyone else needed help. "Last offer, Delilah," I whispered and laid a careful kiss to her brow, "you don't die on me, and I check the other car, okay?" A breath rattled through her lungs, just a little stronger than the previous ones. "I'll take that as a yes."

My left side shot sharp arrows of pain through my chest, but I'd cracked enough ribs in the ring over the years to push through. The driver's door of the silver Volvo hung ajar, window gone, and the man behind the wheel let out a low groan from behind a mop of thin brown hair.

His seat belt gave up on first try and I got him out of the vehicle with a single pull, laying him out in the grass. His hair fell back, and my stomach tightened. "I know you."

"She's not who you think she is," he coughed.

"Childs." His name lurked in the back of my mind alongside the picture Julian had sent me the day before I left for Cape Cod. His face was bruised and swollen now, but I'd dug so deep into this bastard's entire online presence, I could have picked him out from a lineup with a hood over his face. "Roger Childs."

"You better hope she's dead or she'll ruin your life like she ruined mine." His breath spluttered as he coughed up droplets of blood.

He won't bother me anymore.

I still didn't have details on *how* he'd bothered Del. Childs had been her boss up until a few months ago. He hadn't even cropped up when we first ran a background check on her, because Del's records stated that she'd left her job due to mental health issues. No reason to doubt that when you knew about her anxiety…

After I told Julian to dig deeper, he'd found Childs' life in shambles. Somehow, over the course of a few weeks - the same few weeks in which Del had taken on Cordelia's name - he'd lost everything.

It didn't take much to put two and two together.

Someone had simply failed to tell Del that there was nothing more dangerous than a man with nothing left to lose.

"You followed her." Followed us.

"I did you a fucking favor, man. Her name's Delilah, not Cordelia. Fucking bitch."

"A favor," I mused, cold creeping into my bones. Only a few feet away, Delilah, who stole soap from rich people on principle, who came up with wildly sweeping fantasy tales about friendships to beat the odds, and who had given up her own identity for an agoraphobic heiress without so much as a penny flowing into her accounts - spending her own money on dress alterations instead - was barely breathing. Because of him. "Funny. Doesn't feel like a favor."

"I just rammed the passenger side. You're going to be fine."

"You know what's a real shame, Roger?" I pushed myself up to look over the wreckage of his car. Sirens had pulled up on the street, but nobody had made their way down the slope yet.

"To waste such a pretty face on such a prickly girl?" He

laughed, choking on the sound. He was severely misreading my alliance here.

"That I ran over here, and I pulled your body from this wreck, and after all that, I wasn't able to save your life."

Confusion marred his features, and understanding flashed just as I gripped his thinning hair and his stubbled chin. His neck snapped like a twig in my hands.

I didn't waste a single second more on him, leaving him in the dirt where he belonged, and dragged myself back to Delilah's side.

FORTY-TWO

Delilah

My head was throbbing, and that goddamn song didn't stop. Beck never listened to music in the morning, and now he had to play that goddamn song. "Can you turn off the music?"

"There's no music, darling," a woman replied, and I tried to pry my eyes open, because she wasn't Beck, and that goddamn song wouldn't stop. And not a single person named Delilah ever wanted to hear that goddamn song again. My eyes didn't open though, and I just sank back into the comforting, warm darkness of Beck's arms around me and his face snuggled into the crook of my neck while he hummed, so cheesy.

"Good song," I mumbled, tongue heavy.

"Good night," he whispered back.

FORTY-THREE

BECK

"I swear to God-"

"If you don't hold still, you'll be meeting God a lot sooner than you might be comfortable with, Mr. Beckett." The white-haired nurse chuckled while holding out a metal container. The doctor dropped another shard into it without saying a word. She'd given up talking to me after the ninth or tenth glass splinter she'd removed from my side. At least they had moved on to my arm now. If they'd just hand me the damn tweezers, I'd dig the tiny pieces of car window out of my flesh myself - after checking on Delilah.

"Is that a threat?" I asked.

"Oh, no, I'm just informing you of the dangers of open wounds getting infected." She snorted but didn't hide her frown when another particularly jagged piece landed in the bowl, laced in a film of blood. "Are you sure you don't want painkillers, honey?"

"I'm sure. How many more?"

The doctor sighed and shook her head. "Not that many," the nurse cooed, clearly unbothered by the fact that I had somewhere else to be. She must have lived through decades of ER bullshit to stay that chipper, but I really didn't care for it.

It had been hours since I'd seen Del. They had wheeled her off to get her patched up and scanned head-to-toe, and the only reason I wasn't with her right now was a different doctor yelling at me that he couldn't do his job if I was getting in his way.

The door to the exam room swung open and Isaac let out a long breath when his eyes landed on me. "Hard man to find."

"Dr. Hunter?" The nurse furrowed her brows, giving Isaac a long once-over. He had thrown his white coat over a Pink Floyd shirt and ripped jeans, which probably wasn't his usual attire.

"Hello Denise, looking lovely as ever." He pasted on a bright, beaming smile and winked at the woman. "Did you get a haircut?"

The doctor next to me snorted and pulled another shard from my arm, wiping blood off my skin with a piece of gauze, while nurse Denise giggled and blushed. "Oh, Dr. Hunter, stop your nonsense."

"Sign this." Isaac held his clipboard out to me, still eye-fucking the woman old enough to be his own mother.

"Self-discharge?" I asked, taking the clipboard from him with my good arm.

"Don't sign that. I'm not done yet," the doctor grumbled without looking up.

Isaac handed me a pen and turned to me for the first time since entering the room, his charming facade dropping. "We have to go."

We hadn't talked since I'd sent Jonas his way, but his words left little room for protest. The back of my neck prickled, because if he didn't elaborate in front of his colleagues on why we had to go, my chances of sitting in a chair next to Del's bed, waiting for her to wake up, had just slimmed to zero. I signed the discharge form on the dotted line. Immediately the doctor dropped the tweezers on the medical tray and held her hands up in surrender.

"Shirt?" Isaac asked.

"Gone."

"Take this until we get to the car." He shrugged out of his lab coat and tossed it at me. I couldn't suppress the grimace as the stiff fabric slid over the open wounds on my arm, but it was better than going half-naked, wherever it was we were going. I glanced down at the tattoo marking the inside of his forearm. *Il ne faut pas réveiller le chat qui dort.* The French version of 'let sleeping dogs lie'. I hadn't, and I was about to face the consequences.

"Care to tell me what's happening?" I asked once we were out of that room and Isaac set a brisk pace down the hospital hallway.

"Cordelia Montgomery was a patient here two years ago with a burst appendix," Isaac spoke fast and low.

"Shit." I could see where this was going. I hadn't thought twice about which name to give the EMTs. Cordelia. If the crash ended up in the papers, our names would be out there - and as far as the rest of the world was concerned, the woman in the passenger seat was the same one I'd been photographed with at various events the last few weeks. The rest of the world had no idea Delilah Edwards existed in *my* world.

"Cordelia needed a blood transfusion back then."

"I'm guessing Del's blood type didn't match the one on record."

He pushed through a heavy door marked 'staff' that led us into a blindingly white stairwell. "You know?"

"Yes," I hissed, jolts of pain shooting through my ribcage with every downward step. "Where is she?"

"That's the other thing." Isaac halted on the landing and

narrowed his eyes at me. "Two years ago, Cordelia gave us an emergency contact and a healthcare power of attorney. Someone who could make decisions for her if she was incapacitated. Victor Yelchin."

"He's here?"

"They're both gone."

The pain ebbed from my body, replaced by the cold instinct that the car crash had only been the first domino to fall.

Within minutes, I sat in the passenger seat of a sleek Tesla that still smelled like new leather and had nothing in common with Isaac's usual old, red Honda with the permanent ketchup stain on the backseat. He'd thrown a plain T-shirt from his trunk at me to replace the lab coat before gunning out of the hospital's garage. "Going somewhere?" I asked, glancing at the sleek black suitcase in the backseat.

"I was."

"How did you find out about the crash?"

"What do you think?" He countered.

"Are *we* good?"

"I'll let you know when my father decides what he wants in exchange for using federal resources on the Russian mob." Despite his words, he shot me an easy grin over his shoulder. "Nice weed farm, by the way."

"Do you know where he took Delilah?" I asked, not ready to banter about the situation until I knew Blondie was safe.

"Delilah," Isaac tested the name in his mouth, "yeah, he took her home, but my guys can't go in. I can't go in. Unless you want to start an international incident."

"Home?"

"Cordelia Montgomery's house." Isaac pointed at the street sign as he rounded the corner onto Beacon Street. "Look, Beck, I have no idea what's going on, and I'd like to keep a shred of plausible deniability, but I had a look at Del's charts. She's stitched up but you should get her back to the hospital. Whether or not she's the real heiress, she deserves that much."

My fingers twitched, clenching into fists. Whether or not she's the real heiress? Did he really think I would deny Del the medical attention she needed just because she wasn't called Montgomery? I forced my hands to relax because Isaac wasn't too far off. We had met when I'd been very much my mother's son, and Georgia Beckett had no problem letting someone bleed out once they ceased to be useful to her. Even if I wanted to pretend that I had distanced myself from her over the years, this whole scheme had her stamp of approval on it. Which should have set off my warning bells weeks ago.

Isaac stopped the car a block away from Cordelia's house and turned in the driver's seat to level a hard gaze on me. "One last thing."

"What?" I barked, already gripping the door handle.

"Julian's the one who took the money and paid off Yelchin. He's in there with them."

Of course, he was. I climbed out of the car and didn't wait to watch Isaac drive off. My mind was reeling a million miles a minute.

Julian had known about Delilah just as long as I had. A former high school teacher, hired as a stand-in for Cordelia. But when had he found out about Yelchin's part in this?

'Three strategies. Go.' My mother's voice echoed in my thoughts, because Julian may have spent many nights at the kitchen table, but he had never tried to leave it early, never hid novels in the dust jackets of his books, never stopped playing the game. He didn't break Georgia's rules. Once, he had gotten so frustrated that he had flipped the table, had picked up some small marble sculpture, and had smashed it into the wood until the table

legs splintered off. Then he sat down on his chair and stayed there until he came up with one last strategy.

That was the Julian I expected to walk in on.

FORTY-FOUR

Delilah

"I'M SURE THE BOSTON MEMORIAL STAFF IS VERY COMPETENT, but I'd rather not have you die due to a hospital infection." Julian sighed and fumbled with the plastic switch on the IV-drip.

I tried to blink through my blurred vision, but all I got was patches of pastel blue walls and a dark sky beyond my windows. Julian's words swam through my hazy thoughts. Hospital. This wasn't the hospital. We were in my bedroom. "I don't..." My voice died a raspy death after just two words and I squeezed my eyes shut, trying to think, trying to piece together the scenes in my head.

"Don't worry. You'll get all the medical attention you need. We have great physical therapists on staff to make sure there's no lasting damage to your range of movement. If you want, I'll set up an appointment for you with one of the country's top therapists, so you can work through today at your own pace," Julian rambled on, his voice grating against my nerves.

His words drifted in and out of my head, as I replayed the snippets. I'd been in a car crash. Then black. I'd been in the back of an ambulance. Then black. I'd been at the hospital. Then black. No. Not I. *We*. We had been in a crash. "Where's Beck?" I croaked.

"He'll be here tomorrow."

Tomorrow. Here? In my room? Why was Julian in my room? My temples ached under the pressure of all the questions. "I'm tired."

"I know, Del. Try to catch some sleep. We can discuss the next few weeks of recovery later."

Julian pulled my blanket higher before leaving me be. He turned off the lights, and I allowed myself to sink deeper into the pillows and close my eyes. Before sleep could catch me, the lock on the door clicked shut.

My eyes flew back open at that one mechanical sound.

I pushed myself up against my headboard and in the dark room. Something tickled the back of my mind. Another dark room. A melody. That goddamn song on Beck's lips as he nuzzled closer to me.

"Good song," I mumbled, tongue heavy.

"Good night," he whispered back.

He knew.

He'd known since the first time I'd slept with him.

The sound of glass shattering would have been poetic if it hadn't been followed by a pained scream. I swung my legs out of bed and stumbled forward. One of my arms was in a thick, blue cast, the other hooked to an IV-drip. I yanked the needle from my wrist with my teeth, barely registering the pain. I was either tripping on some heavy painkillers, or I had become really good at that whole pain channeling thing. Two more steps towards the door confirmed it was the painkillers, my legs wobbling under me.

I leaned on the bedpost and took a few steadying breaths.

Whatever the hell was going on if Beck had known for weeks... I'd asked him to call me Del. Had he ever even referred to me as Cordelia?

I couldn't focus. My head felt like the air above hot asphalt, all thoughts reduced to a dense shimmering mirage. Julian was here. At Cordelia's house. And there was a chance he knew I wasn't really me. No, *hold on*, I was still me, but I wasn't really Cordelia. Cordelia was somewhere in this house though.

Pressing a hand against my forehead as if that could steady my mind, I stumbled towards the door. Of course, it was locked. What on earth had he locked me in here for? Where had he even gotten the key? The scream. Someone had screamed. Oh god. I leaned my forehead against the cooling wood of the door. *Okay, okay, okay, think, Del. Don't panic.*

Julian had said something about the next few weeks, right? That meant, he couldn't be planning to hand me over to the authorities for impersonating Cordelia.

Whatever he had planned, I knew in my gut that I didn't want to lie in bed and wait. I had no intention to find out *what* Julian was, as Beck had put it.

If Beck had known- *nope*. No. *Focus*.

I glanced down at myself. I was in an old, oversized t-shirt that reached down to my knees, that I usually only wore as a nightgown when I knew nobody was going to see me in it. Mostly due to the holes all around the collar. It would have to do, because my legs were too unsteady to even consider putting on pants. I had one burst of energy in me, and I wouldn't waste it on leggings. Instead, I trotted towards the window, crawled onto the window seat, and wedged the sliding glass open. A wall of stale, warm summer air pressed against me.

I looked down. Second floor with a garden view. Also, a prime view through the roof of Cordelia's small winter garden, just a few feet beneath my window. Alright. I sucked in a breath and pushed my feet through the opening. Apparently, I'd rather die by falling through a glass roof and cutting all my veins open than wait for Julian. Or Beck.

I didn't wait for the panic to creep through my clouded brain. Harvesting whatever momentary lapse in judgement the pain killers afforded me, I turned onto my stomach and let myself slide out. A dull ache throbbed in my side as I lowered myself and all my weight hang off my upper body. Then my toes connected with smooth glass.

"Oh god," I whimpered. There was no going back. I would die. Winter gardens weren't constructed to be walked around on. The second I let go, I was in for certain death by a thousand glass shards.

I squeezed my eyes shut and let the rest of my weight drop. The glass groaned beneath me, then... Nothing happened.

My subconscious took over, some old knowledge about weight distribution on unstable surfaces making me lower myself onto my stomach, flat palms pressing against the cool glass. This way, I pushed myself to the side of the roof, only to realize I'd forgotten a little detail in my escape plan. It was an 8ft drop to the ground. If I fell and hit my head- If the wounds from the car crash reopened- *Nope. No.* Teens climbed out of windows and off roofs all the time. It was going to be fine. I pushed myself further, feet dangling first, then legs, and then I just had to let go and gravity pulled me off the roof.

I landed on my butt, a sharp pain radiating up my tailbone and clearing some of the haze from my head.

"You're such an idiot," Cordelia laughed, voice bitter, and I forgot all about the pain. I couldn't see into the house from where I'd landed, because potted plants lined the glass walls of the winter garden, but I could still hear the shuffling of feet and clatter of cutlery inside. My eyes landed on the glass door a few feet away from me, which stood ajar by just an inch. Weird. I'd never seen that door open. I crawled towards it, listening to Cordelia's words. "Even if Delilah marries your brother, *you* won't get access to the Montgomery estate."

Marry? Who the hell was marrying who? Not *this* Delilah.

"Well, not yet," Julian mumbled through a full mouth. Was he eating? What the hell? Having dinner with the real Cordelia Montgomery and discussing her inheritance? "She'll pop out a child two or three years from now. And then if something were to happen to *Cordelia Montgomery*, her child would inherit the whole lot. Sure, the inheritance would be tied up in a trust, but who better to oversee the trust than Daddy dearest. You know, women die in childbirth all the time, right?"

My stomach soured at his words. Women died in childbirth all the time? Like what? Eclampsia? Preventable if only you knew what to look out for? I was beginning to see what Beck had implied. *Just another woman that should do her hair, open her legs, and stand behind her man.* Julian probably didn't think much better of Cordelia, and if it had been her scream earlier…

I shot a look around the backyard, but the shed with the potential weapons of self-defense was at the other end - God, why did rich people have such large backyards? I wouldn't make it that far without collapsing or someone inside spotting me. Fine. I studied the plants right by the door, and decided the peace lily in the square pot with the sharp edges would be perfect.

"As of Friday morning, 8am, all the assets that were tied up in the Montgomery name will be gone, Beckett. Except for my house and my personal trust, which is probably less than what you take home in a year."

He wouldn't see me. He wouldn't see me. He wouldn't see me. Manifestations in my thoughts, I bent forward to shoot a look through the glass door. Julian and Cordelia sat across from each other at the dinner table. Him, with a sandwich on his plate. Her, with her hands tied behind the chair.

"Gone? What do you mean *gone*? You couldn't have bankrupted your father's company in six months. You had no access to it while it was legally tied up."

"Oh no, that's the best part. Delilah was going to give a big speech at the White Ball next week. All the money is funneled into the Theresa Montgomery foundation to stop violence against women." She tossed her head back, shaking the hair from her face. "Do you see the irony of this situation?"

And once the company was gone, Cordelia Montgomery could disappear from the public eye forever. She could run the day to day of the foundation from her home. She could focus on direct action instead of fundraising galas. It had been a very persuasive 34-page PowerPoint presentation.

"Bullshit. Nobody would be that stupid. You and that girl have been lying to everyone for weeks." He grabbed something from the table as casually as one would a saltshaker - except, it was a gun, and he was pointing it right at Cordelia. "This is just another lie, trying to weasel your way out of here, so you can crawl back to your little boytoy and pretend the world doesn't exist."

Boytoy? Did he mean Victor? Where the hell was Victor anyway?

I wasn't going to wait for that gun to go off. As fast as my shaking limbs allowed, I jumped up, swung through the door, and grabbed the peace lily. "Hey!" I chucked the plant at him, aiming for the gun, but it crashed at his feet instead. Soil exploded all over the floor.

Julian raised an unimpressed brow and shook the dirt off his leather shoe. "Didn't I tell you to go to sleep?"

"Has nobody ever taught you how to treat a lady?" I countered, slowly stepping forward. I had no plan other than keeping him talking to keep the gun down.

"Lady? Her?" He swiveled out of his chair and waved his gun in the general direction of Cordelia. "That's rich coming from you. Weren't you pretending to be her?"

"Is that what this is about? You're pissed because you didn't get to meet the real Cordelia Montgomery?"

"Please," he grunted. "I'm glad you replaced her. I doubt the real Cordelia would have dropped her panties within three weeks of meeting my brother. She might actually be more of a lady than you are. You barely hesitated to dump your precious boyfriend, so Beck can finger your little cunt in *her* living room. You're going to be much easier to handle than that frigid ice princess."

What did you tell him about me?

I told him fucking nothing. You're mine.

My stomach flipped, but I pushed all thoughts of Beck aside. I could try to make sense of that later. When there wasn't a gun in the room. Cordelia's split lip quivered. "What happened to you?" she asked in the moment of silence.

"Car accident. What's going on here?"

"Oh, you know. He wants to wine and dine me, rape me, kill me, and make *you* the only real Cordelia."

"Busy schedule, Julian, huh?" The gun whacked me in the face faster than I could react, and I stumbled, falling back over the drink cart. Whiskey and Tequila soaked my nightgown. I struggled to push myself back to my feet, vision spinning and tears shooting up at the sharp stench of alcohol.

"Go back to your room Delilah. Beck will come check on you in the morning. At least we can now all stop pretending."

"Pretending?" I blinked and blinked but my vision remained blurred. I reached up to stop my brain from whirring in my skull and my hand came back bloody.

"Oh dear, you really are as blonde as you look, huh?"

"Julian, what the fuck?" Beck's voice droned from the door.

"Oh good, there you are. You can catch your future wife up on our plans. Didn't happen to bring the engagement ring, did you?"

"Delilah belongs in a hospital." There it was. My name. On his lips. I could hardly make him out beyond vague shapes and colors, but his voice was crystal. He stepped past his brother and then his arms were around me to pull me to my feet, and for a moment that was so easy. His scent. His warmth. But reality washed over me in a cold wave.

"Don't touch me," I hissed, struggling to break out of his arms without falling over.

"You're bleeding. You need to see a doctor." He wouldn't let go, and his arms were too much, because Julian was right there. And he was taunting me, because I was weak and naive, and Beck... Beck knew who I was.

"Stop," I winced, and Beck froze, letting me stumble for Cordelia's chair, which had to be enough support until the world stopped spinning.

The room was silent for a moment before Julian's grating voice piped up again. "Cordelia, dearest - *real* Cordelia, that is - why don't you tell *fake* Cordelia why you wanted her to go out with August Beckett?"

"Good press," Cordelia replied, short and to the point. "Good for the image."

"I'm not stupid," I pressed out, closing my eyes because my stomach was starting to rile up against the spinning room.

"Beck, care to fill in the blanks?"

"Julian, why the fuck is Delilah not in the hospital?"

"If I didn't dissolve the company, I would have to take over as the owner," Cordelia cut in, "my father's papers are airtight. The Montgomery business stays in the Montgomery family. Dating Beck was good for the image, because even the idea of *August Beckett* marrying into the Montgomery family put stakeholders at ease. Until I could move forward with the foundation."

"Stays in the Montgomery family," I repeated. Julian's words from before clicked. Get married. Pop out a child. Die. Daddy dearest. "So you planned to marry Cordelia?" I blinked against the room that was getting way too bright, pointing my finger at Beck, then back at me. "But I was officially Cordelia."

"Yes," Beck said.

"You would have married me while I pretended to be Cordelia?"

"Yes."

"Well, at least the 'waiting at the altar' comment makes sense now. I just- I-" I toppled over, the contents of my stomach shooting up my throat.

"I'm taking you back to the hospital," Beck's arms were there, and I was still heaving, unable to tell him to get off me. Instead, I fumbled for Cordelia's bound hands, folding my fingers around hers. Even if her voice had been steady through all this, she was trembling and locked her hand tight around mine once we touched.

"When old Montgomery died, I really was going to let you play this out, Beck, but then I realized we weren't the only ones in this game. You really should have gotten her pregnant. It would have been such a quick solution. It was never Beckett vs. Montgomery. It was Beckett vs. Yelchin with the Montgomery name as the prize."

"Leave Victor out of this," Cordelia hissed, harsher than I'd ever heard her. "You want my name? You can have it. I'll marry either one of you right now."

"Too late." Julian shrugged. "His family picked him up right after he got Delilah released from the hospital for me. He really thought he was hiding, huh? They only let him stay here for this long because they knew how valuable of an asset *you* were. It cost me quite a bit to get them to pull him off, but he was just never going to leave your side."

My whirring brain was struggling to keep up. Whoever wanted the Montgomery fortune had to marry into the family. Beck had planned to marry Cordelia-*me*. And Victor's family had planned for him to marry Cordelia-*Cordelia*? Or something. So, Julian had Victor taken out of the equation?! God, that was screwed up.

"We're leaving," Beck said in an authoritative tone.

"I'm not going anywhere without Cordelia," I gasped, wiping the sour taste from my mouth with the back of my hand, "and I'm not going anywhere with you." I shot Beck a withering glare, or at least hoped I did. Everything was still so blurry. But he was right next to me, holding me upright when my knees were struggling to do the same. "Get off me," I muttered, well aware that I would drop to the ground if he did, "stop."

"Fuck, Julian, at least get a first aid kit before she loses any more blood."

"I said, stop." I tried to push against Beck. He'd played me. He'd gotten close to me because he wanted Cordelia's inheritance. "I say stop, you stop."

"Del, not now. You need help."

"I say stop, you stop," I repeated, my voice dying in my throat as I wavered on my feet.

"Julian. Now."

"Jesus fuck. Always so dramatic. She'll live. You don't need her to be fully functioning to marry her," Julian moaned but angled for the door. A bitter laugh crept up my throat, because who the hell was *he* calling dramatic? My laugh died a moment later, when three muffled mechanical blows pierced the air, followed by the thump of a body hitting the ground. *Julian* hitting the ground.

Beck's arms stiffened around me.

"He sure likes the sound of his own voice."

"Victor," Cordelia gasped, her hand jerking around mine.

"See? This is what happens when you start messing with my family." Victor stepped through the open door of the winter garden. I felt his eyes more than I could discern them. His hands wove through mine and Cordelia's as he started untying her. "Delilah, you look like shit."

"Thanks," I huffed, a tired grin pushing against my lips.

"Let's get you out of here, Blondie," Beck said and wrapped an arm around the back of my knees, ready to sweep me up.

I slapped him across the cheek with whatever strength I still had. The sharp sound stilled the room. "I told you to stop touching me."

"Cordelia?" Victor asked.

"I'm fine."

"I'll take Del," Victor said, and I wrapped my arm around his neck the second he was close enough, "clean up your mess, Beckett."

FORTY-FIVE

Delilah

THE DAYS IN THE HOSPITAL BLURRED PAST AS I DRIFTED IN AND out of a deep, exhausted sleep. Victor was there a lot. Tabitha and Defne visited. But I rarely had the energy and brain space to talk to them. I barely even had the energy to process everything that had happened the day of the car accident.

I didn't hear from Beck besides flowers and chocolates being delivered to my hospital room. I gave all of it to the nurses.

Victor just said I didn't have to worry about the Becketts anymore. Not to worry was his standard answer, no matter what question I asked.

Was he really tied to organized crime? *Don't worry about it.*

What had happened to Julian? *You shouldn't worry about him.*

Was Cordelia okay? *Let* me *worry about Cordelia.*

The day I was released from the hospital, he helped me into the backseat of Cordelia's town car, only to take me back to her place. I'd figured the whole ruse was over now, considering they'd checked me into the hospital under my own name, but apparently, I was still a resident of the Montgomery mansion.

Victor wordlessly stemmed most of my weight as I struggled up the stairs to my room and brought me a bottle of orange juice and a fresh cream cheese bagel on a tray, as if he was still just running around and doing chores. But I figured if I asked him about it, he'd tell me not to worry.

So, I forced myself to worry about the one thing that seemed within my control. I tucked myself into bed, ripped open the large envelope from Truman Academy, and spilled its contents onto the blanket. I was going back to being Delilah Edwards full-time. No more launch parties, just the teacher's lounge. No more small talk about private islands with the upper-class, just discussing Treasure Island in a classroom.

Once I had the onboarding package sorted into categories, I heaved my backpack onto my bed, got out my highlighters and page flags, and got to work.

"I'VE BEEN THINKING." CORDELIA SAT DOWN AT THE FOOT OF MY bed that night and smoothed her skirt out. No matter how unwrinkled her clothes, the crescent indents on her cheeks betrayed how hard she'd been thinking. Still following her like a shadow, Fitzwilliam launched his thick, gray body up onto the bed as well, curling into the space between my feet and Cordelia's thighs.

"About what?" I asked.

"You see, I think it would be cruel to make Fitzi move again, now that he's gotten used to such a large house."

I blinked. We'd been caught in some hostile takeover scheme. She had been held at gunpoint. Victor had shot a man. And Cordelia was thinking about my cat? Then again, I couldn't fault her, when I'd spent the afternoon doing everything *not* to think about all of that.

"You want to keep my cat?" It wasn't an outlandish request, considering she was the only person in the world allowed to pet him without getting half her arm torn off.

"I wouldn't expect you to give up your cat, silly." She looked up from her skirt smoothing. "It would only be logical for you to stay, too."

"Cordelia Montgomery, are you asking me to move in with you?"

"Maybe? Yes."

"I'm not going to be your employee anymore. You know that, right? I'm done pretending to be you."

"I was thinking more of a roommate situation." She pulled her shoulders up. "My house comes with many perks. Number one, it's rent-free. Number two, excellent on-premise security staff with great cooking skills. Number three, discreet housekeeping."

I opened and closed my mouth again, trying to puzzle out the catch. "What about visitors?"

"My proposal is, Defne, Tabitha and any serious romantic partners can come and go as you please. Further visitors must be discussed two weeks in advance, so Victor can vet them, and I can make arrangements to stay upstairs if need be."

"Does that mean no spontaneous Tinder hookups?"

She cringed. "I'm open to letting you have the house to yourself every first weekend of the month, so you can have multiple people over, throw a party or do whatever else you might have need for."

"And where will you go? There won't be any more Montgomery hotel VIP suites."

"I can stay with Victor," she said as nonchalantly as if that didn't put a million more questions in my head. Starting with:

"Victor has his own place?"

"Of course. I bought him the house next door for his birthday a few years ago."

"You bought- you- next door- the whole house?"

"Yes. Anyway, no rush, you can think about it."

"Of course, I'm moving in," I said although I had some more questions about Victor's living arrangements, because he was here when I woke up and he usually went upstairs with Cordelia at night. I'd figured he had a room right across the hall from her.

"Are you serious?"

I reached for her hand, and she placed it in my palm, lips quivering into an exhausted smile. "You had me at *it would be logical*."

"Delilah, when I said you're my employee…"

"You don't have to explain," I squeezed her hand, "it's fine."

"I want to, please. I've not had friends since my *first time* being held hostage." She rolled her glistening eyes at the sound of that. "And even though I was always friendly with our staff, the cooks, the maids, the drivers, none of them were ever truly my friends. They moved on without so much as a goodbye, or they would talk behind closed doors about how much they pitied me. I knew you would move on, too. And when I told you that you should remember that you're my employee, I was also talking to myself, because I knew that our relationship was first and foremost transactional. I don't want it to stay that way though."

"Cordelia." I scooted closer, causing Fitzwilliam to hiss and sink his claws into the blanket over my feet. "This was never just transactional. That first night in the bathroom at Truman, I didn't agree to wear that dress because of its resale value. I saw so much of myself in you, and I'm not talking about the hair or the eyes or the nose. All of which are kind of weird though."

"Don't worry. I had our DNA checked. We're not actually related."

"You had our- you know what, never mind. Just because we're

not biologically related, doesn't mean anything. You let me borrow your clothes and you offer to buy me condoms and we eat ice cream when you have nightmares. I only have books for reference, but that sounds very sisterly to me."

"I'm also the one who ate your Pringles. Not Victor. I had a midnight craving."

"Are you kidding me? I gave him shit for days."

"I know. He's been covering for me. He doesn't even like chips."

"So when he put like 30 rolls of Pringles in the pantry..."

"He's very good at being passive aggressive."

We both laughed, days' worth of tension rippling off our shoulders. When our laughter fizzled out, a single happy tear running down my cheek, I gave her hand another soft squeeze. "Have you talked to him? What happened with his family?"

"I'm not sure." She nodded slowly. "It's fine. We'll be back to normal soon."

"Don't you want more than that?"

"It doesn't matter what I want if it's not reciprocated."

"I see the way he looks at you, Cordelia, and I know the two of you have kissed before. Before you say anything, I tricked him into admitting that."

"It doesn't matter." She stiffened and pulled her hand back, only to continue smoothing out her already smooth skirt. "For what it's worth, Julian didn't lie. Victor has a complicated past and an even more complicated family. He was upfront with me about it the day he interviewed for the job. I told him that I wasn't going to leave this house unless there was an emergency, and he said that he needed a place to hide from the people that want his head on a platter."

A knock on the doorframe had our heads snap up. "Sorry to interrupt," Victor leaned against the door. "A messenger dropped this off for you, Del."

He held up a gift box. I recognized its shape and the matte black color. No big red ribbon this time. My spine straightened at the memory of the last time I saw that box. Or a box just like it - depending on whether the original had survived the accident. "I don't want it."

"Are you sure?"

"Yes. Could you send it back?"

"Of course." He wedged the box under his arm and shot a quick look at Cordelia, who was suddenly very distracted by a non-existent piece of lint on her sleeve. "I'll get started on dinner."

"Thanks," Cordelia said without looking up.

I tried to offer him a reassuring smile, but his eyes were solely transfixed on Cordelia before he turned and left. Once he was gone, she let out a long, shaky breath.

"That didn't look like it was *fine*," I whispered.

"Yeah," she choked on a bitter laugh, "I'll work harder on getting over the fact that he killed a man for me."

Her words cracked my carefully built mental dam, and all the thoughts I've been walling up, the things I've been told not to worry about, broke flooded through me. "Julian's dead?"

FORTY-SIX

BECK

11 DAYS.

That's how long it took for my life to be irrevocably changed, only to fall back into a daily routine.

Access to his personal computers made it easy to link Julian to the money taken out of Axent's accounts to pay off the Yelchin family, and with that in hand, it was even easier to make it look like he'd fled the country.

I'd expected to mourn him more, but despite being brothers, it had been a long time since we'd been family. *Brothers first* had been our mother's words over and over again, until the word 'brother' had lost all meaning. The Julian who had held my hand while our parents threw books and vases at each other, who lay in the twin bed next to mine at Casa de Camila while our father and grandfather argued business, who spent countless nights sleeping at the dining table with me - that Julian had been long gone.

Once that was settled, Brody and I moved into an apartment halfway between her house and mine. My place had been too small, but there was no way in hell I was moving into Julian's rooms. Movers had us packed and unpacked in the span of two days, and then life just continued.

I had meetings from dusk till dawn to tie up the embezzlement, and Brody was prepping to go back to school and stayed with friends more than I probably should have allowed but I wasn't her goddamn father.

11 nights and I spent every single one reliving that moment. The slap. Delilah's bloodied hand striking my cheek with enough fervor to make my head snap. The hurt in her glazed ocean eyes.

I'd sent flowers and letters to the hospital. Sent her another notebook, since the first one had burned in the car crash. I'd even sent her a first edition of Emma, hoping that Mr. Knightley would be enough to at least get her to pick up the phone, but the box came back the next day.

If she'd just let me explain.

On the 12th night, I realized that I could be facing my last chance to ever see her again if I didn't want to stalk her at home or at her workplace, so I put on the ivory suit I'd gotten tailored weeks ago, and I went to the last event Cordelia Montgomery had RSVP'd 'yes' to.

The White Ball was a gaudy excuse for people to pretend they cared about the 'no white after Labor Day' rule. The ballroom was decked in white orchids, crystals, and gauzy fabrics, while the people sipped their white wines and martinis. As far as social events went, balls were still preferable to any alternative. If you went to a ball, you brought a date, and you danced. Which kept the socializing to a minimum. Not that I didn't feel their stares or saw them leaning into each other to whisper their hushed opinions about my family - but nobody approached me as I sat in my chair near the front of the stage and nursed my whiskey until they finally got to the opening speech.

An older woman rambled on about traditions and the long history of the ball, before finally ending on the words: "And now, I'm pleased to welcome our guest of honor, Cordelia Montgomery."

The room erupted into cheers. A silver white gown swept over the stage. Delicate shoulders, gold hair swept into an updo, red lips. Wrong Cordelia. I saw a few people exchange glances at the front tables, but from afar Cordelia and Delilah looked eerily alike.

"Thank you for having me," Cordelia said, her voice clear and coldly melodic like a wind chime, none of the warmth and bubbly energy that carried Del's every word. "My name is Cordelia Montgomery, and I'm sure some of you are confused by my appearance because I look a little different from the Cordelia Montgomery many of you have met over the last few weeks. I will get to that in a second. Most of you know that I have not left my house in 15 years, since my mother, Theresa, was murdered." Her knuckles turned white around the podium as she steadied herself. "What you may not know is that I was kidnapped that day and held for ransom. My mother's life was taken as a means to an end, to show that my life, too, was disposable if my father didn't pay my kidnappers. My mother's life wasn't worth a cent. My life was priced at twenty million dollars because I was born a Montgomery. That is why, to this day, leaving my house gives me panic attacks. I just had one backstage, and I'm sure I'll have another one once I step off the stage."

She took a trembling breath but the whole audience was hanging onto her every word. "Earlier this year, my father died and left his entire legacy to me, but most of his assets were tied up in probate up until a few days ago. During the last six months, I was fighting tooth and nail to make our stakeholders see that I was capable of running his company without leaving my house. For a lot of people, including many in attendance today, that wasn't good enough. I wasn't rubbing shoulders with the right people, shaking hands with them, or even dating the right people." Her eyes found mine across the room without searching. She'd done her homework on the seating chart. "So, I gave my name to my sister, who wasn't born a Montgomery." A low murmur passed through the crowd, but Cordelia continued unfazed. "A lot of you met *that* Cordelia, liked her, and invited her to your parties. You saw her date a powerful man, and you saw her wear exclusive designer clothes. And even though nothing changed in the way I handled the Montgomery business, stakeholders were appeased and I was taken more seriously in every phone conference."

She swallowed, and worked her jaw, and her eyes flitted to the side of the stage. Yelchin stood in the shadows, arms crossed, nodding at her. "I'm sorry to have deceived many of you, but I'm more sorry that I was pushed to go that far because it's further proof that a capitalist company is not able to protect those of us who require health and safety accommodations, not even at the executive top. That is why I am proud to announce today's birth of the Theresa Montgomery foundation to prevent violence against women, and help survivors of violence, abuse and exploitation, abduction and human trafficking." A few people started to clap, but Cordelia didn't give them more than a breath for their reaction, pushing through her speech. "I am proud to announce that, in my mother's name, I have dissolved my father's company as I am striving for my legacy to have social, not monetary value. Thank you."

The second she stepped away from the podium, I was moving.

The ballroom had fallen silent, but neither Cordelia nor I were waiting around for people's reactions. I swung myself up on stage and followed her through a side door.

My steps faltered when I entered the smaller, vacant event

room with its chairs tucked in and its lights dimmed, and Del was right there. She had her arms wrapped around a trembling Cordelia, rubbing soothing circles into her back with the hand that wasn't still in a blue cast. She was in denim shorts that revealed the paling bruises on her legs, and an oversized t-shirt, and any woman in a white ball gown still paled against her.

"Get out." Victor stepped into my line of sight, causing both girls to swivel in my direction. Del's eyes widened a fraction, but the rest of her face was schooled into a stoic mask that didn't look anything like her.

"Just give me one minute."

Victor glanced over his shoulder and Del shook her head. "That's a no."

"What the fuck are you even still doing here, Yelchin?" I tried to push past him, but the second my hand connected with his shoulder, the bastard twisted it around and kicked my leg out. I fell to my knees, but the pain striking through my bones had nothing on the ache in my chest caused by Delilah's unblinking, empty eyes on me.

"I suggest you turn around, go back to being everyone's favorite most eligible bachelor, and forget you ever laid eyes on Delilah Edwards." Victor's warning rumbled close to my ear.

I could have fought him off. He was broader than me, but I'd watched dozens of his fights. I knew his moves. I knew how he left the right side of his chin exposed when he kicked out. I also knew about the injury that had taken him out of the ring a couple of years ago. Back then, I'd expected him to go work for his family - not find an actual job. He might even be out of practice, improving my chances... I just doubted that knocking him unconscious would earn me any points with Del. But she was right there, and this was possibly my last chance.

"I didn't know he was going to-" A fist slammed into my jaw, whipping my head aside. Copper taste exploded in my mouth. I didn't even look at Victor. "Julian didn't-" another hit followed, and blood speckled the lapels of my new suit.

"Let's go," Cordelia hissed and wrapped her arm around Delilah, pulling her to the door.

"Wait." Del stopped, hand on Cordelia's arm as she turned and found my gaze.

My chest spluttered at the tinge of warmth that flitted into her mask. "Brody?"

"She doesn't know. It's better that way." I spat the blood coating my tongue onto the pristine, polished marble. The sarcastic asshole in the back of my mind reminded me that we'd discussed what Brody should or shouldn't know just a few weeks ago. And I was once again on the side of keeping her in the dark. "She's safe, and she's strong. She'll get through it."

"I think so, too." Delilah nodded, her mask slipping back into place before she turned and left with Cordelia.

My thoughts hadn't caught up with me yet when another hit caught me in the jaw and pummeled me sideways. "The first ones were for the girls. This one was from me," Victor said. "Stay the fuck away from my family."

The way he said it left little doubt that he didn't mean the family that shared his last name. "Hey, Yelchin," I called after him. A bitter laugh wrecked my chest as I pushed myself back to my feet. "You should come to the Vortex some time. If you ever want to get back into the ring."

"Thanks, but I changed careers a long time ago, Beckett."

FORTY-SEVEN

Delilah

"Oh my god," Brody gasped and slapped a stack of paper down on my desk. "I can't believe they didn't kiss. They were so close. So close." She held up her thumb and index finger, tightly pressed together.

"Frustrating, isn't it?" I laughed.

I'd meant to throw myself into my new job. I'd meant to pretend the entire summer hadn't happened, no matter how much my chest ached every morning. I'd meant to forget all about the haunting image of Beck's darkened eyes and split lip when he'd knelt and pleaded for just a minute of my time. I was going to spend my days at school and my nights with Defne, Tabitha and Cordelia, who had worked out a Del-sitting schedule all by themselves to keep me busy. - And then Brody had popped into my classroom the third day of her sophomore year, and asked to stay there during lunch break because she couldn't stomach another question about her father.

Somehow the one distraction that managed to keep my mind off August Beckett, turned out to be the same distraction Brody Beckett had needed. At the end of the day, nothing compared to a little escapism.

"Can they please just kiss in the next chapter? Please? Cerulean deserves some nice things in his life."

"And ruin all the tension?"

"What good is tension if there's no pay-off?" she scoffed.

"Have you ever heard the term delayed gratification?"

"I have, and I'm not a fan. I'm sorry, do you know me at all? Instant gratification or bust, Del." She slapped the stack of paper. "Make them kiss."

"Brody," I rolled my eyes at her, "you know it's Ms. Edwards now. And I will consider your feedback."

"Also, I think you made a mistake with the memory spell. I page-flagged it."

"Thank you."

"I gotta go. I'm going to make Penny Crawford wish she hadn't gotten out of bed this morning." Brody slammed her fist into her palm and jumped backwards out of my classroom, braids whipping in all directions.

"Good luck," I called after her and slipped chapter six into my bag before switching the lights off for the day.

I just stepped out of my classroom, when Brody came to a screeching halt in front of me, almost crashing into me. "Shitballs, sorry, fuck, shit."

"No problem," I laughed at the cacophony of profanities.

"I think I dropped my phone in there. Can I?"

"Sure," I stepped aside to let her in, and when I looked up, Beck was standing a few feet away. I sucked in a breath. He didn't move. Despite Brody having been part of my life again for over a month, I hadn't seen him.

One blink. Two blinks. The seconds stretched between us like hours. None of my perfectly suppressed memories did justice to him, to those sharp features or the heat in his gray eyes.

"Got it." Brody zapped past me with all that bundled-up energy only to do a 180-jump and face me again. "Hey, you wanna come?"

I shook my head, mostly to shake off the weight of Beck's gaze. "I don't think so, but thanks."

"You could consider it research for the fight between Cerulean and Firth, because that was lacking some oomph. Come on." She grinned and bobbed on her heels.

"Brody, lay off. She's not coming," Beck said in a stern voice and turned to leave.

Defiance prickled in the pit of my stomach. After having been a pawn in his hands, I didn't want him to have the final word over any of my decisions. "Actually, I am. Brody's right. I need some oomph."

I regretted the words as soon as I'd said them, but now I had to go on principle. At least Brody made for a good buffer, talking like a waterfall for the entire ride to the gym. When she disappeared into the changing rooms, I made sure to stand three feet away from Beck, arms crossed with my hands tucked in to avoid any and all accidental contact.

Not that it mattered.

I felt him.

I may have tried to concentrate on the young women punching each other in the ring, but my every thought was occupied by how hyperaware I was of his presence. Every hair on my body angled towards him. My skin prickled whenever he moved so much as an inch. It was as if Beck was the North Pole, and my body was the needle on a compass. But worst of all, with every reaction he drew from my body, my chest ached under the weight of every lie he'd told me to hone me into this pathetic, delicate needle that had no mind of its own and would always spin for the North Pole.

"You're writing the book?" He asked, voice lowered, when the first fight ended.

"I'm not talking to you," I hissed through my teeth. "I'm here for research."

"You should talk to me about that missing oomph. I have had notable success as your research assistant before."

"Are you seriously trying to flirt with me?" How could he even bring that up? How could he offer something like that?

"Maybe, but I'm serious. I'm Brody's coach. I can help if you want to go over a fight scene."

"I don't want your help." I tightened my grip around myself, my fingernails finding the thin skin on the underside of my arm and pinching. It barely helped to keep my thoughts from spiraling into the past.

"I didn't know he was going to hurt Cordelia."

No. Nope. I was so not doing that. I wasn't going to listen to any more lies. "I'm going to go stand over there," I gritted out before walking to the other side of the ring. I stopped next some blonde guy who was whooping and hollering loud enough to drown out my thoughts.

"That's my daughter," the man said, leaning in and pointing at a young girl with a whole lot of energy, jumping up and down beside the ring, ready to go next, "I signed her up after the divorce, so she could work through some of those feelings."

I blinked. Subtle. Very subtle. "I hope it works." I tried to offer a genuine smile for the sake of his daughter, but my face was frozen into a frown.

"Do you fight? Are you one of the girls' coaches?"

"Me? Oh, no. I'm just here as moral support."

"That's a shame. I'm sure you would look good in the ring."

"Here." A bottle of apple juice popped up in front of me and I instinctively shrank back from the hand holding it. The blonde guy blanched, blinking up at the towering presence throwing its shadow over me.

"Thank you. I'm not thirsty," I glared at Beck, leaning away from him. "Beck, this is-" I turned to introduce the guy, but he was gone. Great. What a chicken.

"He's not wrong," Beck said. "You should get in the ring."

"Yeah, right."

"I think it would help."

"Plenty of writers come up with epic battle scenes without getting themselves punched in the face."

His lips twitched. "I'm not talking about your skills as a writer. I'm talking about your anxiety. Although I'm glad to hear you finally consider yourself a writer."

"What are you even- I came over here, so I didn't have to talk to you."

"You say stop, I stop."

The familiar words sent goosebumps racing down my neck. "That doesn't work on me anymore. You have gone far beyond any line of consent and communication."

"Think about it. You won't even have to see me. I'll set you up with a great beginner's coach." He pulled a business card for the Vortex out, sleek and minimalist, including the club's contact details and opening times, along with his name listed as owner.

"This is your place?" I shot a look past him at the girls that had taken over the entire gym.

"I only own it. Scarlett runs it."

The squealing, screaming, jumpy energy of all the little girls around me didn't match the Axent business models at all. Neither did the gym. No luxury amenities, no VIP lounges. I wasn't about to agree with Beck - but that blonde guy had signed his daughter up to punch her way through her feelings. Maybe that would work on mine, too. "I'm going to pay the membership fee and everything. I don't want anything from you, Beck."

"If that's what you want."

"Jesus H. Roosevelt Christ, you have to stop holding back!"

"I'm literally kicking as hard as I can," I huffed.

"Maybe with your foot, but you need to put your goshdarn hip into it, nugget." Sometimes, when Scarlett yelled at me, it felt like getting yelled at in a black and white movie. She wore her black hair in victory rolls, and her lips in a shade of red that made my favorite lipstick look bland, and she cursed like she was about to get censored for impropriety. Just last week she'd asked me if I was 'on the fudging rag', which turned out to be her way of asking if I was on my fucking period, because apparently, I was punching like a *bloated raccoon.*

"Excuse me, Mrs. Ashton, your eight o'clock is here." Scarlett's assistant, a mousy girl with big glasses blinked up at us.

Scarlett didn't usually do one-on-one sessions and her assistant hadn't gotten the hang of dealing with this setup yet. When I'd asked her about it, she'd said she preferred it when Beck owed her a favor, not the other way around, and hadn't elaborated further. Maybe I should have asked, but even if I tried to evict him, Beck was already living on my mind rent-free. I didn't feel like upping his square-footage on top of that. Even if he had arranged for Scarlett to be my private teacher, I was still paying through the nose for these lessons.

"Alright, Del, time to hit the shower. We'll try again next week."

"Okay." I deflated. I wasn't good at not being good at something.

"Mind if I give it a shot?" The low, familiar rumble of his voice ran down my spine like a shiver. Beck slid his suit jacket off his shoulders and threw it over the ropes of the ring.

"Be my guest, but I'm out of here in twenty, whether you've talked numbers to me or not." She tossed him her pads. "I have dinner with Harlan and his parents tonight."

"No, it's fine," I said, backing away from Beck as he climbed into the ring. All that damn height and muscle mass and unfair bone structure wouldn't get anywhere near me. "I'm done for tonight."

"Come on, Blondie, hit me. Let out some of that anger."

"I'm not angry at you."

Scarlett cleared her throat. "I'll be in my office if you need me."

I should have left. I should have gone home instead of waiting for Scarlett and her assistant to disappear in her office. I shouldn't have said: "Why can't you just leave me alone?"

"I want to explain."

"You don't have to. I get it. We both lied. I pretended to be Cordelia and you pretended to be human. But you see how one of these lies involved putting on pretty dresses, and the other involved double homicide plans, right?"

"I keep trying to tell you. I didn't know Julian was going to harm Cordelia."

"What did you think was going to happen? Once you figured out that I wasn't her, how did Cordelia factor into your plans?"

"Institutionalized." He threw his arms out as if that answer was so obvious. Of course. When someone doesn't fit into your plans, you just put them in a straight jacket. "Private clinic in Switzerland. More fucking luxurious than her own house. Double homicide? What the fuck are you on about?"

"Eclampsia. Unfortunate but not uncommon."

"What?"

"Don't play stupid, asshole. How big is Brody's trust, huh?" My voice exploded out of me. Okay, so maybe there was anger simmering in my veins. I ran my thick, fingerless gloves over my face before the tears of frustration could well up. If we were doing this, I was going to get through it clear-headed. "Half of that donut franchise her grandparents established along the west coast, right? I googled it. Estimated annual revenue is 120 million. Her half is 60 million. Over 18 years? Roughly a billion dollars in Julian's pocket. It's a good fucking play. Keeping it in the family."

"We'll go over how revenues work some other time, but-"

"You set me up to die. Did your mother inspire that plan? Kill the spouse, keep the kids?"

"Sweetheart-"

"Shut up." I barreled into him. I didn't even pretend to aim for the soft pads on his hands. My fists drummed into him, and he didn't even flinch. "Shut up, shut up, shut up." My voice broke. "You told him."

"I didn't tell him anything."

"Stop. Fucking. Lying. Beck." Sobs cracked through my chest. "He knew. He knew how I let you touch me. Did you have a good time mocking me behind my back? Discuss how many fingers you needed to make me come?"

His head snapped sideways as if I'd slapped him. "Fuck," he breathed. Caught red-fucking-handed.

"Yeah. I know you told him." My voice hiccupped and I brushed the tears from my face. "What was the plan here? Teach Delilah how to climax, because once she'd been fucked by the great August Beckett, she wouldn't want any other dick ever again? If you're the only one, who does it for me, I'd have to marry you, right?"

"Something along those lines."

"Thank you. Finally, an honest answer."

"I was honest with you when you asked me what I wanted."

He stripped the pads off his hands and tossed them aside. "I wanted to meet you because of your name, the Montgomery name, and my interest in you was mainly sexual when we first met. It was never meant to get more complicated than that."

"Alright. Then fuck me." I tore the Velcro of my gloves open with my teeth and let them fall to the ground.

"No."

"I want you to fuck me. Right now. Right here. All cards on the table. August Beckett and Delilah Edwards. No more lies. Come on." I pushed him and he dropped a step back, putting some distance between us.

"No."

"What? Scared you won't make me come?" I pushed him again, his back colliding with the elastic ropes. "Or were you only turned on by my naïveté? Is that what gets you going? The lies? Wide-eyed Delilah lapping them up?"

"Delilah, stop." My hands froze and hovered over his chest before I could give him another push. In one swift move, he grabbed my wrists and spun me around, pushed against the corner post of the ring. His body pressed into my back, air wedged from my lungs. One hand like iron around my wrists, the other slipped around my waist and into my pants, pinching my clit between his fingers. Sharp pain shot through my nerves, along with a spark of heat. "Is this what you want?"

"Yes," I gasped, squeezing my eyes shut.

He tugged my workout shorts down to my thighs, not letting go of his grip on my wrists. He pushed two fingers into me, painfully fast. "You want this?" I couldn't spread my legs with my pants tying my knees together, but he pumped in and out, the slick sound filling the gym.

"Yes," I moaned when a new wave of tears spilled down my cheeks, "more."

A zipper. The rustle of fabric. He pulled my hips back,

bending me in the middle, and then he pushed into me. It was the worst pain I'd ever experienced during sex. I bit my tongue so hard, a bitter metallic taste welled up in my mouth. I couldn't open far enough. I wasn't wet enough. He was just fucking into me, too big and too fast. And I started doing what I always did: Moan when the dick hit deep, clench when it was pulled out. Throw in an "Oh god, yes." every now and again and clench down harder. Within a few minutes, he groaned and spilled himself into me.

The second he pulled out, I straightened, tugged my pants back into place and climbed out of the ring. "Goodbye, Beck," I yelled over my shoulder before disappearing into the shower. Never had I ever wanted to scrub a man off my body faster.

FORTY-EIGHT

BECK

I shouldn't have fucked her.

I should not have fucked her.

I. Should. Not. Have. Fucked. Her.

Fuck, fuck, fuck, fuck.

I wanted to bang my head against the wall until my brain started rattling, because that thing was clearly not working. The same thought had been on repeat since last night. *I shouldn't have fucked her.* But I was a fucking idiot.

"Working from home today?" Brody asked.

I snapped my head up from where I'd pressed it against the cool metal of the refrigerator - which hadn't helped either - and watched her snatch an apple from the fruit bowl. "No, and you're not going to school. I actually need you to go and pack an overnight bag."

"What?" Her brows furrowed just before a stubborn hope

unfolded on her features. "Do you know where Dad is?" I really didn't and it was better that way. I'd spent a lot of money to retain that plausible deniability.

"We're going to see your aunt Eva."

"We're what now?"

Eight hours later, our jet landed in Portland, and Eva greeted us with a big, pink, sparkling sign that read 'Brody' in neon letters. She pulled Brody into a tight, motherly hug the second we were close enough. "Oh, it's so good to see you," she squealed, bobbing from side to side with Brody in her arms.

I hadn't spoken to Eva since the wedding, 17 years ago, until last night, after I came home from the Vortex. Turned out, Julian had done his fair share of damage to ensure her side of the family wanted nothing to do with ours and vice versa. He'd also done his fair share of damage to Brody's trust.

Which meant I owed Del a bigger apology than I'd thought. No wonder she hadn't picked up the phone for a few measly flowers.

Eva wrapped an arm around Brody's side and led us to her car. "Your uncle's told me that you're into sports. Your mother and I actually used to be competitive figure skaters, you know?" Okay, so maybe they wouldn't bond over their favorite sports, but Brody's eyes lit up at the mention of her mother.

I didn't let her out of my sight, but I gave her space that weekend. Space to meet her cousins and show the 8-year-old how to kick-punch his bullies into oblivion. Space to look through old pictures of her mother and try on her horrible 2001 prom dress - and keep it. Space to learn her grandparents' traditional donut recipe that sparked an entire business. I may have given her less space for that last one, crowding around the kitchen island with her.

"You never told me what happened between you and Del." Brody plopped down on the porch bench beside me that evening, another donut speared onto her pinky. She pulled my phone out of my hands, sliding it face-down onto the table.

"We broke up. There's not much more to tell."

"You fucked up, didn't you?" She raised her brows at me.

"Yes." No point in lying. Brody would just keep poking.

"How bad?"

With her big brown eyes on me, with her mother's family living a perfectly happy life just a few feet away, I couldn't even pretend it wasn't bad. That I had just gotten close to Del for the wrong reasons. The reminder of what Julian might have pulled fifteen years ago was sitting right here. I hadn't plotted a murder - or two - but that was the only reason I was alive, and he wasn't.

"Well, shit," she sighed when I didn't reply.

"Any advice?" I asked, both because she talked to Del more than I did, and because her last relationship advice had actually been sound.

"Groveling?"

"Tried that."

"Grand romantic gesture?"

I chuckled. "Did you get that from your smutty books?"

"Judge my books all you want," Brody jumped back to her feet and flipped me off with a big grin as she retreated back inside, "but in case you forgot, Del reads those books, too."

"Fair point," I sighed and added, "smart-ass."

I wasn't sure there was a gesture big enough to make up for what I had done - or almost done. There was no way to show Del that she had it wrong and I was the hero from her romance novels all along, because none of my intentions had been noble and just misinterpreted. Whatever we had, it had been built on lies and greed. But the most fucked up thing about the whole situation was that, even knowing the outcome, knowing how much pain I'd caused, knowing how wrong I'd been, I would do it again in a heartbeat if it gave me just another second with Del, a single smile, a single hug. That probably made me an even bigger asshole because I wasn't even reformed. I was a fucking addict, and I'd do anything to get a fix.

"I need to make one last stop before we leave," I told Brody Sunday afternoon when we got in the car, "and I'm going to need your help with it."

"Cryptic much?"

"How much of Delilah's book have you read?"

FORTY-NINE

Delilah

"This is just tasteless. It's called Underwater Sex." I wouldn't even have accepted the books. Just another gift, more over-the-top than that first edition of Emma he'd sent a while back. There were boxes upon boxes of them, all delivered while I was at work. Since they weighed about a bazillion pounds, sending them back would have been more expensive than just going through them and deciding which ones to keep and which ones to donate.

At least we'd made it a group project.

Tabitha whisked the Underwater Sex book out of my hands and read the back. "Oh, it's just about how fish procreate. I expected kinkier from him."

Defne skimmed the description over Tab's shoulder. "Wait, did you know the male seahorse gets pregnant? Not the female one?"

"Yes," Cordelia and Victor replied in unison, pulling all attention to them. Cordelia threw her hands up. "What? I like watching the Discovery Channel."

"I watch her watch the Discovery Channel." Victor shrugged.

All five of us sat between stacks of books in the second bedroom on my floor, which had become more of a reading room since I'd moved in, bed replaced by a cozy armchair.

"How many books is this?" Defne asked, pulling a large photo book on coral reefs into her lap.

"999," I replied, waving the delivery slip. Tabitha picked that out of my hands as well.

"That's weird," Cordelia mused, "did they miss one?"

"It says they were paid for in the shop," Tabitha said, dissecting the details of the order.

"Why did he go to Portland to buy you 999 books?" Defne asked.

I dropped my head back against the shelf that had housed antique China up until three hours ago. "Because 1000 books make a library."

"Then you're still missing one- oooh." Defne slapped her palm against her forehead.

"999 books to help me write mine." I drummed my fingers against the thick book of mermaid mythology that had been sitting in my lap for the last 20 minutes.

"I'm not saying we should forgive him," Tabitha prefaced, "but I think this is a way more romantic gift than a vibrator."

"A vibrator?" Cordelia gaped, hand stilling on Fitzwilliam's back, while Victor was suddenly very interested in Hydrographic Survey Methods 101.

"It was a thing." I waved her off.

"Not a big thing," Tabitha added, indicating a three-inch length between her fingers.

"The size doesn't really matter when it's an air pressure vibrator," I pointed out.

"I think I left the ice cream in the car," Victor said and swung himself to his feet in an enviable show of athleticism. He power-walked out of the room fast enough for his shoes to squeak against the wooden floors.

The second he was through the door, the rest of us burst into laughter.

VICTOR POKED HIS HEAD BACK INTO THE CHINA-GALLERY-TURNED-almost-library a few hours later. "Safe to come in?"

"Promise not to talk about sex toys," I replied, re-shelving the coral reef book someone had put in the seabed section, when it should be with the flora and fauna books. The others had cleared out half an hour ago, and I was still fixing the shelving system.

"Good, although you'd probably prefer talking about sex toys to this." He held up a manila envelope and crossed the room to me. "I should warn you, there's very graphic images in there."

"Are you giving me porn?" I grinned and pulled a file folder from the envelope. My smile faltered when I realized what he was giving me. "I already know what happened the day of the accident. How did you even get your hands on a *police report*?"

"You don't know everything. I added notes. You should burn this after reading." He nodded at the fireplace on the other wall.

"Okay. Thanks?"

He left me with a curt nod.

I knew he was a man of few words, but sometimes, being less cryptic wouldn't hurt.

I dragged the armchair from the window to the bookshelves and curled up in it, flipping the police report open like a novel. My stomach churned at the images of Beck's car, lying on its side, metal crinkled like paper. The passenger side of the Porsche was bent inwards like a pop-it toy. Automatically my fingers, no longer broken, slipped into my shirt to trace the scar along my ribs. I'd been half an inch from drowning in my own blood.

The other car didn't seem as badly damaged with only its front folded in, but I'd been told the driver hadn't survived the crash.

I flipped the pages until I got to the actual report and stopped breathing. Roger Childs. The name was glaring at me from the top of the page. My insides tightened, stomach souring, and my mind immediately conjured up images of his hand on my thigh. I shook my head to ward the memories off like annoying flies. What the heck was his name- I flipped back to the images of the cars. Silver Volvo. Maybe it would have looked more familiar if it hadn't been as damaged, but it wasn't a car that stood out until seeing it in front of your workplace turned your tongue to sandpaper in the morning.

Roger had been the one who rammed into us. The police report said his phone was found near his seat and he must have been texting when leaving the rest stop. There was no note about his ties to me because there was no *me* in this. Roger didn't know Cordelia Montgomery. I doubted the policemen involved in a closed-and-shut accident were interested in the society pages enough to care about Delilah-me and follow up on this... What would they even find? The man who had once tried to coerce me into spreading my legs had his neck snapped by his own airbag when he tried to run me off the road? Suited him fucking right.

The page tore in the cramping grasp of my fingers and I sucked in a deep breath and focused back on the words. I'd known Beck pulled me out of the car. The nurses had been swooning over him every second they got when I'd gone back to the hospital. A proper knight in shining armor. Yeah right. He'd still needed me to marry him. If I'd died, Cordelia could have simply branded me an imposter, but Beck couldn't have just started dating the real Cordelia without looking suspicious.

I hadn't known he'd also pulled the other driver out. Too late for Roger though.

I finally got to the page Victor had promised. The one with his notes. A play-by-play account of how they had hired private investigators to look into Roger and had used that information to get him fired - and had sent a copy to his wife. He didn't go into detail about what the investigators had found, but it must have been bad enough to cause a divorce - and make Roger mad enough to follow me and run me off the road when he saw an opening. He was vindictive enough for that. Or... had been. Good riddance.

Victor also detailed how Julian had blackmailed him, threatened to reveal his location to his family if he didn't get me out of the hospital - only to find out Julian had been working with his family for a while. Nothing about Beck.

After burning the pages, as instructed, I went to the garage and stared at the red Porsche waiting next to Cordelia's town car. Turns out, sending back a car wasn't as easy as sending back a notebook or regifting flower bouquets. I'd considered just dropping it off in front of Axent's headquarters, but... I climbed into the passenger seat, trying hard not to let the scent of fresh car and rich leather seduce me, and pulled the papers from the glove compartment. Registered to two owners. Cordelia Montgomery. Delilah Edwards.

Fine. He wanted to get my attention. He had my attention. And I needed some straight answers.

An hour later, I stood in front of a nervous doorman while he tried to get through to the penthouse. "I'm very sorry Miss Edwards, but it appears he's unavailable."

"Fine, then just give him this." I smacked the key to the Porsche down on the counter and just pulled the registration from my bag, when his voice poured over me like honey.

"I believe this lovely lady is looking for me." I turned around to see Beck with his sleeves rolled up and a takeout bag in one hand. He placed the food on the counter and took the key instead. "Dinner's on me, Henry, and feel free to put Delilah on the approved visitors list. She can come up whenever she wants."

"I do not need to be on any list, Henry," I said but Beck was already directing me to the elevator with a hand between my shoulders. I twisted around to shoot the trembling doorman another look. "Take me off the list!"

The elevator doors shut and by the fifth floor, the moment had sunk in, and I turned to see Beck smile at the ground. "Did you just go out and buy food for your doorman?"

He chuckled. "No, but I'm not going to expose you to chicken satay."

"Oh." Yeah, I could do without another allergic shock. "Thanks."

"That means you owe me dinner."

"No, this just means we're even for the dinner you canceled on me."

"What I'm hearing is, we need to catch up on two dinners."

"I think you need hearing aids, Casanova." I hated how easily I slipped back into conversation with him. This wasn't supposed to be easy. For goodness' sake. We had spent almost as much time *not* talking since the White Ball as we had spent time getting to know each other. The fake versions of each other.

The elevator pinged and let us out on his floor. His new place was bigger than the old one, but most of his sleek, dark wood furniture had carried over. It was also a lot more cluttered, and I clutched the strap of my bag to refrain from starting piles for scattered clothes and books. Beck led me through the living room, a separate dining room, and into kitchen. "Where's Brody?" I asked, picking up the single red converse that had been abandoned on the bar stool of the kitchen island.

"She's with a friend. She's…" He sighed and pulled one of those small orange juice bottles from the fridge, placing it in front of me. I'd never actually told him that I preferred juice to any other drink. It was something he had just picked up on. "She's spending a lot of time with friends. Which the therapist tells me is good, because it means she's seeking out the familiar instead of acting out."

"For what it's worth, she seems okay in school. All things considered."

"Yeah," he sighed, "I think she knows more about her father than she lets on."

I should have been asking about him. And how are you doing, Beck? How are you coping with his death? How do you feel considering your brother was shot right in front of you?

"You were right about Brody's trust," he said, while collecting a mixing bowl and various ingredients around his kitchen, "I don't think anyone would benefit from looking into her mother's death, but you were right about her inheritance going to Brody, and Julian taking control of the trust. We met with her mother's family in Portland. Her aunt will help if Brody ever wants to go into the Donut business."

"Portland. That's why you sent the books from Powell's."

"Buy indie, right? You came here because of this?" He slid the car key across the counter. "I'm not taking the car back. Or the books. In fact, I'm not accepting any further gift returns."

"You had the car registered in two names."

"I wasn't sure if you had a license with Cordelia's name on it."

"Your whole scheme was one speed check away from blowing up in your face."

"Yes, it was."

I let that confirmation fester in the air between us before I asked the question I came here to ask: "When did you find out who I was?"

"First day of meeting you."

"What?"

"Not quite, actually. We had someone monitor Cordelia's house since this was going to be the first time she'd attended an event in years. Imagine my surprise when, after dancing and dining with you, I received the alert that Cordelia had already made it back home an hour earlier. In a change of clothes," while explaining, he added eggs and flour and other ingredients to his bowl, before finally getting out a whisk, "I didn't figure out you were *you* until money from the Montgomery estate was used to pay rent on a small studio in Mission Hill."

"And when did you find out about Roger?"

He halted in his whisking, gray eyes bleeding to black as he fixed me in place with his stare. "When you told me."

"I didn't tell you about him."

"I picked you up from High Tea. You were chatty. I did my research with what info you gave me."

"So, you knew? When you pulled him from his car after the crash?" I refused to call it an accident now.

"I knew who he was. I didn't need all the details of what happened, but after the crash, I made sure you were *safe*."

He poured a spoonful of dough into the pan. Pancakes. Comfort food, he'd called them. "I punched him," I said, watching the dough turn gold, "that's why I got fired. He gave me a negative teacher evaluation and then asked me to meet him to go over my performance."

"Delilah, you don't have to tell me any of this. You don't owe me an explanation."

"I know. I want you to know." I nodded and kept my eyes on the pancake as Beck flipped it. "Roger made it quite clear how my performance could improve and how he could be swayed to re-evaluate my skills. I punched him. Obviously, I couldn't prove that he shoved me into a corner and pushed his hand up my skirt. He, on the other hand, had security footage that showed me walking into his office, and the broken nose to prove I'd gotten violent over my negative performance review."

"You broke his nose with one hit?"

"Yep." I furrowed my brows and looked up from the pan. That wasn't even close to any of the other questions I'd gotten about that day. When I told people what happened, if they believed me, they tried to push the victim role on me. *Poor little Delilah, how do you feel, are you hurt, do you want to talk?* Yeah, it had fucking sucked, and I'd needed to work through it, but the crunch of Roger's nose under my fist? His shocked face as he tried to stop the bleeding? God, that had been the most satisfying moment of my life.

"I'm impressed." He chuckled. "Maybe I should upgrade your status at Vortex from student to teacher."

"Beck, about the other day at Vortex."

"I shouldn't have touched you."

"No, I'm glad you did." He looked confused. "I needed to know that you're not the magical key to my lock."

"I never was."

"Actually, do you still have the- nevermind. I'll get one. Sorry." What was I thinking? We were not back there. God. My tongue had moved faster than rational thought.

He eyed me, and switched the flame off, pancake still a bit wobbly. "You want the vibrator?"

"It's a really good one. And it's really expensive. I looked it up. Why would you pay that much for a vibrator?"

"Because it's a really good one." Beck smirked. "Come on. I actually have a couple of your things."

I followed him through the living room and upstairs, only to stop in the doorway of the room he led me into. "You keep a used vibrator in your office?"

My eyes raked over the familiar bookshelves and his desk, and narrowed at the wide leather sofa pushed against one wall, decked with throw pillows and a soft blanket. "It's a library, not an office. It's supposed to invite people to stay and read." He gestured at the sofa, shooting me that damn signature Beckett grin, with the mischief hiding in its corners. My traitorous stomach did a silly flip at the sight of it, combined with the fact that he had created a *library,* but I stayed glued to the doorframe. "And yes, I do. Here." He pulled a large gray box from the shelf and placed it on his desk.

Okay, fine. A few steps into the room wouldn't make me do anything stupid. I was in full control of my actions here.

I kept the desk between us and pulled the box over to me. Something inside clattered and I drew my brows up as I flipped the lid off. Alongside the small blue box I'd become familiar with, lay a pink Taylor Swift shirt, a plaid pajama top, a certain leather-bound notebook, a handful of page flags and pens, and a Ziploc bag with around a dozen sea shells.

"I won't lie. Bernard didn't survive the move, but he died an honorable death."

I raised the Ziploc bag against the light. "Bernard is right there. With the yellow speck. Oh. Ooh. Dorothy is gone."

"Have dinner with me, Blondie."

"No, thank you." My stomach did another flip, and I forced myself to keep breathing, keep my eyes on my hands as I carefully nestled the sea shells between the clothes. I'd gotten the answers I'd wanted. I didn't have to spend even one more second thinking about Beck from here on out. I could be civil on school grounds, and for Brody's sake, but he was otherwise banned from my mind. "I'm busy."

"I didn't say when."

I put the lid back on the box and carried it out the door without looking back. "I'll be busy then, too."

FIFTY

Delilah

Cordelia had stuck true to her word and gave me the house every first weekend of the month, staying with Victor, so I could have people over. I had spent all evening on Tinder, swiping left on douchy tagline after douchy tagline.

Defne and Tabitha had helped me set up a profile that boiled down to 'want to get laid without getting murdered please' before both of them had left me to my own devices - Tabitha to get laid herself, Defne to go to family dinner.

I swiped right on a handful of profiles. However, by my second glass of wine and yet another 'unmatch' after the most uninspiring three lines of conversation, I understood that someone could look like they fucked (thanks Tabitha) but their spelling made it virtually impossible to even think about fucking them. I really wanted to fuck them, too. Just to test the waters. Test some of my newfound knowledge. But how could my loins catch on fire if this guy didn't even know the difference between *their* and *they're*?

I grabbed the half empty wine bottle from the counter and took it upstairs with me, where I tossed my phone onto the sheets before pulling a certain blue box out from under the bed. This was how far I'd sunk- sunken- sinked- oh god, maybe I shouldn't be judging anyone on their spelling when the wine messed with my head like this. Further proof of my far-sunken-ness.

Tried to be all casual, get drunk and laid, and it was going to be yet another night alone in my room - with the added bonus of major alcohol-induced anxiety spirals tomorrow.

Well, that was tomorrow-Delilah's problem.

I tossed the lid of the blue box aside and tested the weight of the vibrator in my hand. Its handle was a smooth curve, with the little air nozzle at the top jutting out at the perfect angle. Between the minimalist design and the metallic sheen, it almost looked like a fancy skincare tool rather than a sex toy.

The floor swayed a little as I climbed into bed, but I somehow made it out of my clothes and under the soft covers without toppling over. At least the buzz of the wine behind my temples quieted my anxieties when the first air blast hit my clit.

I let the warmth between my legs carry me, let my eyes drift close as I feathered my fingertips over my chest. But the second I shut the room out, I saw Beck's head between my legs, the flicks of his tongue so close to the vibrator's bursts of pressure. My back arched, and my eyes flew open.

Okay. No.

This was about me, not him.

I shook my head, as if that could clear out any thoughts of him, and I thought back to how I'd come really close *on my own* at Clandestine. I could imagine that. I could put myself back there.

Readjusting the vibrator against my clit, and dialing up the speed, I let my eyes fall shut again. The memory of the island room was still vibrant in my mind: the dark space, dotted with beds covered in sheer curtains that allowed glances at the writhing bodies on them. I imagined myself on one of those beds, exposed but still safe, imagined the weight of people's eyes sliding over my skin like ghost touches. And I imagined Beck sinking into me, stretching me, claiming me for all to see. I let out a startled gasp, toes curling into my sheets.

No.

Hell no.

I didn't want that. I didn't want him back in my life, didn't want to give my body to someone who had so little regard for the lives of others. Why on earth did my brain conjure up images of someone who, for all intents and purposes, would have been an accessory to murder just to get his hands on a company? How could I even think about sleeping with someone, about being vulnerable with someone, who valued money more than people?

I couldn't rationalize my way out of this, and before I knew it, I had my phone in hand and was dialing Beck's number. Shit. I should probably- I fumbled with the buttons of the vibrator to switch off the buzzing. My phone tumbled somewhere into my pillows, just as I heard Beck pick up on the other end.

"Oops, hi," I gasped once I had my phone in hand again, vibrator switched off successfully, "hello you. I have a queue – I have a – a question for you."

"What the fuck? Del, you sound drunk. Where are you?"

"I'm slightly tipsy. Slightly. And I'm at home, and I just think that all the guys on Tinder suck."

"You don't drink."

My heckles raised, because maybe I didn't usually drink but maybe I also wasn't super boring and predictable and easily exploitable. "You don't know my life, okay?"

On the other end of the line, Beck heaved a deep sigh. "You called to ask a question."

"Yes! I wanted to know you. Know from you." Wow. Words were hard after half a bottle of wine. "Why do I think about you when I masturbate?" I shifted and accidentally pressed the button on the vibrator again, squealing at the sudden blow against my center. "Shit, sorry. I. Yes. Question."

"Are you doing what I think you're doing?" His voice dropped low, and the rumble mixed with the soft pressure against my clit, sent a shiver down my spine. I should have just switched the vibrator off again, but I wanted to be bold. I wanted to show him that I wasn't just a red ribbon girl.

"I need to know, please. I tried to rationalize, but I can't. It's not rational for me to think about you, but my brain just keeps doing it. Is that okay?"

"Alright sweetheart, are you asking for my consent or are you asking me on an intellectual level?"

"I don't know. Both?" I pressed my lips together, as the heat in my abdomen started welling up.

"Yes, it's okay. Consensually and intellectually. Your fantasies don't have to be rational. They don't even have to be something you want to happen in real life."

"They don't?"

"No, because in your head, you're safe. Even if you think about me, it's a fantasy version of me. The scenarios you fantasize about would likely still play out differently if we were to actually have sex. In your head, you're the director. You're in full control."

"Oh, I rarely am." I laughed.

"Well, you know, keep practicing."

"Okay, alright - oh god, oh - I am going to go now."

"Have fun."

"Thank you-oh." I flung my phone across the mattress, my back arching as the buzzing inside me grew stronger. I couldn't deny that Beck's voice had added to that. And I let my head fall back into the pillows, squeezed my eyes shut and allowed the thought of his hand wrapped around my throat to carry me deeper.

FIFTY-ONE

BECK

THE SECOND TIME I STEPPED INTO THE EVENT SPACE AT TRUMAN Academy, the florals and luxurious gold decor from the first time had been switched out for swiveling disco lights and glittering rainbow streamers. Where a string quartet had played, a DJ was currently remixing a song I'd never heard, but it had all the teenagers jumping up and down and singing along.

I spotted Del on the other side of the room before she had the chance to notice me. At least that gave me a moment to drink her in. Her hair had been curled and swept into an updo, leaving just a few strands to frame her face, which really put the focus on those devastating red lips. My eyes dropped lower to the pale green empire-waist dress - and I knew the exact moment her eyes found me, because her chest strained against the scooping neckline in a deep, long sigh.

She made her way along the edge of the dance floor, but while my eyes never left her, she was intently focused on the kids before stopping next to me. "What are you doing here?"

"I was roped into chaperoning," I replied, watching her face for any trace of uncertainty or blush, considering our last conversation.

"How?" She furrowed her brows. "Brody's not even a junior yet."

I hesitated, waiting for the realization to sink in that she hadn't spoken to me since drunk dialing while masturbating, but she'd either blacked the memory out, or she was comfortable enough with the action not to show remorse. I fucking hoped it was the latter, for her own sake, but selfishly also for mine. I dragged my eyes from her to the kids twirling and jumping around on the dance floor. "Apparently, there's a whole pecking order among the parents here, and as a newcomer who didn't introduce themselves to the PTA with personalized gift baskets, I'm at the bottom of the food chain."

"Wow." She laughed. A light, genuine laugh that I hadn't heard in weeks. "Couldn't negotiate your way out of this one?"

"I negotiated my way out of chaperoning the ski trip." I grinned. "This is the compromise."

"Really? Why? I can't wait for the ski trip."

"You're going?" I immediately regretted choosing one night of Homecoming over five days of mountain air.

"I negotiated that compromise myself. I'm covering all four dances for Rhonda this year to take her spot, because new teachers usually don't get to. But they do a day-trip to the Niagara Falls every year on the ski trip, and I wasn't passing up that chance."

"You didn't even want to leave the city with me."

"Yeah, but that was *Cordelia-me*."

"I kind of figured."

"How so?"

"A Janeite who wouldn't jump at the chance to go to England?" I raised my brows at her. "Come on."

"You know, August Beckett almost sounds like a name from a regency novel. *Oh dear Mr. Beckett.*" She said that last part in a horrible English accent that sounded almost German.

"In that case, I would like to make use of my advantage as a man and ask you to dance, and leave you the power to refuse me." I held out a hand for her.

"Are you misquoting Northanger Abbey to me?"

"Would you do me the honour of dancing with me, Miss Edwards?" I asked in a fake English accent a lot crisper than hers thanks to my boarding school years.

"Uh…" A rush of blood tinted her cheeks pink and she stared intently at her nails, throat bobbing. English accent. I'd have to remember that. "Alright."

I was prepared to make a total fool of myself, trying to dance to whatever remix the DJ would put on, but the second Delilah stepped onto the dance floor with me, a literal record scratch filled the room, followed by the announcement: "DJ Day has decided it's about time for all the lovebirds to get in their obligatory slow dance."

Del's head whipped around, and she shot the DJ a death-glare through narrowed eyes, but that man just grinned and winked at her.

"Friend of yours?" I asked, my voice as tight as my clenched jaw. He only got away with that wink because he was clearly putting on Ronan Keating for our benefit.

"Fellow English-teacher," she replied and turned, face still stony, "and self-proclaimed matchmaker. He's read Emma a few too many times."

"You can still refuse me," I said and held out my open hand.

After a moment, Del placed her palm in mine and let herself be swept into a slow sway. Her other hand curled around my shoulder, nails digging in hard enough to betray her nerves. I started running soothing circles over the small of her back, but it had the opposite effect. Her spine stiffened under the touch, so I stopped.

The hollow ache in my gut deepened. It had been there since the night she found out what I'd done, and it grew deeper every single time she reminded me that my hope was futile when it came to any kind of future with her.

Even our very first dance had been more intimate than this. She'd let herself melt into the movements then. Tonight, I could have been dancing with a mannequin and it would have been just as deep.

"I would like to tell you something, but I don't think you'll like it," I said.

"Beck." Del shuddered in my arms. "Can't you just let this go?"

"Can you?"

Her eyes found mine, swimming with the promise of tears. Instead of replying, she shook her head and pulled her shoulders up. She couldn't have pretended to be over me, considering our phone call the other night, but having her confirm as much stitched up a small part of my hollow gut.

"What I'm about to tell you is not an excuse. I don't expect you to forgive me, but I think you deserve the full story of how we got here. If only to stop beating yourself up, because I know that I've made you doubt yourself."

Lips quivering, she nodded.

"Ah, perfect. Man. Woman." Principal Baker, who I'd met with to discuss Brody's situation, clapped his hands over both our shoulders. "Boys' room. Girls' room. Toilet check. Now." Not a word wasted before he blazed on, completely oblivious to the moment he'd just wrecked. Nobody at Axent talked to me that way. Hell, nobody outside this room talked to me that way, but I was learning that schools operated on a whole different social level.

"We're on it!" Delilah called over her shoulder with enough enthusiasm to send a troupe of soldiers to battle and pulled herself out of my arms.

It took us all of four minutes to check the only set of unlocked bathrooms, but when Del was about to breeze back to the dance, I wrapped my hand around her wrist and gently pulled her back. She shot a quick look up and down the hallway, only to realize we were alone. All the previous pep dissipated from her features. "Okay," she sighed and dropped back against the row of lockers, "tell me."

"Do you remember what I told you about my mother?" She nodded, and I told her about Georgia. Once I started, the words kept tumbling over my lips. I told her about growing up in a house, where my father ignored his children, but kept their mother on a leash like she was a dog and he expected her to heel. I told her about Georgia in turn training us just as ruthlessly, withholding sleep and food if we didn't perform. I told her that my secret reading materials gave me an escapism and different perspectives that Julian never got. He'd always been our mother's son, playing her game to win instead of outplaying her by changing the rules - until he decided that I was no longer a player on his team. I told her about Sternberg's theory of love.

That last one finally cracked her careful composure. "You rationalized love?" She smiled.

"Yes."

"For someone as smart as you are, that's really dumb."

"Why? You can hardly deny that our feelings got mixed into this."

She rolled her eyes at me. "Commitment, passion and intimacy aren't enough. Parker was committed to me. He was passionate about me. We shared intimacy, being open about our pasts and family histories. We didn't match because he doubted my commitment to him. I couldn't bring myself to be passionately swept up by him because of my self-doubts. He projected his hang-ups about his family's financials onto me." She furrowed her brows, then raised her hand into the space between us, flashing me the smooth skin on the back of it. "The first night we met, you understood what I was doing. You got me out of the conversation. It took Parker eight weeks to notice I was pinching myself, and even then, he didn't understand."

"All I'm hearing is that your ex didn't deserve a shred of your time, Blondie."

"Maybe," she chuckled, "but I don't think you can manufacture love. We matched. You didn't *pretend* to have a library full of books to woo me with your literary prowess. You didn't go out and buy 200 nonfiction books about sex just so I could intellectually work through my very specific issues. And you may be a good liar, but I never felt judged by you. I think we share the idea of 'curiosity not judgement' and that allowed us to be curious about each other and fall for each other. We matched. Just not enough to make it work. Not when it mattered." She pushed herself off the lockers with a soft smile. "For what it's worth, I'm sorry you had abusive parents, but you're right. It's not an excuse. You're a grown man who makes his own decisions."

I followed her back to the ballroom, where the kids were back to their previous upbeat dance moves. To my surprise, Del waited for me, glancing over her shoulder to make sure I was still following her when she took over drinks' duty from one of the other chaperones.

"Would you ever consider giving up Axent to do something else?" She asked and handed me a plastic cup filled with neon red punch.

"No."

"You didn't even take a second to think about that."

"Just because I hate what it took to get there, doesn't mean I hate where I am. I like it. I like negotiations and contracts and 5am meetings with our team in Hong Kong. I could do without board meetings, but I doubt everyone likes every aspect of their job."

"Hmm." She hummed and filled the cup of a girl with ringlet curls and braces.

"Why do you teach?"

"Because I like it," she grinned, throwing my words back at me.

"I read your introduction in the school newsletter. You got your master's at Harvard on a full academic scholarship, and yet you decided to become an English teacher."

"Not prestigious enough for you?"

"You could have gone into journalism, or publishing. I simply don't know a lot of teachers with an ivy league background."

"Do you know many teachers?"

"Touché."

"I grew up without books. My parents just weren't big readers. I later fell in love with reading because of my English teachers. I started making up stories because of my English teachers. I want to help kids find the story they didn't know they were looking for, whether that's in a book or in their own writing. I don't want to negotiate deals or discuss marketing strategies, sit in an office and stare at contracts all day." She tilted her head from side to side and waited for a giggling group of girls to get their drinks and leave, before she continued: "I could have gone to any school to become a teacher, I suppose, but you know me. Inquisitive by nature, so if I can learn from the best, I'll learn from the best."

"Would you consider giving it up when you sell your book?"

"I don't know. I can't even consider that yet." She shrugged. "I'll have to finish writing the damn thing first."

"Alright, I'll ask again when you do."

We continued working side by side until the punch ran out and the overhead lights flickered on. The last students trickled out, while I handed Del empty cups and she tossed them in a big bin.

"Good night, folks. Another one for the books. I'll see you all on Monday." Principal Baker clapped his hands together and beelined out the door when the roughest mess was cleared up, the rest to be left for the custodians and cleaning crew.

"We never got to finish our dance," I said and held out my hand again. "Miss Edwards?"

"There's no music, *Mr. Beckett.*"

"We'll make do."

This time, I didn't bother with the proper placement for my hands, letting them slip around her waist instead. After hovering in the air for a heartbeat, hers folded around my upper arms. I began swaying from foot to foot lightly, only for her head to drop against my chest. If she heard the erratic beating she caused behind my ribs, she didn't show it. Instead, the tension rippled from her body, rigid muscles softening in my arms as I slowly turned us in a circle.

I stifled any hopeful thought that wanted to flicker up, because Delilah had few reservations about physical closeness. It was as agonizing as it was addicting.

People cleared out around us, and DJ Day hovered in the door just a moment longer than the rest, but I kept us moving. As long as we were dancing, I had her. "I did it, by the way." She pulled her head back and blinked up at me. "After our phone call? I got there by myself."

"Are you serious?" A big, genuine smile shot to my face. Not only because she still trusted me enough to share, but because I was so fucking proud of her. She may have needed to talk her anxieties through, but in the end, she got to the climax all by herself. She'd figured out how to quiet her mind enough to enjoy the physical side of sex without anyone guiding her through. "That's amazing, Del."

She laughed and shot a quick look around, before lowering her voice. "I don't know if I would call drunkenly masturbating *amazing*."

"Don't do that."

"What?"

"Downplay your achievement just because it's something that might come easier to other people." I tilted her chin up, forcing her to meet my gaze, because I meant it when I said: "Congratulations, sweetheart."

"Thank you." Her breath stuttered as our eyes locked and the air between us thickened with the understanding and familiarity that led to this very conversation.

My fingertip trailed from her chin, down her jaw, until I could wrap my hand around the back of her neck. Her lips trembled, but her eyes stayed on mine as I leaned down. She didn't turn her head, didn't ask me to stop, didn't flinch until my lips brushed over hers. A desperate sigh passed from her mouth to mine before she melted into me.

All rational thought left my body when I tasted her. I crushed my mouth over hers. She whimpered into the kiss and her tongue swept over my lips, sending a hot spark through my veins. Her arms closed around my neck as she pulled herself against me. With her body pressed into mine, we kissed like two people starved by a hunger that only the other could sate.

"Stop." She jerked back without warning and pushed me off. The word stung worse than her slap had, but I didn't try to bridge the distance when she stumbled back. Her chest was rising fast as she closed a hand around her blue pearl necklace. "I'm sorry. I can't."

FIFTY-TWO

BECK

Something Del had said at the dance had wedged itself into my mind in the way something got caught between your molars. Annoying, invisible, and damn near impossible to get out, no matter how much you poked and prodded it with your tongue. You'd be stuck with it until you got your hands on floss.

That was Cordelia-me.

Not: That was when I was pretending to be Cordelia.

Not: That was part of Cordelia's character.

Cordelia-me.

It occupied the same corner of my brain as Cordelia's debut/farewell speech at the White Ball. She had introduced Delilah to the world as her sister. Even though they shared no blood relation, a whole lot of people now thought they did.

It had, surprisingly, only taken one email to be invited to Cordelia's home office. Which was a cluttered mess. She sat between piles of paper, cat toys, brochures, and half-empty smoothie bottles, but based on Yelchin's glower across her shoulder, I decided not to point out that Delilah could probably get her on a color-coded system within a few hours.

"I'm not putting in a good word for you with her," she said after offering a drink - which I declined based on the amount of cat hair on her clothes.

"That's not why I'm here."

"In that case, let's hear it." She leaned back and folded her hands in her lap. They looked similar enough, but the way they moved was nothing alike. Where Del's mind was whirring a million miles per hour, her body sometimes moving as if it was an afterthought, Cordelia's every muscle twitch seemed controlled. Even her slow blinks seemed deliberate to make me feel watched.

Maybe Del had been right. Maybe I was a good liar, and I'd lied to myself above all. Because *this* Cordelia Montgomery, I couldn't picture myself longing for, not even if Sternberg himself published a manual for falling in love.

This Cordelia Montgomery was, however, the reason I came here. I inhaled and met her eyes. "I'm sorry."

She tilted her chin up, a small smile curling around the corners of her lips. "I think I misheard you. Repeat, please."

Alright, they may not have moved alike, but Delilah and Cordelia were two peas in a pod. "I'm sorry," I repeated, "I think we both know why I've been putting my efforts into making amends with Delilah, but I realized that you deserve an apology as well. The original plan was to facilitate an Axent-Montgomery merger through marriage between you and me. I came to that charity dinner prepared to sweep you off your feet and I thought it would be easy because of your mental health. And when we found out you had gotten yourself a stand-in, I had arrangements made to ship you off to a mental institution for the rest of your life. A very nice one with horses and art classes, but I still hadn't considered… you. You're great at what you do. I've been keeping an eye on your foundation. I underestimated you in the worst way possible."

"Hmm." Cordelia leaned back in her chair and tapped a pen against her lips. "So, you're admitting that you were an ableist pig?"

"Yes."

"Good. What are you doing to make up for it?"

"Excuse me?"

"An apology is worth nothing if you don't do the work to back it up."

She *was* great at what she did. I had been the fool to walk into the wolf's den without prepping on an economical level. "I suppose you have something in mind."

"I'm glad you asked." She beamed and straightened in her chair. "I want three free self-defense classes at one of your gyms for every survivor benefitting from our foundation. We invite all of them to join fully sponsored group seminars in our centers on the east and west cost twice a year, so don't think just because they live in South Dakota or Texas, they won't make use of their free classes. I need a majority of these classes to be taught by women. All instructors have to be trained on dealing with vulnerable people who might experience mental health issues during the class, such as PTSD flashbacks. We're willing to provide that training through our foundation, but you'll pay for it." She handed me a piece of paper across the desk.

"Done." I pulled my pen from my jacket pocket and signed on the dotted line.

"Just like that? No negotiation? You didn't even read the contract." She narrowed her eyes at me, waiting for the other shoe to drop.

"I signed Delilah up at the club," I said.

"I know. That's what gave me the idea. I don't understand the relevance though."

"I've seen her train with a professional fighter, and it doesn't work. You can't tell someone who needs to work through a mental block that they just have to turn their hips and kick harder. So, no. No negotiation. I want that training for my instructors. All of them, not just the ones teaching self-defense. Can your foundation accommodate that?"

"Yes." She shot a quick look over her shoulder, but Yelchin's expression remained stoic. Whatever silent exchange passed between them, she turned back to me with a smile. "I like that energy, but you're not getting a friends and family discount."

"Name your price. You can work out the details with Scarlett. She runs the day-to-day." I handed the contract back along with a Vortex card that had Scarlett's details on it. She'd rip my head off for giving out free classes like candy, while throwing money at Cordelia for that mental health training. Maybe she'd have to get that regional manager back. Anna? Hannah? That girl that had been harping on about inclusivity.

"Amazing. Perfect." Cordelia stuck the business card to her monitor with a piece of pink tape. "Del isn't here by the way. She's at work."

"I know. This wasn't for her benefit."

"Well, consider your amends to me made." She stood from her chair and shook my hand as she dismissed me. "I'll see you around, Beck."

"I thought you didn't show your face outside your house." Confused, I turned in the doorway just to see her big toothpaste-commercial-worthy grin.

"That's correct."

FIFTY-THREE

Delilah

Vortex was closing for the whole week, and when Scarlett called to cancel my lessons, she had some choice words about the Montgomery foundation hijacking her ovulation window, when she had originally taken three days off just to spend them in bed with Harlan. That was already way more information than I needed from her, so I decided not to ask any more questions. Instead, I went right to the source of the hijacking.

"This is a conversation that requires a lot more ice cream." Cordelia sighed and swung herself out of her desk chair.

We were in the middle of pumpkin spice season, but for Cordelia that just meant she'd chase her ice cream with a hot chocolate (extra marshmallows). I thought my Starbucks order was bad, but Cordelia trumped me on sugar consumption in almost every way possible. The only exception being that disgusting tea Victor kept making for her.

"Why didn't you tell me?" I asked, halfway through my single scoop of caramel fudge, while Cordelia was swirling gummy bears and whipped cream around in her bowl.

She pulled her shoulders up. "Because I don't get a vote here."

"Vote on what?"

"Your feelings for Beck."

"Excuse me?" I scoffed. "This doesn't change what he did in the first place."

"No, it doesn't." She scooped a mountain of ice cream and gummy bears and rainbow sprinkles into her mouth.

"I can't have feelings for him," I said, knowing exactly what look that would earn me from her. Because I said *'can't'* not *'don't'*. Because even if I hated everything he'd done and had planned to do in the name of a business merger, I couldn't pretend that I had detached myself from him. How could a person willing to manipulate me, and get rid of Cordelia, be the same person who put my own name on a car registration just to make sure I wouldn't get arrested for Grand Theft Auto?

"I'm not saying you should be with him. I'm on your side, no matter what you decide to do." Cordelia set down her spoon and folded her hands under her chin to look at me across the new dining table, replaced after that night with Julian. "I think, there are actions that are inexcusable, and then there are mindsets we can grow out of."

"You think someone can grow out of planning to abduct you and lock you up for the rest of their life?"

"Yes." Cordelia let that one word sink in. "I think a lot of people are raised to believe that anyone with disabilities and mental health issues is worthless, and that can lead to harmful action. But I do believe that people's concept of health, and its worth, can change. Which will lead towards a change in their actions. If I didn't believe that people can change, I'd be running a high security prison, not a social organization. The question is whether a person has previously crossed a line they can't uncross. That's something you have to figure out for yourself."

"That sounded rehearsed."

"I've actually thought about the same thing a lot since he emailed me."

"And?"

"And he hasn't crossed my lines. His brother has, may he rot in hell, but I know first-hand that a shared last name doesn't mean you're on the same page about how much money a person's life is worth to you." Cordelia picked her spoon up again. "Planning to commit a crime and actually committing it are two very different things. You don't know if he would have gone through with his plans."

"He didn't stop his brother when he waved a gun around. Victor did."

"You didn't see yourself. You were barely standing up, bleeding, throwing up. Beck tried to get you out. He prioritized the person he loved over anything else going on in that room."

"He tried to get me out because he still needed to marry me-as-you."

"Did he?" Cordelia's voice was all innocent and chipper, as she shoveled another mountain of rocky road onto her spoon, but she knew exactly what she was asking.

FIFTY-FOUR

BECK

I OPENED THE DOOR, NOT SURE WHO TO EXPECT AS THE SOURCE OF incessant knocking on a Wednesday night, but it definitely hadn't been Delilah. Her hair was hanging limp and soaked around her face, and her wet jacket stuck to her like a second skin.

"Jesus, Blondie, you're drenched." I stepped aside to let her in. She left a trail of puddles on the hardwood floors.

"Yeah, well, the idea of getting me a car was good. There's just no parking anywhere." She unwrapped her scarf, holding it up like a wet rag. "Also, Henry didn't take me off the approved visitors list even though I told him to last time. I feel like that's a security oversight."

I threw the scarf over the coat rack, not giving two shits whether it would ruin my jackets. Delilah's hands trembled and her cheeks had taken on a bright pink hue as she fumbled with her zipper. I couldn't care less about keeping an appropriate distance, and covered her hands with mine to undo the zipper. I peeled her out of the jacket, my knuckles grazing over her bare underarms. "You're freezing."

"Again. Parking," she stuttered. "Had to walk five blocks."

"You should get out of those clothes." Even the shirt underneath her jacket hadn't been spared. I'd have to get her a better parking spot, and an umbrella, and possibly a better jacket. For now, I boxed her into the living room, where the gas fireplace flickered on high. "Let me find you something dry to wear. Do you want a bath? Tea?"

"No, actually, I came here with a purpose." She sniffed and pulled her bag around, digging through her number of colorful pouches. "Ha. Good thing I laminated it."

She dropped her bag on the sofa and held up a small rectangular piece of plastic. Her picture was on it, but I had to pluck it from her hands and hold it up to the light to read her neat, tiny handwriting. "August Beckett Library Membership Card?"

"It has my photo and everything."

"I can see that. Did you draw a logo for a fake library?" I narrowed my eyes at the letters AB drawn onto the pages of an open book.

"That card is very real. It gives me access to your library, whenever I want."

"I see. The opening times are 24/7, huh? And you are…" I tapped the corner where her makeshift library card said as much, my mouth twitching into a smile. "…entitled to personalized book recommendations by a qualified librarian at least twice a month?"

"If it says so on the card." She pulled her shoulders up. "Sounds like that's the library policy. And it's laminated, so it can't be changed."

I laughed. I couldn't help myself. Delilah was putting down clear rules about where, how, and how much she wanted to interact with me - and she wasn't giving me a choice. Not that I wanted one. I would have agreed to far less than two monthly conversations about books as long as it meant getting to spend time with her at all. "I do appreciate a clear policy."

"I want to make use of my membership and borrow a book."

"Okay, well," my eyes slid down her body to the small lake that had formed at her feet, "you're not setting foot in a room full of paper."

"Fine," she huffed and pulled at her thin sweater, only for it to snap back against her skin, "can you bring me your robe? The fluffy blue one?"

"Sure."

When I came back to the living room, towels and robe in hand, Delilah stood in the exact same spot where I'd left her, eyes on the growing puddle beneath her. I tossed a towel down at her feet and it was soaked instantly. She slipped out of her shoes and stepped onto the dry corner of the towel.

"How much do you want to crawl out of your skin right now?" I asked, handing her a towel. She may have looked calm and collected, but I had a feeling she was going through sensory hell.

"I'm okay-ish," she replied as she clamped the towel through her hair, "better once the wet clothes are off, but at least it's just water." She handed the towel back and before I had a second to even consider turning around, she wiggled her jeans down her legs. They squelched against the floor. Her legs had turned as pink as her face, her veins working overtime to keep her warm. Even though I figured it was coming next, I didn't even pretend to look away when she pulled the sweater off and dropped it onto the towel. Judging by the mismatched cotton underwear, she hadn't planned tonight to go this way, but that didn't stop my body from coming alive at the sight of her smooth skin and soft curves.

"Robe?"

She held out a hand, but instead of passing the robe, I opened it and stepped toward her. She slipped one arm in, then the other, and I fixed the collar around her neck.

"Thank you," she whispered into the narrow space between us.

"The August Beckett Library frowns upon its members dying of hypothermia."

"I didn't read about that in the policy." She giggled and watched as I tugged the fabric around her middle.

"It's an unspoken rule."

She laughed, but the sound died in her throat, replaced by a hitched gasp when I tightened the belt around her waist. That sound burrowed straight down my center to my hips, and I had to focus hard on tying a simple bow and letting my hands fall to my sides afterward. Just to be safe, I pushed them into my pockets. "All done."

"Books please."

I led her upstairs, aware of every inch of space between us. Her fingers trailed over some of the book spines before she turned to the one shelf she'd always turned to, and deliberately pulled one book from its rows.

"The Milkmaid Diaries?" I asked, brows raised, as she held up the pornstar's autobiography.

"Yep." She flipped it open, not even acknowledging my skeptical tone.

"You made a fake library card, laminated it, drove here at 9pm, walked five blocks through the rain, for the Milkmaid Diaries?"

"Yep. Hold on. I marked the passage."

"Sure."

"Got it," she smiled and tapped her finger against the page. "For a lot of people sex and love go hand-in-hand. You can certainly have sex without love, and you can love without sex. Yet, most people would argue that the best sex they have ever had has been with a loved one. To me, however, sex has always been about trust. I am able to trust my co-stars because we often have long-standing relationships and understand each other and the roles we play. I am unable to trust the guy I just met on Tinder who claimed to be 6ft tall but, in reality, barely matches my 5'8". Trust is built and earned, and once I trust someone, I can allow myself to be vulnerable with them in a way that makes sex worth having."

"Good quote."

"I marked this the first day I spent at your apartment." She swallowed and lowered the book, her azure eyes finding me across the room, swimming with a warmth she hadn't shown in two months.

The deep hollow inside me gnawed at my stomach, eating away at me with every flicker of useless, stubborn hope. My voice came out raspy, strained: "Delilah, why are you here?"

She took a step closer, then another one, before flipping the book over. "Read the margin."

Next to the paragraph she'd highlighted in pastel blue, she had written three little words: "I trust Beck."

"I did then, and I still do. I trust you. I know that you're not Prince Charming, or a white knight in shining armor, or even Mr. Knightley, but I don't think you would ever intentionally hurt me. I trust you with my life and with my body, Beck, but if I'm going to trust you with my love, I need to know when this stopped being about Cordelia."

With her love.

My breath stilled in my lungs as I watched her, waited for her to pull back again, braced myself for the other shoe to drop - but it didn't come. She was offering me more than two monthly conversations about books. Tongue dry, and my heart hammering hard enough to break straight from my ribcage, I took a tentative step towards her. She didn't flinch. "It started being about you when you put your hands down your shorts to get a rise out of me. That was clearly not Cordelia-you. *You* played me at my own game. I'm not easily intrigued but that got me." I took another step, close enough to force her to tilt her head back to keep her eyes on me. "It stopped being about Cordelia on July 24th when you almost died on my kitchen floor and put on a bunch of sappy romance movies for comfort afterwards, while simultaneously asking about spreader bars. I mean, who looks at ball gowns and ringlet curls, and thinks '*I should learn more about BDSM from the guy whose blankets I'm hogging even though he isn't my boyfriend*'? Your inquisitive nature and your honest curiosity are intoxicating." I took one last step, allowing me to brush the wet hair from her face and tuck it behind her ears. Her cheeks fit perfectly into the curve of my palms. "And by the time I took you to Casa de Camila, I was already looking forward to spending the rest of my life with *you*, because I love you, Delilah Edwards."

"That was a good answer," she breathed.

"Thank you."

"Beck?"

"Yes, Delilah?"

She tilted her head, eyes falling shut as she nestled into my palms. "Can you kiss me please?"

"Isn't kissing frowned upon by library staff?" I smiled, barely holding myself back. She may not have said those three little words back, but she'd promised to trust me with her love, and whether that was today, tomorrow, or six years from now, I'd take it.

"Shut up and kiss me."

She didn't have to tell me again. I pulled her to me and leaned down simultaneously, closing the gap between us. Her lips were still cold, and I mentally set myself the goal to kiss her until they were hot and swollen. Del's plans seemed to align with that, because the second our mouths connected, her hands were on me. They roamed my hair, pulled at my shirt, grasping for a hold, and pulling me closer. Each feverish touch tightening the pressure in my hips. Fuck, I'd missed her. Her taste, her hands, her everything. When her teeth joined in on the kiss, pulling at my lower lip, I growled against her. "You're testing my restraint, Blondie."

"What if I told you to shut up and fuck me sensele-" I stifled her words with my tongue against hers.

Her spine collided with the shelves behind her, and I made quick work of the belt around her waist while she fumbled with the buttons of my shirt. Nothing compared to Del's velvet skin under my fingertips, or to her strangled gasp when my hands dug into her ass, or to her breath hitching against my mouth when I pulled her bra down and ran my thumb over her hardened nipple.

She pulled out of the kiss, arching her back into my touch. "Can I keep the robe on?"

"Really?"

"I still can't feel my toes," she half-gasped, half-laughed, "just until I'm warmed up."

"Your wish is my command," I laughed and helped her peel out of her bra without dropping the robe. "Actually, this is kind of hot."

"Me in a huge bathrobe?"

"You, naked, in *my* bathrobe. You think I'll be able to think about anything else whenever I wear it from now on?"

"I'm not naked yet."

"Easy fix," I grinned and leaned down to close into another kiss, but Del titled her chin up, making my lips collide with her jawbone.

"Wait. I forgot. What about Brody?"

"Staying with her girlfriend," I replied, wiping my thumb over the accidental wet kiss I'd left on her chin.

"Oh, thank god." She laughed at my incredulous expression. "What? I want you to make me come at least three times. Do you really think I'd even manage once if I was worried about being overheard?"

"*At least* three times?"

"Minimum," she laughed, and shimmied her own panties down her legs, "unless you're not up for the challenge."

"Oh, you're going to regret those words." I plucked her hands from my shirt and placed them on the shelf behind her. "You don't get to touch me until I've made you come *at least* three times."

"That's not fair," she laughed but kept her hands in place.

"I don't play fair. I play to win." I nipped at her bottom lip, causing a shudder to ripple down her spine. Any answer she had for me was cut short by a high-pitched yelp when my teeth dug into her neck next. I was careful to keep my tongue back, leaving nothing but dry indents behind. Her delicate skin turned bright red in my wake, as I cut my path down her shoulder, to her chest. With every bite, her breaths came faster. My hands smoothed over every patch of skin after my mouth, just to make sure I didn't leave any unwanted traces.

"Oh god," she gasped and arched into me when I bit down on her nipple. It snapped out of my teeth. My fingers quickly replaced my mouth, digging into her soft flesh.

"Mine," I growled before pulling her second nipple between my teeth and nipping harder. She moaned, her knees wobbling enough for my hands to close around her waist, just to keep her upright.

I took that as my sign to sink onto my knees before her. Our eyes stayed locked as I positioned myself. "Put your leg on me, sweetheart." She let me lift her knee to hook around my shoulder, granting me a prime view of her glistening arousal. "Fuck, I missed you."

"Are you talking to me or my vagina?" Del laughed and reached out for me, but I caught her by the wrists. Her stomach trembled, when I pushed them back against the shelf with a warning growl.

"Hands off." I cut a quick look up at her before biting hard into the flesh on the inside of her thigh. Del winced at the sharp pain, but it definitely worked for the heated muscles twitching between her legs.

"Beck," she gasped.

"Hands on the shelf," I reminded her. She looked down at her hovering hands as if surprised to find them halfway between us. She flexed her fingers and curled them around the sides of the shelf until her knuckles turned white. "There you go," I said, "that's good."

She whimpered, her leg twitching on my shoulder. So eager for a few words of praise. "Please."

I repositioned her leg until her thigh pressed against my ear and she was open and fully exposed to me. The anticipation trembled through her muscles. Her entrance was already glistening, ready to welcome me back. "You're doing so good, getting that gorgeous pussy so wet for me. And I don't even have to do anything."

"Do you like torturing me?"

Instead of answering with words, I delved forward and let my tongue slowly trace the length of her slit. I'd dined in Michelin-star restaurants across the globe, but the salty sweetness of her had quickly become my favorite taste in the world. Her leg tightened around my shoulder when I hit her clit, spurring me on. I sucked her into my mouth, and she moaned. I played with her, nibbled, licked, thrust my tongue into her until her leg started shaking, and only then did I push a single finger into her tight entrance. She moaned and pulsed around me as I slid in and out of her while devouring her.

I added a second finger, and she cried my name. When her

standing leg gave out, I held her by the hips to keep her steady through her climax.

The tremors stopped, and I gave her one breath, two breaths, three breaths, before I pulled my fingers out of her and hoisted her second leg over my shoulder.

"What are you doing?" She stuttered through ragged inhales.

"You might want to hold on to something," I warned just before I stood up.

"Wha- hah." Del's hands scrambled for a hold on the shelves as I balanced her between them and my shoulders. I pushed her ass on the edge of one of the higher ones that put her pussy at the perfect height for my face.

With her legs on my shoulders, I braced both arms on the shelves before leaning forward again. "Oh god," she whimpered when my tongue entered her, "wait."

I paused and pressed a soft kiss to her clit. "What are you thinking?"

Her lashes fluttered as she tried to find her vocabulary through the haze of her orgasm. "This doesn't feel safe. What if I fall? What if your shelves break?"

"I've got you," I promised and whispered another kiss to her pelvic bone, "I won't let anything happen to you."

She hesitated for a second before letting out a single breathy "Okay."

Slowly sweeping my tongue over her entrance up to her most sensitive spot, I gave her another moment to consider, but she just gasped and tightened her legs. "Your pussy tastes so fucking good, sweetheart," I said and flicked my tongue against her faster.

"Beck," she whimpered, bucking against my face.

I drew my movements out the second time. Settling between her thighs, I let my tongue linger and my teeth tease her tender flesh, until her moans were reduced to a voiceless chain of pleas.

"Please. Please, Beck, please."

"What do you want, sweetheart?" I asked, a smirk playing out over my lips as I leaned back to look at her all flushed and trembling.

"I want you to make me come," she rasped.

"Who's allowed to make you come, Delilah?"

"Just you."

I gave her what she asked for, working my tongue and teeth against her more aggressively. I ravished as much of her taste as I could before Delilah bucked into me and fell apart a second time. Even as the tension bled from her body with each erratic jerk of her hips, I kept her steady. And when she finally stilled, I wrapped my arms around her waist and lowered her just enough to keep her at eye level.

"Oh. Hi," she breathed before sinking against me, face buried in the crook of my neck.

"Hi."

"Hmm…" She crossed her legs behind me, pulling me tight against her. Tight enough for the pulsing erection in my pants to press into her flesh. I groaned and she laughed against my collar. "I vote third orgasm should happen in bed."

"Sure," I laughed, "but don't think you're getting your hands on me just yet."

FIFTY-FIVE

Delilah

I was still a little dazed and breathing hard when Beck sat me down on the edge of his bed and peeled the robe off, trailing kisses along my shoulders. I hummed, leaning into him, grasping for his shirt. He pushed my hands back down, pressing them against the mattress. "Not yet."

"Fine."

His kisses trailed up my throat, sending a warm shiver down my spine. "Do you remember the first night you stayed over?"

"Are you going to feed me peanut curry again?"

Beck stepped to his nightstand and the second he pulled the drawer open, I knew. A moment later, he pulled out the silver bar with the leather cuffs on each end, and my throat tightened. "May I?" I watched him extend the bar like a telescope, tripling its lengths to somewhere between four and five feet. And even though I understood the concept, I was struggling to come up with positions *that* would be comfortable in or that even required this kind of tool, because I was more than happy to open my legs for him. "You can say no," he added after a moment of silence.

"I'll try it on, but I think I need you to explain it to me again, because it makes no sense to me."

He carried it over and showed it to me up close. The silver metal looked a lot sturdier than I'd thought. Less selfie stick, more car jack. Thick chain links hooked the cuffs to each end of it.

"It's for you to give up control to me," he said and lowered himself to his knees, directing one of my feet into his lap. The cushioned leather slipped around my ankle way too easily, and he closed the clasps just loose enough to give me some wiggle room. "To me, it's less about the fact that your legs stay apart and more about the fact that you are putting your body in my hands. Figuratively and literally." He pulled my second foot into the cuff, my legs parting wide, my butt sliding to the edge of the mattress. My pulse spiked at the physical sensation of opening my body like that, and I was thrown back to the beach, to him watching me writhe, anticipating how he might touch me. "You're giving yourself to me and I get to decide how I fuck you, how you come, how often you come…" A mischievous glint sparked in his eyes as he looked up at me. "How does it feel?"

Giving myself to him. That possessive streak of his. Maybe it should have scared me, but I tested the cuffs, trying to close my legs, the soft leather digging in to keep them apart, and the warmth that had just died down, simmered back up. "Okay, I guess," I replied, still unsure about how much that thing would do sexually.

I should have known he'd take *that* as a challenge, too.

Beck gripped the bar, stood, and yanked it up. I was thrown back onto the mattress, yelping, my ass suspended in the air. My legs were *up*. And spread. And my weight was pushed onto my shoulders. Oh god, I was just… Lying there. Or hanging there.

And Beck was grinning down at me as my fingers scrambled for support, digging into his sheets. He barely had to lift the bar to his shoulder level for this.

"How does it feel now?"

"Uh... I... uh..." Words. I needed words, but I was barely able to compute how I felt, caught between the novelty of the position my body was in, and the knowledge that Beck was seeing every muscle spasm between my legs.

"How is this?" He dipped two fingers back into me. Downwards. And my insides immediately clenched, still tender from five minutes ago, sending a ripple of pleasure down my spine. And I didn't have to – no – I couldn't do anything but let him touch me.

"Yes," I panted when he drew back out, "that's good."

"You're so wet for me, sweetheart, you couldn't lie about that if you tried." He pushed the fingers back in curling them just right to hit my G-spot and I moaned, my legs jerking on the bar as I scrambled to find hold on something other than his sheets. "I think we need to do something about those flailing hands of yours." He dropped the bar, my ass hitting the mattress and my feet the floor.

His words had just sunk in when he grabbed the back of my neck and pulled me back upright. He took the soft belt of the bathrobe and slung it around my wrists on either side of me, just to tie both ends around my middle. Belt, yes, but with my arms strapped to my sides. Fuck. I was *really* tied up. And God, I felt myself getting wetter just testing the new restraint. "Beck," I gasped.

"Yes, Blondie?" He wore such a smug smile on his lips, and I couldn't wait to wipe it off.

I inhaled deeply and smiled up at him. "If we do this, you're mine. I'm the only girl you ever touch from here on out, so you better make the most of it."

Surprise flashed across his features, followed by a devilish grin that already made me wonder how much I'd regret my words in the morning. "You're not doubting me, are you?" He leaned down, his face a breath from mine, and those dark stormy eyes scalding on me. "Because, Blondie," he thrust those fingers back into me and I gasped, but I barely had room to buck in this position, "I am more than happy to remind you how only I can make you scream. Now, open your mouth."

I did as I was told without hesitation, only for him to slip his fingers from my pussy to my mouth, my own salty taste dissolving on my tongue.

"I'm the only one who will make you taste like that, sweetheart," he rasped and pulled his hand from my mouth, only to suck on his fingers himself. His eyes were on me, while he savored every inch of my taste. The sight did things to me, every muscle tensing. "Take this." He grabbed a short chain from his nightstand and pressed the cold metal in my palm. "Drop it on the floor if you need me to stop."

I had no chance to ask why I couldn't just tell him to stop, because he picked me off the bed like I was nothing and whipped me around. Next thing I knew, my chest hit the mattress, face buried in the sheets, and he pulled my hips back until the tips of my toes scraped against the floor. I had no hold. Zero leverage. And each sound would be muffled by rich cotton. My heart sped up, as I realized that I *had* given him full control - and the excitement outweighed any anxious thought, because I wanted him to touch me. More than that, I just wanted him. I wanted to stop thinking and let myself be consumed by him.

"You're so fucking beautiful." His hands smoothed over my ass cheeks, their tenderness hiding the promise of what I'd gotten myself into. He spread me open with one hand before something cold hit my skin, wetness trickling from my tailbone down my center. I squirmed, trying to turn my head, trying to figure out what he was- but all I could see was my own blonde hair and cotton sheets. Damn his expensive thick bedding. The slick wetness trickled over my throbbing clit, and I winced. It was heating up. Oh God. Within seconds of touching my skin, the lube was prickling, my skin burning, and it was- I was- I was gasping into the sheets, trying to push myself against his hand or the bed, because the prickling was good, but it wasn't enough. I needed friction.

"Patience, Blondie." Beck laughed behind me and patted my ass check. Goddammit.

"Please," I begged, but my voice was swallowed by his bed.

He had barely started, and I was begging again already.

I jerked when something cold and hard pushed against my clit, chasing off the heat for just a second before he dragged it up my fold. It was small, too small to make much of an impact if he- I yelped when he dragged it past my entrance and positioned the cold tip against my ass instead.

He pushed slowly, and the image formed in my head. I'd seen enough of them on the pages of his books to recognize the small teardrop shape of a plug. The strain against my muscles rippled up my entire spine. Each inch widened me further, pain sharpening.

My fingers jerked around the chain.

But then the ache eased as the plug slotted into place.

Beck's hands dug into my cheeks as he pulled them apart, thumbs rubbing circles around my tense opening. "The prettiest damn jewel you'll ever wear. Fuck. I want you to wear that every damn day, sweetheart."

Jewel? Right. I'd seen those. The plugs with a sparkling stone at the end. Not the jewelry I'd usually opt for… He pulled it back again and my insides pulsed painfully around it. My cry was suffocated, and every thought fled my mind. He slid it back and forth, the thickest part of it pulling taut against my entrance and plunging back, until the pain ebbed into a strange, different pleasure. The pressure in my lower back humming.

"Beck," I whined into the fabric, knowing fully well the plea was lost. With the last thrust of the plug, he pushed something hard and cold against my pussy. I barely registered it, before the dildo thrust into me and a white-hot pain exploded through me. I screamed into his mattress. My toes scraped against the floor and my free hand pulled on my restraints. I held the chain tight though. I could feel the butt plug pressing down against the dildo. I wasn't even sure if it was large or if it was just the double pressure that made it feel like I was stretched to a breaking point.

"You feel that, Del? You're mine." His teeth scraped over the curve of my ass, and I jerked, then whimpered because even that tiny movement sent a pulse of hot pain through my insides. "Mine to play with." He bit down, my cheek in his mouth, and I twitched again, moaning as my walls tightened around the toys. That hadn't been a gentle bite either, sharp pain throbbing where his teeth had dug in. "Mine to pleasure however I want." He bit down hard on my other cheek and gave the dildo another push, sliding it deeper. The heat between my legs was boiling, every sensation blurring into the feeling of pulsing, hot fullness. I whimpered quietly as he kept biting, kept thrusting the hard length into me.

"Please," I moaned into the sheets, "please," not entirely sure what I was begging for. For him to stop? For more?

Something clicked, and the thick toy inside me started buzzing. The vibrations pushed against the plug and rippled up my spine. Shoulders flexing, neck bending, I bit down on a mouthful on cotton and dissolved into a whimpering, squirming mess, unable to move, to push back. My legs tried to jerk up, but Beck had the bar pinned against the bed. The orgasm quaked through my bones, all senses short-circuiting until I was nothing but the tremors rocking through my body.

I blinked and somehow found myself on my back, head on the pillows, heaving air and staring up into Beck's beautiful slate eyes. "God, you're gorgeous," I breathed.

He chuckled. "That's your first thought after coming like that?"

"Yeah, mh-hmm," I hummed, thoughts clearing enough for the dull pressure in my hips to seep through. He'd left the plug in. And lying on my back, it pushed deep against my insides.

"Sounds like I need to up my game."

"Oh no, don't worry. That was number three." My gaze raked down the smooth ridges of his body to the thick erection outlined in his pants. "I think we can end the night here," I grinned.

"We're done when I say we're done." His fingers were on the belt, but he just opened the knot around my waist. My hands were still caught in it. And instead of taking it off, he wrapped the ends around his headboard.

"Beck," I mumbled, "you said I could touch you after three orgasms."

"I said *at least* three orgasms." He grinned and crushed his mouth into mine painfully hard as he yanked my wrists tight against the headboard. The chain links bit into my palm and I winced, which only seemed to spur him on, his tongue sweeping past my lips to claim mine. "I think we can make it five," he rasped after breaking out of the kiss.

I shot a quick look up at the knots keeping my arms up, and another tremor of anticipation rocked through my body. I was stretched out in all directions, completely exposed to him. "You can take the chain."

"Keep it. You might still need it." My stomach tightened just knowing he had plans that would make it impossible to use my words. "Give me two seconds."

He left the bed but even raking my head, I couldn't make out anything past my knees. I heard a drawer opening and closing though before Beck came back to me. He trailed a hand from my collar to my navel. My spine arched for him on its own accord, needing his touch like a flower needed the sun. "I've been wanting to try this since you let me tie you up at the beach," he announced, and I didn't get the chance to ask what he meant before a sharp pain pierced through my nipple. I cried out, tears springing to my eyes, and I almost dropped the safety chain - until I saw what he'd done. A small silver clamp with rubber edges was fastened to the tip of my breast. It was connected to a second one with a thin silver chain.

"Oh god," I breathed just before Beck locked the second one in place. Head thrown back, I gasped through the pain. It didn't ebb off either. This wasn't his teeth, piercing me in place for a hot moment, and it wasn't a slap that left nothing but an afterburn. This was a continuous, throbbing strain.

"Eyes on me." He tugged on the slim chain, sending a new flash through the peaks of my breasts.

I forced my neck to bend down even though every part of me wanted to recoil from the pain, just to see Beck grin at me with the chain between his teeth. If I'd had any doubts before, they were well and truly diminished by that sight. I was his. Completely. Mind, body, and soul.

"Beck," I whimpered, needing him, needing his touch, needing to connect with him.

"Ssh." His warm thumbs smoothed over my cheeks, clearing away the tears that had sprung up, and I tilted for his soft touch. The thin chain dropped from his mouth to my chest. "I know you can give me one more, sweetheart."

He didn't give me the chance to protest before he grabbed hold of the spreader bar and whipped it up. Air spluttered from my lungs. My own weight pressed into me. It took him less than ten seconds to fasten the metal rod to the ends of the belt that kept my hands in place. There were maybe eight or nine inches between my wrists and my ankles. For all intents and purposes, he'd folded me in half.

I dragged my gaze back to him, his dark, hungry eyes roaming over me.

"You're mine," Beck said, just before his hand whipped against my center.

Blinding pain shot through me. The slap pierced my clit and shoved the plug deeper. My scream was only stifled by the weight of my own thighs pressing into my lungs. "Yes," I moaned, no longer sure where my body started and ended. I was being reduced to all my nerves burning.

"Mine," Beck repeated, and another slap hit me between the legs. I bucked against my restraints, whimpering.

"Your pretty pink pussy is all mine," he said, and I was barely aware of his fingers spreading me wide, until his next slap hit my exposed clit. I almost choked on my own cries. My body was burning, and I knew how to find relief. He just didn't grant it yet.

"I need you," I breathed, blinking up at him through blurred vision, "please."

"Say it." His thumb smoothed over my throbbing clit, drawing a deep-rooted moan from my lungs, as my entire searing nerve system honed in on that one spot. With that being the only sound coming from my mouth, he pulled his hand back. The anticipation rattled through me before the pain did, and I arched and bucked against his slap.

"Fuck me," I whimpered.

"No." Another slap hit me. The pain morphed into something else entirely, when he pushed two fingers into my tight entrance. He curled them where the plug pushed into me from the other side, just before his second hand delivered another slap. "Say it," he demanded loud over my moans.

"I'm yours," I groaned, the burn between my legs consuming me. "Just yours."

He added a third finger, stretching me, and slapped me hard enough for my vision to turn black as I quivered around him. I gasped for air through burning lungs. Beck delivered another blow, and I dropped over the edge.

I was still shaking when I felt *him*. I blinked rapidly, trying to clear my vision. Beck knelt over me, clothes gone, all beautiful bronze skin and flexing muscles. He had one hand hooked into the headboard, the other on his shaft, as he slid it between my folds. Another tremor rocked through me, as his tip pushed against my sore clit.

"Do you want me to use a condom?"

"God, no," I gasped. I wanted to feel him, and I wanted nothing between us.

He buried himself in me with one quick thrust and drew another loud cry from my lips. I'd thought the vibrator had been a taut stretch against the plug, but that was nothing in comparison to Beck's size. And all the pain that had just chased through me in a wave of euphoria flamed up again - with the added strain deep inside me.

Beck stilled above me. "Breathe."

I sucked in a deep breath, not realizing I'd even stopped.

"Good girl," he rasped, my muscles clenching around him at those two simple words, "keep breathing, Del."

I nodded, incapable of bringing coherent thoughts to my tongue. Beck started moving. Slow at first, until my insides relaxed, and he found an angle that allowed him to shift deeper than before. Once he had that, he plunged into me without mercy. I moaned under his hard, relentless thrusts, and tried to tilt my hips against him. I wanted- no, I needed- I couldn't go a second longer without-

"Fuck, you take that so well, sweetheart."

"Beck!" He hit an angle that had his shaft push against the plug, while his tip stroked over my G-spot. The fire in my veins burst through me, and I pulsed and trembled through another climax.

The next orgasm chased that one within a few thrusts.

My entire body was limp when my ankles came free and dropped against the mattress. Maybe there was a dull throbbing in them, or maybe in my hips, or in my knees - every single bone ached in the best way possible, and I wasn't sure which painful sensation originated where.

Beck's rhythm had slowed, and he took the safety chain from my stiff fingers, then made quick work of the knots. He tossed all of it aside before coming back to me, a beautiful, small smile on his lips.

"Why do you always do that?" I asked, as my swimming thoughts slowly cleared.

"Do what?"

"Loosen the restraints before you even come."

"I told you." He caressed my chest with soft kisses after he loosened the clamps from my nipples. "I want to make *you* feel with every cell in your body that you're mine. I'm in control. You come."

"I think that's kind of how I feel when you come inside me." My tired, quivering fingers raked into his hair, finding soft spots to rest. "Like you're completely giving yourself to me."

"I've actually never done that before you," he breathed, his pace speeding up again.

"Never?" I gasped.

"No." He moaned and leaned down to close his lips over mine. Unable to hold the swelling in my chest, I laughed, completely wrecking the kiss. Not just a small laugh either. A deep, honest laugh that made fresh tears spring to my eyes.

"Something wrong?"

"No, quite the opposite." I wiped the tears from my cheeks. "These are happy tears. I can't believe I got to be one of your firsts."

"Delilah," he grabbed hold of my knees and pushed them into

the mattress, opening me wide again for him to deliver a devastating deep thrust that killed the last laugh on my lips, "I fully plan on making you my last." As if the words weren't enough, Beck spilled himself into me. Giving me exactly what I'd asked of him. A last quiver trembled up my spine when his hips stilled.

With his charcoal eyes on me, Beck's lips formed a simple five-letter-word:

Yours.

FIFTY-SIX

BECK

FOUR WEEKS LATER

"Hey Blondie, what do I get if I win?"

"We don't even have to discuss that, because you're going to eat my dust."

"Alright, then you'll have no issue to agree that if I win, you get back in the ring with me. For real this time." She'd gotten better over the last few weeks, since our staff had gotten mental health awareness training, but she still refused to let me go anywhere near her at the gym. I got that it brought back complicated emotions, but I hated the way she'd be happy and energetic with everyone at Vortex, only for her face to fall whenever she spotted me.

"That's not going to happen because you're not going to win." Her chirpy voice filled my car.

"So you agree on the prize?"

"Fine." She looked over, squinting at me through the windows of our cars. I saw her lips move, but her voice came through the speakers connected to my phone. "*When* I win, you wear a red ribbon the next time we go to Clandestine."

Isaac cleared his throat. "You are aware that this is group call, right?"

"Done," I said, ignoring Isaac.

"What's Clandestine?" Tabitha piped up.

"Sex club," both Cordelia and Defne replied.

"Why do you guys know about a sex club, and I don't?"

"It's quite expensive and exclusive to members only," Cordelia explained.

"More than happy to take you some time," Isaac replied.

"How do *you* get into an exclusive-"

"Excuse me? Can we please get back to the real reason we're here?" I could practically hear Delilah roll her eyes. "Preferably before the cars grow roots."

"I got it. Don't worry, I'm here." Defne stepped up onto the road, positioning herself in line with the ten-foot gap between our cars. She'd dressed up in a black and white checkered mini dress and held flags in the same pattern in each hand. She fumbled with her headset that made her look more like she was about to give a pop concert than start a race. "Everyone ready?"

"Yep," Del quipped.

"Yes," I agreed.

We had gotten her father's car out of storage, and it was almost entirely fixed up by now, but for this occasion both Del and I sat in much newer sports cars. After complaining about my driving one too many times, I'd finally told her to follow through on her promise from summer and race me. It had taken a while, her hand always falling back to the jagged scar along her ribs when I brought it up, but two days ago, she'd looked up from the papers she'd been grading and said, "I'll beat you so bad, you'll never get behind a wheel again."

We'd driven two hours out of town, to acres upon acres of dirt that had been acquired by my grandfather but had never been developed.

"On your marks. Set." Defne raised the flags above her head. "Go!" She brought the flags down and we tore off.

The gravel crunched beneath my tires and my engine roared as I ripped my car past Delilah's. But then she easily slipped past at the first corner when my tires skidded over dust, her bubbly laughter ringing through the speakers.

She stayed in front of me, kept swerving to cut me off whenever I tried to make a move, but by the last turn we were neck-and-neck again. We shot over the finish line, and I had no idea who won, but Del's loud hollering over the phone was infectious enough to make me laugh along with her.

"Ohmygod." Del climbed out of her seat, only to drop back against the side of her car. Her pupils were blown wide, and her chest was rising fast.

"You good?" I asked as I stepped in front of her, trying to differentiate between adrenaline rush and panic attack.

"That was amazing." She grabbed me by the collar and pulled me down into a feverish kiss. Adrenaline rush. Definitely. And I had no problem with that, kissing her like the fate of the entire Formula One depended on it. Once she had her fill, she shoved me back again with just as much fervor, lips trembling. "I want to go again. And I want to tear your clothes off. And I want donuts. Not in that order."

"I think we can manage all three, starting with the food." I took her hand and led her over to the useless block of concrete, where our friends had set up camp.

Defne was now swaddled in two winter coats and a sleeping bag, gripping an iPad, while Isaac and Tabitha sat on either side of her - Tabitha with her camera, and Isaac with half a box of donuts.

"So, who won?" Del asked, climbing up on the platform to narrow her eyes at Tabitha's camera screen.

"It's a tie," she said.

"Oh, come on." I settled onto the platform and glanced over Delilah's shoulder at the paused video.

"Does that mean you both lose?" Isaac asked.

"I think we both win." Del shrugged and leaned over her friends to grab a donut, before she unceremoniously climbed into my lap, one arm wrapped around my neck. My arms automatically found their way around her waist, where they belonged.

"I only have one trophy." Defne held up a small golden matchbox car.

"Give it to Delilah," Victor piped up and all heads swiveled to the iPad in Defne's lap. Cordelia, on the other side of the video call, tilted her camera to bring Victor into view. "If she hadn't slowed down on the last turn, she would have won."

"I did *not* slow down." Even though she delivered the words with a straight face, her throat hitched, giving away her blatant lie. "We both won. We can share custody of the trophy."

I stayed silent and pressed a kiss to the back of her head. I had a feeling I'd spend the rest of my life trying to keep up with her.

Tabitha queued up the footage of the race again and they started bickering about whether or not Del had actually slowed down. When they all started speaking over one another, Del shook her head and leaned back, wiggling to slide deeper into my lap. If she wasn't careful, I'd end up whisking her back into the car and parking it on the other side of the property - just to show her how much fun seat belts could be.

"August Beckett," she sighed and pressed a kiss to the dip between my jaw and ear. I hummed in appreciation. "I have a confession."

"Delilah Edwards," I replied, smiling down at her, and stealing a kiss from her lips, "I already know that you lied about slowing down."

She scrunched up her nose at me. "No."

"No?"

"I trust you and... I love you," she whispered. It was the first time she said those words. I had told her many times since that night she showed up on my doorstep with a library card, but I'd made it very clear that she didn't have to say it back. That I'd rather know she trusted me than lie about loving me. And yet, hearing her say those words, my chest felt too small for the warmth flooding it.

Her big ocean eyes roamed over my face, waiting for me, watching my reaction. I had no reason to stop the smile spreading on my lips. "I love you, too, Delilah, and I trust you."

EPILOGUE

Delilah

FEBRUARY 21ST

BRODY LEANED OVER THE COUNTER, BROWS DRAWN UP TO HER hairline. "Please," I laughed, "I'm not messing it up. Back off."

"Are you sure about that?"

I rolled my eyes at her and placed the small piece of green garnish on top of the frittata slice. "Look. It's perfect."

To be fair, she'd done most of the cooking after witnessing me crack one egg and most of it landing on the kitchen floor. She had allowed me to plate the food though, but she generally trusted me in the kitchen just as much as her uncle did: not at all.

"What's going on here?" Beck asked when he stepped into the kitchen mid-tie-knot. Neither Brody, nor I usually got up before him, let alone prepped breakfast. I'd snuck out of bed at 4:30 to make this work.

"We made frittata," I replied with a big smile. He grimaced.

"*I* made frittata," Brody cackled.

"Idea," I pointed at myself, then at Brody, "execution."

"Does that make me an executioner?" She grinned and placed the plate on the kitchen island in front of Beck. "Happy Birthday!"

"My birthday isn't until next week." He furrowed his brows, but I could hardly tell him that I had plans to whisk him off to London for his birthday. That was a well-kept secret between me, Brody, Cordelia, and Beck's assistant, who had filled his calendar with bogus meetings while blocking all actual appointments.

"It's technically the practice run for your birthday," I said and set a fork and napkin down for him, "surprise."

"Come here." He caught my wrist and pulled me around the kitchen island to steal a quick kiss from my lips. My heart fluttered in response, still as easily swayed as if I couldn't get all the kisses I ever wanted from him. "I don't like waking up without you next to me."

My cheeks heated but Brody's gagging sound made both of us laugh. "Will you try the damn food already, so I can go back to bed?"

"Alright, alright," he picked up the fork and I held my breath as he cut off the very tip of his slice.

"No, no, no, you have to take a bigger bite," Brody protested, pointing her finger at an imaginary line on the frittata.

"Brody," I breathed a warning.

"Just cut through like here," Brody's finger swiveled over the cheesy eggs on his plate.

"Here?" Beck laughed and deliberately brought is fork down half an inch away from her finger, but he stilled at the sound of metal hitting metal.

For a moment, the entire kitchen fell silent. Even the refrigerator seemed to stop humming. The only sound was the blood rushing in my ears while I waited. It was probably five seconds, but it felt like five hours before Beck broke through the frittata with his fingers.

He pulled out a simple dark platinum ring, an exact match for the color of his eyes. I'd walked past it in a shop window and had to double back because of its distinct hue. That had been two days before our car race last year, and I'd kept it safe since.

"You see," I said, finally pulling his attention from the ring to me. "I'm 27 years old. I have no money, no company, and no prospects. But with you Beck, I'm not frightened."

"Are you misquoting the Pride and Prejudice movie to me?" He chuckled. "Not even the book?"

"Fine. Let me try a Delilah Edwards original." My breath trembled in my lungs. I couldn't get this wrong. I wanted this to be perfect. I wanted him to say yes. Taking a moment to steady myself, I took the ring from him and cleaned it with the napkin. Once it was spotless, I looked up at him again. His steel eyes softened as a small smile twitched over his lips, and that hint of hope was encouragement enough. "I *adore* you in a way that if anyone tried to insult your eyes, I'd start a club called Ice - I C E - and make it the most sought-after club in the world. I *trust* you in a way that makes the rest of the world inconsequential as long as you're holding me. And I *love* you in a way that makes me not want to waste another second not being your wife." I held out my open palm with the ring in it. "August Beckett, will you marry me?"

He cleared his throat. "Brody, could you?"

"On it!"

"What's happening?" I asked, turning to see Brody zap through the kitchen, then back to Beck who was suddenly very intent on avoiding my gaze. My heart skidded in my chest. "Are you saying *no*?"

"One second, Blondie."

Brody returned from the freezer with an ice cube tray in hand. Beck wordlessly broke out one of the cubes and placed it on the counter.

"He was going to put it in champagne," Brody squealed.

"You don't put ice cubes in champagne," I replied, not quite tracking why they were showing me an ice cube, when Beck still hadn't replied to my question. *The* question.

"Uuuuh, wine?"

"I'm actually very relieved that you don't know which drinks go with ice cubes," Beck said, tipping his head at Brody.

He hadn't said yes. He wouldn't say yes. Whatever was happening, he wasn't answering my question, and there really was only one reason you would avoid answering a proposal.

"I don't even drink," I squeaked, nerves fluttering until Beck picked up the ice cube and switched it out with his ring on my palm. The cold snapped the string on my panicked thoughts, and I gasped, staring at the small piece of ice. "Wait, that's a ring in there."

"Yes. I haven't actually gotten to the speech portion of the proposal yet, but yours was very good."

"I-" He'd bought me a ring. He'd been preparing for the same damn question. Tears welled up in my eyes as I smoothed my thumb over the melting ice cube, trying to make out the details of the golden metal inside, getting small winks of blue. "Oh, it looks like it's pretty."

"It is," he chuckled. "It's a regency era sapphire and pearl ring."

"I've not heard anyone say *yes, I do*," Brody chirped.

"Of course, I do." Beck took the ice cube from me again, only to hand me the titanium ring and stretch out his hand.

"Yes, very much. God, yes." I slipped the ring onto his finger.

"Brody, can you get the hair dryer from my bathroom? Let's get that ring out of the ice."

"Sure can!" She dashed past us and tore through the kitchen door at a speed that smashed the door into the wall hard enough to deepen the dent already there.

As soon as she was out of earshot, I raised my brows at Beck. "I don't drink ice cube drinks."

"I know." He grinned and leaned in to press his lips to the corner of my mouth.

"You were going to propose to me in bed, weren't you?"

"There was never going to be a speech." His hands slid around me, giving my backside a slight squeeze before pulling me forward. My chest collided with his as he grinned down at me. His voice dropped to a low rumble. "I was planning on finding creative ways to use nine ice cubes to make you come until you were such a spluttering mess, you would have said yes to anything I asked you by the time the tenth ice cube melted." I shuddered at the idea, and he placed the ice cube with my ring back in my hand.

"Well…" I extracted myself from his embrace and grabbed the ice cube tray. "I'll put these back in the freezer and remember that strategy for when I ask you for a themed wedding."

"Sweetheart, you get to have any wedding you want as long as I'm the one waiting by the altar." He followed me across the kitchen, hands sliding back around my waist the second I stopped in front of the fridge.

"Any wedding?" I laughed as I barely managed to wedge the door open enough to slip the ice cube tray back inside, because his body was blocking me in. I turned and smiled up at the stupidly tall and beautiful man I'd call my husband one day soon. "White ducks included?"

Using his left hand, with his ring glistening in the first morning light, he brushed the hair from my face, before leaning down to kiss me. I melted into him with a sigh.

"White ducks included," he promised against my lips.

THE END

Cinderella found her perfect fit.

Now it's time for Rapunzel to let her hair down.

AUTHOR'S NOTE

In the extended epilogue, Beck develops a whole new appreciation for the regency era when Del shows him just how many ribbons are on her wedding corset.

Head to **www.dilandyer.com** to access this exclusive bonus chapter.

ACKNOWLEDGMENTS

In true ND fashion, I looked at around 50 different acknowledgement sections from different authors, and I still don't know the 'correct' way to start one.

Let's just jump right in!

To PB: 20 years is a hella long time to stick with someone. Thank you for growing up with me. Thank you for doing the dishes when my brain won't let me. Thank you for watching Magic Mike with me when I have no spoons. Thank you for reading every single line I've ever written. I love you.

The biggest thanks to my lovely beta readers who trusted me with their love for spicy romance and jumped on this ride with me: JD, Adrian, Meg and Cat. Your feedback was invaluable and you made this book so much better (and so much longer).

Shout-out to Edith, who has proof-read this book many times, and whose eagle eyes caught many small inconsistencies. Your editorial brain is unmatched. Your hype keeps me going. I am so grateful to be able to call you my friend.

This book wouldn't be published without Bethany. One of the first people to know about this book's existence, she has been championing this book for months, virtually holding my hand through the self-publishing process. We'll try to reduce the amount of 2am phone calls for the sequel, ok?

Thank you to the *neurodivergent baddies* GC for everything. Y'all are a constant source or inspiration and motivation, and you give me the warm and fuzzies. I can't wait for us all to be rich and famous :D

The romance community has been incredibly welcoming and supportive. Thank you especially to Ki, Aubrey, Philippa, Janni, Akwaah, Ruby and Amelie for answering my many questions about this process. Thank you to Nyla for cheering me on and helping me make this book even better. And a huge thank you to the besties on Insta and TikTok - y'all know how to make a girl feel special.

Most of all: THANK YOU for taking a chance on my debut novel, for reading, for letting me sweep you off to my fairy tale for a little bit. It really does mean the world.

ABOUT THE AUTHOR

Dilan is the future bestselling author (manifesting) of the Princess Crossover series. Constantly on the move, she has lived in countless cities across five countries and dreams of a camper van to take her life on the road. She just needs to find one big enough for her pets, her vintage tea cup collection and her staggering TBR.

Having outgrown her slut phase, Dilan now channels her thirst in spicy romance novels with swoon-worthy HEAs.

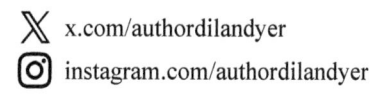

X x.com/authordilandyer
instagram.com/authordilandyer

www.ingramcontent.com/pod-product-compliance
Ingram Content Group UK Ltd.
Pitfield, Milton Keynes, MK11 3LW, UK
UKHW042204060625
6286UKWH00002B/169

9 783982 606705